Runefell
The Trials of War

I0657879

Shawn Sodman

ISBN: 0-578-45975-2
ISBN-13: 978-0-578-45975-2

Dedicated to Kathy, Autumn, Amber and Kyle.

I'd be forever lost without you.

CONTENTS

Acknowledgments

I would like to thank Leonardo Borazio for the fine artwork that he custom-made for each of the three books in the series so far. I look forward to seeing his vision for future books.

I would also like to thank Caitlin for once again helping me edit and improve my writing. I'd also like to acknowledge my secondary editors, Linda and Lydia, for going over everything again before it went to print.

And finally, I'd like to thank everyone who sat and listened to me read as I self-edited. Being able to get into the characters' personalities with their accents and voices not only gave me great joy, but allowed me to improve my writing, as well.

Chapter 1
The Beginning of the End

It is a little after 9:00 am when Lyra knocks at the apartment door were Kel'ana lives with Laura, Josh, and Haley. Under her arm is the ancient account of the Third Orcnea War. It doesn't take long before the door opens to reveal Josh, still in his pajamas.

"Good morning, Aunt Nica," greets Josh cheerfully, using the only name he has ever known Lyra as. Then after spotting the book under her arm, adds, "You brought it. Sweet!"

"Is everyone else awake?" asks Lyra.

"Yeah, we're all up," answers Josh. "I just didn't get dressed yet. Come in." Lyra enters the apartment as Josh runs down the hall and calls to his sisters, "Laura! Haley! Aunt Nica is here."

Lyra enters the living room and is greeted by Kel'ana sitting on the couch. "Good morning," says Kel'ana.

"Good morning, Danielle," says Lyra, keeping with their aliases even though they are alone in the room.

Kel'ana says, "Thanks for helping Laura get through her headache yesterday."

"How long has she been having them?"

"I don't remember her ever having a problem before."

"The book must have triggered it."

"How?" asks Kel'ana. "Isn't it just a normal book?"

"Most historical accounts have spells to protect them from damage," says Lyra.

"Huh. Oh! that reminds me," says Kel'ana. "Did Kelik tell you what we found in Bermuda?"

"Yes!" exclaims Lyra. "I can hardly believe it."

"Do you think Ariella is still alive?"

"I don't know. I suppose it's possible. She would've needed to drain the youth from a lot of people to keep from aging all these years. Four hundred years' worth."

"Sounds like something a vampire would do," laughs Kel'ana.

"I am so glad we don't have to do that to stay young," says Lyra.

"Me too," agrees Kel'ana. "If Ariella is still alive, I wonder... What is she doing now?"

In the warm tropic sun of Bermuda, Ariella and Garret wait to be picked up in front of the L.F. Wade International Airport. Ariella says impatiently, "What's taking your sister so long?"

Garret spots a vehicle approaching. "There she is."

A sedan pulls up and stops in front of them. The driver's side window rolls down. "I'm sorry it took so long," says Annalee from inside the vehicle. "They were giving me a hassle about paying with cash."

"I have never had an issue with that before," says Ariella.

The passenger side door opens and Fidelma McMurphy emerges. "Don't worry, I persuaded the manager that U.S. currency was acceptable."

"Well, then, let's get to the marina," says Ariella. "I want to reach the coordinates that Eric gave me before noon."

Back at the apartment, Lyra and Kel'ana are joined by Josh and his two sisters. Lyra sits on the couch with the book open on a coffee table before her. Kel'ana says, "I'll leave you all to the story while I go shopping. Don't worry, Nica. If you need to go, Laura can watch them."

"All right," says Lyra. "But I should be able to stay until the book is done. We're at the beginning of the end now, so it shouldn't be too long."

"Well, maybe I'll see you when I get back," Kel'ana says as she grabs her purse.

"Bye, Aunt Danielle," says Josh as he sits next to Lyra on the couch.

Kel'ana leaves as Laura makes herself comfortable in a chair. Haley sits on the floor and plays with two dolls. Lyra asks, "Do you remember where you left off?"

"Yes," says Josh, sounding disgruntled. "They just killed Chance and took over Sheathelm."

Lyra looks down at the pages. "Then I have marked the correct spot. Are you ready?"

The three nod, and Lyra begins reading where they left off the day before.

Day 22
Continued

At the stronghold to the south of Sheathelm, Arioch calls for a gathering of generals and captains. As they prepare to meet, the soldiers are busy on the hillside placing spikes. On the outside, the stronghold is not much more than a tower on a hill. Its walls follow the crest of the hill before turning southward, where they extend down to the bay where two docks are located.

Other than the bay, there is only one entrance: a gate next to the tower. Beneath the tower are ancient subterranean levels carved into the bluff. One entrance to these levels is located at the base of tower. The other is at sea level near the docks. It is here that king Arioch and the others enter making their way to an old military planning room.

Still on the hillside with Kianna and Isen, Ya'leigh continues to watch the horizon as smoke rises from Sheathelm. Va'leen and Nicari join them. "I am sorry about your loss, Ya'leigh," says Va'leen. Ya'leigh wipes away tears as she tries to gather herself. "Your father was a wonderful man," continues Va'leen. "He treated me with more kindness and respect than anyone. If you need anything at all, don't hesitate to ask. We are family."

"Thank you," replies Ya'leigh with a sniffle.

Va'leen spots Kristieana making her way over and decides to leave to avoid any possible conflict. The raven-haired Amazon excuses herself just as the fiery redhead joins them. Kristieana says quietly to Isen, "How is Ya'leigh holding up?"

"I don't know," he replies.

"Maybe we should get everyone behind the wall," suggests Kristieana.

"Good idea," replies Isen. "If those drakes move in to attack, we shouldn't be out here in the open."

Princess Kianna leads her friends to the gate, and soon the four of them find refuge within the walls of the outpost.

Down below, King Arioch is about to begin discussing strategy with his generals and captains in a dimly lit room around a long stone table with enough room for about ten people to stand along its edge. Among those gathered are the captain of the Silver Tide, Resif, along with a few other captains from the elven fleet. Lord Damion and Levin are also there.

Ariella enters the room and looks around for Chance, unaware of what has happened. While the others talk amongst themselves, Ariella approaches Arioch and asks, "Where's Chance?"

A hush falls over the men and women as Arioch answers, "I'm afraid he was still inside the atrium when the gate was destroyed."

"What!" she gasps.

Arioch sighs. "He didn't make it."

The gathering erupts with chatter. "What are we going to do now?" asks General Reigns over the crowd.

While Arioch tries to gain control over the talk, Ariella retreats into the hall. Her hands shake as her legs become weak. She nearly falls, but manages to lean on the cold stone walls. The voices of the men inside the chamber fade from her senses as the sound of her own heart beating fills her head. Her breaths are short and shallow, and tears fill her eyes, making it difficult to see where she is going.

In her hasty exit from the underground lair, Ariella runs into a bearded figure. She hears the voice of her father ask, "Ariella, what's the matter?"

She is so distraught that she can barely speak. "H-he's gone," she finally manages to say.

Noticing the anguish on her face, Red Beard does not need to ask who. "I'm sorry, my dear," he says as he puts his arms around her. "Let's get you back to the ship."

"No," she replies. She takes a deep breath and wipes her face. "We should join the meeting and see what we are going to do next."

"Are you certain?"

"Yes, I'll be all right now. Thank you."

Red Beard leads his daughter back down the hall, and they enter the room where Arioch and the others are still gathered. Prince River says to Arioch, "We have sent word to my father of the recent events. It is my hope that he will commit more forces to the effort."

"Thank you," says Arioch. "Do we have any update on the

troop counts?"

The captain of the drake riders, Belron, says, "As near as we can estimate, they still have ten thousand troops to our six thousand."

Arioch nods, acknowledging Belron. The room is silent as the group ponders. Arioch asks, "Is there any word on new reinforcements from Artos?" When no one answers, he says, "We have to get word to them."

"I can go," says Belron.

"No," says A'ranah. "If the drakes attack again, you and the other riders will be our best hope against them. I'll find an Amazon to deliver the message."

"I'll go," volunteers Kristieana from the doorway. Everyone turns their attention to the tall Amazon. "If I leave soon, I may be able to reach them before the end of the day."

Arioch looks to A'ranah, who gives a nod of approval. "Very well," says the king. "I'll prepare a message at once."

A'ranah says, "We should also communicate with Dicean and warn them not to use the gate to Sheathelm."

"I thought the gate was destroyed," says General Reigns.

A'ranah explains, "Yes, the gate at Sheathelm was destroyed, but as long as the gates in Dicean and Elonfar still stand, those cities still have access to Sheathelm."

"We could use this to our advantage," says Arioch.

"I was thinking the same thing," A'ranah agrees. "In the meantime, we must make sure that those in Dicean do not unwittingly open the gate to Sheathelm and put themselves in danger."

Prince River says, "Elonfar is already aware of the situation. Perhaps I can ask them to deliver a message to Dicean as well."

"Thank you," says Arioch.

Ariella turns to her father. "I wish Fidelma was here. Two of her crew are students at Dicean. They study teleportation magic and could most likely get word to the school in minutes."

"Where is Fidelma?" asks Red Beard.

"I don't know," Ariella answers.

In the seas off the southeastern coast of Bruen is an island with a tall mountain in the center. The top of the mountain is relatively flat. The first explorers named this place Plateau Island. On the western shores of the island is the large town of New Waterford.

Built in, and on, the steep rocky slope of the mountain, the town is taller than it is wide. The main road winds back and forth like a giant serpent climbing a hill. Homes and other buildings are built along the road, while others are carved into stone's surface. Where the land and sea meet, the terrain is a broken one. The town constructed buildings on top of enormous boulders and connected them all with a variety of wooden and rope bridges.

Because it is a mining town, the sturdiest bridges run from the main road out to the docks. Currently, the only ship at the docks is the Sea Griffin. Captain McMurphy disembarks from her ship with Samantha and Fernando close behind. The twins Fay and Janette, along with Vindalia, stay behind.

"Why do we have to watch the ship?" whines Janette. "I doubt anyone will try to take it."

"Don't worry," says Vindalia. "There really isn't much to see here unless you go to the top of the mountain."

"Does the captain come here often?" asks Fay.

"We come here every couple months," Vindalia answers. "Her parents still live here, and she likes to visit them."

Minutes later, Fidelma stops outside a modest dwelling. She says to Fernando, "This is my home, or at least where I grew up."

"It is very nice," says Fernando, admiring the well-kept house.

Fidelma opens the door and as she enters she calls out, "Mother, are you home?"

"Fidelma? Is that you?" a voice calls down from a stairway.

"Yes, Mother," she replies as they enter.

From the entry, Fernando can see one large room that acts as both a kitchen and dining area. A stairway next to the door leads to a second level. A woman, resembling Fidelma but older, makes her way down the stairs and gives her daughter a hug.

"It is so good to see you," says the woman.

"Mother," says Fidelma. "I would like you to meet Fernando Greythorn. Fernando, this is my mother."

Fernando takes Mrs. McMurphy's hand, kisses it, and says, "It is an absolute pleasure to meet you, Mrs. McMurphy. I see now where Fidelma gets her beauty."

"Oh my," she says with a laugh. "Aren't you sweet. Please, call me Deborah."

"If you insist," replies Fernando.

Deborah says to Fidelma, "It's about time that you brought a gentleman home. Your father and I were beginning to worry."

Samantha involuntarily snickers. Fidelma, glaring at her friend, says, "It's not funny."

"Yes, it is," laughs Samantha.

Deborah, confused, says, "I'm sorry, I must have misunderstood."

"Yes, Mother," Fidelma replies sternly. "You did."

"So," Deborah says to Fernando. "You and Samantha are together, then?"

"What!" exclaims Samantha. "No, that's not it at all."

Fidelma and Fernando both laugh at the confusion. Fidelma explains, "Mother, Fernando is not involved with anyone. He is just... a friend."

"I see," Deborah replies. She leans in and whispers loudly enough for the others to hear, "That's too bad, he is a handsome one. Maybe if you smiled more, he might notice you."

"Mother, please..." begs Fidelma, embarrassed.

Deborah replies, "Your father won't be back for a few more hours. Please, everyone, make yourselves at home."

Samantha and Fernando make their way to the dining table and sit down. Fidelma says, "Mother, I'm going to step out for a few minutes. I have something I must take care of."

Samantha asks, "Are you sure you don't want us to go with you?"

"I'm sure," she replies. "There's no need. I can handle this on my own. Just keep an eye on Fernando."

Fernando says, "I promise I am not going anywhere."

"Good," says Fidelma as she reaches the door. "I'll be back soon." Fidelma walks out the door, closing it behind her.

"Samantha," says Deborah, "what does she need to take care of?"

"I'm not certain," Samantha lies, knowing the real reason for their return to New Waterford.

"Well, whatever it is," Deborah replies, "she didn't seem too happy about it."

With a wooden road beneath her feet, Fidelma makes her way through the lower portion of the town. After crossing a couple bridges over the water, she finds herself standing in front of the Smelters Inn.

The Inn is busy with people eating lunch. Fidelma is looking around when she is greeted by Ami. "What can I do for you?" Ami asks, not recognizing her.

"I came to see you," replies Fidelma.

"Oh, hello, Fidelma," says Ami, sounding disappointed. "What do you want?"

"I need to ask you about the night before my wedding."

Confused, Ami replies, "That was a long time ago. What about it?"

"Did you try to use a love potion on Sven?"

"I tried," Ami admits, shrugging her shoulders. "But that friend of yours came in and ruined everything."

Fidelma is taken aback by the honest answer. She takes a few moments before grabbing the other woman by her neck and slamming her against the wall. "How could you?!" she shouts. "You had no right."

"Let go of me!" demands Ami, struggling to breathe.

Fidelma releases her, but continues to stand in her way. "Why would you do such a thing?"

Ami adjusts her blouse and replies, "You didn't deserve him."

"What makes you say that?"

"Where did Sven go when he wanted to eat?" Ami asks, already knowing the answer.

Fidelma clenches her fists. Trying to stay calm, she says, "He only liked you for your food."

Ami laughs. "I don't know how you ever expected to keep him satisfied when you don't even know how to prepare a proper meal."

"We loved each other," snaps Fidelma. "And that was more than enough for him."

Ami, with a smirk on her face, says, "If he was truly satisfied with you, then he wouldn't have come to me when you were too busy."

"If he truly wanted to be with you," retorts Fidelma, "you

wouldn't have needed to use a potion."

"I could have made him happy," says Ami. "I just needed one chance to prove it."

"By drugging him?"

"I was going to give him a night of passion that he would never forget."

Shaking her head, Fidelma chuckles. "Then you chose the wrong potion."

"What do you mean?" asks Ami.

"I mean," explains Fidelma, "that the potion you chose to use on Sven causes the subject to lose all memories while under its influence. Sven didn't remember anything from that night. Anything you would have done with him would have been forgotten."

"Well, it didn't matter anyway," says Ami. "Now, if there isn't anything else..."

"Actually, there is one more thing I'd like to know."

"What is that?"

Fidelma waves her hand in front of Ami's face, saying, "I just need you to hold still for a moment."

"All right," says Ami, in a trance.

Fidelma places her hand on Ami's forehead and casts the spell to read through her thoughts to make sure she has the complete story. After a few moments, Fidelma smiles and says, "Thank you." She then removes her hand from Ami's head and snaps her fingers.

Ami, waking from the spell, asks, "Why are you still here?" She pushes her way past Fidelma.

"Oh, I almost forgot," says Fidelma.

Ami turns around again, irritated. "What?"

Fidelma slams her fist straight into Ami's face, breaking her nose and splitting open her lip. Ami cries out as she falls to the ground. She covers her face as blood begins to flow through her fingers. The crowd at the Inn looks on in disbelief as Fidelma leaves with a smile on her face.

Chapter 2
The Deep Connection

At Fidelma's childhood home, Fernando and Samantha are led upstairs by Debora to a small bedroom. "This is Fidelma's old room," says Debora.

There is window directly opposite the doorway, and a bed next to it in the left corner. On the windowsill is a wooden trough filled with dirt. Fernando walks over picks up handful of the soil and lets it run through his fingers.

"Fidelma liked to grow plants," Debora says. "She was always fond of strawberries. When she left, we had to move them outside."

Samantha comments, "She still grows them on the *Sea Griffin*."

"She always had a talent for plant magic," says Debora. "She was five years old when she made a flower blossom."

Fernando asks, "Did she ever go to Dicean?"

"No," Debora answers. "We didn't have enough money to send her. Even without formal training, she could always make plants grow faster. She was ten when a friend of hers started to teach her new spells."

"Was her friend Ariella Stormrage?" asks Samantha.

"Ugh," groans Debora. "I don't like that woman. My daughter would be happily married right now if not for her."

Samantha and Fernando do not reply. Instead, Fernando walks over to a dresser and picks up a hand-sewn doll. It is worn from many years of use, but still in good repair.

"That's Roxy," says Debora, reminiscing. "Fidelma didn't play with her very much. She preferred to climb the mountainside."

Fidelma enters the room and asks, "What are you all doing in here?"

"I thought it would be nice to show them your old room," says Debora.

Fernando teases, "Nice doll. I can almost imagine you as a child, brushing her hair."

"Well, don't," says Fidelma, snatching Roxy away from him.

"That's just strange. Besides, I didn't play with her all that much. My grandmother made it for my mother, then she passed it down to me. I remember re-naming her Roxanne or Roxy. I don't remember what her name was before that."

"Her name was Ariella, the same as your former friend," says Debora.

"Oh, that's right," says Fidelma. "I remember now."

Fernando says to Debora, "I am sorry to ask, but did you by chance have a sister when you were younger?"

Debora, confused, replies, "Yes, how did you know?"

"Wait," says Fidelma, surprised. "Mother, I didn't know you had a sister. Why didn't you ever tell me?"

"It was too hard to talk about," says Debora sadly. "She left when I was fifteen. I never saw her again."

Fidelma asks Fernando, "How did you know about it?"

Fernando asks, "Did you read the letter that Ariella got from her mother?"

"No," replies Fidelma. "Why?"

"Perhaps the two of you should sit down," says Fernando. The two women sit on the bed as Fernando explains. "Ariella's mother died on the *White Feather* many years ago, right after giving birth to her. Red Beard was there, of course. We all know that. But what we did not know was that he found a letter nearby. Red Beard assumed it was written by Ariella's mother to her parents. We are not sure why he never gave it to her."

"What does this have to do with my doll?" asks Fidelma.

"While the letter did not reveal the names of Ariella's mother or grandparents," says Fernando, "it did have two other names. The letter mentioned that Ariella's mother planned on naming her after a doll that she used to play with."

Debora starts to become overwhelmed by the story. Fidelma puts her arm around her and asks, "Mother, could it be true?"

"I think so," she replies, her voice cracking.

"What else did the letter say?" Fidelma asks.

"There wasn't much more," answers Fernando. "The only other name mentioned was someone named Lana."

"By the gods!" Debora gasps.

Fidelma asks, "Mother, who is Lana?"

"My middle name is Alannah," she answers. "My sister,

Bridget, used to call me Lana.”

"So does this mean that Ariella's mother was your sister?” ponders Fidelma.

Debora replies, "If what Mr. Greythorn is saying is true, then yes. The doll belonged to Bridget and me both. I never thought anything of it when Fidelma changed its name.”

"Why did she leave?”

"My mother always told me that Bridget chased after a man who was the father of her unborn child.”

"That would have been your father,” Fidelma says to Fernando.

"Wait,” says Debora. "Fernando is Ariella's brother?”

"Half-brother,” Fernando replies. "We confirmed it with a mystic seer. He was killed on the *White Feather*, as well.”

"I'm sorry,” Debora says.

"It is all right,” says Fernando.

"This is so much to take in at once,” says Fidelma. "I can hardly believe it.”

"Me neither,” says Debora. "Ariella visited so many times, and we never knew. I always thought there was something familiar about her eyes.”

"What was Bridget like?” asks Fernando.

Debora laughs. "She was a handful for our parents, that's for sure. She liked playing around the docks, even though we were told to stay away from them. She was good with magic. In fact, I was jealous of her. I never could cast a spell. That's why I was so happy when we learned that Fidelma had the ability.”

"That must be where Ariella got her magic from,” says Fidelma.

Debora nods. "Bridget was very much like Ariella. She had red hair, and green eyes. I can't believe that all this time my niece was right there in front of us. I also can't believe it was your own cousin that came between you and Sven.”

Fidelma takes her mother's hand. "As it turns out, Sven was given a potion that night by Ami.”

"Ami, at the Smelters Inn?”

"Yes.”

"That little wench.”

"Don't worry about her, mother. I already dealt with it.”

Fernando asks, "What did you do?"

"Did you kill her?" asks Samantha.

"No!" replies Fidelma, offended. "I only broke her nose."

Deborah says, "Please, tell Ariella that I would love for her to visit. I could answer any questions she might have about her mother."

Fernando says, "I think she would like that."

"We should be leaving now," says Fidelma. "I have to get to Ariella and tell her the news."

"Be careful," warns Debora. "I don't like that you are returning to a war."

"I'm not fond of it, myself," says Fidelma. "But I have to get to her."

Debora gives her daughter a hug before the three head back to the *Sea Griffin*. When they finally board the ship, Faye greets them, "Captain, there is a noise coming from your quarters. It sounds like someone is blowing into an ocarina."

Fidelma hurries down the stairs and enters her quarters. Fernando and Samantha follow her while the others watch from the doorway. On Fidelma's desk is the crystal necklace that she uses to communicate with her two former crewmen, Trisha and Lee. The crystal is glowing and making a high-pitched sound. Fidelma picks it up and places it in a crystal bowl filled with water. An image of the two young women appears in the bowl.

"What can I do for you?" asks Fidelma.

"Shh," replies Lee, putting her finger over her lips. She then says quietly, "Captain, Trisha and I are trapped in the King's Shield Inn. Sheathelm has been taken over by the orcneas."

"Are you all right?" asks Fidelma, trying to speak quietly.

"For now," answers Trisha. "We are hiding in our room. I think everyone evacuated to the south somewhere. Please tell someone where we are."

Fidelma sighs. "I'm not near Sheathelm right now, but I promise to return as soon as I can. Just try to keep quiet, and maybe they won't find you. Do you have anything to eat?"

"Yes," replies Lee. "Please hurry."

"We will," says Fidelma. Lee takes out the amulet from her bowl and image of the women disappears.

"All right, everyone," says Fidelma. "We need to make haste

for Sheathelm. Vindalia, I'm sorry, but we are going to need you to push your limits."

"Yes, ma'am," she replies.

"I cannot believe that Sheathelm has fallen," says Fernando.

Fidelma replies, "I just pray to the gods that Ariella is all right."

Chapter 3
A Token of Respect

Later, at the stronghold, Ariella approaches a small gathering of people. King Arioch hands a letter to Kristieana and says, "It is important that you make our case to the entire council of Artos. First, seek out Michael Tren. I marked his home on the map I gave you earlier. He will call an emergency council meeting."

"I understand," replies Kristieana.

Namos steps forward and hands Kristieana a pouch, saying, "I have a few potions left over that may be of some use to you. One is for hunger, and two more will revitalize you if you grow tired."

"Thank you," says Kristieana, taking the pouch.

Ariella pushes her way through the people until she reaches Kristieana. Holding out a letter, she says, "One of my crew told me that if you get this letter to Lord Myron Reonia, it might help the council decide in our favor."

Arioch asks, "What does it say?"

Ariella shakes her head. "He didn't tell me, but I trust him."

Kristieana takes the letter from Ariella. The two women gaze at each other momentarily. Each is a reminder to the other of Chance. Kristieana places the letter in her bag and says, "I should hurry if I am to reach Artos before midnight."

Isen, pulling Kristieana aside, says, "Be careful."

Kristieana laughs. "I will be in far less danger than you. You make sure you take care of yourself and watch over the Princess and Ya'leigh."

"I will," says Isen as he looks to Kianna and Chance's eldest child.

Overhearing the conversation, Ariella also looks over at the two young women. As Kristieana steps back to transform into an eagle, Ariella makes her way over to Ya'leigh. Kristieana takes flight as the crowd begins to disperse.

"Excuse me," Ariella says to Ya'leigh.

The princess and Ya'leigh stop. "Can I help you?" Ya'leigh asks.

"Are you Ya'leigh Na'Moon?" asks Ariella.

"Yes, I am," she answers.

Ariella suddenly finds it difficult to speak. She stands there, silent, as Ya'leigh waits for her to say more. "I... I'm sorry about father," Ariella finally says.

"Oh, thank you," Ya'leigh replies, almost instinctively.

"I knew him years ago," Ariella says as Isen joins them. There is silence again as Ariella struggles with what to say next. "Anyway, I just wanted to say that I was sorry, and that he will be missed."

Before Ya'leigh can reply, Isen asks, "Are you Red Beard's Daughter?"

"My name is Ariella," she answers. "Yes, Red Beard is my father."

"Chance spoke fondly of you," says Isen.

"That is kind of you to say," Ariella replies. "Thank you. Now, if you'll excuse me, I should be getting back to my ship."

Ariella starts to walk back to the docks when a guard calls down from the tower, "Orcnea messenger approaching!"

King Arioch and A'ranah run up the hill to the tower, followed by Isen and a crowd of others. When they reach the top, Arioch walks out through the open door next to the tower. Looking out over the land, he can see one orcnea, approaching on horseback.

Arioch starts down the hill when Isen says, "Your, Majesty, let me speak with him."

"No," says Arioch. "I must be the one who talks with him, but you are more than welcome to come with me. If it is some sort of deception, then you can kill him."

Isen and Arioch make their way down the hill through the men laying spikes. Belron and A'ranah watch from the tower. "That doesn't look like the general we spoke with last time," says Belron.

"It isn't," agrees A'ranah. "He was fighting with Chance in the atrium when the gate was destroyed."

The orcnea messenger is dressed the same as any common warrior within the orcnea ranks. He continues to get closer to King Arioch and Isen, who are now waiting at the base of the hill. When he is within forty paces, Arioch says, "That's far enough."

The orcnea stops his horse. "I bring a message from our people."

"We are listening," says Arioch.

"I am here to offer you a cease-fire," he says.

Confused by the offer, Arioch asks, "And why would you offer this?"

"Both sides have lost many fighters this day," replies the orange-skinned soldier. "We offer time to properly care for the dead."

"And what would you do with our fallen?" asks Arioch.

"That is up to you," says the orcnea. "Our tradition is to burn the bodies, but if you wish, we could return them to you."

"That is a kind offer," says Arioch. "How long do you think it would take?"

The orcnea answers, "We could have them ready for you by sunset in front of the main gate to the city."

"How long do you propose the cease-fire to last?" asks Arioch.

"We promise not to attack until dawn if you promise the same," says the messenger.

"Very well," Arioch says reluctantly. "We will send some men to the west gate to collect our dead."

"We will treat them with proper respect," says the orcnea.

Arioch and messenger give each other a nod. The King backs away slowly while the orcnea turns his horse and rides away.

"Why did we agree to another cease-fire?" asks Isen. "It didn't work out well for us last time."

"I am more interested in retrieving the bodies of the dead," says Arioch. "The last thing I want is for them to display Chance's body like a trophy, or worse, mount his head on a battle standard. At this point, we have no choice but to hold out and hope that more help will arrive."

Hours pass without incident. Near the end of the day, Isen and about one hundred men and women begin to haul away wagons full of dead soldiers. The task is a gruesome one that is both exhausting and demoralizing. For hours they take their fallen back to the stronghold, where others do their best to identify them. Headmaster Grunwalt inscribes the names of the fallen into a book before the bodies are incinerated in one of three massive pyres outside the walls of the stronghold.

Isen looks over every wagon, hoping to find the body of his friend. An orcnea approaches him and says, "That is all we have for you."

Isen, while checking over the last wagon, asks, "Are you sure of that? A friend of mine should be among them, yet I have not seen his body."

"We have brought you all that we could recover," says the orcnea. "Perhaps there was not enough left of your friend for us to find."

Isen fights the urge to attack the orcnea. Instead of fighting, Isen nods his head and leaves with the last wagon. When he arrives at the stronghold, he is greeted outside the door next to the tower by Arioch.

"I'm sorry, Your Majesty," says Isen. "Chance was not among the recovered."

A'ranah, standing alongside the king, asks, "Did you see any of the generals?"

"No," says Isen. "I didn't see anyone that looked to be in charge."

"Chance told me that there were three generals near the gate just before he destroyed it," says A'ranah.

"Then they are without their leaders," says Arioch. "We must make sure that Chance's sacrifice was not in vain. We will attack them as soon as the sun rises."

Baeldeth and Prince River come out through the door. The prince says, "Your Majesty, I'm afraid that I bear bad news."

"What is it?" asks Arioch.

"I'm sorry, but my father is recalling our troops," says River.

"Why?" asks Arioch.

Baeldeth answers, "King Nomari feels that the war is lost."

"It will be if you leave," replies Arioch angrily.

"I tried to convince him to let us stay," says River. "But he told me that if we could not protect Sheathelm, then he did not see how it would be possible to take it back."

Arioch sighs. "If it were not for the goblin airships being used against us, Sheathelm's defenses would have held. Still, I understand your father's doubt."

"You are welcome to come to Elonfar," offers River.

"And what of my men?" asks Arioch.

Baeldeth answers, "After you take out all the elves and the forces from East Artos, you only have about three thousand men.

While we cannot accommodate all of them at Elonfar, perhaps we could take the ones who have sent their families there. The rest could go to Artos where the other families have gone."

"Are you suggesting that we just give up?" asks Arioch.

"I am simply giving you options other than certain defeat," replies Baeldeth.

A'ranah interjects, "Baeldeth, this war is far from over."

"I'm afraid it is for us, Mother," explains Baeldeth.

River sighs. "Again, I'm sorry, Your Majesty. I did all that I could."

"I appreciate your efforts," says Arioch. "I do have one request when you leave."

"What can I do for you?"

"Please, take my daughter and Ya'leigh with you to Elonfar."

"Of course," the prince replies.

Baeldeth says, "We will leave later tonight, under the cloak of darkness. We will travel southwest until morning. That way, the orcneas may think we are still here."

"What about the ships?" asks A'ranah.

"With any luck," says Baeldeth, "they will believe that we dispersed them for protection."

"I do have some fortunate news," says River. "Captain Belron and the other drake riders have elected to stay, despite the orders of my father. If the rest of the troops would follow my lead, we would stay as well, but they have little respect for me."

A'ranah says to her son, "Baeldeth, couldn't you get the troops to stay?"

"Perhaps," he replies. "But I side with King Nomari on this. I think we have spent enough time here. It is time for us to start thinking of our own people."

"I'm sorry you feel that way," says Arioch.

"Shall I tell the princess that she is coming with us?" asks River.

"No," Arioch says as he looks down at the burning pyres on the hillside. "I'd better tell her myself. Otherwise, she may not listen."

Later, Ya'leigh is with Kianna and the young Amazons of the Silver Moon, watching over the pyres. Lyra says, "According to

Headmaster Grunwalt, there was no sign of Chance."

"Then he could be alive," says Rehma.

"No," says Ya'leigh sadly. "My father was safe from fire, but not the force of an explosion. Nothing could have protected him from the blast, or the collapsing of the atrium."

Gelana says, "They're saying that the orcneas are without generals. It would seem your father's sacrifice may have turned the tide of the war."

Evelena shakes her head. "Not if the rumors are true that the elves are returning to Elonfar."

"Why would they do that?" asks Rehma.

Kianna says, "River told me that his father thinks the war is lost."

"But if their leaders are dead, they will be disorganized."

"You're right," agrees the princess. "But they still have Sheathelm, not to mention the floating fortress."

Ja'noa flips one of her Star Steel daggers around in her hand. She tosses it into the air before calling it back to her hand. "I don't understand why the orcneas don't just move in with the floating city."

"Because it may be risky," says Evelena. "Right now, that city is keeping our navy away. There isn't much that city could do to this stronghold. We'd be safe underground."

"I think it's because the orcnea leaders are dead and they don't know what to do," says Rehma.

As the sun begins to set, a guard approaches them. He says to Kianna, "Your Majesty, King Arioch requests your presence at the gate, along with Ya'leigh."

Kianna looks at her friend. "I'll bet I can guess what he wants."

Chapter 4
Night Journeys

As the elves gather outside the fortress along the west wall, out of view from Sheathelm, Princess Kianna and Ya'leigh arrive at the gate. They are met by the king, A'ranah, Baeldeth, and River.

"I am NOT leaving with them," says Princess Kianna to her father.

"Yes, you are," insists Arioch. "It's not safe for you here."

"So why are you staying?"

Arioch replies, "If more help arrives from Artos, then we may have a chance to take back the city. If they don't send help, then we may be forced to abandon this post as well."

A'ranah says, "This underground fortress will keep us protected from the floating city. It is full of long passages that will allow us to fight effectively against the orcneas. Their ogres will not be as useful to them underground."

Ya'leigh says, "If it's that safe, then why can't we stay?"

Arioch explains, "We will most likely be engaged in close combat. That is not the place for the two of you. Besides, I already lost a close friend today. I will not lose my daughter, or his."

River says, "Your Majesty, I promise to keep her safe."

Kianna asks River, "Why are you leaving in the first place? Is this because we're not getting married?"

"This was my parents' decision."

Baeldeth mutters under his breath, "Though her refusal probably didn't help much."

Kianna, concerned, asks, "Is that true? Are your parents angry with me?"

"No," says River reassuringly.

Kianna, not believing him, says, "We can take our vows right now if it will change their minds."

River shakes his head. "It won't make any difference."

"But if we're married," says Kianna, "Sheathelm would be your kingdom as well. They would have to keep forces here."

Arioch says, "I will not let my daughter take vows just so Elonfar will feel an obligation to keep their troops here. We will find another way."

"I have an obligation to our people to protect them," says Kianna. "If that means I have to take my vows with Prince River, then I will do so without hesitation."

"That is not necessary," says River.

"Please," Kianna says desperately. "This is all my fault. I should never have refused our engagement. I beg of you now, please marry me."

River sighs. "Kianna, don't do this to yourself. This isn't your fault. I swear to the gods, nothing would make me happier than to take my vows with you, but how could I possibly do so under these circumstances? Kianna, most of your people are already safe, and your father will be, too."

"How can you know that?" she asks. "The orcneas outnumber us greatly."

Arioch says, "I promise we will be safe underground."

A'ranah adds, "We have three gate-stones to our village in the Mana Forest. If things should get out of hand, we have a way out."

Kianna, now feeling less worried, says, "All right, I'll go."

Arioch embraces her, saying, "I love you."

"I love you, too, father," says Kianna.

River, Baeldeth, Ya'leigh, and Kianna make their way along the wall and join the other elves. They begin their journey away from the stronghold through the night, while to the south, Captain McMurphy and her crew are continuing their journey to the stronghold.

The fire in the brazier burns low as Vindalia focuses on increasing the speed of the wind. She plays a tune on her fiddle at a quickened pace. Her fingers move swiftly along the neck of her instrument as she changes notes. Several strings on her bow have worn through as it glides back and forth across the strings of the fiddle.

Fernando and Fidelma sit near the fire across from Vindalia. Samantha watches over the edge of the ship to monitor their elevation. The moonless night sky makes it more difficult to see the ground from above.

Fidelma says to Vindalia, "Why don't you rest for a little while?"

Vindalia stops playing and asks, "Are you sure, Captain?"

Fidelma looks at a small flag-like piece of cloth that is tied to one of the ropes that secure the ship to the balloon above. The cloth continues to sway from a strong breeze. Fidelma says, "It looks like we have the wind at our backs for now, so you can take a nap if you like."

"Thank you, Captain," Vindalia says as she stands up and stretches her arms. "I am rather tired."

"We're making good time, thanks to you," says Fidelma. "We'll try to manage the rest of the journey without waking you."

Vindalia says, "If the wind should slow too much, just let me know."

"I will," says Fidelma as Vindalia climbs down the stairs below deck.

Fernando asks, "How would you fly this ship if you did not have her?"

Fidelma replies, "The *Sea Griffin* was designed to fly without the assistance of spell casters." Pointing to the wheel, she continues, "From there you can make the flames of the brazier go higher or lower. It can burn continuously at its lowest level."

"And what about the wind?" asks Fernando.

Fidelma says, "There's nothing on the ship that can control it. So, in that aspect we are somewhat dependent on Vindalia. If I had to, I could create wind for about an hour."

"How long has Vindalia worked for you?"

"This is her fourth year. Before her, I had recruited young spell-casters from Dicean."

"Like Faye and Janette?"

"Exactly."

Samantha says, "Fidelma, we are passing over South Haven."

"Good," replies Fidelma. "We're over halfway there. We should be there before noon tomorrow. I just hope we're not too late."

"I am sure that Ariella is fine," says Fernando.

"I hope so," replies Fidelma. "There's so much I have to tell her."

On board the *Red Dawn,* Ariella is sitting at the table in the captain's lounge. She fills a glass with wine before setting the bottle in front of her. Spread over the table are the letters from Chance. Ariella drinks the entire glass of wine without taking a breath. She picks up the bottle when there is a knock on her door.

Ariella stares at the bottle for a moment before setting it down, saying, "Enter."

The door opens, and Red Beard enters. He says to her, "My dear, you have a visitor."

"Fidelma?" she asks with a smile.

"No," answers Red Beard.

Disappointed, Ariella sighs, "All right, send them in."

Red Beard turns and nods to someone outside the door. The fair-skinned Amazon of the Silver Moon, Va'leen, enters.

"I'm sorry if I'm disturbing you," says Va'leen.

"Do I know you?" Ariella asks.

"No, we have never met," Va'leen replies as she looks around the room. "My name is Va'leen."

Confused by the visit of a stranger, Ariella asks, "Forgive me for sounding rude, but what do you need, Va'leen?"

Va'leen looks back at Red Beard, who still stands protectively in the doorway. She asks, "May we speak alone?"

Ariella looks at her father and says, "Thank you, Father, but I'll be fine." Red Beards closes the door behind him as he leaves. Ariella says, "It's just the two of us now, so what is it you wish to discuss?"

Va'leen approaches the table and looks down at the letters. She asks, "These are from Chance, aren't they?"

Suspicious, Ariella says, "If you're here to tell me that you were involved with Chance..."

"Oh, no," says Va'leen. "Chance and I were just friends. He never thought of me in that way, and he certainly never adored me the way that he did you."

"I don't understand," says Ariella. "How do you know what Chance thought of me?"

"Chance and I go way back," explains Va'leen. "Not quite as far as the two of you. We met in the Dragon War."

Ariella says, "That's when he met his wife."

Va'leen nods. "Sha'al was my youngest sibling. I must say it took me by surprise when I found out that she laid claim to him."

"If this is supposed to make me feel better, it's not," says

Ariella.

"I'm sorry," says Va'leen. "It's not my intention to bring up bitter memories. I just wanted to meet you. In all the time I spent getting to know Chance, you were all he ever went on about."

"He did?" she asks, trying to hold back her tears.

"Yes," says Va'leen as she makes her way around the table. "He described you in great detail. He would also create your image in the flames of our campfires whenever he talked about you." Va'leen reaches out and brushes Ariella's hair back from her face. "I see you are as beautiful as he portrayed."

"Thank you," Ariella says softly. "Would you like a drink?"

Va'leen eyes the bottle of wine on the table and replies, "Yes, thank you."

Ariella gets another glass from her desk. She fills them both, lifts hers, and says, "To Chance."

Va'leen takes her glass and says, "To Chance."

The women drink their wine. Ariella says, "Please, sit. I am curious now about what else Chance told you."

Va'leen pulls out one of the chairs from around the table and sits. She says, "His stories were always bittersweet. It was easy to see how much he was in love, but, at the same time, he suffered incredible pain."

Ariella sighs, "Chance and I wrote to each other often, but my father saw it fit to keep those letters from reaching each of us." Pointing at the letters on the table, she says, "I didn't get these until a couple weeks ago."

"That's terrible," says Va'leen. "Did Chance ever get your letters?"

"Yes," says Ariella. "We received them at the same time. My father's friend, Torgus, held onto them all these years."

Va'leen says, "I am certain that had Chance known that you were writing to him, things would have turned out differently."

"It doesn't matter now," says Ariella sadly. "I'm just glad to know how much he thought of me before he met her... his wife, I mean."

"I suppose it was partly my fault that he ended up with her," says Va'leen.

"How so?" she asks as she refills their glasses.

"I told him numerous times that he should move on. After all, it had been years since he had heard from you. It was nothing against you, of course, I just wanted to see him smile for someone who was still there. I had no idea that my sister would be the one he'd end up smiling for."

Ariella takes another drink. "You were in love with him, weren't you?"

Va'leen hurriedly finishes the wine in her glass. "Like I said, we were just friends."

"That's not an answer," says Ariella.

"I suppose not," says Va'leen as she stands up. "Thank you for the drink."

"You don't have to leave," says Ariella. "I didn't mean to make you uncomfortable."

"You didn't," says Va'leen. "But I should go now. If there is to be war again tomorrow, I wish to be well rested. I just hope that our message to Artos is well received."

Chapter 5
Council of Artos

Built over the river that divides East and West Artos is the grand palace. It is the center point of the city and is one of only a few places that someone can cross from one side of the city to the other. The city of Artos is not ruled by a king, and, instead of a throne room, there is the council chamber at the very center of the palace.

A diamond-shaped table with eight seats around it sits in the middle of the council chamber. Each side of the table represents one of four districts with two chairs for their representatives.

Kristieana waits as the last two council members take their place at the table. They are more dressed for sleeping than conducting business. Their clothes are hastily thrown on. Three of them only wear robes.

One of the members, a gray-haired woman from northwest Artos, says, "Can someone please explain to me what we are all doing here at this late hour?"

Romnelius, the tall, thin man who visited Sheathelm before the fighting began, asks, "Yes, Michael, you are the one who called this meeting. Why?"

Michael, the other man who visited Sheathelm weeks earlier, says, "I am sorry to have disturbed you all, but we have just received urgent news. My fellow councilmen, I would like you all to meet Kristieana from the house of Ree. She has brought news from Sheathelm."

"Welcome, Kristieana," says the man next to Michael. "I am Richard. Michael and I are from southeast Artos."

"I am Olivia," says a dark-haired woman. Motioning to the man next to her, she continues, "Fredrick and I are from the northeast district."

Impatient from the introductions, Romnelius says, "What news did she bring?"

"Don't be rude, Romnelius," says Micheal. "She has traveled a great distance to be here."

Olivia says to Kristieana, "I am sorry about Romnelius. He

and Lucinda are from the northwest district."

"It's all right," says Kristieana as she eyes Romnelius and the gray-haired woman that spoke earlier.

"You must be exhausted, coming all the way from Sheathelm," says Olivia. "Would you like some food or drink?"

"No, but thank you," says Kristieana. "I'm afraid I bring unfortunate news. The city of Sheathelm was overrun today by an orcnea attack."

The councilmen are stunned by the news. "How is that possible?" Fredrick asks.

"How many orcneas were there?" asks Richard.

Michael says, "According to the letter we received from King Arioch, the city and castle were taken swiftly when large breaches in the walls were formed. To save as many lives as he could, Arioch retreated to the southern stronghold on the coast. He says they are still outnumbered, but they are confident that they can take the city back if we were to send more help."

"We have already sent as many men as we can spare," says Olivia.

"Yes," says Michael. "East Artos has sent plenty of men already. The West, however, has yet to send assistance."

Romnelius says, "The western forces are all that stand between Artos and those savages from Bastion."

Fredrick replies, "There are no reports of any activity from Bastion. You are just using them as an excuse to keep your forces back."

Michael says, "Arioch also has requested that we send our naval forces. He says that the orcneas have raised another floating city. So far, they have kept it out to sea, but with little presence in the water, the orcneas may feel emboldened to bring the floating city over land."

"Our navy wouldn't stand a chance against that city," says one of the two remaining councilmen yet to be introduced.

Kristieana says, "We do not expect you to take on the city. We only hope that your presence there will keep them from turning the floating city to those on shore."

The man replies, "I'm sorry, we have not been introduced. I am David. Myron and I represent the southwest district. Most of the ships belong to our people."

Kristieana looks at other man and asks, "Are you Myron Reonia?"

"Yes," answers Myron. "Why?"

Kristieana, remembering the letter that Ariella had given her, quickly fetches it from her bag. "I was told to give this to you," she says holding out the parchment.

"What is it?" he asks.

"I don't know," replies Kristieana. "I was only told to pass it along to you."

Myron takes the letter and unrolls it. He looks it over and says, "It is from my son."

"Seth?" asks Lucinda. "What does it say?"

Myron rapidly scans the letter. "He says he is serving aboard the *Red Dawn*. He says that they plan to stay and fight the orcneas in Sheathelm. He asks us to send all the help we can."

"Your son should be married to my daughter," says Lucinda, "not gallivanting around the ocean with some pirate whore."

Kristieana says, "With all due respect, ma'am, Ariella Stormrage is risking her life to fight an enemy that is a threat to everyone on this continent, including you."

"Well! I never," huffs Lucinda.

Myron, amused with someone standing up to Lucinda, says, "If a pirate is willing to risk her life to protect these lands, then who are we to hold back our forces?"

Romnelius says, "I doubt you would be so willing to risk our troops if your son was not aboard that ship."

"Perhaps not," admits Myron. "But then again, you may not be so willing to hold back assistance if you cared for anyone other than yourself."

"So, shall we bring this to a vote?" asks Michael.

"This is ridiculous," protests Romnelius. "Are we going to send off our men just because of one man's son?"

Olivia replies, "What of the sons and daughters of Sheathelm? What of the families whose sons we already sent to war?"

Myron says, "If it makes you feel any better, Romnelius, I will be risking my other sons' lives as well. Marcus and Harold both captain their own ships."

"I will vote in favor of sending troops on one condition," says Lucinda. "After the war, I want Seth to marry my daughter, Julia."

"I support a union between them," says Myron, "but that is not a promise that I can make. I can tell you, though, that if we do not send enough help, Seth could very well be killed."

"Fine," says Lucinda. "I vote to send our navy and men."

"As do I," says Myron.

"Am I the only one opposed to this?" asks Romnelius.

Michael asks, "Is there anyone else voting against the proposal of sending more reinforcements to Sheathelm?" No one raises their hand other than Romnelius.

"We will need to leave some forces to defend our own city," says Fredrick. "If Romnelius would like, I propose that he may leave behind half of his legions."

"Does that agree with you?" Michael asks.

"Very well," relents Romnelius.

"I will send word that our forces are to leave first thing in the morning," says Richard.

"Thank you all, and goodnight," says Michael. The council begins to break up as the members head back to their homes. Michael says to Kristieana, "I will arrange for a room to be prepared for you."

"Thank you," says Kristieana.

"It is I who should be thanking you," says Michael. "I think your words swayed the others to vote in favor of helping."

Kristieana replies, "I think it was more the letter from Seth."

"Excuse me," says Myron. "But I was wondering if you have seen my son."

"I am sorry," says Kristieana. "The letter was given to me by Ariella. I did not see him personally, but I am sure he is all right for now."

"If I were to write a letter to him tonight, would it be possible for you to take it back with you in the morning?" asks, Myron.

"Of course," says Kristieana. "I will do what I can to make sure he receives it."

"Thank you," says Myron. "His mother and I have been worried about him. A few weeks ago, he left without any word. We weren't even sure he was still alive. I just hope he stays safe."

Day 23
Chapter 6
Awakening

The room is blurry at first. With great effort, the bars of the cell come into focus. "So, you're finally awake," says a nearby voice. "We were getting worried."

After looking around, he finally locates the source of the voice. Standing outside the cell, General Lortec Ka says, "You look surprised to see me, Na'Moon."

Chance tries to move, but finds that he is bound in heavy chains. "What happened?"

Lortec explains, "Your attempt to kill us all failed, though you did manage to destroy the gate."

As Chance becomes more coherent, he realizes that his armor has been stripped from him, along with his amulet. A thick iron collar is affixed around his neck. The chains around his wrists anchor him to the ground. While he can move, it takes extra effort to do so. Chance opens his hands and stares into his palms. He tries to concentrate on a spell, but nothing happens.

"Don't waste your strength, Slayer," says Lortec. "Your spells won't work so long as you have that collar around your neck."

"How did we survive?" asks Chance, leaning his head back against the wall.

Lortec replies, "Fortunately for us, we were next to the stairs to the throne room. When I realized what was happening, I dove for cover. The other generals were able to escape, as well."

"So what do you plan to do with me now?"

"We have something very special planned for you," answers Lortec. "In fact, General Vork and Cron should be discussing the matter with your king now."

At the base of the stronghold's hill, King Arioch is with Isen, A'ranah, and several guards. They are meeting face to face with Carr Vork and the behemoth ogre, Cron.

"You were wise not to attack this morning," says Carr.

"Make no mistake," says Arioch, "we will retake what is

ours."

Carr laughs. "What makes you think that these lands were ever yours to begin with?"

"For hundreds of years humans have occupied the east of Bruen," says Arioch.

"Until now," adds Carr. He looks at Cron and gives a nod. Cron opens a sack and takes out the breastplate belonging to Chance. Carr says, "Don't worry, your precious hero is alive. For now. If you decide to attack us, he will be the first to be killed."

Arioch says, "Chance would be the first to tell us not to hold back on his account."

"That may be true," says Carr. "But he is not here, and I doubt you will risk your friend's life knowing that we orcneas do not plan to pursue any further aggression at this time."

A'ranah asks, "Are you proposing another cease-fire?"

"Nothing that formal," answers Carr. "But for now, you may rest easy. Tomorrow there will be a trial, and we invite you to watch." Carr takes off two necklaces and offers them to A'ranah. "I assume you know how to use these."

"I do," says the Queen of the Amazons as she takes the necklaces.

Arioch asks, "What sort of trial?"

Carr replies, "Tomorrow, Chance Na'Moon will have to answer for his crimes against our people."

"Are you referring to what he did during the Second Orcnea War?" asks Arioch.

Carr replies, "We are not as concerned about his actions during the war."

"Then why a trial?" asks A'ranah.

Carr looks at the Amazon queen and says, "Chance Na'Moon will be on trial for the war itself."

"That is ludicrous," snaps Arioch. "He didn't start the war. Your people did."

"Then Chance should have nothing to worry about," says Carr. "Tomorrow, at noon, the trial begins. I suggest you find a large pool of water so that all of your people can watch. I have given you two crystals to ensure that more can witness this monumental event. I should warn you, though, that if any attempt is made to free him, we will not hesitate to execute him immediately."

"At least he wouldn't have to endure your fictitious trial," says Arioch.

"I assure you that our trial is very real," says Carr.

"You have already found him guilty," says A'ranah.

"I have done no such thing," says Carr. "Chance will have his opportunity to make his case."

Isen asks, "What if he is found guilty?"

"You will have to watch tomorrow and find out," says Carr. The two generals turn and walk away as Isen keeps a close watch.

Back in the dungeons of Sheathelm, Lortec sets a bowl of stew in front of Chance and says, "You should eat." Chance looks at the bowl suspiciously. Lortec laughs. "It is not poisoned. If we wanted you dead, you would be."

Chance takes a drink of the stew. "So, you plan on making a spectacle of my death tomorrow."

"We will make the world see the truth."

"*The* truth, or just yours?"

"There is only one truth."

Chance drinks the rest of the stew before placing the bowl on the floor. "How old were you when your village was burned?"

The question surprises Lortec. "So, you want to hear my story?"

"I'm not going anywhere for a while," says Chance. "But first, why don't you tell me your name?"

Lortec picks up the empty bowl from the floor and exits the cell. He closes the iron door behind him. "My name is Lortec Ka. I was twelve years of age when you came to my village. It is a day I shall never forget. I was in the fields, gathering some beans for my mother, when I heard a scream. I looked toward our village and saw smoke rising into the air. I ran as fast as I could, expecting to find one of the huts on fire, but by the time I got there, nearly half of our village was ablaze. My people were running through the streets, pointing at the sky. I looked up. That is when I saw you for the first time. You were in the form of a giant eagle. You flew from one of the rooftops and landed in front of my house. You ended your shape-shifting spell, and I saw your true form. I had never seen an elf before that day. Your demonic ears and pale skin were as terrifying as the stories told." Lortec pauses as he chuckles to himself. "I am sure that to you, we orcneas appear to be monsters, as well."

Chance replies, "Perhaps it is simply a matter of perspective."

"Indeed," Lortec nods. "Despite how frightened I was, I did not run from you. Even as you set my house on fire, I charged in. I wanted to stop you, but before I could even try, my father moved in and attacked you." Lortec sighs as he shakes his head. "You just raised your hand and flames engulfed him. He stumbled around for a few moments before you ended his suffering by impaling his skull on your sword." Chance, hearing the story of one of his victims for the first time, can't help but feel empathy. He sits quietly as his enemy continues. "My mother cried out in agony as my father perished by your hand. I tried to attack you myself, but my mother grabbed me and held me tight. You turned to us, and, using our own language, you told us to leave these lands and never return. Then you turned your back to me and walked away, throwing fireballs at the rest of the huts. The moment my mother's grip weakened, I broke free. I ran to my father and picked up his sword. I let out a yell that even you couldn't ignore. You looked back at me, holding a fireball in your hand. My mother grabbed my arm again and begged you not to kill me. She said that I was only a child, and that I was not a threat to you. I never felt so small in all my life than the moment you turned your back to me again and left in your eagle from. I made a vow to myself that someday not only would I be a threat to you, but I would be the death of you."

After staring at the floor for a few moments, Chance finally looks up at his captor through the bars. "After all these years, it looks like you will make good on that vow."

"Tomorrow," Lortec says as he draws his sword, "you will meet your fate. I will use this very sword—my father's sword—to put an end to you."

"And once that is done," says Chance, "do you really believe that your pain will end?"

"Perhaps not," says Lortec, "but my father will be avenged."

Lortec begins to leave when Chance says, "Vengeance will not bring our loved ones back. Believe me, I know."

"You would say anything to save yourself!" snaps Lortec.

"That is where you're wrong," replies Chance. "I'm ready to join my wife in the great light, if that is my fate. I'm just thinking about the future for my children. Tell me, Lortec, do you have any children?"

"I have a son," Lortec reluctantly answers.

"He couldn't be much older than my daughter was when her mother was killed," says Chance.

"What is the point of this?"

"Have you ever thought about his future?" asks Chance. When the general doesn't answer, Chance continues, "Have you ever wondered if we are just condemning our children to a future of war and hate?"

"My son has no future if we are forced to live beyond the sea," says Lortec. "The lands that you have banished us to are barren. I fight for his future."

Chance sighs. "I guess the only question left is: is it really necessary to fight?"

Lortec, surprised by Chance's words, replies, "Who would have imagined that the 'Slayer of Orcneas,' the infamous Chance Na'Moon, would have thoughts deeper than war?"

"You only know a small part of who I am," says Chance. "Perhaps if we weren't so consumed by rage, we could have done things differently."

Lortec stands in silence at the door for moment before opening it. He motions to three guards to enter and says, "I will see you later, Na'Moon."

"I look forward to our next chat," replies Chance.

Far to the southwest, in East Artos, two of Ariella's former crew, Allen and Marie, have been staying in an inn for the last few days. As they make their way down to the docks, they come across a large gathering of people.

Allen asks a man, "What's going on?"

"You didn't hear? Sheathelm fell to the orcneas yesterday."

Marie gasps, "By the gods." She takes Allen's hand.

Allen asks, "Are the orcneas on their way here?"

"No," he answers. "At least, not yet. Arioch and most of his men are now in an old stronghold just to the south of Sheathelm. They don't have enough forces to take back the city. Apparently last night the Council voted to send reinforcements."

Marie asks, "So, what's going on here?"

"They're assigning us to generals or to a ship depending on our skills," he explains. "I'm surprised you didn't know. They went to every house in Artos this morning."

"We aren't from here," explains Allen. "We're staying at the Artos River Inn."

"Well, lucky for you, then. Most of us have no choice," says the man before turning his attention back to the front of the gathering.

Marie says, "We should go back to the inn." She starts to walk, but as she tries to pull Allen, he doesn't budge. "Allen, come on."

He shakes his head. "I don't know, maybe I should help."

"What are you saying, Allen?"

"Maybe I should go with them, to help take Sheathelm back."

"No," protests Marie. "They don't need you as much as I do."

Allen sighs. "South Haven is so close to Sheathelm. It will most likely be the next settlement to fall if the orcneas are not stopped." He pulls her close and kisses her forehead. "I love you, Marie, and I want to build a life with you just like the one we've talked about."

"Then stay with me," she argues. "One more soldier won't make a difference."

"I know, but what kind of man runs away and lets everyone else fight for his future? If we ever have children, what would I tell them when they ask what I did during the Third Orcnea War?"

"Ariella didn't give us all that coin so that you could go and get yourself killed."

"She didn't know that Sheathelm would fall."

Marie shakes her head. "Still, she would want us to stay safe."

A soldier interrupts the conversation. "You there, do you have any weapon skills?"

Allen turns to the man. "I served aboard a ship until recently."

"Report to Captain Reonia," he says, pointing to a dark-haired man with a trimmed beard.

"Yes, sir."

Marie begins to cry. "Allen, please don't do this. Don't leave me."

"You'll be fine without me. Just stay at the inn until I return."

"What if you don't come back? How will I know if you're all

right?"

"After the war, I'll come for you. If you don't hear from me within a week of the war ending..."

Marie throws her arms around him. "Promise me you'll come back."

"I promise." They kiss as Marie clings to him tightly. When they finally separate, Allen says, "I don't really need to bring anything I don't already have. I have my sword already. I suppose I should go see Captain Reonia."

"I love you," says Marie, still clinging to his hands.

"I love you, too." They kiss a final time before Allen forces himself to leave her behind and approach the captain. "Captain Reonia," he says to the man, "my name is Allen. I was told to report to you."

The captain, though not much taller than Allen, is fit. The sleeves of his white shirt fit tightly around his hefty arms. "I'm sorry," he replies, "I don't recognize you. Have you served aboard a ship before?"

"Yes, sir. Until recently, I was member of the *Red Dawn's* crew."

"Really? So you've served under Ariella Stormrage?"

"Yes, sir, for about a year."

"And now you want to go back out to sea?"

"I want to do what I can to help keep the orcneas from overrunning Bruen."

"Very well. This is my ship, the *Trident*." He points the galleon behind them. "We are about full to capacity, but I believe you can find an empty hammock below. We will be leaving soon, so if you need to get anything else..."

"No, Captain, I'm ready now. With your permission, I'd like to board."

"Permission granted. Welcome aboard."

Allen walks up the boarding plank and sets his foot onto the deck. He looks back over the railing and spots Marie, sobbing among the other women gathered on the docks to see their husbands, sons, and fathers off.

Another sailor standing next to Allen says, "I wonder how many of those women will lose a loved one."

"Too many," replies Allen.

"My name's Jack."

"I'm Allen."

"You're new?"

"Yes," Allen replies as he turns his attention to the ship. "The captain said I would find an open hammock below deck."

"Yeah, there are a few," replies Jack. "I'll show you around. Follow me."

As Jack leads the way, Allen looks back one last time at the woman he loves. He whispers, "I promise you, Marie… you will not lose me."

Chapter 7
Family Reunion

Back at the stronghold, word has spread that Chance is still alive. With the *Red Dawn* still docked within the walled cove, Ariella makes haste to the king. "Arioch!" she calls, forgetting to properly address the king. "Is it true?" Arioch turns to greet her as she asks, "Is Chance really alive?"

"That's what they told us," says Arioch.

"We're going to get him back, right?"

"At this point we can't risk it. They said that if we attempt a rescue, they will kill him."

Frustrated, Ariella asks, "Well, what are we going to do, then? We can't just sit here and do nothing."

"We're working on a plan now," says Arioch. "They plan to hold some sort of trial tomorrow. We may try to use that time to strike."

"Well, if you need me for anything, let me know," she says.

"I will," says the king.

As Ariella heads back to the *Red Dawn*, A'ranah joins Arioch and says, "Belron is on his way to inform Baeldeth and Prince River."

Arioch says, "I just hope that Ya'leigh doesn't get her hopes up. It's not likely that Chance will survive the day tomorrow."

Outside the walls of the stronghold, Fidelma and Fernando are making their way around to the gate on foot. Fernando says, "It was a good idea to land the ship over that hill. Everyone looks on edge. They probably would have shot us down."

Fidelma replies, "It's not exactly a brilliant plan to fly over a fortress unannounced. Even if we used our invisibility, they are most likely prepared for that as well."

Fernando nods to a guard as they enter the interior of the stronghold. Fidelma says, "Good, Ariella is docked. I can hardly wait to tell her the news."

"You may want to make sure she is no longer angry with you first," suggests Fernando as they walk down the hill to the water.

"You're right," Fidelma replies. "After everything that's happened lately, I almost forgot that I took you from her."

Looking around at the soldiers, Fernando says, "I still cannot believe that Sheathelm has fallen."

"We need to tell Ariella about her mother, then convince her to leave," says Fidelma as they reach the *Red Dawn*.

Fernando looks up the plank to the ship. "I'll go first."

As they board, Ariella rushes to her brother and holds him tight. Fidelma nervously stands behind them and waits.

"I'm so glad to see you," says Ariella as she steps back.

Fidelma says, "Ariella, I owe you an apology."

Ariella throws her arms around her friend and says, "Don't give it another thought. I'm just happy to see you both."

Confused, Fidelma says, "I thought you would be angry with me."

Ariella shakes her head and the smile on her face quickly fades as she dissolves into tears. Between sobs, Ariella frantically explains, "They have Chance. Yesterday the orcneas took Sheathelm, and Chance stayed behind to destroy a magic gate. We all thought he was dead until this morning when the orcneas said that Chance was their prisoner. Arioch just told me that there's going to be a trial tomorrow, and they'll probably kill him then. I don't know what to do."

Distraught, Ariella is comforted by Fernando and Fidelma. Slowly, her tears dry.

"I am sorry," says Fernando. "Perhaps I can try to speak with the king."

"I already have," responds Ariella, wiping at her face. "They said they're trying to come up with a way to use the trial as a distraction tomorrow."

Fidelma says, "I'm sure Arioch will come up with something."

"I hope so," says Ariella.

Fernando says, "I don't suppose there is any way we could convince you to leave this war behind."

Shaking her head, Ariella answers, "Absolutely not. As long as Chance is alive, I can't leave."

"I understand," says Fernando. "Look, Fidelma and I have something important to tell you, but it hardly seems appropriate now."

"What is it?" she asks, now curious.

Fidelma smiles. "You remember the letter that you got from your mother?"

"Yes," replies Ariella. "What about it?"

Fidelma looks at Fernando. "You tell her."

Ariella, now more intrigued, asks, "Tell me what?"

Fernando takes a deep breath before saying, "I happen to know that the letter your mother wrote to you said that you were named after a doll your mother used to play with when she was little." Ariella, now hanging on every word, waits for Fernando to continue.

Fidelma, unable to contain her excitement, interrupts. "We're cousins!"

"What?" asks Ariella, confused.

Blurting out words so fast that they're almost incoherent, Fidelma says, "The doll that I had when I was young used to be my mothers. It was named Ariella. She had a sister named Bridget that I didn't know about. Bridget is your mother."

Ariella doesn't know what to make of her friend's ramblings. "I don't understand," she says.

Fernando turns to Fidelma and says, "Perhaps you had better let me try to explain."

"All right," says Fidelma excitedly.

Fernando turns to Ariella. "In the letter, your mother referred to someone named Lana, correct?"

"Yes," answers Ariella. "She said that she was going to name me after the doll that she and someone named Lana used to play with as a child."

"We found out who Lana is," says Fernando.

"Are you sure?" she asks, cautiously optimistic.

"Fidelma's mother used to have a sister named Bridget. Bridget left when Fidelma's mother was young to search for the father of her unborn child."

"But who is Lana?" asks Ariella. "Fidelma's mother's name is Deborah."

Fidelma takes Ariella's hand. Trying to remain calm, she explains, "My mother's middle name is Alannah. She told me that her sister used to call her Lana. Ariella, they shared the doll that my mother gave to me. I named it Roxanne, but originally the doll was named Ariella. Don't you see? It all fits. My mother is the same Lana that your mother spoke of. They were sisters. We're family."

"By the gods," gasps Ariella. "Are you certain?"

"Yes," replies Fidelma. "We can confirm it later with a seer, but I have no doubt."

Ariella embraces her cousin. "I can hardly believe it. Less than a month ago, I didn't have any family left. Now, I have a brother and a cousin. I finally know where I come from."

"My mother is anxious to see you again," says Fidelma.

"Of course," replies Ariella. "I can't wait to see her, either."

Fernando says, "Now, we just have to make sure we survive this war."

"Right," says Ariella, her smile fading. "I just hope they can find a way to rescue Chance."

Chapter 8
Old Habits

Sitting on the hillside within the walls of the stronghold, Lyra is reading a book. Next to her are the other six young women on their Rite of Passage.

Rehma says, "I can't believe the orcneas are going to put Chance on trial for the Second Orcnea War."

"It's no more than an execution," says Gelana. "The trial is just for show."

Rehma, frustrated, says, "The whole thing is ridiculous. What is he guilty of, anyway? Fighting in the war that they started?"

Evelena says, "When we stayed at Copper Pass, Kel'ana and I couldn't sleep. We ended up talking with Chance that night. He told us about the things he did in the war that he wasn't proud of."

"It's not like he killed the women and children," replies Rehma. "He showed them mercy. Which is more than they showed his wife."

"I know," says Evelena. "But, still, he did attack towns and villages that were not defended by soldiers."

"Whose side are you on?" snaps Rehma.

"I'm not saying that Chance is guilty of doing anything wrong," says Evelena. "But I'm sure the orcneas feel very strongly that his actions were questionable."

Rehma says, "I also can't believe that we're just going to wait and do nothing."

Gelana replies, "There's not much we can do. At least until more help arrives."

"Besides," says Kel'ana, "didn't they tell Arioch that they would kill Chance if we attacked or attempted a rescue?"

"Well, I hate waiting," grumbles Rehma.

They are sitting quietly, looking out at the docks, when Yentroc spots Sven. She says to Lyra, "Have you talked with Sven since we evacuated yesterday?"

Lyra looks up from her book. She, too, sees Sven down by the water's edge. "No, I haven't," she replies before burying her nose in the book again.

"I thought we weren't talking about him anymore," says Gelana.

"I'm sorry," replies Yentroc. "I just thought that, after yesterday, she might have spoken with him."

"I would have," says Lyra, not looking up this time, "if there was anything more to say to him."

Wanting to change the subject, Yentroc looks around for something to discuss. Next to the docks, she sees water flowing into the harbor from a small man made tunnel. "Where do you suppose that water comes from?"

Gelana replies, "From the underground portions of the fortress."

"I know that," says Yentroc. "I meant, what is the source of the water?"

Evelena says, "Most likely a spring."

"I wonder if we could find it," ponders Yentroc.

Lyra closes her book. "I have already been through most of the stronghold. It's impressive."

"Well, let's go look for it," suggests Ja'noa.

Kel'ana adds, "That sounds like fun to me."

Gelana says, "You lead the way, Lyra, since you're already familiar with it."

Lyra stands up and glances at Sven. In a melancholy mood, she says, "I can do that."

As the seven sisters make their way up the hill to the entrance of the stronghold, the group of people making plans with Arioch is beginning to break up. Ariella, along with Fernando and Fidelma, approach the king.

"Arioch!" calls Ariella, once again ignoring protocol.

The king sighs. "What can I do for you now, Ariella?"

"What did you decide we're going to do?"

"Until help arrives," says Arioch, "our options are limited. We would like to attack the floating fortress directly, but we have no way of getting troops up there. We *would* open a magic gate, but it is protected just like Sheathelm. The goblins inform us that if one of their airships could land next to one of the towers around the outside edge, we may be able to destroy it with black powder and create an opening in their magical defense."

Fernando asks, "When will their airships arrive?"

"Unfortunately," says Arioch, "the closest one is over two days away. Even if it were here, the orcnea drakes would most likely bring it down before it ever got close. We have no way of approaching it undetected."

Ariella and Fernando both look at Fidelma. "Oh, no," Fidelma says. "I don't think so."

Fernando says, "Your ship might be our only chance to destroy one of those towers."

"Not if it gets destroyed by the drakes first," she retorts.

Arioch interjects, "You have an airship?"

Ariella answers, "Yes, she does. It's a smaller one, but it can become invisible."

"Wait," says Fidelma. "This is *my* ship you're talking about. I've worked very hard to get it."

"You will be compensated," says Arioch. "I promise."

"Where would we get enough black powder?" asks Fernando.

"There is a goblin ship out to sea," replies Arioch. "It can't fly, but it does carry enough black powder to destroy one of those guard towers."

Ariella looks at Fidelma hopefully. "Well, what do you say?"

Fidelma sighs. "I'd better be very well compensated for this. That ship is like a home to me."

Arioch says, "I'll make sure that you are given a ship of equal or greater worth."

"Until then," says Ariella, "you can stay on the *Red Dawn.*"

"I don't think that's a very safe place for my crew," says Fidelma. "Where would we sleep?"

"We can convert the lounge," suggests Ariella. "There's only the five of you."

"All right," Fidelma relents. "I'll bring my ship in and dock it. But first, I have two former crewmen trapped in the King's Shield Inn that need to be rescued."

"I'm sorry about your crew," says Arioch. "If they're trapped in the city, I'm afraid you won't be able to get to them."

"Why not?" asks Fidelma. "If we can use my ship to attack that floating fortress, then we should be able to use it to fly over Sheathelm."

Arioch replies, "We're not even certain this is going to work. The orcneas have been prepared for invisible attacks, but if they try to bring down your ship when we attack, we may still be able to control where it lands and destroy their magical defense. If you lose the ship trying to rescue your crew, we won't even be able to try. I'm sorry, but it's too risky. They'll just have to try to stay hidden."

Fidelma says to Fernando, "Go tell Sam to bring the ship into the harbor."

"Of course," he replies.

Arioch says, "I'll go make sure the guards are aware of what's happening."

As the king and Fernando leave, Ariella says to her cousin, "It's a very noble thing that you're doing."

"It's hardly noble," says Fidelma. "I expect the king to make good on his promise."

"I'm sure he will," Ariella replies. "I'm going to go clear some things out of the lounge."

Fidelma sees Sven walking along the docks. She says to Ariella, "I'll join you shortly."

While Ariella makes her way back to her ship, Fidelma catches up with the half-giant from the north. "Sven!" she calls as she nears him.

Sven turns, surprised to see her. "Fidelma? What are you doing here?"

"It's a long story," she says. "Look, Sven, I owe you an apology for the other day."

"You only spoke truth."

"Still," says Fidelma, "It was not right for me to cause problems between you and that elven girl. Please tell her that I'm sorry."

"Lyra is not speaking to Sven."

"Oh, I'm sorry to hear that," Fidelma replies genuinely. "This is all my fault."

"No," says Sven. "Lyra is not speaking to Sven because of what Sven did later that night."

"What did you do?" she inquires, almost afraid of the answer.

"After Lyra left Sven on docks," he begins, "Sven went to Rusty Dagger to be alone. Then, woman showed up and bought Sven drinks."

"I don't need to hear any more of this," says Fidelma.

"No, it's not like that," insists Sven. "Nothing happened between Sven and other woman."

"Then why is Lyra not speaking with you?"

"Because Sven still took woman to his room. Sven remembers being tempted by other woman, but she told Sven that nothing happened."

"And you don't remember?"

"Sven remembers most of night, but not much after returning to his room." Sven shakes his head. "It is just like night at Smelters Inn."

"Believe me, it's not," says Fidelma.

"Why do you say this?"

"First of all, this other woman told you nothing happened, correct?"

"Yes."

"Well, that's one difference," says Fidelma. "Secondly, you should know that you weren't drunk the night before our wedding. You were drugged."

"Drugged? By whom?"

Fidelma sighs before explaining, "Do you remember that flower Ami had that night? The white one?"

"Yes."

"It's called the passion blossom," says Fidelma. "It can be used to make someone fall passionately in love with someone, but they don't remember anything the next day."

"Ami would not do that to Sven."

"She did," says Fidelma. "I just got back from New Waterford. I confronted her, and she admitted to me what she had done. She wanted you for herself. She thought that if you slept with her, she would take you from me. Unfortunately for her, Ariella showed up just as she was serving you that drink."

Sven nods. "That is why Sven cannot remember what happened after that."

"Exactly," says Fidelma. "I'm sorry I never believed you. I know now that it wasn't your fault. I even tried the potion on myself, and I understand that you were not in control of your actions."

"Sven cannot believe that Ami would do that."

"I have already dealt with her."

"You did not kill her, did you?"

"What? No, of course not," scoffs Fidelma, offended. "I just broke her nose."

Sven chuckles. "So what happens now?"

Fidelma smiles, "Well, I could make you dinner as a way of saying I'm sorry."

"That would be nice," Sven replies. "When did you learn to cook?"

She playfully slaps his arm. "I always knew how to cook, you just didn't appreciate my recipes."

Sven jokes, "If your recipes called for not enough spices and overcooking, then no, Sven did not appreciate them."

Fidelma smiles. "Well, at least you liked it when I brought you lunch."

"They were usually leftovers from your mother's cooking," he laughs.

"I don't know why I even try," she says, holding back her own laughter.

"If you wish to make Sven dinner," he says more seriously, "then Sven would be happy to join you."

"How about this evening?" she replies. "I'm going to be staying with Ariella on the *Red Dawn* for a while. You can find me there."

"Sven is looking forward to it," he replies.

Fidelma smiles. "So am I."

Chapter 9
Walk Through History

Below the hilltop of the stronghold, Lyra leads her friends to a room within the labyrinth of stone walls. Having cast a light spell on the end of her staff, Lyra allows the others to see within the chamber that has long since been abandoned.

"Where are we?" asks Ja'noa.

"I think this was where they prepared their food," says Lyra.

"Who lived here?" Gelana asks.

"Dwarves," answers Lyra.

"I thought the writing looked familiar," says Evelena.

"Can't you read it?" asks Kel'ana.

"Only some of it," Evelena replies. "When I was learning how to speak it, we read from translated texts that used letters from the Common language. We weren't taught the ancient runic lettering."

"This is as far as I've been able to follow the water's source," says Lyra, pointing to the far wall. On the other side of the room, water flows out from a round tunnel that is carved into the wall. A gate made up of iron bars allows water to pass through the entrance of the tunnel while keeping trespassers out. Over many years, minerals have built up on the bars below the water's surface. The water pours into a stone trough, about as high as the women's knees, that runs along the left wall. It is carried the entire length of the room before it escapes through a smaller tunnel.

Lyra points to a lock fastened to the rusted gate and says, "I wasn't able to go any further."

Ja'noa steps forward to examine the lock. "It's probably too rusted. I doubt I could pick that."

Gelana stands on the edge of the trough peering through the bars. She draws her sword and uses the hilt to break the aged lock.

"That works, too," Ja'noa laughs.

Gelana pulls on the iron gate, forcing it open. The hinges creak loudly, forcing Kel'ana and Lyra to cover their ears. After the obstacle is out of the way, Gelana says to Lyra, "Do you want to lead, or would you like me to go first?"

"I can do that," says Lyra. She climbs onto the edge of the

trough as Gelana steps down to get out of her way. The tunnel is high enough that the women do not have to duck down to walk through it. The water flows to the left side of the tunnel while the right side is higher, presumably to walk on. Lyra steps inside. "I don't think anyone has been down here since it was built."

"How old is this place?" asks Evelena.

"It's not really that old," replies Lyra. "About five hundred years."

"What happened to them?" Evelena asks. "The dwarves, I mean."

"They moved on after the gold ran out," says Lyra. "Most of them went north and helped build Coldrock, in the Northwind Range."

"How do you know all this?" asks Ja'noa.

Lyra laughs. "History was one of the few subjects I enjoyed."

While walking through the tunnels, Lyra stops and notices a change in the walls. "Look, the tunnel is no longer carved out of stone."

Evelena notes, "These are bricks."

"I wonder why they changed," ponders Yentroc.

Evelena replies, "We're probably no longer under a solid stone."

"How far do you think this tunnel goes?" asks Kel'ana.

"It might go all the way to King's River," suggests Lyra.

"Why would they build a tunnel that long for water?" asks Yentroc as they continue on.

Kel'ana replies, "To keep it from freezing in the winter."

"They could have just dug a well," says Yentroc.

"True," says Evelena. "But long tunnels like this would be useful for escape, as well."

Lyra says, "It also wouldn't have been very hard for them to build these tunnels. Many dwarves were, and still are, masters of earth magic."

"I would have loved to have seen Coldrock," says Gelana. "Kelik was telling me that it was as big as Sheathelm, but underground."

"From what I read," says Lyra, "Coldrock was the largest underground city since the Great Collapse. Before then, the largest subterranean city was the Dwarven capital of Rune."

"Isn't that the city that this realm is named after?" asks Yentroc.

"Yes," answers Lyra.

"So, is it Rune, or Runefell?" asks Gelana.

As Lyra carefully makes her way along the water's edge, she tells the others what she remembers. "When the dwarves first arrived from their home world of Nidavellir, they found the lands of Runefell untamed by any other race, with the exception of dragons. They settled in the first mountainside they came across and built the city of Rune. The mountain was rich with iron, gold, and other valuable metals. It took ten years for them to build a magic gateway back to their home world, but once it was established, the city of Rune prospered greatly. Goblins were the next to arrive, followed by the orcneas. Humans and elves arrived much later. By that time, the city of Rune was as vast as the mountain it was under, and the dwarves dominated the land."

Evelena asks, "This was all before the Great Collapse?"

"Yes," confirms Lyra. "It was during the golden age of magic. Every major city built magic gates to other cities and worlds."

Evelena adds, "And it was those very gates that caused the Great Collapse."

"Is that how Runefell got its name?" asks Yentroc.

Lyra nods. "When the gates were destroyed, the magic forces ripped out parts of each world and scattered them to other realms. Entire cities were destroyed and their people were left stranded in strange new lands. A group of humans came across what was left of the city of Rune. The stories say that King Demetrius Ravenguard looked upon the mountain that had collapsed on the city, and noted that it looked as if the city of Rune fell. His squire mistakenly wrote it down as one word."

"Wait," interrupts Kel'ana. "This realm got its name due to a squire's error?"

"That's the story, anyway," replies Lyra. "Later, the squire asked the king if he should correct his mistake. King Demetrius proclaimed that the city of Rune was no longer, and that the realm's name should accurately reflect that fact."

Gelana suggests, "Maybe we could go to the old city."

"Assuming we survive this," says Ja'noa.

"Now, let's not think like that," replies Evelena before

changing the subject back. "Where is the city of Rune?"

Lyra answers, "It's deep within the broken hills of Nechorez, across the eastern sea."

Gelana laughs. "I guess we won't be seeing it anytime soon."

Looking ahead, Lyra can see the tunnel open up into a chamber. "I think we're at the end," she says.

The women enter the cavern and find a small body of water feeding the tunnel that leads back to the fortress. It is no more than twenty paces in diameter. Evelena says, "This must be it."

"I wonder how deep it is," says Kel'ana.

Lyra picks up a small rock from the ground and casts a light spell on it. With the rock now glowing brightly, she tosses it into the water.

"You dropped something," Kel'ana jests, as they watch the rock sink to the bottom, revealing the pool's depth.

"It's certainly too deep to walk across," says Evelena as she looks at the submerged glowing rock. The water is clear, and the light from Lyra's stone allows them to see that the rocky edge of the pool drops off steeply.

"There isn't anything on the other side, anyway," says Yentroc, pointing across to a small ledge.

Lyra points her staff at the opposite side of the small cave and can see where time has ravaged this underground reservoir. Boulders from the ceiling of the cavern have fallen around the edges.

Evelena says, "I'm amazed that this whole cavern hasn't collapsed."

"Maybe we should get out of here," suggests Yentroc.

"I agree," says Jan'oa.

The seven sisters begin to backtrack when Yentroc asks, "When the Great Collapse happened, what caused the magic gates to be destroyed?"

Lyra, leading the way back to the stronghold, answers, "The great city of Atlantis, in Midguard, hosted a grand festival. During the celebration, every magic gate in the center of the city was opened at once. Elders speculate that the amount of magic being used was so great that it caused the gates to amplify their power, and instead of transporting what passed through them, they began to move everything around them. Every realm that hosted a magic gate was affected. They say that other gates nearby activated themselves and spread the problem. Countless lives were lost, and even though over the years we have been able to rebuild new gates and locate the ruins of most of the cities, some have never been found."

Evelena adds, "Elonfar was lucky. It was originally located in Alfheim. Much of it was destroyed, but our ancestors were able to rebuild it."

"I don't understand," says Ja'noa. "We open multiple gates all the time. Why hasn't it happened again?"

Evelena answers, "Because those gates don't take us very far. The amount of magic used to move someone from one city to another is nothing compared to the amount it takes to travel to another realm."

Lyra says, "The capital cities before the Great Collapse had multiple gates to other realms. Rune had three, and Atlantis had over a dozen. They were all located in one room. Now we try to build such gates further apart to prevent it from happening again."

The women soon find themselves back in the stronghold. They climb down from the trough and Lyra immediately heads for the door. "Where are you going?" asks Gelana.

Lyra answers, "I'm going to check if one of the books or scrolls that Grunwalt and I saved from the library at Sheathelm has any more information about this place. I have a feeling that we're missing something."

Chapter 10
A Message From Home

Later in the afternoon, Fidelma and Samantha carry the last of their belongings aboard the *Red Dawn*. Fidelma pauses to look back at the *Sea Griffin,* which is also docked in the small harbor. Soldiers are busy loading the flying vessel with barrels of black powder.

"Are you going to be all right?" asks Samantha.

Fidelma sighs, "I will be. It's just hard to say goodbye."

"I know," replies her friend. "I'll miss her, too."

Ariella welcomes them. "Is that the last of your belongings?"

"Yes," answers Fidelma, setting down a backpack stuffed with clothing.

"Let me get someone to help," says Ariella. She looks around the deck and spots her newest crewman, Seth, talking with one of the twins, Janette. Ariella calls his name. Seth excuses himself from the young lady's presence and rushes over.

"Yes, Ma'am?" he replies before noticing the other two women.

Samantha's eyes widen. "Seth, is that you?"

Both Fidelma and Ariella are surprised that the two know each other. "Samantha?" Seth replies, equally taken aback.

"What are you doing here?" Samantha asks.

"I should ask you the same thing," says Seth.

"You know the answer to that," she replies.

Fidelma interrupts, "How do you two know each other?"

Samantha answers, "This is Marcus's younger brother."

"Oh," says Fidelma. "Now I understand."

"Well, I don't," says Ariella. "Who's Marcus?"

"Marcus is my brother," says Seth.

"Don't get smart with me, boy," warns Ariella. "I've figured that much out."

"I'm sorry, Captain," apologizes Seth. "That was not my intention. Samantha was betrothed to my brother, Marcus, several years ago, but she disappeared."

Samantha says, "I had no intention of taking my vows with

54

someone without any say in the matter."

"I don't blame you," says Ariella.

"Besides," continues Samantha, "I couldn't imagine a life just sitting at home while he was out to sea."

"He was a sailor?" asks Ariella.

"A captain, actually," replies Samantha.

Ariella ponders for a moment before asking, "Are you talking about Marcus Reonia?"

"Yes," answers Samantha. "Why? Do you know him?"

With all attention shifted to her, Ariella begins to feel a bit unnerved. She answers vaguely, "I may have met him once... or twice." After the others continue to look at her in silence, she adds, "I don't feel the need to explain myself any further."

Samantha turns to Seth and says, "Well, now that you know why I'm here, what about you?"

Seth replies, "You could say that I'm just following your lead."

"You ran away? Why?" asks Samantha.

"My parents arranged a marriage between myself and Julia Koehn," Seth answers.

Samantha laughs uncontrollably. The others watch her as she regains her composure. "I don't blame you for running away," she finally says between laughs.

Ariella asks, "Is she that bad?"

Samantha replies, "She's an insufferable little wench. You'd be tempted to throw her overboard in less than a day."

"She's not that bad," says Seth politely.

"Oh, yes, she is," insists Samantha.

The conversation is interrupted by the arrival of Kristieana. The tall red-headed Amazon walks up the plank to the ship.

Ariella asks, "Is Artos sending any forces?"

Kristieana nods, "Yes, thanks to the letter you had me deliver. It seemed to make the difference in the Council's vote." She holds out a sealed letter to Ariella. "Lord Myron asked me to deliver this. Please see to it that it reaches his son. Now, if you will all excuse me, I'm rather tired from flying all day."

"Of course," says Ariella. "Thank you."

Kristieana turns and leaves. Ariella hands to letter to Seth, saying, "I had no idea when you gave me that letter that it was to your father. I don't know how to thank you."

"Allowing me to serve aboard your ship is thanks enough, Captain," replies Seth. "But, if you don't need me any further, I would like to see what my father has written."

"I understand," says Ariella. "We'll manage these bags. You're dismissed."

"Thank you, Captain," replies Seth. He takes his letter, walks to the stem of the ship, and sits down on the deck, leaning back against the railing.

While Seth begins to read the message from his father, Ariella, Samantha, and Fidelma enter the lounge of the ship.

"I know it will be a bit cramped," says Ariella, "but you're free to stay here as long as you need to."

"Thank you," says Fidelma. "If you don't mind, I'd like to use the galley this evening. I invited a guest for dinner."

"Oh? Who?" asks Ariella.

"Sven," she answers.

Ariella, shaking her head, says, "I don't think that's a good idea. I know that you said what happened wasn't his fault, but still..."

"I need to do this," says Fidelma.

"If you say so," says Ariella. "Well, this place is all yours, including the galley. I'll leave you to get settled."

Ariella steps outside and looks across the deck of her ship. She spies Seth, just finishing his letter, folding the parchment and putting it in his pants pocket. She makes her way down the stairs from the quarterdeck, and as Seth looks out at the horizon of the sea, she approaches him.

"Why didn't you tell me you were the son of a councilman?" she asks once she reaches him.

Seth replies, "Because I didn't want to be treated any different, and I also feared that you might try to send me back."

"Why would I do that?"

"I have no doubt that my father has posted a handsome reward for my safe return."

"What did your father say... in the letter, I mean?"

Seth laughs to himself. "He told me to be safe, and that I was to return with Marcus to West Artos."

Ariella says, "So, not only are you a son of a councilman, but you're from the west side of the city. You may as well be a prince. You took quite a risk joining Rineheart's crew. You're lucky they didn't find out who you were, or they would have held you for ransom."

"I guess I'm fortunate that you came along."

"I suppose it all worked out well."

"At least until I have to go back to Artos."

"You know, there are worse places you could be. Most people would give anything to live the life that you must have there."

Seth nods his head. "I know. I should be thankful for all that fate has given me. But still, when most of your choices are made for you, life can feel like a prison no matter how much wealth you have. Tell me, Captain, do you know what it's like for a parent to decide who you can and cannot spend the rest of your life with?"

Ariella smiles. "Boy, you have no idea just how much I understand."

Seth notices Samantha standing at a slight distance behind Ariella. She says, "Captain, if I may have a word with Seth."

"Of course," replies Ariella before leaving the two alone.

"Is your brother coming?" Samantha asks.

"Yes," Seth answers. "Marcus should be here in a couple days."

"Does he know I'm here?"

"No."

"Please," says Samantha, "don't tell him that you found me."

"I don't understand," says Seth. "You and my brother were happy together. Why did you leave?"

"It's like you were just telling Ariella," Samantha replies. "If the choices are made for you, life can feel like a prison. Besides, I wanted to see the world, and if I were his wife, I would have been forced to stay at home and perform my 'wifely duties.' Now, I'm living the life I always wanted."

"Well, I certainly understand that."

"Promise me that you won't tell him."

"I won't. I promise."

"Thank you," replies Samantha. As she turns to leave, Samantha almost runs into Fidelma.

With a smile on her face, Fidelma says, "I just heard from Lee and Trisha. They managed to get down to the cellar. I'm so relieved that they're still fine."

"Good," sighs Samantha. "I've been worried about them, too."

"They said there's plenty of food for them down there."

"Hopefully they can stay hidden until we can reach them."

Changing the subject, Fidelma says, "Speaking of food, I have everything I need to prepare Sven's meal, except one small detail. The whitefish."

Seth says, "We had whitefish last night. I can ask Torgus if there's any left over."

"It has to be fresh."

"I'm certain that Torgus has them well preserved."

Fidelma sighs, "I suppose it will have to do."

"Great," replies Seth. "I'll go ask him."

As Seth walks away, Samantha notices Fidelma's cheerful demeanor. "Well, someone's in a good mood," she teases.

"I'm just glad that Lee and Trisha are all right."

"I'm sure you are," replies Samantha. "But I think you're more excited about having dinner with Sven than you want to admit."

"Perhaps," says Fidelma. "But I don't want to get my hopes up. The last time I did, I was hurt. I promised myself I wouldn't let that happen again."

In galley of the *Trident,* the captain, Marcus Reonia, is having dinner at a long table with several others. Allen, holding his plate, looks around for a place to sit. "Allen," the captain calls, "come sit over here."

Allen makes his way over to the captain's table. "Thank you, Captain. It would be an honor."

Marcus says to the others, "If you haven't already met him, I would like you all to meet Allen. He used to serve aboard the *Red Dawn.*"

A balding man with a thin goatee asks, "Under Red Beard, or his daughter?"

"Ariella was my captain."

Marcus says, "Allen, this is James. He is one of our wind masters."

"Nice to meet you," says Allen as he shakes his hand.

James replies, "The pleasure is mine."

A taller, thin man says, "I'm Alex." Allen shakes his hand and nods.

"I'm Matthew," says a man with sandy brown hair and a short, thick beard. "I'm the other wind master."

Allen greets him with a handshake before sitting. Marcus asks, "So, Allen, what do you think of the ship?"

"It's much larger than the *Red Dawn*. It's hard to tell we're even out to sea."

James asks, "What was it like on the *Red Dawn*?"

Allen shrugs. "I don't have much to compare it to, so I can't rightly say."

Marcus asks, "How is Ariella these days? I haven't seen her since her father was killed."

"Oh, her father's..." Allen cuts his sentence short, then says, "I mean, she's doing well, I suppose."

"I guess I can ask her myself when we arrive in a couple days."

"Wait, Ariella is there?"

"Yes," Marcus replies. "In fact, my brother is on her ship now. His name is Seth."

Allen shakes his head, "I don't think I've met him."

"From what he wrote to our father, he recently joined her crew just outside Bastion. He asked that Artos send support."

"I'm not surprised she went to Sheathelm, but I didn't think she would stay around for long."

Marcus laughs. "Ariella Stormrage hates orcneas with a passion. They killed her mother."

"Yes, I'm aware," says Allen, wondering how his former captain will react to him leaving Marie in Artos to fight.

"Is something wrong?" asks Marcus, noticing the distant look on Allen's face.

"Yes," he answers honestly. "I must tell you, Captain, that while Ariella and I parted on good terms, we did so with the understanding that I would stay safe and look after a woman who was also a member of her crew."

Marcus asks, "And this woman... where is she now?"

"She's back in Artos."

"And you think Ariella will be upset with you for leaving her and choosing to join my crew?"

Allen nods. "I think there's a very good possibility of that."

Marcus jests, "Are you trying to get Ariella angry with me, too?"

"No, sir, I'm sorry."

"I'm only joking," Marcus reassures him. "But seriously, I would not want her angry with me."

"You're right about that, Captain," says Allen, thinking back to the morning after Fernando fled. "So, how do you know Ariella?"

"Oh, I've met her once or twice."

"I suppose you could call it 'meeting,'" says James. He and Matthew laugh.

Marcus shakes his head. "Pay them no attention. So, tell me, Allen, has any man been able to win over her heart yet?"

Allen thinks of Fernando and then Chance. "Well, I don't know if anyone won her over, but a few days before I left, she did get a visit from Chance Na'Moon. Apparently they had a past together of some sort."

"Of course. She mentioned him when we first met. She said that she had moved on, but I could tell by the way she spoke with such loving disdain that she still had feelings for him. It must have broken her heart."

Confused, Allen asks, "What must have broken her heart?"

"Oh, you didn't hear? Chance Na'Moon was killed in Sheathelm."

"By the gods, really?"

Marcus explains, "The rumor is he sacrificed himself to destroy the lunar gate."

Allen, stunned by the news, says, "I met him only days ago on the *Red Dawn*."

James asks, "What was he like?"

"I don't know, normal, I guess. Sad, maybe. I was there when he set an entire orcnea ship ablaze."

Alex asks, "Really? You got to see the Slayer fight in battle?"

"Actually, no," he admits. "I didn't see it. I was in the captain's quarters fighting at the time."

"You fought an orcnea?" asks Marcus.

"Yes, Captain. Four, to be exact." He looks around the table at the doubtful faces. "Not at the same time, of course, and I'm not boasting. I'm lucky to be alive."

"You killed them all?"

"Yes, but it's not that big of a deal. There were far more than we could handle. If Chance hadn't arrived, I may not even be here to tell the tale. I can't believe he's gone."

Marcus nods. "Unfortunately, not only is the Slayer dead, but the word is the other elves have also pulled back their forces. It hasn't been confirmed yet, but if it's true, I'm not certain that we will be able to take back Sheathelm."

Chapter 11
Dinner for Two

Chance is woken by the sound of the iron gate of his cell opening. Lortec Ka enters holding a large platter covered with enough food to feed several people. Still bound by his chains, Chance watches as three guards enter the cell, bringing with them a table and two chairs. After placing them in the center of the cell, the guards leave, locking the door behind them.

Lortec places the platter on the table and asks, "If I release you from your bonds, will you try to kill me?"

Chance looks at the guards around the cell. Each has a crossbow drawn. He looks up at Lortec. "Even if I did attack you, my magic is useless with this collar around my neck."

"You are correct," replies Lortec as he kneels next to Chance. "I also have no weapon with me for you to try to steal. If you were to try to fight me, you would lose."

Chance lifts his chains, holding the locks out to the general. Lortec takes a key and unlocks the bindings. Chance rubs the irritated skin of his wrists. As he gets to his feet, Chance asks, "Am I to understand that you and I are going to eat together?"

Lortec sits at the table. "Unless you refuse to eat."

Chance eyes the roasted turkey on the platter surrounded by an assortment of vegetables. He sits in the other chair and says, "I suppose that as long as you eat first, I can be sure that it's safe."

"This is no more dangerous than the food this morning," replies Lortec. "I do *not* care for trickery, but if it will make you feel better..." Lortec tears a leg from the turkey and places it on his plate. With a serving fork, he loads his plate with vegetables. "If you still do not trust me, then I will let you decide whether I eat this food, or you do."

"You eat it," replies Chance. "I'll serve my own, thank you." He takes the other leg from the platter, along with a small pile of vegetables. "I don't understand why you're here. Surely my well-being is not that important if I am only to be put to death tomorrow."

Lortec chuckles to himself. "You seem to be convinced that

your trial tomorrow is going to be nothing more than an execution."

"Are you telling me that it's not?"

"You will be given time to speak."

"What difference will my words make to those who have already made up their minds?"

"You do not give my people enough respect. We are a fair and just people. If you are found guilty tomorrow, you will still have a chance to save yourself."

"By fighting you?"

"Yes."

"You want me well fed so that I will not have an excuse for losing to you in combat."

Lortec laughs again to himself. "Now you are beginning to understand me."

"And what of my injuries?"

"You will be healed before combat begins."

"Will I be able to use magic?"

"It is a part of you, so yes."

"And what if I flee?"

"You will not," replies Lortec shortly. "Now, eat, and ask no more questions."

While Chance and the orcnea general begin to eat, Fidelma is busy aboard the *Red Dawn,* preparing a very special meal. The personal galley of Ariella is a mess, as Fidelma rushes about putting spices in a pot that sits atop a cast iron stove. She sniffs the rising steam before removing the pot and setting it aside.

Samantha enters saying, "It sure smells nice."

Fidelma laughs. "I only hope it tastes as good as it smells."

"I'm sure it will," says Samantha as she looks around at the mess. She walks over to the counter and spots an open book. Within the pages are the white petals of a passion blossom. "Fidelma, please tell me that you didn't put this in the food."

Fidelma looks at the open book before rushing over and closing it. "Of course not," she mutters.

Samantha, unsure of her answer, says, "Fidelma..."

"I promise," says Fidelma. "I didn't use the passion blossom. I'll admit I was tempted, though."

"Why?"

"I don't know," she sighs. "I guess I just wanted Sven to treat me as passionately as he did Ariella the night before our wedding. I can still see her memories of that night."

"But those memories aren't real," says Samantha. "At least, his actions weren't. Sure, he slept with her, but he wouldn't have had he not been drugged."

"I know," relents Fidelma.

Samantha says, "Besides, if something happens tonight, don't you want Sven to remember it?"

"You're right," replies Fidelma as she walks back over to the stove. "That's why I decided not to use it. I want everything tonight to be genuine and honest."

Annalee knocks at the galley door, surprising the two women. "Excuse me," says Annalee to Fidelma, "but there's huge man outside. He says he's here to see you."

"Thank you," says Fidelma, smiling, as she exits the galley.

The adjacent lounge is now cluttered with the belongings of the women of the *Sea Griffin*. As the three women walk to the door, Annalee asks, "He wouldn't happen to have any brothers, would he?"

Fidelma laughs, "He has two brothers, but they are older, and not nearly as handsome."

They reach the door, and Samantha opens it. Fidelma says, "You're just in time."

"It smells good," says Sven, as he enters. "Did you make it, or did they?" He nods toward Annalee and Samantha.

Samantha snickers as she and Annalee exit. Fidelma replies, "I'll have you know that I made it all on my own."

"Sven cannot wait to try it," he says as he enters.

Fidelma closes the door, leaving Samantha and Annalee on the quarterdeck with Fernando and Ariella. Samantha teases, "Well, Fernando, it looks like your chance to be with Fidelma just got a little smaller." She holds out her hands to simulate the height difference between him and Sven.

"That is all right by me," replies Fernando. "Even though I did not get to know him well, I can tell that Sven is a good man, and Fidelma needs a good man."

"Are you sure you're not jealous?" asks Samantha.

"On the contrary," says Fernando. "I am happy for her."

"Well, I'm jealous," interrupts Annalee.

Samantha laughs. "If you like goliaths, you should travel to the north."

"I thought goliaths were much larger than him," says Annalee.

"They are," replies Samantha. "Sven is one of the smallest."

"Oh," sighs Annalee. "Well, then, going north wouldn't do me much good. I wouldn't want anyone taller than Sven. If you haven't noticed, I'm a bit short myself."

Fernando says, "You are rather adorable."

"Please," replies Annalee, disgruntled. "Don't ever use that word to describe me again."

"*Lo siento,*" Fernando apologizes.

Inside the lounge, Sven sits at the table that has been set for two. He looks around at the piles of women's clothing. Fidelma emerges from the private galley, carrying the pot from the stove. "I'm sorry about the mess. We haven't had a chance to organize since moving to the *Red Dawn.*"

"Why are you staying here now?"

"My ship can fly, and the king wants to use it to attack the floating city," she explains as she sets the pot in the center of the table.

Sven, unaware of Arioch's plan, asks, "But what could your ship do against that city?"

"He plans to use something called black powder—that's what caused the goblin airships to explode when they landed in Sheathelm—to destroy one of the guard towers on the city. They suspect that if one of them is destroyed, it will allow them to open a gate there. They plan to attack tomorrow. Ariella and I are going with them."

"You should let the goblins handle this."

"It's *my* ship. I have to go."

"After it is done, what will you do with no ship?"

"King Arioch promised to reimburse me," explains Fidelma. "It sounded like a fair deal. Especially if it works." Fidelma takes the lid off the food. "Now, it's time to eat."

Sven deeply inhales the air to smell the fish better. "It is making Sven's mouth water."

"I hope you like it," she says as she serves him one of the

fillets. "I borrowed the recipe from an old friend." Fidelma continues to stand next to him, waiting for Sven to take a bite. "Go on, try it."

Sven uses his fork to break up the tender fish before eating one of the pieces. Fidelma waits nervously for his reaction as he chews. "It is very good," says Sven. "It tastes like fish at..." He stops and looks up at Fidelma. She smiles as he asks, "Where did you get recipe?"

"I told you," she replies. "I got it from an old friend."

Sven laughs. "Ami was *not* your friend."

"No, I suppose she wasn't," says Fidelma. "So, you like it, then?"

Sven nods. "It is best fish that Sven has ever had."

"Did you forget that I can tell when you're lying?"

Sven looks at her, smiles warmly, and says, "Sven would never lie to you."

Fidelma finds herself momentarily speechless. Fighting back her emotions, she finally says, "I know that, now. I'm sorry it took me so long to learn it."

"Do not be sad, Sven's sweet midnight daisy," he says softly. "Please sit, and eat."

Fidelma, forces a smile, trying not to cry. She serves herself one of the fillets and sits opposite Sven.

As Sven and Fidelma begin their meal, Chance and the orcnea general, Lortec Ka, are finishing theirs.

Chance, continuing their ongoing conversation, says, "Are you telling me that out of all the shamans you trained, none could make the soil of your lands fertile?"

"Water and air are easy to learn compared to the earth spells," argues Lortec.

"Still," replies Chance, "plant spells aren't that difficult to learn. Just a few shamans could feed large cities."

Lortec replies, "That is true. But tell me, how many plant spells do *you* know?"

After thinking a moment, Chance nods. "You make an excellent point."

Lortec laughs. "You misunderstand, Slayer, we do have shamans that can feed us, but they are overworked, and orcneas do not like to rely too much on others for their food. If something were to happen to them, or the mana around us, we would perish."

"So is that why you've come back?" asks Chance. "To secure fertile land for farming?"

Lortec sits back in his chair. "That, and to avenge those who were killed in the last war."

The door to the room opens and General Carr Vork enters. He holds out Chance's talisman that was given to him by the red dragon, Feonvear. "This amulet will not obey me."

"Perhaps after you kill me tomorrow, it will," Chance suggests.

Carr replies, "I have already checked. It is not that sort of magic. This gift from your red dragon friend is only useful to you." Carr drops the talisman on the floor. He says to one of the guards, "Give me your sword." Chance watches as the guard hands his sword over to the shaman general. Carr says, "If it cannot be of use to us, then I will make certain that it will no longer be of use to you." Carr strikes the amulet with the sword. A flash of light temporarily blinds everyone in the room as a red mist rises from the shattered necklace.

Chance stands up from his chair as the mist floats through the bars of the cell and approaches him. He reaches out his hand and the mist abruptly envelops him. Chance falls to his knees in agony. The generals look on as Chance struggles to breathe.

"What is it doing?" Lortec asks.

Carr replies, "It is binding to him. I was foolish to destroy it in his presence."

Chance coughs as he breathes in the smoke. As it is absorbed into his body, red lines begin to appear on his skin. After a few moments, the pain subsides. Chance takes a deep breath and gathers himself. As he rises, he looks at his forearms, which are now covered with fiery red markings similar to the war paint that the Amazons from the house of La'harn apply to themselves.

"We will have to cancel the trial," says Carr.

"No," replies Lortec as he looks at Chance, who is clearly as confused as they are.

Carr says, "If he possesses the power of the red dragon..."

"Then he will be no more dangerous to me than when he held the talisman," says Lortec. "This will make the trial that much more glorious."

"I think you are making a mistake," protests Carr.

"You made the mistake when you brought that talisman in here," snaps Lortec. "But fear not, I will make sure that everything goes as planned."

Chance says nothing as Lortec motions for the guards to open the door to the cell. They enter and remove the table and chairs as Lortec stares down his captive, saying, "Tomorrow, Slayer, you will be held accountable for your crimes. The blessings from your fire dragon will not save you."

Lortec closes the door to the cell and leaves Chance, still stunned by what just happened. He walks over to the bed and sits down, still staring at his arms.

Back in the harbor of the stronghold, Sven is walking along the docks with Fidelma. "What is it like to read minds?" he asks.

Fidelma ponders momentarily before answering. "When looking at the past, it's like remembering your own memories, except more dream-like."

"Is it confusing?"

"At first it was, but I became used to it."

"Do you always know what people are thinking?"

"Most of the time it's not hard to tell," she laughs. "I rarely need to use a spell anymore to tell when they're lying."

"Can you tell what someone is feeling?"

Fidelma stops walking. She looks up at him, and answers, "Only when I'm inside their thoughts, and even then I can only tell what they're feeling about the specific memory I'm seeing or the current thought I'm seeing through them. I don't know if that made any sense."

"It does."

"Why do you ask?"

"No reason," Sven replies as he looks at the *Sea Griffin*. "Sven is going with you tomorrow."

"What are you talking about?"

"When you go to floating city, Sven is going with you."

"We don't really need your help, but thanks."

"Sven just wants to be sure nothing will happen to you."

"That's sweet of you, but I'll be all right."

Sven leans in close and says sternly, "Sven is sure that you will be, but Sven is going anyway."

"Well, if you insist," says Fidelma with a smirk. "I always liked when you were overprotective of me, even when you didn't need to be. It made me feel... loved."

As the two draw nearer, Sven replies, "You were always loved. Sven never stopped."

No more than twenty paces away, Yentroc watches Sven and Fidelma. Lyra approaches her friend, carrying a scroll. Unaware of Sven's presence, Lyra says, "Yentroc, I have to show you something."

"Come on," says Yentroc as she tries to lead her away. "You can show me inside."

Lyra spots the half giant, just as he takes Fidelma in his arms. Lyra, heartbroken, stands there unable to move as the two begin to kiss. "I'm so sorry," says Yentroc. "What did you want to show me?"

"It's nothing," she says distantly, as she starts to walk away. "Never mind."

Yentroc begins to chase after Lyra, unnoticed by Sven, who is looking sadly at the woman he was supposed to marry many years before.

Fidelma says, "I don't have to read your mind to know what you're thinking now."

"Sven is sorry," he apologizes.

"You don't need to explain," says Fidelma.

"All these years," Sven says with a heavy sigh, "Sven has wondered what he would do if he could hold you in his arms one more time. Sven has dreamed of your kiss countless times, and yet, now that those dreams have become real..." Sven drops his gaze.

Fidelma reaches up and tenderly brushes back his long locks. "I know. It felt like a distant memory."

"Fidelma, you know Sven still loves you."

"I know," she replies as she takes a step back. "When I read your memories on the dock the other day, I could feel it. I still love you as well."

Sven nods. "But it is not going work between us, is it?"

"I think your heart belongs to someone else right now."

"Lyra?"

"Of course," she laughs. "When I asked you if you ever felt anything for any of the women you were with, your thoughts went straight to her."

"Sven is sorry."

"Don't be," Fidelma says, shaking her head. "What you have with Lyra is wonderful. I could feel your love for her. Honestly, I don't know if it would have made a difference with us or not. My feelings are far from clear, too. So many years have passed us by. I'm just glad that one of us has found love again."

"Sven never expected to find it," he replies. "For years Sven has wandered about Bruen. Every time he got close with woman, he would leave. Sven was coward and ran from them."

"You're not a coward."

"When it comes to love, Sven is."

"But that changed when you met her."

Sven chuckles to himself as he remembers first meeting the young Amazons at Copper Pass. He recalls, "When Sven first met them, he did not think much of it. Chance made Sven promise not to touch them, and Sven kept his word, somewhat."

"I don't think Chance would have objected to you keeping Lyra warm at night."

"On first night, Lyra was freezing. All Sven could think about was keeping her alive. In morning Sven noticed her beauty, but it was sweet, and child-like. Sven felt need to protect her. Few days later, she was mad with Sven for calling her child. She threw snow at Sven."

Fidelma laughs. "I know, I saw that memory, too."

Sven says, "It was then that Sven saw something else in her. He saw her no longer as child that needed protecting, and instead saw young woman with fierce passion. After that, it became more and more difficult to keep her warm at night and get good sleep, as you were so quick to mention to her."

"I'm sorry about that too," sighs Fidelma. "If you'd like, I can speak with her."

"No," replies Sven. "It is best this way."

"For who?"

"Please," says Sven, almost begging. "Let us not speak of this anymore."

"As you wish," replies Fidelma.

Within the depths of the fortress, Lyra lies down on her furs. Evelena notices her wiping away tears from her cheeks when

Yentroc joins them, asking, "Lyra, are you all right?"

"What happened?" asks Evelena.

Yentroc says, "We just saw Sven with another woman. He was kissing her."

Gelana, who is not far away, pipes up, "I guess we were wrong about him."

"No," says Lyra as she sits up. "It wasn't just another woman. It was Fidelma, the one he was going to take his vows with."

"She didn't waste any time, did she," says Yentroc.

"It doesn't matter," says Lyra. "Maybe it's best this way. I know he loved her. Maybe they can finally be happy together."

Gelana says, "You're taking this rather well."

"Please," says Lyra. "I would prefer not to talk about this anymore. I'd like to get some sleep."

"I'm sorry," says Yentroc. "May your dreams guide you safely."

To the southwest, aboard the *Trident,* Allen watches the sun begin to set, paying little attention to the goings-on around him. A conversation nearby escalates as Mathew argues with a man. "I'm telling you, Jack, orcneas are not green."

Jack, smaller than most of the crew, replies, "How do you know? Have you ever seen one?"

"No, but everyone knows that."

"Well, I don't," says Jack. "But I've heard stories that they're green, like goblins."

Allen, unable to ignore the voices, says, "Actually, the orcneas I've seen were reddish-orange."

Jack scoffs. "You haven't seen any orcneas."

"Actually, he has," Mathew says, defending him. "He used to serve aboard the *Red Dawn.*"

"I don't believe it," he says dismissively.

"He even killed a few."

Other men gather around. One of them asks Allen, "Is that true?"

Allen looks nervously at the others. Modestly, he answers, "I did, but it was nothing, really."

The men chatter among themselves for a bit. Jack asks, "Well, what were they like?"

Allen thinks back to his encounter. "They were big."

The crew laughs. "That's it?" Jack replies. "They were big? What happened?"

Allen shakes his head. "The first one lost his footing, so I had an opening. The second one only had a whip. After that, I don't really remember clearly. It all happened so fast."

"What color is their blood?"

Allen shrugs. "Red, same as ours."

Another man asks, "Is it true that they sail inside killer storms?"

Allen nods. "That part is true."

Growing concern among the men can be felt. Mathew says to them, "Let's not get overly worried about the weather. We've sailed in storms before, and besides, Allen survived."

"But he was on the *Red Dawn*," says Jack.

Allen says, "This ship is larger and more sturdy than the *Red Dawn*. I wouldn't be worried so long as you have spell-casters." He looks at the others, who don't seem to be put at ease by his words. "You do have other spell-casters, don't you?"

"No," answers Mathew. "It's just me and James."

"Oh... Well, that's fine. The *Red Dawn* only had Ariella and Torgus."

Mathew laughs, "Well, I'm certainly no Ariella Stormrage, or Torgus, for that matter, but I can take a sizable piece of a ship's hull out with a speeding chunk of rock."

"Well, that's no different than Torgus," says Allen. Trying to put the rest of the crew at ease, he adds, "Believe me, we'll be fine."

Chapter 12
Eve of the Trial

Sitting near his campfire, Baeldeth is eating a roasted chicken leg for a late dinner. Prince River, Ya'leigh, and Princess Kianna are also eating. After having traveled the night before and most of the day, they are exhausted. Just outside camp, the captain of the drake riders, Belron, lands his flying steed. He is met by a couple of guards before being escorted over to Baeldeth and the prince.

River stands to greet him while Baeldeth continues eating. "Good evening, Belron," says the prince.

"Good evening, my prince," says Belron. "I'm sorry to have arrived so late, but I was not sure exactly where to find you."

Kianna asks, "Is everything all right?"

"Yes, princess," answers Belron. "The orcneas have not made any move on the stronghold as of yet."

"So, what brings you here?" asks Baeldeth.

"It is regarding Chance Na'Moon," says Belron. "He's alive."

Ya'leigh jumps to her feet. "He is?"

Not wanting for Ya'leigh to get her hopes too high, Belron adds, "He is, but I am afraid he may not be for much longer."

Baeldeth tosses the bone of his meal into the fire and gets to his feet. "The orcneas still have him, then?"

"Yes," answers Belron. "They plan to have some sort of trial tomorrow."

"For what?" asks Ya'leigh.

Belron answers, "They claim it is for the Second Orcnea War."

"They would make such a claim," says Baeldeth.

"They gave us two viewing crystals," says Belron as he holds out one of the necklaces that General Vork gave A'ranah.

"They just want everyone to see him executed," says Baeldeth.

River says to Ya'leigh, "I'm sorry. I wish there was something we could do."

Baeldeth asks, "Is Arioch going to attempt a rescue?"

Belron shakes his head. "No. We do not have enough forces to take the castle, but we're going to try to destroy the magical protections of the floating city. We hope that the orcneas will be distracted enough by the trial that we can get a flying ship, filled with black powder, close enough to one of the guard towers. If it works, we should be able to open a gate and attack."

Ya'leigh asks, "What about my father?"

"They warned us that if we attacked or tried to rescue Chance, they would kill him," says Belron. "Despite this threat, Arioch believes that our best hope is to attack just before the trial while everyone is distracted. If we are successful, we will bring down the floating city and change the tide of the war itself. Then, we may be able to rescue him."

Baeldeth adds, "Assuming they don't kill him the moment you attack."

"Chance's trial seems to be important to the orcneas," replies Belron. "We don't believe they will simply kill him without making a showing of it."

"I hope you're right," says Baeldeth. "Still, I feel Arioch should have some sort of plan to rescue him."

"We don't have many options," replies Belron. "You left us to return to Elonfar."

"Taking back that city is not something we were in a position to do," Baeldeth retorts. "We wouldn't have had enough forces even if we had stayed."

Kianna asks, "What are we going to do now?"

Baeldeth replies, "So long as those monsters have one of my brothers, I will not leave him behind."

"So we're going back?" asks River.

"Yes," answers Baeldeth. "Can they open a gate for us to return?"

Belron replies, "At the moment, those with gate magic are creating gate stones, but I will inform A'ranah of your request. I will be leaving shortly to make sure I'm back before dawn."

"We will be leaving at first light," says Baeldeth. "If they can return us before the trial, I will offer my assistance. If we are unable to save Chance, then we will return to Elonfar."

Kianna asks, "So out of all of the reasons to fight the orcneas, you're doing so for one person?"

Baeldeth replies, "That one person is my brother, even if not by blood."

Belron asks, "Do you think your men will follow your order if they go against the king's wishes?"

Baeldeth nods. "Yes, they will. Just as your drake riders followed your orders. Many of these soldiers belong to the Brotherhood of the Silver Moon. They would rather die than abandon a fellow brother."

"Thank you," says Ya'leigh, trying to hold back her tears.

Kianna puts her arm around her friend and says, "I'm sure my father will do everything he can to save him."

"I know," replies Ya'leigh. "I'm just worried about what they might be doing to him right now."

In his cell at Sheathelm, Chance is once again visited by Lortec Ka, who is carrying a mug full of an unknown beverage. The orcnea general says, "I brought you something to help you sleep. You should get a full night's rest."

Chance approaches the iron bars. Without question, he holds out his hands and takes the mug from Lortec. He smells the contents and recoils from the odor. Lortec laughs. "I know it smells awful, but it will help you rest. It should even heal the remainder of your wounds."

Chance closes his eyes and forces down the drink. He coughs several times as he hands back the empty mug. "You know, it seems futile to heal me, only to kill me tomorrow."

"That may be," replies Lortec, "but as I said before, I want you to be at your best so when I do kill you, there will be no doubt in anyone's mind who the better warrior is."

"I imagine your reputation would be greatly increased with my death," says Chance as he sits on the bed in the cell. "You may even rise to the status of High Chief."

"No," Lortec refutes. "I have no desire to lead the orcneas. I only want to provide a future for my family. Speaking of family, mine will be watching the trial tomorrow."

"You brought your family here from across the sea?"

"No, they will be watching through magic. So will your king and his people. We delivered two crystals to them so that they may witness your fate."

"Don't you mean my execution?"

Lortec shakes his head. "You have little faith in your skills."

"That's not it at all," replies Chance, now showing signs of fatigue. "I just don't expect it to be a fair fight."

"I assure you, it will be."

Chance lies down. "What is your son's name?"

"His name is Quoven," answers Lortec. "It was my father's name."

"Quoven," Chance repeats softly as he drifts off to sleep.

Within the underground fortress, the Amazons of the Silver Moon have occupied several rooms as sleeping quarters. Nicari finds Va'leen sitting alone on her bedding in one of the corners. Nicari carries her backpack over to her friend. "May I join you?"

Va'leen looks up and smiles. "Of course."

Nicari pulls a fur blanket from her backpack and lays it on the ground. "I always have a hard time falling asleep when Belron is gone."

"I'm sure he's safe," says Va'leen reassuringly. "It's not like he was sent on a dangerous mission."

"I know," Nicari sighs. "I was just hoping that he would be back by now." Va'leen nods, and they sit in silence for a while. Nicari lies back on her blanket and looks up at the dark ceiling above. "Did I see you leaving the *Red Dawn* last night?"

"I was there, yes."

"Why?"

Va'leen lies down, as well. "I just wanted to meet the woman Chance would always go on about."

"Oh," replies Nicari. "And what did you think of her?"

"Well, she is beautiful," says Va'leen. "Her hair is as red as the fires Chance used to shape her images years ago. It's easy to see why he was taken by her."

Nicari shakes her head. "I don't understand why you'd torture yourself by seeing her."

"Perhaps I'm just drawn to the flame, like a moth. I can't stay away even though I know it could burn me."

Aboard the *Trident*, the men are changing shifts. The night crew are coming up from below deck while Allen and others are waiting to go downstairs to get some sleep. With the entire crew gathered, Marcus shouts, "I need everyone's attention!" The men quiet themselves and turn to their captain. "We have just received word that Chance Na'Moon still lives." Allen and the others listen, cautiously optimistic, as Marcus continues. "Unfortunately, he is being held prisoner by the orcneas." The crew's disappointment can be heard in their whispers.

One of the crewmen asks, "Is it true the elves abandoned the war?"

Marcus reluctantly nods. "Yes, it is true that the elves have pulled back their forces."

The crew grumbles with disapproval. Jack asks, "Are we still going to fight?"

"Yes," answers the captain. "The stronghold that they're in is well fortified. It's better to keep the war away from Artos, and our presence should keep the orcneas from advancing any further. Now, everyone back to work."

The crew carry on with their duties as Allen and Jack head below deck. Jack says, "I sure hope we can do this without the elves."

Allen sits in his hammock. "So do I."

Day 24
Chapter 13
Anticipation

As the first morning's light begins to burn away the fog, Lyra is eating breakfast with her friends under a canopy that has been set up for serving meals. The soldiers have crafted two long tables for people to eat on with only crates and barrels for seating. It is far from the luxurious dining hall of the castle.

The young women are conversing among themselves when they hear a woman's voice. "Mind if I join you?"

Lyra looks up and sees Re'ann, one of the three remaining drake riders. "Of course not," Lyra says as she moves a small pile of books off of the table next to her.

"Thank you," says Re'ann before setting down her plate and sitting next to Lyra. "My name is Re'ann."

Evelena comments, "You're one of the drake riders."

"Yes," she replies.

"My name is Evelena," she says.

Lyra adds, "And I'm Lyra."

The others introduce themselves. Re'ann says, "It's a pleasure to meet you all. If you don't mind my asking, aren't you girls a bit young to be fighting in a war?"

"We're on our Rite of Passage," says Gelana.

"Oh, that explains it, then," replies Re'ann. "I've always been fascinated by the Amazons of the Silver Moon. I wish I could join, but I understand you have to be related to one of the three houses."

"Actually, there is another way to join," says Lyra.

"I didn't know that," says Kel'ana. "How?"

"You have to take a blood oath," says Lyra. "But first you have to decide what house you want to swear yourself to. Then, you have to find someone who will stand with you at the ceremony, as well as gain the blessing of an elder from that house."

"That doesn't sound too bad," says Re'ann.

Gelana says, "I guess the hardest part would be impressing an elder enough to gain their blessing, but since you're the first female drake rider that Elonfar has ever had..."

Rehma adds, "And I heard that you pulled Chance Na'Moon from the sea when the orcnea ship he was on exploded."

"She did?" asks Evelena, impressed.

"Yes," answers Re'ann. "He was unconscious and sinking when I spotted him. I dove in with a rope that I had tied to my drake's saddle. I secured the other end to Chance and pulled him out."

"I'll stand with you," says Rehma, "if you decide to choose the house of La'harn."

"Why would she want to choose the house of La'harn," jests Yentroc, "when she could join the house of Ree?"

"Or, she could choose Dri'el," suggests Ja'noa.

Evelena laughs. "She won't join any of our houses if we scare her off."

Re'ann looks at Lyra, and asks. "What house are you from?"

Lyra points to the markings painted on her face. "This leaf represents the house of Dri'el, and the stars are for the house of Ree."

"You can belong to two houses?" asks Re'ann.

"It's not very common," answers Lyra, "but yes. I'm not sure if blood sisters are allowed to join more than one."

Evelena asks, "I assume you know at least a few spells?"

Re'ann nods. "Yes, I can heal my drake. I can communicate with him as well. I can also throw a stone missile."

Evelena smiles. "I also know earth spells."

Gelana says, "Rehma and I only know combat spells. We weren't taught the elemental college."

"They usually leave the elemental spells to the Dri'els and Rees," says Ja'noa. "I can throw lightning, and Kel'ana can create daggers of ice."

Re'ann looks at Lyra, "What can you cast?"

Lyra replies, "I studied light magic."

"She can even make herself invisible," adds Evelena.

Re'ann eyes widen. "Really? Can you make others invisible?"

"I can do that," replies Lyra.

"Do you think you could make a drake invisible?" she asks.

"I don't see why not," Lyra answers. "But it would be very tiring."

"I have an idea," says Re'ann, "but I'll have to speak with

Captain Belron and the king. If they agree, we might be able to rescue Chance."

Hours later, in his cell, Chance wakes to find his armor stacked neatly by the door. On the other side of the bars, Lortec says, "Your trial will begin soon."

Chance stands and checks himself for injuries. "Whatever you gave me last night seems to have worked."

"I told you," says the orcnea general, "I want there to be no excuses when I beat you."

Chance picks up his breastplate. "You went through a lot of trouble cleaning this."

"You need to look your best. If we were to drag you out there looking like you do now, no one would recognize you for the brutal murderer that you are. With your armor, however, there will be no mistaking you."

"This seems more about presentation than holding me accountable for my past."

"It's about giving my people hope, while taking it away from yours."

"You're not interested in killing me. You just want to destroy the symbol I've become."

Lortec laughs. "Now you are beginning to understand. It would have been easy to kill you, Chance Na'Moon, but I am more interested in killing the Orcnea Slayer."

Chance, looking down at his armor, says, "I cannot put this on as long as I wear this iron collar around my neck."

"I will remove it," says Lortec, "but be warned. If you attack anyone, or try to flee, there will be consequences."

"I understand."

"Good. You should also know that your friends will most likely attempt a rescue. They may even create an opportunity for you to escape. I am sure the thought of leaving with them is tempting to you now. However, you may change your mind after you see what I am about to show you."

To the west, Prince River has begun to head back to the fortress along with the remaining elven forces. Ya'leigh, Kianna, and Baeldeth walk alongside him in the lead. A sudden burst of air surprises them as Eveoh magically appears.

Baeldeth instinctively reaches for his sword before realizing who it is. "You shouldn't teleport so close to us."

"Normally I wouldn't have," Eveoh replies, "but I can only appear in places I've been, or places I can see clearly. We used magic to find you, so under the circumstances this is best I could do."

Baeldeth asks, "Are they ready to open a gate to bring us back?"

"Almost," she answers as the rest of the army begins to come to a halt. "First, we need to make sure everyone is ready to move quickly once it opens. This is going to be a very exhausting spell to maintain. We may not get everyone through on one try."

"I'll make the preparations," says Baeldeth.

"There's one other thing," says Eveoh as Baeldeth turns to leave.

The commander looks back. "What's that?"

"King Arioch wants the princess and and Ya'leigh to continue towards Elonfar. They said that you would only need to send a small escort with them."

"I'm not going," argues Ya'leigh.

Eveoh nods. "They said you would resist the idea."

Kianna says, "You can't make us go."

Baeldeth sighs. "With all due respect, Princess, we could force you, but that's not what we're going to do." He looks at Eveoh. "If anyone asks, you can tell them they are returning to Elonfar." Baeldeth says to Kianna and Ya'leigh, "Now then, we're going to have to get you two changed into something that won't draw so much attention."

In the harbor of the fortress, Fidelma and her crew are aboard the *Sea Griffin* along with Sven and Fernando. Fidelma says to the twins, "I want you two to stay safe. If anything happens to me, I want you to return to your family. Sam is going to stay behind with you."

"I am?" asks Samantha, confused.

"Yes," replies Fidelma. "There isn't much for you to do, anyway."

Samantha points to the men. "Why are they going?"

Fernando states, "I am going wherever my sister is going."

Sven adds, "And Sven is going to make sure Fidelma is safe."

Samantha shakes her head and sighs. "That's all I want to do."

Fidelma places her hand on her friend's shoulder. "I know, but I need you to look out for the twins."

"I understand," Samantha relents. She turns to leave as Isen and Kristieana make their way aboard along with a goblin.

Fidelma asks, "And just who are you?"

"I'm Isen, and this is Kristieana."

The goblin says, "I'm Qheon."

"We were about ready to leave," says Fidelma.

"I know," replies Isen. "We're going with you."

"We don't need any more help," says Fidelma.

Kristieana says, "Actually, I think you might." She looks at Vindalia. "You need to use your fiddle to be effective at creating wind. They will hear you coming."

Ariella speaks up. "I don't need to use an instrument."

"That may be," replies Kristieana, "but, if you use my staff, it will make things a lot easier." Kristieana hands Ariella the Staff of Storms.

Ariella studies the magical weapon, looking closely at the blue crystals affixed to each end. "This is an amazing staff. Can you create wind as well?"

"No," answers Kristieana. "At least, not very well. My talents are more with healing."

Fidelma asks Qheon, "I assume you are here to make sure the explosives are set off properly?"

"Of course," the goblin answers.

Fidelma turns to Isen. "So what are you here for?"

Isen shrugs. "Protection, I suppose. King Arioch ordered me to come."

Sven says, "Isen is good fighter. He was with us in northern territory."

Ariella asks Isen, "Oh, so you're the friend of Chance?"

"Yes," Isen answers, confused. "How did you know?"

Ariella glances at Kristieana and grins. "Chance told me about you the other night."

Isen laughs, "I hope he mentioned *good* things about me."

Fidelma says impatiently, "Let's get underway before anyone

else decides to join us." She walks to the railing of the ship holding an hourglass sideways in her hands. One quarter of the sand was already on one side. She waves to Arioch, who is holding an identical timing device. Arioch and Fidelma both stand their hourglasses on end with the majority of the sand on the top. Fidelma says, "Let's go. We have less than an hour to get this done." She places her hand on a large gem at the center of the wheel. She concentrates, and soon the *Sea Griffin* disappears from sight.

Chapter 14
Preparations

It is just before midday on the *Trident* as Allen makes his way up the stairs to the quarter deck. The captain and Mathew are there, along with James, who is in a state of meditation. Allen asks, "Is he searching for the presence of orcneas nearby?"

"Sort of," answers Matthew. "He has shifted his consciousness to his falcon, and is scouting up ahead."

"That must be a very effective way to be on the lookout."

Marcus chuckles. "We are very rarely surprised."

The flapping of wings is heard as James's falcon lands on the ship's railing. James opens his eyes. "There is a damaged ship ahead. It looks like they were in a battle not too long ago."

"Are they orcneas?" asks Marcus.

James shakes his head. "No, they're dwarves and humans."

"How long 'til we reach them?"

"About an hour."

Far inland, Baeldeth and Prince River wait patiently with the troops from Elonfar for the magic gate that will take them back to the stronghold to appear.

Kianna and Ya'leigh, now wearing brown cloaks over their armor, look no different than the elven archers. Ya'leigh asks, "When are they going to open the gate?"

"Eveoh said it would open shortly," replies the prince.

Baeldeth looks back at his men. They are lined up tightly in two long rows. "When the gate opens," he hollers, "be ready to move quickly. Once you are through the gate, continue to move forward and out of the way so everyone can come through. They cannot hold this gate open as long as the Lunar Gate."

A popping noise and a gust of wind signals the arrival of Chance's sister, Eveoh. "Is everyone ready?"

River nods. "We are."

"Good," she replies. "I'll go back and tell them to start casting the spell." In an instant, she is gone once again.

Baeldeth looks ahead and waits.

Back at the fortress, Eveoh appears before King Arioch and A'ranah just outside the walls. She says, "They're ready."

A'ranah looks at a dozen Amazons who have gathered for the collective casting of the spell. "Hold open the gate as long as you can, or until everyone has made it through."

Eveoh joins the other women as they clasp hands and begin to concentrate. Moments later, a magical gateway appears and the soldiers from Elonfar begin to run though. Baeldeth and the prince are the first two. They break off of the formation and Baeldeth commands the others, "Keep moving! Go all the way into the fortress."

Arioch says, "Thank you for returning."

"Don't thank me," replies Baeldeth. "I didn't return for you. I came back for my brother, and if we are unable to save him from execution, then I will depart once again."

"I understand," replies the king.

A'ranah interrupts, "If you will excuse me, I have something I must attend to before we begin the next phase of our plan."

As the Amazon queen walks away, Baeldeth asks Arioch, "So there is a plan, then?"

"Yes, though I have my doubts it will succeed."

"What do you want me to do?"

"For now, all we can do is wait and see if your sisters are successful. If they are, it could make all the difference in this war."

Inside the fortress, Ya'leigh and Kianna are doing their best to blend in with the other soldiers. "I don't think anyone noticed us," says Ya'leigh.

"Good," replies Kianna. "My father is going to be upset when he finds out."

"You are certainly right about that," says the Amazon queen, standing behind them. A'ranah pulls back their cloaks. "Did you really think you would fool me?"

Ya'leigh pleads, "Grandmother, I just couldn't go back to Elonfar. Not when they still have my father."

"I know," A'ranah replies with a nod. "Now, let's put you both to better use than hiding." She points to harbor, where the drake riders are gathered with the seven young Amazons on their Rite of

Passage. "We're going to begin shortly."

Aboard the *Sea Griffin,* Vindalia and Ariella both cling to the Staff of Storms as they concentrate on a spell, making the winds carry them toward the floating fortress. The goblin, Qheon, uses his magic to maintain a modest fire in the brazier in the center of the deck.

Fidelma and the others look at the levitating mass of land just above them off the port bow. Fidelma looks at the hourglass, noting the amount of sand remaining. "We're making good time. As soon as we pass by, we will take the ship higher so the sun will be at our backs as we come down on them."

"Don't you think they would have spotted us by now?" asks Isen.

Fernando says, "We are low enough that most of the watchtowers cannot see us."

"He's correct," says Fidelma. "But be on the lookout for any drakes that may try to attack us."

Kristieana looks back at the shore. "Speaking of drakes, it looks like Belron and Ashden have begun their distraction."

High above the city of Sheathelm, Belron and one of the last remaining drake riders, Ashden, have begun to fly their drakes around the edges of the city. As they fly side by side, Belron, looking down at the Colosseum full of orcneas, says, "It looks like they're about to begin. Make sure you avoid flying directly over the city. We don't want them to feel like we're a threat. If they do, they may make good on their promise to kill Chance."

"Yes, sir," Ashden replies.

"Let me know if you see any sign of other drakes."

At the fortress, A'ranah stands down by the water with more of the Amazon sisterhood and the third remaining drake rider, Re'ann.

Lyra looks nervously at Re'ann's drake, Cirrus. "I don't know if I can do this."

"Sure you can," Yentroc says reassuringly.

"What if they dispel it?" asks Lyra.

Re'ann says, "Since Kristieana let me borrow her invisibility cloak, you don't need to worry about me. And with your sisters protecting Cirrus with other spells, he'll be safe. You just need to give us time to approach. Cirrus is fast, so it won't take long."

"I just wish Leanara was still here," says Lyra.

Nicari says to Lyra, "From what others have told me, Lyra, you are very talented with light spells. You can do this."

"Thanks," sighs Lyra.

A'ranah says to Re'ann, "I will communicate with you through the same spell I'm using on Belron and Kristieana. It may be confusing at first, hearing other voices in your head, but you'll get accustomed to it soon." A'ranah touches Re'ann's forehead. *"Can you hear me? Try to answer with your thoughts."*

"Yes," she answers in her mind. *"Am I doing this correctly?"*

"You are doing well," A'ranah says aloud. "Now, everyone else, be ready to cast your spells. There's no telling when Re'ann will have to leave."

A guard in the tower calls down, "Drakes are leaving the floating city!"

The Amazon queen shifts her attention to Belron. *"Are you ready?"*

"Yes, we see them now," Berlon answers. He says to Ashden, "Let's keep those drakes occupied."

Belron and Ashden begin to engage the orcneas' flying forces as A'ranah checks in with Jadelyn, who is sitting on the ground with a small bowl of water in front of her. Within the water is an image of the Colosseum from above.

A'ranah asks, "Is there any sign of Chance yet?"

"No, Mother Elder."

"Can you get a closer look?"

"If I get any closer, my spell will be disrupted by the magical protections of Sheathelm. Don't worry, I can see well enough."

Arioch joins A'ranah. Seeing Ya'leigh and Kianna, he asks, "What are they doing here?"

He starts toward them when A'ranah grabs his arm. "Now isn't the time." Arioch turns to face her as she continues, "Let them help. Ya'leigh can increase the speed of Re'ann's drake, and Kianna can lend her strength to help maintain those spells."

"They should be on their way to Elonfar right now."

"Is that what you were doing at her age? Fleeing to safety?"

Arioch sighs. "I've put my life in danger so that others, like my daughter, wouldn't have to."

"I understand, my love, but right now they are useful to this war. If things go badly, we can still escape."

Arioch looks at the hourglass, which is now almost empty. "I hope this works. I'm afraid of what will happen to Chance if it doesn't."

In the southern sea, the *Trident* has secured lines to a damaged ship. A weary crew greets them as a dark haired dwarf calls, "Thank you for coming to our aid."

The crew lay down planks. Marcus, looking at the damage, says, "Were you attacked by orcneas?"

"Yes, last night. We managed to sink 'em, but they nearly took us with 'em."

"Are you the captain?"

"No," he replies as he shakes his head. "He was killed in the attack. My name is Vardik Craghammer. I'm the ship's healer."

"Are there any other spell-casters?"

"Most of the dwarves on board can throw stone with the best of 'em. We're from New Waterford, and most of us are miners. We were on our way to help the king of Sheathelm when we were attacked."

"Good, we could use more help. We're on our way there now." Marcus looks again at the damaged ship before continuing. "I think it would be best if you boarded our ships. We don't have time to make proper repairs to your ship."

Vardik nods. "Agreed."

James says to Marcus, "Captain, there is a fleet of ships approaching from the stern. I think it's the elves."

"Perhaps they've changed their minds about retreating."

"They'll be here soon enough to ask."

Marcus calls out to his crew, "Everyone make room for their crew! We'll reassign everyone later to best make use of their skills." He turns to Vardik. "If that's all right by you and your men."

Vardik replies, "Whatever we can do to help."

Chapter 15
The Descent

Commander Belron and Ashden fly their steeds ahead of the pursuing enemy drakes. After splitting up, Belron says to A'ranah through his thoughts, *"How much longer do we have to keep this up?"*

"The Sea Griffin is waiting to descend," she answers. *"How are you holding up?"*

"We're doing well," he replies. *"So far we've been able to keep them following us. Is there any word on Chance?"*

"Jadelyn hasn't seen him yet. I'm getting concerned that the invisibility of the Sea Griffin will expire before they bring Chance out for the trial."

At the fortress, A'ranah is interrupted by the high-pitched sound of the image crystal. King Arioch rushes over and says, "No doubt they are upset about our drake riders."

A'ranah walks over to where a bucket of water sits on the ground. She takes the crystal that was given to them by the orcneas the day before and places it in the water.

An image of General Vork appears on the surface of the water. Not only can they see him, they hear him as well. "What are your drake riders doing?" he demands.

Arioch bends over and looks into the bucket. "They're just trying to get a better view of this 'trial' of yours."

Vork laughs. "Be warned that if they approach the city, we are more than capable of taking them out of the air." Vork lifts his crystal out of the water. The image begins to shift as the general continues to speak. "I will no longer be able to see or hear you, Arioch, but you will still be able to watch your hero." The orcnea general hangs the crystal, which has been fashioned into a necklace, around the end of his staff.

A'ranah calls to Ja'noa and Kel'ana. When the young women arrive, the Amazon queen says, "I want you to shape the water in this bucket into a thin wall."

"Yes, Mother Elder," replies Ja'noa.

The two of them begin to shape the water, and as they do, the image of the Colosseum can be seen stretched across the liquid wall. A large crowd of soldiers begins to gather around. A'ranah and Arioch make their way over to Re'ann and the Amazons waiting to cast their spells.

"It's almost time," A'ranah says to them. Anxious, the young women only nod.

There is a roar from the crowd of orcneas as Chance is brought out onto the Colosseum grounds. "There he is," says a voice from the crowd of elves and humans.

A'ranah nods to Ya'leigh and the others and says, "Now." As the women begin to cast their spells on Re'ann and her drake, A'ranah communicates with Kristieana. *"Begin your descent. Chance is on the field."*

Aboard the *Sea Griffin,* Kristieana announces, "They spotted Chance. We have to drop down now."

Fidelma rushes to look over the railing. Directly below them is one of the towers. She smiles as she makes her way back to the center of the ship and pulls down on the rope that releases the air. She ties it down and says, "Light the fuse and ready the gate-stone."

Qheon says, "I'll check the black powder one last time." He runs down the stairs and looks at the barrels of black powder that are stacked along the sides of the ship. A long, thin white fuse runs along the floor. He calls up to Fidelma, "Everything is ready! Come down here and we can activate the gate as I ignite the fuse."

Fidelma motions for the others to follow her. Kristieana pulls out a sandstone amulet and says, "Let's hope this gate-stone works."

They make their way down the steps one by one. As Fernando begins to climb down the steps, he nearly falls as the ship shutters. A deafening cracking sound is heard as a man-sized harpoon crashes through the lower hull of the ship and up through stairway. Small splinters and dust fill the air. The deck begins to creak as the harpoon snares the planks, pulling them down into lower deck. Fernando is completely cut off from the others.

"Ariella!" he yells through the debris. "Are you all right?"

He listens for moment before hearing the voice of his sister.

"Yes, we are. We're going to try to get through to you."

The ship moves suddenly to the side. Fernando looks over the railing and can see that one of the ballistae has been fired at the *Sea Griffin* and a rope attached to the oversized harpoon is now pulling the ship off course. He looks down and can see the tower still beneath them.

He runs back to the damaged deck and calls down, "You don't have time. Light the fuse and go. I will make sure we hit the tower."

Below deck, Ariella frantically tries to move a wooden beam. "No! We can get to you!"

Isen tries to use his strength to move it, but with the added pressure from the harpoon pulling down, it is no use.

Kristieana says, "I'm sorry, but we have to go."

Qheon casts a spell and the fuse is lit. Ariella screams, "We can't leave him! We just can't."

Kristieana takes a couple steps away from the others. She holds out the gate-stone and crushes it in her hands. A magic gate appears before them. "I'm sorry," she says before entering the gate.

Qheon follows behind the red-headed Amazon. Fidelma says to her friend, "We have to go."

"No," Ariella insists. "I can't lose him. Not when I just found him."

Fernando looks down through a small hole. "Ariella, you have to leave me. There is no need for us both to die." With tears streaming down her face, Ariella shakes her head. Fernando looks at Sven. "My friend, will you please make sure my sister makes it out."

"Of course," Sven replies. He looks at Ariella and says, "Sven is sorry." He scoops her up and begins to carry her to the gate.

As Ariella kicks and screams, Isen and Vindalia exit through the magic porthole. Fernando, continuing to pull on the rope to let the hot air out faster, listens to the agonizing yells of his sister until she is carried away.

Fernando looks back through the hole at Fidelma. She says to him, "You know, a part of me is going miss you."

Fernando laughs. "Goodbye, Captain."

"You can call me Fidelma."

"Goodbye, Fidelma. I hope that you can find someone who

makes you happy and cares about you the way that I have grown to. Now go, before the gate closes."

"Goodbye, Fernando," Fidelma says sadly, turning and walking through the gate.

The ship lands hard. Fernando gets to his feet and looks over to find that he has landed over forty paces from the tower. He sighs. "We have failed."

At the fortress, Arioch says to A'ranah, "The drakes have turned back toward the floating city." He looks over to where the gate-stone has brought the crew of the *Sea Griffin*.

Sven sets Ariella down as the gate closes. She promptly proceeds to hit him. "We could have saved him!"

Arioch rushes over. "What happened?"

"We were spotted," says Isen. "A harpoon struck the ship, separating us from Fernando. We had to leave him behind."

"What about the black powder?" Arioch asks Qheon.

"It should be going off any second," he says, looking back at the floating fortress.

"No, it won't," says Ariella. Everyone turns their attention to her as she adds, "I put out the fuse before we left."

"Why did you do that?" asks Arioch.

"I couldn't kill my brother," she replies.

Isen asks, "And just what do you think the orcneas will do to him?"

Ariella doesn't answer. She looks up at the sky, where the drakes have made it back to the orcnea base in the air.

A'ranah uses her spell to communicate to Belron and Re'ann. *"Belron, you must circle back and destroy the Sea Griffin. It is far too dangerous to let it fall into their hands. Have Ashden fly high over the Colosseum to keep their attention. Re'ann, move in now."*

"I'm on my way," replies Re'ann. Sitting in a field west of Sheathelm, Re'ann commands her drake, "Up, Cirrus. Let's get Chance." The drake takes flight toward the city.

In the Colosseum, Chance is led to the center by Lortec. Two orcneas with crossbows follow behind them. Carr makes his way to the center, as well, carrying his staff. The orcneas filling the seats within the arena jeer loudly.

Back at the fortress, Baeldeth comments, "Why doesn't he just fly away? They don't have him chained up at all." The others look closely and confirm his observations. Chance is unbound. The collar that inhibited his magic has been removed. The watchers spot it in Lortec's hands.

Arioch says, "If he were to try to flee, they would most likely shoot him down."

"We don't have our protections on him," A'ranah adds. "He would never make it out of there."

Carr stops thirty paces from Chance. He drives his staff into the ground. He walks around so that Arioch can see his face. Facing the crystal, he says, "Your assault on the floating city has failed. Just like all of your attempts to win this war will fail." His eyes shift to the sky. Seeing Belron and Ashden, he calls out to his forces, "Keep an eye on those riders, and get our drakes back here now!"

Rapidly approaching, Re'ann flies over the outer walls of Sheathelm. Skimming the tops of the buildings, she makes her way to the Colosseum. Cirrus glides over the arena's wall as Re'ann prepares to jump. The sky drake descends into the bowl-shaped structure. Low to the ground, Re'ann pats her mount on its neck and says, "Good boy. Now return to the fortress." She jumps down as her drake ascends once again.

Re'ann lands behind the two crossbowmen and rolls safely to a stop. The two orcneas and Chance turn when they hear the sound of her hitting the ground. Puzzled, the soldiers draw up their weapons.

Shamans begin to point to the sky and call out in their native language. One of them casts a spell and Lyra's invisibility enchantment is broken.

At the fortress, Lyra gasps, "Oh no! They dispelled it."

Jadelyn, still watching the events unfold through magic, says, "Don't worry, Cirrus got away."

"Good," Lyra sighs.

Evelena says, "Now let's just hope Re'ann can get to Chance."

Chapter 16
Pretrial

Re'ann draws her sword and charges at the orcnea to the right. She impales him before grabbing his crossbow and aiming it at the second soldier. Before the other orcnea can react, Re'ann pulls the trigger, firing the weapon.

With both crossbowmen down, Re'ann calls to Chance. "Chance, run to my voice! Hurry!"

Though he can hear her clearly, Chance does not move. Re'ann grasps a gate-stone hanging around her neck and crushes it. As a new gate opens to the fortress, Chance can see through to the other side. Arioch, Baeldeth, and A'ranah, motion for Chance to come to them. They yell to him as well, though the sound does not travel through.

Baeldeth says, "I'm going after him."

He takes a step towards the gate when A'ranah stops him. "You would only put yourself in danger."

"Why is he just standing there?" he asks.

Arioch answers, "There must be some reason."

An explosion is heard off in the distance as the *Sea Griffin* is destroyed. Belron flees, still clutching a fire elixir in his hand.

Ariella looks out at the horizon to where the floating city hangs in the sky. A'ranah says to her, "Belron told me that he saw Fernando taken prisoner. He's alive... for now." Ariella sighs with relief.

In the arena, many, including Chance, glance up at the sky when they hear the explosion. Re'ann calls for Chance again. He looks back towards the gate and replies, "I can't go."

Re'ann pulls back the hood of the cloak, becoming visible. "What do you mean you can't go? Come on." She holds out her hand, beckoning him.

"Save yourself," he replies. "Get out of here before it's too late."

"I'm not going without you," she insists.

Carr interjects, "Then you will not be going at all." He casts a spell and the magic gate closes.

Re'ann looks around the arena. Five orcneas are rapidly approaching. She looks at Chance, bewildered. "I'm sorry," he mutters. "I tried to tell you."

Re'ann draws her sword, only to place it on the ground before her. She raises her hands to surrender.

Chance yells out, "If you harm her, the deal is off!"

Carr looks back at Lortec, who is standing behind Chance. Lortec grunts. "Take her alive."

At the fortress, Baeldeth is furious. "What deal? Why isn't he helping her?"

No one has the answer to his inquiry. The crowd continues to watch the images as the orcneas move in. One of them throws a net over her while two more grab her arms.

Seeing that Re'ann is in danger, Cirrus circles back and begins to enter the arena of the Colosseum. Re'ann, looks up and tries to dissuade her mount from coming to her rescue. "Go back, Cirrus! Stay away!"

Her loyal steed dives into the arena. Archers fire their arrows, but with the added protection from Rehma's spell, they have no effect. The sky drake lands next to Re'ann and bites down on an orcnea holding the netting. Cirrus swipes his tail, striking two more soldiers.

Re'ann tries to free herself from the net, but another orcnea grabs her. He stays behind her, keeping her between him and the drake. Cirrus hisses, trying to circle around the enemy holding Re'ann. She calls to her steed once more, "Go back, please. They'll kill you."

A dark stream of energy strikes the drake. Cirrus screeches in pain. Chance looks at Carr holding his staff as the dark spell continues.

Chance considers casting a spell when he hears Lortec say, "Don't interfere, or you know what will happen." Carr ends the spell, leaving the drake extremely weak and unable to move.

Back at the fortress, Arioch asks, "What did he just use against the drake?"

A'ranah approaches the bucket of water that continues to show images from inside the arena. She motions with her hands and turns the view displayed on wall of water. They see the crystal used to send the images hanging on the necklace around the end of the staff. She then moves the image closer to the staff itself.

Arioch recognizes something familiar about it. He spots a sizable crystal affixed to the staff. "That looks like a Dragon Slayer weapon."

"I thought they were all destroyed," says River.

"So did I," replies the king.

Back in the arena, Carr approaches the downed drake. Its chest is heaving as it struggles to breathe. It hisses as Carr stands before its enormous head. Re'ann, helplessly watching, pleads, "Please, don't kill him."

"What choice did it leave me?" Carr asks.

She replies, "He was only trying to protect me."

"They are magnificent creatures, aren't they? So loyal." Carr looks back at Re'ann. "Don't worry, drakes are so similar to dragons that his soul will live on forever inside this crystal. His life force will be made to serve me."

Re'ann tries desperately to break free as Carr prepares to use the staff again. The orcnea holding her bludgeons the back of her head with the hilt of his sword. Chance steps forward, but before he can act, Lortec secures the collar around his neck, rendering his spells useless.

Chance tries to draw his sword, but the orcnea general tackles him. Lortec, pinning him to the ground says, "This won't take long."

Chance looks up and watches as the shaman general uses the staff once again on the defenseless drake. Cirrus screeches as it writhes in pain. It is a sight that many back in the fortress find too difficult to watch. They are forced to turn away. After a few moments, the drake ceases to move. The spell ends as Cirrus's life force is trapped in the dragon crystal. Carr walks back several paces before driving the base of his staff back into the ground of the arena.

He walks around the staff and looks at the viewing crystal. "We warned you what would happen if you tried to rescue him."

Re'ann, dazed but conscious, remains on her knees. She looks at Cirrus, its body, no longer moving. She looks at Chance, who is now being dragged to his feet. An orcnea pulls the netting from Re'ann and secures a collar around her neck just like the one on

Chance. Other orcneas join, attaching two chains to the collar before standing off to her sides. Re'ann rubs the back of her head. She can feel warmth from an open wound where she was struck. Looking at her hand, she can see blood.

Lortec says to Chance, "If you move, she dies." He then walks over to the drake rider. Re'ann glares up at her captor, her body trembling with rage. He draws his sword and places the tip under her chin. "You are brave, I'll give you that. I would have been disappointed had no one come for him. You must be asking yourself why he didn't leave with you." Re'ann shifts her gaze to Chance, who stands only a few paces from her. Lortec motions to the guards at the gates of the Colosseum. "Bring them out!"

Through the wall of water, everyone at the fortress watches as the gates open in the arena and five humans are dragged out in chains. "By the Gods," says Arioch. "No wonder Chance didn't leave."

Fidelma and Ariella watch as three men and two women are brought closer into view. Ariella asks, "Aren't those your former crew?"

Fidelma gasps at the sight of Trisha and Lee among the prisoners. "No, it can't be. They were safe."

In the arena, Lortec looks at the image crystal that hangs from Carr's staff. He addresses those watching at the fortress. "We warned you what would happen if you attempted a rescue." He motions to one of the soldiers holding the prisoners. "Bring me one of the women."

The young blonde, Lee, is ushered forward by one of the guards. Her friend begs for them to stop. Terrified, Lee collapses to the ground, crying. The orcnea begins to drag her.

Chance angrily states, "This was not part of our agreement. You told me that if I stayed, they would be spared. I upheld my end of the bargain. If you have any honor at all, you will uphold yours."

Lortec nods. "Very well." He looks back at his soldier. "Put her back with the others." Lee stumbles to her feet. The soldier shoves her back to the line, where Trisha huddles close to her.

Lortec shifts his attention to Re'ann. "I made no promise about those who would rescue you."

Chance replies, "I already stated that if she was harmed our deal was off. If you want me to stand trial peacefully, you will leave them out of this."

Lortec, frustrated, looks back at the image crystal. "If there is any further attempt to rescue Chance, this drake rider will be the first to die." He points to the men and women bound in chains. "They will be next." The general walks back to Chance. "Would you like to say anything to your people before the trial begins?"

Chance faces the staff and crystal. He clears his throat and says, "Arioch, my friend, please do not risk any more lives by coming after me. I'm not worth it."

Though Chance cannot hear it, the king replies, "Like hell you're not."

Chance continues, "I want to face these charges against me, even if they hold no truth." Looking at Lortec, he says, "If I may address them further *after* the trial, I would prefer to do so then."

Lortec nods. "That is reasonable enough."

Orcneas begin to clear the arena floor. They haul off the few dead soldiers and begin to pull the fallen sky drake away with chains. Re'ann watches tearfully before glancing at the staff that drained the life from her trusted steed.

Carr announces, "It is time for the trial of Chance Na'Moon to begin!"

Drums are struck and the crowd of orcneas cheers wildly. Two shamans shape water into two large walls, much like the ones Ja'noa and Kel'ana had set up at the fortress. Chance watches, wide-eyed, wondering what's to come.

Chapter 17
The Trials of War

Carr, still standing before his staff, says, "I am General Carr Vork, and I represent the orcnea nation." He looks at Chance and says, "You, Chance Na'Moon, are accused of atrocities against my people. You are also accused of starting the Second Great War, or as you call it, 'The Second Orcnea War.' What do you say to these accusations?"

"I deny them," Chance answers. Though his words are spoken plainly, the image crystal amplifies his voice through the two walls of water. The entire Colosseum can hear him. The crowd erupts with jeers.

Re'ann looks around at the angered assemblage. She checks the collar around her neck as two orcneas continue to hold the chains. She gets to her feet to take the pressure off her knees.

Lortec, standing behind Chance, says to him, "I will remove the collar now." He uses a key to unlock the iron binding around his neck. Lortec walks over to Carr and places the collar on the ground next to the staff. He then addresses the audience through the viewing crystal. "I am General Lortec Ka." The orcneas cheer as he continues to speak. "I also represent the orcnea nation. I would like to start by asking the Slayer a question." He turns to Chance. "Do you remember how many villages you burned during the war?"

Chance hesitantly answers, "About a dozen, I would guess."

"That is very close," replies Lortec as he unrolls a parchment. "There were fourteen, to be exact. You do not deny burning them?"

Chance shakes his head. "No. But I was careful not to let any women or children perish."

"Yes," replies Lortec. "I, myself, was spared from your onslaught, as were many that surround you today."

Chance looks around the filled seats of the arena, while at the fortress, Evelena says to Kel'ana, "It's just like Chance said to us at Copper Pass."

"What did my father say?" asks Ya'leigh.

Evelena says, "He practically blames himself for this war. He told us about all the women and children he left behind and how they must have grown up hating him."

Kel'ana comments, "It looks like they did."

Chance looks up at the orcneas filling the seats. "You have every reason to hate me. I don't blame you. But if you are going to accuse me of atrocities, you may want to make sure that you are not guilty of the same actions. Your attack on the city of Dury was no different than what I did. You killed every adult male there."

A dull roar is heard from the gathering in the arena as they talk amongst themselves. Lortec steps forward and replies, "You are right, Slayer, our actions in the city of Dury are no different than what you did, years ago, to our cities. In fact, many of us hold a certain level of respect for you for allowing us, the children, to live. The destruction of our villages and towns are not the atrocities that you are accused of."

Confused, Chance asks, "Then what exactly *am* I accused of?"

Lortec stands before Chance, stoically. He looks him in eyes. "The true crime that you committed years ago was the burning of our fields."

"I don't understand," says Chance.

"It was autumn," says Lortec, "and we were only beginning to harvest our food supply for the winter. When you set our fields ablaze, you took from us what we needed most to survive."

"You must have had food," retorts Chance. "Otherwise, how would you eat throughout the rest of the year?"

"When you burnt our villages you also burnt our food stores. We did save *some* food, but you made us march all the way across our lands to the northeast. How much do you think we, as children, could carry with us? The animals all fled, and fruits and vegetables were all but completely destroyed."

"I can't imagine what you must have went through," says Chance sorrowfully.

"Well, Slayer, let me tell you about it. The nights were cold, but you left of plenty us fires to stay warm by. Some villages burned for days. It was exhaustion that killed most who didn't make it." Chance looks at the general, shocked by his words. Lortec continues, "Did you really think that everyone you spared would survive under the conditions you left our lands in?"

"I'm sorry," says Chance. "That was never my intention."

"Your intentions are not in question," Lortec replies. "Only your actions. Nearly one thousand women and children died in what we have come to call the March Through Flames. Those that did make it to safety were then exiled from this continent to the Red Rock Plains across the sea. More died before we could sustain ourselves on what little that barren land had to offer. It is for these reasons that we accuse you of atrocities against our people."

Chance takes a moment to gather his thoughts. He's never considered the possibility that any of the children he left behind would still die from his actions. As disheartening as the news is, however, Chance manages to pull himself together. "We were at war, and while my actions were not perfect, I did the best I could. I'm sorry for the losses that you and your people suffered. If I could to it again, I would make certain that everyone was able to make it to safety."

Lortec asks, "But you would still banish us to a barren land?"

Chance nods, "I would, but I would have done more to make sure that somehow you were able to receive the food necessary for survival."

Carr, having been silent until now, says, "That is thoughtful of you to say, now that it's in the past."

"I know you don't believe me," says Chance. "But why would I go through all the trouble of making sure buildings were empty before I burned them? If I didn't care about the women and children, why would I have bothered?"

"And what of the war itself?" Carr asks.

"The war was not my fault," Chances scoffs. "Your people were attacking us for weeks before we finally had enough."

Lortec says, "We are aware that your wife was killed by an orcnea raid. I find it interesting that you never declared war against us before that day."

"That's not fair," snaps Chance. "Every life that was lost before that day mattered to us."

"I am sure they did, but it was the loss of her life that moved you to action."

Chance sighs. "I'll admit that I was more driven by her loss, just as you were driven after the loss of your father." Lortec, seething with anger, resists the urge to strike at Chance as he continues to speak. "We are no different, you and I. You seek to avenge your father's death, just as I sought to avenge the loss of my wife. As I said before, if you are going to accuse me of wrongdoing, then you should be certain that you are not guilty of the same."

Lortec looks around at Colosseum. The rage that fills him subsides as a grin forms on his face. "There are similarities between you and I, and our actions, but we are *not* the same." He begins to address the crowd and viewing crystal with a confidence not seen until now. "Yes, we orcneas are here now to seek not only vengeance for the loss of our family members, but also to hold those accountable who started the *unjust* war that took their lives in the first place."

"Our war against you was just. You killed my wife and many others."

"And for that, you and King Arioch conspired with the Amazons of the Silver Moon to enact your revenge. Do you deny it?"

"No."

"So it was you who was responsible for declaring open war?"

"King Arioch and I felt it was necessary after your continued raids."

"The raids that plundered small villages of yours to the north?"

"Yes."

"The same raids that attacked caravans?"

"Yes."

"And, of course, the raid that killed your wife."

"Yes," Chance replies, becoming annoyed.

"The raids by my people?"

"Yes."

Lortec laughs. "That, Slayer, is where you are wrong." The orcnea general moves within inches of Chance's face. "Those raiders may have been orcneas, but they did not represent our people." Chance and those watching at the fortress are baffled. Lortec begins to pace as he questions Chance again. "When your people killed the raiders, did you ever find a banner of our nation among them?"

Chance ponders for a moment. "No."

"Are you responsible for the actions of every elf and human in

Runefell?"

"No," he admits.

"Just as we are not responsible for the individual actions of rogue orcneas. Did it ever occur to you that the orcneas you killed were wanted for crimes against our people as well?"

Chance hesitantly answers, "No."

"No, you didn't," says Lortec. "Just so you know, the leader of that band of orcneas was Kwoi Spearbreaker. He was wanted by our people for multiple murders similar to the ones he carried out against your people. He and his group were every bit as much an enemy of ours as he was to you. You just assumed that because they were orcneas, our nation was responsible. You blamed an entire population for what happened to your wife." Chance does not speak, as the weight of his past actions sinks in. "I'll take your silence as a yes."

At the fortress, A'ranah grasps Arioch's hands. "By the gods, what have we done?"

Arioch looks back at Chance's daughter. With tears streaming down her cheeks, she sobs, "They're going to kill him."

Baeldeth says, "Not as long as I have any say in the matter. I say we attack now!"

The soldiers give a united shout, showing their support. Arioch looks at A'ranah. "I'll follow your lead," she says.

Baeldeth joins the king at his side and says, "You wanted us here to fight. Now is the time."

Kel'ana calls out over the noise, "Chance is going to say something!"

A hush quickly falls over the men and women as they turn their attention to the image on the water. Back at the Colosseum, Chance is standing before the staff with the viewing crystal. He takes a moment as he ponders.

Lortec asks him, "Is there something you wish to say?"

"There is," says Chance. He looks directly at the viewing crystal. "I, Chance Na'Moon, accept full responsibility for my actions that lead to the deaths of innocent lives of orcnea women and children in the second war." Those at the arena and at the fortress listen in disbelief.

Ya'leigh watches the image of her father, shaking her head as she begs, "Please, Father, don't do this."

Arioch yells. "I want a way to communicate with them now!"

Fidelma says, "If we use a crystal bowl, we should be able to signal them."

"Get one, please. Hurry."

Fidelma rushes off to fetch a bowl from the *Red Dawn.*

Once the noise dies down, Chance continues, "Furthermore, I accept full responsibility for the war itself." Arioch hangs his head as he listens to Chance explain, "I was the one who convinced King Arioch and the Amazons of the Silver Moon to participate in the war. I and I alone bear the blame."

Chance looks over at Lortec. The orcnea general is as surprised by Chance's admission as everyone else. After a moment Lortec gives Chance a nod of respect. Chance says to him, "I freely offer you my life, in exchange for releasing the prisoners. Please, there is no need to keep them any longer."

As Lortec ponders the request, Carr speaks up. "No, Slayer, you will not dictate the terms of their release. They will only go free when this war is done."

"Then end it!" Chance yells. "You say that I am the one responsible for it all, and I have accepted that. I am the one you want to hold accountable. Everyone else is innocent. Let my life be the last one taken between our peoples."

Chance's words stir the orcnea crowd. Just then, the viewing crystal hanging from the staff begins to emit a high-pitched sound. Carr magically summons a pool of water on the ground at the base of his staff. He shapes it like the others to form a small wall, about the size of a door, from the water. He forms the water around the viewing crystal and the image of Arioch appears.

Carr says to the king, "Greetings, Arioch. It is good of you to join us."

Arioch says to them, "Chance is not responsible for the war. I am."

"Your Highness," Chance replies. "This is not necessary."

"Yes, it is, my friend. I cannot let you take the blame while I am the one who gave the orders."

"Orders you only gave because I asked you to."

"Chance, we are both to blame."

Carr laughs. "Then perhaps you would like to stand with Chance now."

"No!" Chance barks. "I am the one you call 'the Slayer.' I am the one Lortec seeks vengeance against." He then says to Arioch, "Please, my friend, do not try to stop this."

Arioch sighs. "I don't suppose there is any way to change your mind."

Chance shakes his head. "I am ready to accept my fate."

Arioch bows his head. With a heavy sigh, he says, "May the warmth of the light embrace you."

Ariella pushes her way through to the front of the crowd. She says, "I may have lost my brother, and now I have to lose you too. Please tell me this isn't happening."

Chance, visibly moved by the sight of her, says, "Ariella, I'm so sorry. I want you to know that I am eternally grateful that we got to spend one last night together, with no one keeping us apart. I just wish that it didn't have to be our last. I love you now just as I always have."

"I love you, too," she sobs. "May the warmth of the light..." she struggles to say as sorrow overwhelms her. Fidelma does her best to comfort her friend.

Arioch steps aside as Ya'leigh comes forward. "Father!"

"Ya'leigh, why are you still there?"

"I couldn't go back to Elonfar."

Chance, now distraught, says, "I know you may not understand what I am doing right now, but I am doing this for you and your brother and sister. I want peace in your future, and if my death can bring some semblance of closure to these orcneas, then I would gladly give my life for it." Ya'leigh touches the water's surface. The image ripples as he continues. "No matter what happens to me, please don't seek vengeance. Vengeance is the path that led us to where we are now. I'm not saying you shouldn't fight for what you believe is a worthy cause, but revenge is not worthy. Please take care of your brother and sister. I love you all, never forget that."

"I love you, too," she cries. A'ranah takes Ya'leigh's hand and leads her away.

Chance says to the crowd of people, "Isen, if you're out there, make sure you watch over them, please."

Isen makes it to the front of the gathering and replies, "I will, my friend. You can count on that."

"There are so many of you I would like to thank for being a part of my life," Chance concludes. "I apologize if I didn't get to address you all personally." Watching from the back, Va'leen grasps tightly to Nicari's hand.

Chance turns to Carr, "I have nothing further to say." Carr lets the watery image of those watching in the fortress to fall to the ground, while the image of the Colosseum continues to be displayed on the wall of water that Ja'noa and Kel'ana maintain.

Baeldeth says to Arioch, "Are we really going to do nothing as they butcher my brother?"

Arioch replies, "If we make a move, he will die anyway, as well as the civilians they have captured. If we had any realistic chance at success, it may be worth the risk, but as it stands, we do not yet have the numbers necessary to strike."

Frustrated, Baeldeth says, "Then I have returned for nothing."

"No, you haven't," says Arioch. "In two days, we will have the forces necessary to take back Sheathelm, but only if you stay."

Baeldeth looks at his troops as they still watch the events at the arena. "I'll give you three days. After that, I make no promises. I know what Chance said to Ya'leigh, but one way or another I will avenge my brother's death."

At the arena, Chance faces the viewing crystal and kneels. He says to Lortec, loudly enough that his words are heard by everyone, "You should know that after my death, your pain will still be with you. No matter how many humans and elves you kill, it won't make it go away. Believe me, I know."

Carr says, "You would say anything right now to save your life."

Chance shakes his head. "I don't expect my words to save me. My only hope is that in the future, when you are faced with the option for peace or more war, you will remember that more death will not bring back those already gone. I don't say these things for myself, but for my children." He looks at Lortec and adds, "And your son, Quoven."

Moved by his words, Lortec is unsure what to say. Seeing this, Carr, says, "Do not let his lies fool you, Lortec. Now, carry out his execution."

Lortec looks back at his fellow general. "You do realize that I am not going to kill him outright, don't you? That was never the plan." He looks at Chance. "On your feet, Slayer."

Chance sighs, "I have no desire to fight you. If I am to die, I ask that you make it swift."

Lortec, once again focused, replies, "I will not have someone of your standing simply killed without the opportunity to defend himself. Despite all of our differences, Na'Moon, you deserve that much. You are an honorable warrior, and for that, you shall have an honorable death."

Chance bows his head. "And what if I don't fight back?"

Lortec sighs. "You really don't have any desire to live, do you?"

"I am ready to join the light."

"I understand," says Lortec. "You do not value your own life." He walks over to Re'ann. Pointing his sword at her chest, he asks, "Tell me, Slayer, do you value hers?"

"Why are you doing this?" he asks.

"You already know why, Na'Moon."

"Would you really kill her if I refuse to fight?"

"Not only will I kill her if you don't fight, I will kill her if you lose." The orcneas in the arena cheer with a new-found spirit.

At the fortress, the mood as also shifted from one of sadness to one of hope. Baeldeth grins as he yells at the magical image, "Kill him, brother! Show him no mercy."

A'ranah turns to Arioch. "What are they trying to prove?"

Arioch replies, "They are trying to inspire their troops. They don't want Chance to die as a diplomat of peace, but rather as the feared enemy they have always known him as."

"But they are forcing him to fight," says Ya'leigh.

"I don't think it will matter much once the combat begins," says the king.

At the Colosseum, Chance's frustration is showing. Clenching his fists, he yells, "This is ridiculous! You would slaughter her if I lose?"

"It is the only way to be sure that you don't hold back. Come on, 'Slayer.' Show me a fire in your eyes as bright at as the ones you create in your hands."

"What if I win?"

The question surprises Lortec. "If you win," he replies. "You will remain our prisoner, but will get to live."

"Not good enough," says Chance. "I want the prisoners set free."

"Very well," replies Lortec. He points at Re'ann and adds, "But not her. Either way, she will share your fate. That can be as our prisoner... or in death."

Chance looks at Re'ann. She gives him a reassuring nod. Chance looks back at the orcnea general and says, "I accept your terms."

Chapter 18
The Sentencing

Lortec grins as he walks to the center of the arena to face Chance. Carr takes the staff and moves away from middle while the orcneas holding Re'ann lead her to where the other prisoners are being held.

"It doesn't have to be this way," says Chance as he draws one of his swords. "It's not too late."

Lortec draws the sword that once belonged to his father. "It is for you."

The two warriors circle each other carefully, each watching the movements of the other closely, waiting for just the right moment to strike. Chance summons a small fireball and hurls it at Lortec's head. Though it will not harm him, Lortec instinctively throws up his left arm to prevent the flames from obstructing his view. Chance quickly follows through with a swing of his sword, but Lortec lunges back, staying out of reach.

Chance holds his position as Lortec looks for an opening to attack. The orcnea general steps in and swings his sword. Chance parries, moving backwards to keep his distance. Again, Lortec attacks unsuccessfully.

The combatants continue to duel for some time with neither gaining any advantage. Due to the high importance of the fight, both are cautious to not make a mistake, and the pace is slow. Their swords clash together repeatedly as one attack after another is parried by the defender, the ongoing stalemate continuing.

Chance, studying the face of his enemy, looks for any sign of frustration, but Lortec maintains his calm. In an attempt to break the general's composure, Chance begins to concentrate on a spell while staying vigilant.

Lortec looks around at his surroundings. "What trickery are you up to, Slayer?"

"Perhaps you will find out in a moment."

With the suspicion a of spell being cast, Lortec grows impatient. He lunges at Chance, swinging his weapon once again. Chance ducks and counterattacks. This time he manages to strike

Lortec across his chest. Though the scale armor protects him, Chance has gained the first advantage.

The orcnea general attacks again, this time more carefully. Chance stops his blade with his own when Lortec recognizes the spell that Chance is maintaining. He looks at his father's sword, now glowing from the heat of Chance's spell, and becomes worried.

"What are you doing to my sword?" he demands.

Chance steps in and attacks. Fearful that his sword is compromised, Lortec dodges. Chance pushes forward and swings again. The tip of his sword nicks the general's arm. Blood has now been drawn. With a clear advantage, Chance presses the attack. Lortec is forced to retreat rather than stand his ground.

At the fortress, the enthusiasm can be felt by everyone. Baeldeth cheers on his friend, "Melt his sword into slag, Chance!"

Arioch, cautiously optimistic, says to A'ranah, "I think he's going to pull this off."

At the Colosseum, Lortec's sword is white hot. Chance steps in to attack, but this time the general moves to the side before closing in and slamming his head into Chance's.

The blow stuns them both momentarily. Lortec recovers first and sees an opportunity to strike. He takes it, but instead of swinging his sword, Lortec thrusts it at Chance's throat. Chance narrowly dodges the tip of the blade before swinging his own weapon at the softened steel of the general's sword, cutting it in two.

"No!" Lortec shouts. Chance raises his weapon as the general charges him. The blade impales the general high on his chest near his left shoulder. The scale armor prevents the wound from being a serious one. With his left arm, Lortec swipes at the blade, knocking it out of Chance's hand. Lortec tosses what is left of his sword to the ground.

Chance draws his other sword, but Lortec rushes in, lowering his right shoulder. There is a loud clash of steel colliding as the general's pauldron meets with Chance's breastplate. Lortec knocks him to the ground, causing Chance to lose his other sword.

Lortec, enraged, does not take the time to pick up one of the discarded weapons on the ground. Instead, he tries to stomp on Chance while he is prone. Chance rolls out of the way and sweeps the legs of the orcnea general from beneath him. Lortec falls as Chance jumps to his feet.

Lortec quickly stands before turning around to face his opponent, who waits patiently at a safe distance. "Come and get me!" Chance yells before turning and running the other way. Lortec gives chase and quickly closes the distance. Just as he is about to catch him, Chance drops to the ground and rolls back towards Lortec. The general trips over Chance and falls face first into the dirt of the arena.

At the fortress, the crowd of people cheers. Rehma comments to her sisters, "Chance has made him lose his temper. He's reckless now, and vulnerable... Just like I was."

Chance jumps up and runs over to Lortec before he can stand. He slams his forearm into the side of the general's head. Lortec, now on his hands and knees, is open to attack on his side. Chance takes the opportunity to kick him in his ribs. While the scale armor protects well against blades, it is not very effective against such a crushing blow.

Chance takes a step back to ready himself when Lortec gets to his knees. Despite the two solid hits against him, the general is barely fazed. Chance tries to strike him again with his gauntlet, but Lortec blocks it. Before Chance can get out of reach, Lortec grabs Chance by the collar of his breastplate. No matter how hard he tries to break free, Chance is caught in his grasp. Lortec stands up before throwing Chance to the ground with ease.

Chance wraps his arms around one of Lortec's ankles and tries to take him down, but cannot budge him. Beneath Chance's breastplate is a layer of chain mail. Lortec bends over and grabs Chance by the collar of the steel mesh. As he is pulled up, Chance clings to the general's leg. Lortec punches him in the side, causing Chance to lose his hold.

The orcneas in the Colosseum show their enthusiasm as they roar with applause. Lortec grabs Chance by the sides of his armor and hoists him over his head. Reaching down, Chance manages to rake the eyes of his enemy, forcing Lortec to release him. Instead of just letting go, however, Lortec throws Chance over five paces to the ground.

Chance is able to roll backward to avoid suffering the full impact of the landing. While the general recovers his vision,

Chance removes his breastplate.

"Why is he taking that off?" Baeldeth wonders aloud at the fortress.

Arioch replies, "It's slowing him down and the general is just using it to grab him."

They watch as Chance begins to move back to the center of the arena, where his swords still lie on the ground. As he walks, Chance takes off his gauntlets and finally his chain mail.

Having regained his vision, Lortec charges wildly at Chance. They both sprint back to the center of the arena, where Chance dives to the ground and picks up one of his swords. Instead of falling over his foe, as he did before, Lortec is able to stop and deliver a powerful kick to Chance's side.

Chance can feel one of his ribs crack. He pushes through the pain and swings his sword. Lortec backs up, but is cut across his left thigh. It isn't very deep, and Lortec ignores the pain. He takes a step forward and drives his knee into the elf's chest. Lortec reaches down and grabs Chance by the wrist, forcing the sword to be dropped once more. Then the general grabs Chance by his shirt, but it tears as Chance pulls away.

The markings that were left on Chance from his talisman cover his arms, chest, and back. Having never seen them before, those back at the fortress begin to comment.

Baeldeth asks, "What are those markings? What did they do to him?"

Kianna says to Ya'leigh, "It looks similar to the ones on Headmaster Drakesbane and Dicean. I didn't know your father had those."

"Neither did I," says Ya'leigh as they watch her father continue to keep his distance while blinding the orcnea general with more fire.

A'ranah says, "They certainly do look like a spirit blessing, and I don't see his talisman. I wonder if that's where they're from."

At the arena, Chance continues to use a jet of flame against Lortec as he picks up one of his swords again. Lortec puts his hand before him and rushes toward the source of the fire. Chance steps to the side and slashes Lortec's ribs with his weapon, causing yet another wound on the orcnea general.

Lortec finds the other sword on the ground and picks it up.

Chance uses his flame jet to blind his enemy again when Lortec flings the blade through the air at him. Chance dives out of the way, but he is cut along his left shoulder by his own blade.

As Chance turns to face the general, Lortec wraps his arms around him and lifts him off the ground. Too close to swing his blade effectively, Chance begins to bludgeon Lortec with the hilt of his sword. But, even as blood begins to flow down his face, Lortec is unaffected by the strikes. He breaks his hold on Chance only to grab his wrist to prevent further attacks.

Lortec scoops Chance up and slams him to the ground, still holding his wrist. The general twists Chance's arm as he brings up his knee into the back of Chance's elbow. A sickening crack is heard throughout the arena—and fortress through the magical images—as the joint is dislocated. Even the orcneas, who have no love for Chance, groan and wince.

At the fortress, the mood has once again become a somber one. Any hope that Chance could win this duel fades as the general drives his knee into the back of Chance's elbow a second time, causing more damage. Ya'leigh can no longer watch. As she turns away from the spectacle, Kianna accompanies her.

On the floor of the arena, Chance cries out in pain as Lortec strips him of his weapon before tossing it aside. With his right arm crippled, Chance struggles to get to his feet. Lortec, like a wild animal stalking his prey, slowly walks up to Chance, saying, "If I cannot kill you with my father's blade, then I will kill you with my bare hands." He strikes Chance across the face with his fist.

Face down in the dirt, Chance barely remains conscious. He is dizzy and his ears are ringing as Lortec stomps on his back, knocking the wind out of him. The general kicks his fallen opponent in the ribs, cracking two more before pulling him to his feet. Chance desperately swings his left fist at Lortec. The move surprises everyone as it strikes him in the jaw.

It is a short lived offense, however, as Lortec counters with another crushing blow, knocking Chance to the ground again. Chance looks around for his weapon. When he spots it ten paces away, he tries to crawl over to it. Lortec stands back, watching Chance edge his way closer to his sword until he is within only two paces. The general drags Chance away by his ankles before landing the tip of his boot into elf's ribs once more. Lortec continues to take his time toying with his foe before grabbing Chance by his hair and pulling his head up. He wraps his arm around Chance's neck, choking him from behind. Chance looks ahead as pressure is applied around his neck. He sees Re'ann shouting to him as the other prisoners, distraught, begin to cry.

With only one good arm, Chance cannot pull the stronger arms of the general free from him. Soon the edges of his vision begin to fade as darkness creeps in from the sides. With a final surge of strength, Chance creates flames all around him. Hotter and hotter he makes them, putting every last bit of his life into the inferno as blood begins to flow from his nose.

No one on the outside can see what is happening within the flames. Lortec continues to squeeze Chance's neck when suddenly he loses his grip, as if Chance teleported away. Confused, Lortec stands up as the flames disappear. Once they are gone, everyone is stunned at the sight of Chance, his body made up of flame, standing before Lortec.

Chance is as shocked as everyone else. He looks at his left hand as he moves it about before him, marveling at the flames. He then looks down at the rest of his body. He is completely comprised of fire. He bends down, and as he touches his sword on the ground it, too, becomes ablaze.

Watching at the fortress, A'ranah asks the king, "When did Chance learn how to do that?"

Arioch shrugs. "From the way he's behaving, I would say just now."

At the arena, the orcnea general nods. "Body of flames. Impressive." Lortec calmly stands before the flaming vestige of Chance. He swings his arm at him, but it passes through harmlessly. "Now what?" Lortec asks. "You can't keep that spell going forever. You have only delayed your death."

Chance steps forward into the same space as Lortec. It's as if a living fire were climbing the general. As Lortec moves around, he moves through the flames but is unable to escape them. Chance continues to stay with him.

Annoyed, Lortec yells, "Get off of me!"

Chance creates a ring of fire around the general before moving into the ring himself. Lortec tries to move, but Chance is able to move the fire with them. "Where are you?" demands the general.

"You aren't doing yourself any good. Fire doesn't harm me."

From within the flames, Chance appears behind the general in his normal, corporeal form. His sword is also solid and Chance impales Lortec in the back of his left leg. The sword passes all the way through as the general lets out a yell. "Fire may not harm you," says Chance as he ducks a wild swing from the general, "but steel does." Chance transforms his body back into flame and joins the ring of fire once again. Lortec frantically looks around for Chance, waiting for him to reappear. He tries to limp away, but the fire continues to move with him.

A burst of flames rises up behind the general. Lortec pivots around and raises his fists to attack, but Chance is not there. Instead, Lortec is struck again from behind, this time in the back of the other leg. Lortec falls to his knees.

"Show yourself, coward!" calls Lortec.

The ring of fire forms into six different figures, all of them appearing to be fiery versions of Chance. Lortec studies them carefully, unable to tell which one is real. Each one draws back its flaming sword, preparing to strike. Lortec struggles to get up, but can't. The image facing the general swings its weapon. Lortec puts up his arm to block it when Chance appears on his right rear flank. Before the general can act, Chance drives his sword through Lortec's right shoulder.

As the blade protrudes out the front, Chance releases the handle, leaving it embedded in his enemy. The ring of fire disappears as Chance says, "This isn't what I wanted." Chance walks over to where his second sword lies on the ground. With his right arm still dislocated, he picks it up with his left hand before returning to the disabled general.

With his arm, thigh, and both shoulders and legs either cut or impaled, Lortec remains on his knees, unable to remove the sword that still skewers him. He looks up at Chance, standing before him with his other sword pointed at his neck. "You fought like a coward."

Chance, in a great deal of pain of his own, replies, "I did not wish to fight at all. You forced this to happen. If you want me to admit you are the better warrior, I will do so without shame. All that matters to me is that the prisoners are safe, and if that means resorting to an unsavory tactic, so be it. My pride is not greater than the value of their lives. Now, keep your word and free them."

"You have not killed me yet."

Chance grins, "The agreement was that if I won, they would go free. I never said anything about killing you."

Confused, Lortec asks, "You would spare my life, even now, after I tried to take yours?"

Chance nods. "I would. We cannot build a better future for our children so long as the violence continues. I have killed far too many of your kind already. I do not wish to add your blood to my hands as well. If I did, where would that leave Quoven?"

"Do not bring my son into this!" Lortec warns.

Chance takes a step back and turns to the image crystal. "Quoven, if you are watching this, please know that you and my children do not have to share the same fate that your parents did." Exasperated, Chance looks around the arena. "Why are we even fighting? Vengeance? Yes, that is the short answer, but what before then? Where did it all start? Our ancestors feared each other, because they were different. But are we so different that we cannot coexist? Why must we fight over lands that have more than enough room to support us all? I know you can blame us for exiling you to the north, or banishing you to the barren lands of the Red Rock Plains, and I am willing to accept my part in that. But where we go from here does not have to be the same path that we have always followed."

Unmoved, Carr bellows, "Enough!" The crowd of orcneas is split in their opinion. Some of them are nodding as they talk to those around them, while others are doubtful, and shake their heads.

Carr, trying to get control over the assemblage, says, "It is easy to call for peace, when you are losing. But where were your offers in the last war?" The counterpoint is taken well by the orcneas. As they begin to get riled up, Carr continues, "You had no offers for peace. We were driven from this land completely, only for you to leave the north, our home, abandoned."

"You're right," admits Chance. "We did. I'm not disputing the past. I'm only suggesting that we learn from it."

Carr casts a spell. Electricity sparks between his fingers as he says, "You have said enough, Slayer." Chance is struck with the spell and collapses to the ground.

"No!" Lortec yells.

Carr picks up the magic hampering collar before walking over to Chance. He rolls the elf onto his back and secures it around his neck. He walks back to the viewing crystal to send a message to Arioch. "Your hero is still alive, but know this: if you attack, he and the others will suffer." Carr takes the crystal and removes it from his staff. He places it in a small pouch.

At the fortress, the image from inside the Colosseum ends. Baeldeth, frustrated, says, "Can you believe this? Chance offers them peace and they won't listen. They are nothing more than warmongers."

Arioch argues, "I wouldn't be so sure. It appeared to me that his message was getting through, but that shaman general put an end to it."

"At least Chance is still alive," A'ranah says, still comforting Ya'leigh.

Baeldeth sighs, "At least for now."

Chapter 19
Keeping Their Word

Aboard the *Trident*, a great eagle lands on the main deck before transforming into a male elf. "Welcome aboard," greets Marcus. "I am Captain Reonia."

"Thank you, captain," replies the elf. "I bring a message from the elven fleet. We would like to join with you and sail to Sheathelm together."

"I thought the elves were ordered to pull back."

"After further consideration, it was decided that we will uphold our obligation to our allies."

"This wouldn't have anything to do with the fact that Chance Na'Moon is still alive, would it?"

The elf reluctantly says, "This morning, upon learning of Chance's survival, Captain Baeldeth defied our King's orders and took his men back to the stronghold."

"And now you are doing the same?" asks Marcus.

"We are," replies the elven messenger. "But our return has less to do with Mr. Na'Moon, and more to do with the fact that Artos has now committed a significant force. Without that support, our King saw no victory on the east coast, but now..."

Marcus smiles. "Now, we have more than enough forces to take back the city of Sheathelm."

"Yes," he says. "You should also be aware that Chance Na'Moon was put on trial today by the orcneas. Images were sent out for others to watch."

Allen, interrupting the conversation, asks, "Did they execute him?"

The elf shakes his head. "No. He survived the trial, but remains their prisoner."

The men listening sigh with relief. Marcus asks, "Do we have any ideas about how to deal with the floating city?"

"No, though they are developing a plan as we speak. There is a cease-fire in effect. We assume it means that the orcneas do not have enough forces to take the stronghold."

Marcus sighs. "Let's just hope we can get there before any

orcnea reinforcements arrive."

Hours later, Arioch finishes meeting with his advisers, as well as A'ranah, Baeldeth, and Prince River. The king says, "Until the reinforcements from Artos arrive, all we can do is wait."

"We need to find a way to get that floating city out of the air," says Baeldeth.

River asks, "Couldn't we open a gate above it and drop down?"

"It would be too high," says A'ranah. "Only a few would be able to go through."

Jadelyn says, "I could try to find out how close we can get before the ward spells would interfere. Maybe there's a spot where we can get a gate close enough to the ground that we could safely jump through it."

A'ranah nods. "Start your search."

"Yes, Mother Elder."

Jadelyn excuses herself when a guard calls down, "A small group is approaching!"

Arioch and a group of others rush up the hill to the wall and tower. Peering through the gate, Arioch comments, "It looks like the prisoners."

Others look out towards Sheathelm as the five captives make their way to the fortress. Isen says, "I'll go and help them."

Baeldeth motions to a few of his men. "You there, come with me. We'll help, as well."

Isen and Baeldeth head out through the gate, followed by a few of the elven soldiers. Isen says to the prince's bodyguard, "I'm glad you came back."

"Like I told your king, I didn't do it for you or your people. I was hoping to rescue Chance."

"In a couple more days, we should have the forces necessary to take Sheathelm back."

Baeldeth says, "I just hope our attack doesn't cost my brother his life."

In Sheathelm, Chance wakes in his cell. In pain, he slowly sits up to check his right arm. Re'ann is chained to the opposite side of the cell, sitting on the floor. She says, "They healed your arm."

He flexes his elbow. "Are you all right?"

"No," she answers sadly. "Cirrus is dead."

"I'm sorry."

"I raised him from a pup."

"I'm sorry," he repeats, not knowing what else to say.

"I understand why you didn't leave when you had the opportunity, but you didn't even try to tell us that they had prisoners."

"You're right, I'm—"

"I know, you're sorry. Is that all you have to say?"

Chance sighs. "I didn't really expect anyone to come for me. It all happened so fast. I told you to leave."

"You should have told me why."

"There wasn't time," Chance retorts. "I certainly didn't think you were going to stand there and argue about it. You should have left me."

"Believe me, I wish I had."

Chance hangs his head. "Thank you," he says after a moment of silence, "for risking your life."

Re'ann laughs to herself. "If it had worked, it would mean that I would have rescued you twice. The Amazons of the Silver Moon would have had to let me join them."

Confused by her response, Chance asks, "Was that some kind of joke?"

"Sort of."

Chance notices Re'ann's plain clothing. "They took your armor. Did they hurt you, or do anything else?"

Re'ann shakes her head. "No. Fortunately, we are as repugnant to them as they are to us." She looks at the markings on Chance's body. "When did you get a spirit blessing?"

"They broke my talisman when it wouldn't obey them. The fragment of Feonvaer's spirit inside bound itself to me. Speaking of which, if we can get General Vork's staff, we can free Cirrus's spirit. He doesn't have to remain a prisoner."

Glancing around their prison, Re'ann studies the five orcnea guards outside the bars. "Now we just have to find a way to escape."

The door to the outside opens and Lortec enters. Still suffering from the injuries of his battle with Chance, General Ka is slow to make his way over to the iron bars of the cell.

Chance stands and asks, "What's going to happen to us now?"

Lortec answers, "There is some disagreement as to what we do with you next. Carr would have the two of you tortured to death. I told him that was unacceptable."

"That is kind of you," says Chance humbly. "Thank you."

"Don't thank me yet, Na'Moon," replies the general as he gingerly walks around the cell. "My loss in the Colosseum damaged my reputation with the others. The only reason Carr is not getting what he wants is because Cron still sides with me."

"Cron is the ogre general?"

"Yes. He is older than Carr and myself. He has witnessed true atrocities by enemies far more ruthless than you and your people. It would seem that your call to peace moved him."

"And what about you? Do you desire peace?"

Lortec scoffs at the question. "Of course I do, but sometimes peace requires spilling the blood of those who would oppress you."

"I cannot speak for all my people, but I can promise you that Arioch and myself have no interest in oppressing you. Don't you see? We can build a better future together."

"Enough!" Lortec snaps. "I have already been accused of becoming weak while listening to you. Even as you spared my life, all I could think about was my son, and whether or not I would dishonor him by living. I wish you would have killed me, Na'Moon. At least then, my son could say I died at the hands of the Slayer. There is no shame in that. Still, because of your mercy, there are those like Cron who are beginning to question this war. Carr sees this. He says your words are more dangerous to us than your troops."

"Could you and Cron negotiate a peace?"

"It is not up to us. Nor is it up to Carr. It is the decision of the High Chief. In a few days, you can discuss the matter with him."

"Your High Chief is coming here?"

"Yes, but I would not get your hopes up. He is no more interested in peace than Carr."

At the stronghold, Lee and Trisha are reunited with their former captain, Fidelma. Holding them tightly, Fidelma says, "I'm so glad to see you two. I was so worried."

Lee breaks down in tears. "I thought we were going to die."

As the prisoners are checked on and cared for, Arioch approaches Ya'leigh. "How are you holding up?"

"I'm doing better now that my father survived."

"I promise we will never abandon him."

"I know, thank you."

Looking back at the released prisoners, he says, "It looks like they're keeping their word. I have no doubt Chance is safe so long as we don't attack." Arioch looks down and continues, "In three days, the troops from Artos should arrive."

Ya'leigh nods. "And then we have to attack."

"I'm sorry," says Arioch.

"Don't worry, I understand. I'm sure my father wouldn't want you to delay any attack because of him."

"If there is a way to get him out safely, we will do it."

Lyra and her friends listen nearby. Lyra says to Yentroc, "There has to be a way to sneak in. I just need to find out what it is."

As Lyra begins to walk off, Yentroc asks, "Where are you going?"

"To find Headmaster Grunwalt."

Not far away, Va'leen is walking along the water's edge when she comes upon Baeldeth. She says, "I'm glad you came back, brother."

Baeldeth sighs. "I really wish people would stop saying that. I'm not some hero that came back to save everyone."

"I know why you came back, and that's good enough for me."

Baeldeth sits down on a nearby crate. "He's a hopeless fool, you know."

Confused, Va'leen asks, "Who, Chance?"

"Yes," he replies as his sister sits next to him. "To believe that peace could be achieved after everything that has happened. I don't know what he was thinking."

Va'leen looks at the floating city off in distance. "It might have been desperation. Maybe he feels that we cannot win this war. Maybe he was hoping that because they have been adhering to some honorable code of conduct that he could reason with them."

"What code of conduct?"

"Sparing women and children, honoring the cease-fires, and letting these prisoners go. So far, they have kept every promise. You heard that general. He expressed some sort of respect for Chance."

Baeldeth laughs. "Even then, he still tried to kill him."

"I know," she replies. "I don't think Chance really expected them to accept peace. I think he really was looking to the future. You know, I spent a lot of time with Chance in the Dragon Wars. He was always the optimist. I remember him telling me that he believed if everyone had the opportunity to get to know their perceived enemies, there would be no war, and that conflicts are caused by fear and misunderstandings. Even as we were fighting in a war, his heart was so pure and untainted by the darkness that surrounded us." She looks down and says sadly, "That all changed when we lost Sha'al."

Baeldeth, also saddened, says, "I saw the change in him, too. It's unfortunate that it took the loss of his wife for him to see the world as it really is."

Va'leen shakes her head. "You don't really believe that, do you? That the world is really that cold and unforgiving?"

"I'm just telling you how I see things."

"That's too bad. For years, Chance has been haunted by Sha'al's loss, but when Chance spoke of peace today, I saw the young man he once was. I saw that all the hope in him had not been extinguished. I was once again looking at the man I fell in love with years ago."

Baeldeth looks at her, surprised. "I had no idea you were in love with him."

Va'leen takes a deep breath. "I've only told one other person, so I would appreciate it if you kept that to yourself."

"Of course."

Through the crowd, Va'leen spots Sven talking with Fidelma. "Excuse me, there's something I must attend to." She makes her way over to Sven. She takes him by the arm and says, "Can I speak with you a moment?" Before he can answer, she pulls him away from Fidelma.

"What do you want?" Sven asks.

Glancing over at Fidelma, Va'leen asks, "Who is that woman?"

"She is friend of Sven."

"I see," she replies before looking back at him. "Look, Sven, I'm sorry for what I did the other night. I know how much Lyra means to you."

Sven replies, "Is this what you have come to say? That you are sorry?"

"Yes," she answers. Looking at Fidelma suspiciously, she adds, "If you really care about Lyra, I think you should tell her instead of talking with this woman."

Fidelma, who has been listening, snaps, "I am not just some woman. Sven and I were engaged to be married."

Confused, Va'leen looks at Sven, waiting for him to explain. Sven adds, "It was long ago, but Fidelma and Sven are friends now."

Fidelma asks, "Sven, is this the woman you met at the Rusty Dagger?"

"Yes," he answers. "Her name is Va'leen."

Sizing up the Amazon, Fidelma says, "Well, Va'leen, I think you're right about one thing: Sven does care about Lyra. My question is why does this matter to you? From what I understand, you came between them."

Va'leen retorts, "That's interesting, I heard the same about you."

The two women stare each other down before Sven stands between them, saying, "All right, let us all take moment to calm down. You have both tried to come between Lyra and Sven." Then, addressing Va'leen, he says, "Lyra has made it clear that she does not wish to speak with Sven." Both women laugh to themselves. "What is funny?"

Va'leen says, "I can't speak for Lyra, or anyone else, but when I tell a man that I care about that I want him to leave me alone, I don't really want him to leave me alone."

Sven looks at Fidelma, who is nodding in agreement with Va'leen. Sven shakes his head and says to Fidelma, "All Sven did was try to talk to you years ago. You never gave Sven chance."

"That's because I really didn't want to talk with you," says Fidelma.

"And how does man know when woman does not want to talk?"

Fidelma answers, "She will tell you."

Va'leen adds, "Unless she's testing you."

"Right," agrees Fidelma.

Sven complains, "Women are so confusing."

Fidelma jests, "That's something you just have to deal with if you want to be with one."

Sven laughs, "Life was easier when Sven wanted to be alone."

Chapter 20
Reclamation

Off the coast of Bermuda, Kelik is once again visiting Yentroc on the company's research ship. Gelana and Rehma are still there, as well. Kelik is reading from the captain's log that was brought up from the sea floor the day before.

The tome, now mostly restored, is still blemished with time, though magic has kept it remarkably preserved. Kelik says, "This is amazing. This goes back to the time of the Third Orcnea War. I was just telling that story to the kids."

Yentroc asks, "Isn't Lyra at the apartment today trying to finish it?"

"Yes," he answers as he closes the cover. "It's a long story, but they should be able to get through it today."

"I wonder if Laura's headaches have returned," comments Rehma.

Kelik says, "Ambra is supposed to stop by with a remedy. She grew and harvested the ingredients herself."

Rehma says to Gelana, "I know you aren't looking forward to it, but don't you think it's time we told the kids the truth?"

"They aren't old enough," argues Gelana.

"Laura is," says Kelik. "Josh and Haley may still need some time, but I think Laura is ready."

Gelana says, "It gets harder to believe with each passing generation. What am I supposed to say? 'Hello, I am your eighth great grandmother, and I came here through a magic gate four hundred years ago from another world. You're part elf.'"

Yentroc says, "I understand this is difficult, but we can't put it off forever."

Rehma, distracted, asks, "Do you guys hear that?"

The others listen carefully for a moment when Yentroc says, "It sounds like a boat approaching."

Kelik shakes his head, "Boy, that Mr. Winters is persistent."

Yentroc walks out onto the deck and spots an approaching powerboat. "I don't think it's Eric."

They watch as the boat containing Ariella, Fidelma, Annalee, and Garrett approaches. It slows and Ariella calls up. "I'm sorry to bother you, but I was wondering if we might come aboard for a moment and have a word?"

Though she is skeptical, Rehma replies, "Of course. Is there something we can help you with?"

Garrett tosses ropes up so that the ships can be secured as Ariella says, "As a matter of fact, there is."

Fidelma climbs up first, followed by Garrett and Annalee. Ariella is last to board. She shakes Rehma's hand and says, "A friend of mine said you found something remarkable. It may even belong to my family."

Intrigued but doubtful, Kelik steps forward and asks, "What family do you belong to?"

Ariella answers, "My name is Ariella Stormrage, and I believe you have something that belonged to my ancestor."

The Amazons and Kelik are baffled and stunned. Kelik studies Ariella's face, then says, "Tell me, does the name Chance Na'Moon mean anything to you?"

Now Ariella and her companions are the ones confused. Ariella says hesitantly, "I know of Chance Na'Moon, and you're not him."

Kelik smiles. "No, I'm not. I'm his son, Kelik." As she processes the information, Kelik adds, "Ariella, you don't have to pretend with us. We know each other."

"My god," she says, amazed, "Kelik, is it really you?"

"Yes."

"It's been..." she thinks for a moment, trying to remember, "hundreds of years."

Yentroc steps forward. "You probably don't remember any of us very well, but we served on the *Red Dawn* as part of our Rite of Passage, right after the Third Orcnea War."

"I can't believe it," she gasps. "You're an Amazon of the Silver Moon?"

"Yes, my name is Yentroc."

"I'm sorry if I don't quite remember you all."

Rehma laughs, "Don't worry about that. I can barely remember people I met *one* hundred years ago, let alone *five* hundred."

As they laugh, Kelik brings over the ship's log. "I believe this is yours."

Ariella takes the magically protected tome. "I still can't believe this. After all these years, I never thought the *Red Dawn* would be found. I must admit, I came here not knowing what to expect. I thought we may have to fight to even see it."

"Admittedly, there isn't much down there," says Yentroc.

"You might try looking further up the gulf stream," suggests Ariella. "There was a lot of debris, and we floated along with it for about a half day before we were rescued."

Kelik asks, "How did you even end up here? I didn't think there was a gate big enough to transport a ship."

Ariella says, "It's a long story."

"Why don't we discuss it over lunch?" suggests Yentroc.

"That would be lovely," replies Ariella.

At the apartment, Lyra has taken a break from reading while they, too, get something to eat. There is a knock at the door, and when Laura opens it, she finds Ambra waiting in the hall.

"Hi, Aunt Amber," Laura greets her, using the variant of her name she has always known her as.

Ambra asks, "Is Nica still here?"

"Yes, she's in the kitchen," she answers as she steps back to allow Ambra to enter.

"Great, I brought something she asked for," Ambra says as she walks down the hallway toward the living room.

Lyra comes out of the kitchen. "I thought I heard your voice," she says to Ambra.

Ambra pulls out a pouch from her pocket. "I brought this for you."

"That's great, thank you. Actually, it's not for me, it's for Laura."

"For me?" Laura asks.

Lyra replies, "It's a special kind of tea that should help you with your headaches."

Ambra, trying to hide her enthusiasm, asks, "Laura, you're having headaches?"

"I guess," she answers, confused. "It only started yesterday."

Ambra digs through her purse and pulls out a business card. She hands it Laura. "Do you see anything on the back of the card?"

Laura turns over the card and looks at the back. "I see a smiley face," she says.

"That's great!" exclaims Ambra. "Not everyone can see it."

"What does that mean?" she asks. "Does this have something to do with my headache yesterday?"

"It might," says Lyra. "The best way we can explain it is that you can see a spectrum of light that many others can't, and it can cause headaches."

Josh comes over and says, "Can I see?"

Laura hands him the business card. He stares at the back. "I don't see anything," he says, disappointed.

"Don't worry," Laura laughs. "It's not worth the pain."

"I heard you were reading about the Third Orcnea War," says Ambra.

"We are," says Josh. "It's really cool."

Ambra asks, "Did you read the part about Ambra Na'Moon traveling in the north?"

"Was she one of Chance's children?" Josh asks.

"Don't you remember?" asks Laura. "She and her brother got sent back to the elven city before the attack came."

"Oh, yeah, I remember," says Josh. "She had the giant blueberries."

"Sponge fruit," corrects Ambra. "It sounds like you read past all the fun stuff."

Laura says, "We just got past Chance's trial. Would you like to stay?"

"I don't know," she says, looking at Lyra. "The story gets kind of sad."

"Come on," whines Josh.

"Yeah, stay with us," says Haley.

"Okay," relents Ambra. "I'll stay for a little while."

Lyra says, "If you want to read it to them, I just got to the 25th day. I can clean up from lunch."

Ambra sits down on the couch and leans over the coffee table where the massive tome lies open. "I'm not as good as Kyle when it comes to reading, but I'll try."

Day 25
Chapter 21
The Dark Dwarf

In a darkened cell of the floating city, Fernando sits on the stone floor. The walls are made up of carved stone with one small doorway leading out. The door is a grid of iron bars. In the hall outside, one orcnea stands guard. Torches light the hallway, but not well.

As Fernando ponders what is to become of him, he hears footsteps approaching. He stands when a stout figure appears in the doorway. Unable to see anything other than a silhouette, Fernando says, "If you are the manager of this place, I would like to lodge a complaint." Fernando approaches the door, saying, "I have stayed in my fair share of prisons lately, and this one is by far the worst. I have no bed and it is dark."

The shadowed figure laughs. As Fernando gets closer, he begins to see the visitor is a dwarf with dark hair and beard. The dwarf says, "Mr. Greythorn, it is a pleasure to meet you."

Confused, Fernando replies, "I am sorry, do I know you?"

"No, you do not," replies the dwarf. "But I know who you are, Fernando. You are Ariella's brother."

Fernando ponders for a moment, then deduces, "You must be Corthag."

"Very good," he laughs. "You're right, of course. I watched you through the blue orbs on the *Red Dawn*. It was wise of Ariella to remove them."

"Well, now that the introductions are out of the way," says Fernando, "why are you here?"

Corthag laughs again. "It must baffle you as to why a dwarf would ever work with orcneas. After all, they've been our enemies as long as they've been any other race's."

Fernando replies, "Based on what little I know of you, I can only assume it has to do with personal gain as opposed to anything selfless."

"Your insults are amusing," he replies. "I do not care what you, or anyone, thinks of me. All that matters is that, in exchange for my help, the orcnea high chief is willing to grant me great wealth."

"And what exactly are you offering to them?"

"My magic," he answers. "The dark spells that I know will help them with their victory." Corthag holds out Fernando's sword. "We never thought to see if Ariella could wield this sword. We had always assumed that her father was not on board. It is truly an amazing weapon."

"Why do you say that?"

"I saw it in action that night. The night your father died. He was a good swordsman, that was plain to see, but this sword, it cut through chain-mail like it was nothing more than rags. He was able to parry countless attacks, even damaging the swords that were swung against him. You should be proud of him."

"I am," Fernando replies. "Did he die well?"

"I suppose he did," he replies as he strokes his beard. "He stood in the way of Ariella's mother, protecting her. His persistence is why Ariella is alive today."

"I am sure he took as many orcneas with him as he could."

"Orcneas?" asks Corthag. "There were no orcneas."

"What are you talking about? The *White Feather* was attacked by an orcnea ship."

"Aye, that is how the story goes, but there were no orcneas. It was just us and the *White Feather.*"

"You're lying!"

Corthag unsheathes Fernando's sword. "I'll never forget the pain I felt when your father impaled me with this. I thought for sure I was going to die. In fact, I think I did. It was the first time I realized that the Soul Keeper spell actually worked. Your father thought I was dead, as well, and with good reason. He turned his back to me to check on Ariella's mother. I cast the dark bolt spell, and when he turned back around, I killed him."

"I don't believe you."

Corthag sheathes the sword. "I would tell you to ask Red Beard personally, but that's not possible." As Corthag begins to walk away, he says, "I've always wondered what Ariella would do if she learned the truth. To know that your whole life was built on a lie."

"Wait!" calls Fernando. "Don't walk away from me, I have

more questions."

"I'm sorry, Mr. Greythorn, but I have matters I must attend to."

As the dwarf walks away, Fernando grabs the bars of the cell, shaking them vigorously. It is a futile move, however, as they don't budge. He begins to pace in the small room, wondering about his sister.

Aboard the *Red Dawn,* Ariella sits on the poop deck watching the sun rise over the eastern sea. Red Beard joins her and says, "Mornin', my dear."

"Good morning, Father."

Red Beards sits next to her. "No matter how many times I see it, 'tis always beautiful."

"Yes, it is," she agrees.

"I know you're worried about Chance and Fernando right now."

"Do you think I'll ever see them again?"

"I wish I could tell you."

"With Chance, at least I know he's probably alive, but with Fernando..." She leans on her father's shoulder.

"All my life," says Red Beard, "all I ever wanted to do was protect you from harm. From the moment you were born, I wanted to shield you from darkness. I'm sorry I failed you."

"Father, stop. You kept me safe."

"Not safe enough."

"Some things you can't keep me shielded from. It's not your fault. This is all the orcneas' doing. I know Chance accepted responsibility for the start of the Second Orcnea War, but this war is their doing, just like it was their choice to attack the *White Feather* and kill my mother."

Red Beard sighs. "You know, Chance may be right. Perhaps we shouldn't hold all of the orcneas responsible for the actions of one orcnea ship."

"I know, Father, but I can't help it. I hate them all."

In the floating city, Corthag enters a room and overlooks a reservoir of water in the center. The dark-haired dwarf removes his necklace and places it in the water. Within moments, an image of an orcnea appears on the water's surface. The orcnea wears a headdress made of animal bones, including horns, antlers, and tusks. His face is weathered with age. Instead of armor, he dons simple clothing and a cloak of white fur.

Corthag says, "Greetings, High Chief."

"Corthag," says the orcnea leader, "I understand that you thwarted an attack on the floating city."

"Yes, High Chief. Arioch and the Amazons are desperate. It was nothing we couldn't handle."

"We will be arriving tomorrow, according to schedule. Tonight, I want you to move the floating city out to meet with us and escort us the rest of the journey. There are rumors that ships will be arriving from Artos tomorrow, as well. We cannot allow them to interfere with our plans."

"It will be done."

"Excellent," replies the High Chief. "Once we make landfall, you will join us in the Colosseum, and we shall see if your information is correct regarding the Gate of Banishment."

"The information is correct," says Corthag. "The only question remaining is if the gate is still intact."

"If it is, then we shall offer Chance Na'Moon as a gift to our new ally."

Chapter 22
Endurance

In Sheathelm, Re'ann and Chance are greeted by Carr Vork and four soldiers. Chance stands as they open the door to their cell. While Carr waits outside the iron bars, the four others enter. Without speaking a word, they attack Chance.

One of them kicks him in the stomach, causing him to double over. Two of them grab his arms and force him back against the wall, where the fourth strikes him across the face with his fist.

"Stop!" Re'ann yells as they begin to beat him repeatedly. "Why are you doing this?"

They let Chance fall to the ground as Carr says, "Chance may have won the fight against Lortec, but he is still guilty of his crimes, and must pay the price."

The orcnea soldiers begin to stomp and kick Chance as he lies prone. Re'ann tries to help, but the chains attached to her collar prevent her from getting close enough. The assault continues as she turns to the orcnea general. "Please make them stop. They'll kill him."

"No, he won't die," replies Carr. "I'll make sure of that." After a few moments, Carr orders his men to cease. He enters the cell as the soldiers wait outside. Carr kneels next to Chance and says, "You are fortunate that I am not allowed to kill you. The High Chief has ordered us to keep you alive." He charges an electrical spell in his hand and continues, "However, that doesn't mean we can't make you suffer."

Carr touches Chance's shoulder and the spell begins to shock him. Chance writhes on the floor in pain while Re'ann watches helplessly. The general ends the spell to allow Chance to catch his breath, only to repeat the process again. The crackle of the electrical charge can be heard as the shaman continues to torture the elf.

After pouring his strength into the spell, Carr takes a moment for himself to rest. Soon he resumes the punishment, and begins to shock Chance a third time.

Re'ann cries out, "Please, he can't take any more!"

Carr ends the spell again. He turns to her. "Perhaps you would like to endure the punishment for him?"

"N-no," Chance stutters, barely able to speak. Carr looks down at him as he continues with forced words, "Leave... her... alone."

The general ponders a moment before a sadistic grin stretches across his face. Turning his attention to Re'ann, he asks. "Well? Do you wish to take his place?" Before she can answer he begins to shock Chance again.

As Chance's body twists and convulses on the floor, Re'ann nods. "I will."

Carr stands as Chance tries to grab the general's boots. He is able to throw his arms around them, but is too weak to hold on as the general makes his way over to Re'ann. The drake rider lunges at Carr, but due to the chains, he is just out of reach. Two of the soldiers re-enter the cell. Carr says, "Secure her."

"No!" Chance yells as the soldiers overpower Re'ann.

The orcneas turn Re'ann to face the iron bars before shackling her wrists to them. Carr says to Chance, "You always seem to be more concerned with the well-being of others than your own safety."

Carr walks outside the cell and grabs a whip. As he returns, Chance begins to plead, "Please, just punish me. I'm the guilty one."

Carr replies, "You know, I believe that you will suffer more by watching her in pain than taking punishment yourself." The general tears Re'ann's shirt, exposing her back. Chance turns his head, unable to watch. "If you look away," Carr warns, "I will make it worse on her."

Chance reluctantly turns his gaze back. The general cracks the whip across Re'ann's back. She flinches and whimpers, though her response is subdued. Carr whips her again, but receives the same lackluster response. He laughs. "Now I understand. She is tougher than you, Slayer. But fear not: by the time I'm done with her, she will scream." He strikes her again, this time drawing blood. "Remember, Slayer, she chose this. She suffers for you."

Chance watches through the tears welling in his eyes as the young woman is punished in his place.

Aboard the *Trident*, Allen is gazing at the sea. The dwarf, Vardik, joins him as he leans on the railing, breathing in deeply.

"Are you all right?" Allen asks.

"Yes, I'll be fine, thanks. I'm still getting used to travel on the seas."

Allen laughs lightly. "It took me three months to get to the point where I didn't vomit anymore under normal conditions."

Vardik sits down on the deck and leans back against the railing. "I'm more accustomed to being underground. We dwarves aren't known for seamanship."

"I've met one who is. His name is Torgus, and he's the first mate of the last ship I was on, the *Red Dawn*."

"Red Beard's ship, aye."

"It was his ship, until about a year ago when there was an attempted mutiny. His daughter is the captain now."

"A female dwarf is captain?"

"No," Allen laughs. "Ariella is human. Red Beard took her in after rescuing her when she was an infant."

"Ah, yes, I think I remember hearing about it. Did you ever meet Red Beard?"

"No," he lies. "I didn't join the crew until after he was gone." The two are silent for a while before Allen asks, "Were you a miner in New Waterford?"

"Sort of," Vardik answers. "I help out in the mines, but more for healing when it's needed. Most of the time I help my father run the family brewery. We make the best stout ale in all of Runefell."

"Where did you learn to cast healing spells?"

"I was once a paladin for the Order of the Mountain's Light. I even fought in the last orcnea war. I returned home afterward."

"Do you still have your armor?"

"Yes, it's with me, but I don't wear it when I'm on a ship. The last thing I need is to go overboard while wearing enough steel to make me an anchor."

"My name's Allen, by the way," he says as he extends his hand.

"Vardik Craghammer," he replies as they shake hands.

"We should be arriving tomorrow," says Allen.

"Good," he groans. "I don't know how much more of this I can endure."

In Sheathelm, Re'ann lies on the floor of the cell with her hands still bound to the iron bars. Her back is covered with lacerations from the flogging she received at the hands of Carr. The general, standing over Chance, asks, "Is she your mate?"

Distressed and confused, Chance looks up and shakes his head. "No. I barely know her."

Carr grunts. "Too bad. Women that durable are rare. Still, you seem to care a great deal for her. I wonder how you would react if she were someone you loved."

Chance glares at the general. "You know how I would react, or have you already forgotten what I did in the last war?"

"There he is," mocks Carr. "After all that talk of peace, you are still the Orcnea Slayer."

Chance struggles to get his emotions under control. He says, "I *was* wrong to hold my wife's death against your people, but you," he looks intently in the eyes, "I would gladly watch you burn."

"Burn?" Carr ponders aloud. "What a great idea." Carr says to one of the soldiers, "You, hand me your sword." The orcnea draws his weapon and gives it to the general. Carr magically summons a ball of fire in his hand. As he walks over to Re'ann, he holds the sword over the flame. "I don't have all your talents with fire, Slayer, so I cannot heat this sword like you did Lortec's. I can, however, make it hot enough to burn flesh."

Concerned, Chance looks at Re'ann, who still lies defenseless on the ground. "She's suffered enough, please don't do this."

Carr looks back at Chance. "I am only going to help stop the bleeding." The general kneels next to Re'ann. As the hot steel nears her skin she recoils. Once it makes contact, the blood on the skin boils away as her flesh is seared. Re'ann cries out in anguish.

Chance pulls at the chains that bind him to his side of the cell. "Stop it!" he yells. "I'm the one who burned your people, not her."

Carr drags the tip of the sword down her back before pulling it away. He turns to face Chance. "You're right, it was you who burned our people and our villages. Out of all the wars you have been in, you must have burned hundreds of victims, and yet, you were immune to the flames' effects." Carr stands just outside of Chance's reach. He says to his men, "Bind him like the female."

Three orcneas rush in, tackling Chance to the ground before picking him up and slamming him into the bars. Soon he is bound by his wrists. Carr unlocks the bindings of Re'ann's wrists and says to her, "Now, it is your turn to watch *him* suffer for *you*."

Re'ann, powerless to help, sits while covering herself. "Please, what more do you want from us?" she begs.

Carr laughs, "I want the Slayer to feel what all of his victims felt, though that would kill him. Instead, I will settle for this." Carr takes the sword and begins to heat it once more. He walks over to Chance, who nervously anticipates what is about happen. "This is only a small taste of the suffering you have caused my people." The red-hot sword sears Chance's back as he, too, cries out in agony.

After Carr slowly drags the flat of the blade down his back, the door to the room bursts open as Lortec enters. "What is the meaning of this?!" he demands of his comrade. "This is not how we treat our prisoners."

Carr backs away, but the damage has already been done. Carr says, "You can treat your prisoners as your guests if you wish, but this is how I treat my enemies."

Lortec says to the extra guards, "All of you, out!" He glances at Re'ann, then says to one of the guards, "Search the houses for clothing that will fit her." The orcnea looks at Carr when Lortec moves closer to the soldier. The massive general looks down at his subordinate. "I gave you an order, I suggest you do it."

"Yes, sir," he responds, bowing his head.

Carr leaves, along with the soldiers that came with him. Lortec unbinds Chance's wrists. "I had no idea that Carr was doing this to you."

"Thank you," says Chance.

"Do not thank me."

"Please, let me help her."

Lortec looks at Re'ann. "I'm sorry, but I cannot remove your collar."

"I promise I won't try to escape. I just need to heal her."

"And what of your own wounds?" he asks, looking at Chance's battered face.

"I'll be fine," he insists. "It's too hard to heal myself, anyway."

The general looks back over at Re'ann, who is sitting up and curled into a ball with her arms around her knees. "Is she your mate?"

"Carr asked the same thing. Why do you ask?"

"She does not bear the markings of an Amazon, yet she risked her life trying to save you."

"Tell me, do orcnea women only fight if they are protecting their families?"

Lortec scoffs at the question. "Our women are strong, perhaps stronger than most of your males. But we do not let them fight in wars. They are far too valuable to our people's survival. One male can father a thousand orcneas, but one female can only give birth to a fraction of that. It is for that reason that we protect and cherish them." He looks back over at Re'ann. "It seems wasteful to risk such a precious commodity."

Re'ann angrily says, "I am not livestock."

Lortec nods, "Of course not. I did not mean to make it sound as if our women are treated as such. Perhaps there is not a proper translation that describes the true value of a woman."

"Oh, very well then," replies Re'ann. After thinking a bit, she asks, "What about women who do not want to have children?"

Chance, interrupting, says, "I don't think now is the time to discuss their social structure."

Lortec laughs. "I will return shortly with something to help your wounds."

"Thank you," says Re'ann.

"Do not thank me," repeats Lortec. "I am not doing this to be kind. I am doing it because it is right. There is no need to thank me for that."

Lortec exits the room, leaving Chance and Re'ann alone with the remaining guards outside the cell. Chance asks her, "How are you holding up?"

"My back feels like it's still on fire," replies Re'ann

"I'm sorry."

"You say that a lot, don't you…"

Chance thinks for a bit. "I suppose so, but it doesn't make it any less true."

"Why are you sorry now?"

"Because," he answers as he moves as close as his chains will allow, "this is all my fault."

"No, it's not. I should have heeded your warning and left."

"I'm not talking about that. I'm talking about this entire war. This is all because of what I did."

Re'ann, shakes her head. "You really believe the things they said in that trial?"

"What they said was true," he answers solemnly. "There were no banners on the orcneas that killed my wife. There was nothing at all that linked them to the orcnea people as a whole. I was simply too enraged at the time to notice."

"All right," agrees Re'ann. "So you didn't know the orcneas weren't responsible. Did they ever try to tell you that after the war started?"

"I don't remember."

"I'm not an expert in history, but from what I understand, the orcneas were not taken by surprise when the war started. They were ready for a fight."

"Do you think they were lying about the raiders?"

"I don't know," she answers. "But if they weren't interested in fighting, it seems to me they would have sent someone to negotiate peace early on, instead of waiting until the end. Did they ever ask for peace?"

Chance ponders before answering, "No, but until now, neither have we, and we certainly weren't expecting this."

On his way back to Chance and Re'ann, Lortec encounters Carr. Noticing that Lortec is carrying a leather bag, Carr asks, "Why are you intent on healing them?"

Lortec replies, "Why are you so intent on harming those that cannot defend themselves?"

"The Slayer killed hundreds of our people, including your father."

"I do not need you to remind me of what he has done," Lortec snaps. "He has already claimed responsibility for his actions. The female's only crime is being loyal to her people. Why was she harmed?"

"She chose to take his punishment."

Lortec shakes his head. "Chance Na'Moon faced his trial with honor. He kept his word and did not flee. He was willing to forfeit his life for what he has done."

"And you should have taken it," retorts Carr. "Instead, you made it a game, and now he lives."

"Yes, he does. And as long as he, and the female, remain our prisoners, we will NOT torture them. If we do, then we are no better than the monsters the humans and elves say we are."

As Lortec continues on his way, Carr says, "The Slayer has poisoned your mind. You favor him more than your own people."

Lortec stops suddenly and drops the leather bag on the ground. He turns to Carr, and as he approaches, he says, "You have been telling others that I have become weak since meeting Chance." Now, standing before the other general, he warns, "If you ever question my loyalty to our people again, I will show you which one of us is weak."

Trying not to show that he is intimidated, Carr replies, "All you ever talked about was killing the Slayer, Chance Na'Moon, and now, you protect him and heal his wounds. You may not be weak, but I have never seen you this way. You have let him get to you."

Lortec nods, "Perhaps he has gotten to me, or as you said earlier, 'poisoned my mind.' Then again, who's to say that the hatred I have held for him—and all the elves and humans—isn't the real poison. No matter how much I hated him and tried to kill him, he still spared my life... twice. Once when I was a child, and again only an hour ago."

Confused, Carr asks, "Do you feel as if you owe him?"

Lortec stares Carr down. "I owe Chance Na'Moon nothing. I am not doing this for him. I am doing this because it is the only honorable thing to do. He offered his life, and I refused to take it in that way. He did as I asked and fought for his life. He won, and I will not see him punished for it."

"Very well," relents Carr. "But when the High Chief arrives, the Slayer may yet have to die."

"I will worry about that later," says Lortec as he returns to his bag on the ground.

Carr asks, "Tell me, friend, do you really believe that our people can coexist with humans and elves?"

Lortec picks up the bag. "I am not sure what I believe, but when Chance spoke of peace, I could tell from the look in his eyes that he believed it. And if Chance Na'Moon, the Slayer, can see peace, why should my vision be anything less?"

Back in the cell, Re'ann becomes pale. "I don't feel well," she says as she lies on her side.

"Re'ann?" calls Chance. "Re'ann, say something." When she doesn't respond, Chance appeals to the guards. "She isn't well. Please help her." The three remaining guards look at each other but do nothing. Lortec returns, so Chance pleads with him. "I think she passed out, or worse."

"Not surprising," says Lortec as he enters the cell. "She has lost a lot of blood." He says to one of the guards, "Lock the door." As the orcnea locks the general in the cell, Lortec checks on Re'ann. "She is still breathing."

Chance sighs with relief. "I must ask you again, please let me heal her."

Lortec opens the bag and takes out a vial. "For your magic to be fully effective, I would have to remove both of your collars, and while I want to trust that you will not try to escape, it would be an unnecessary risk." He takes a key and unlocks the collar around Re'ann's neck. "This potion should be effective enough." The general gently shakes her. "I need you to drink this."

Re'ann partially opens her eyes. Lortec holds the vial up to her lips as she opens her mouth to drink its contents. She coughs but manages to drink most of the potion. The guard that was sent to retrieve more clothing returns with a several shirts. Lortec reaches through the bars and takes one. He lays it over Re'ann. "If this does not suit you, he brought others."

Re'ann, beginning to feel better, sits up. "Thank you. I'm sure it will be fine."

Lortec takes another vial from the bag. "These two potions were all I could spare, but I also brought some balm."

Re'ann says, "Give the other potion to Chance."

"I'll be fine," he says. "You need it more."

"Let me see your back."

"It's not bad."

"I said, let me see your back," repeats Re'ann sternly.

Chance reluctantly turns around. Though he cannot see it, there is a wide blistering welt down the entire length of his back. He says, "The balm will help me. It doesn't require a potion."

"Balm won't help your bruises," argues Re'ann. "Drink it."

Chance sighs. "I'm not taking it. Besides, Lortec would have to remove my collar for it to be effective. The balm will work even with it on."

Lortec shakes his head. "Are you two sure you aren't mates? You argue like a pair."

Re'ann holds back laughter as she takes the shirt and begins to put it on. Chance and Lortec look away as she dresses. She shudders in pain as the shirt rubs on her back. "All right, I'll take the other potion."

Lortec hands her the other vial. She drinks it down, then finishes buttoning the shirt. Lortec says, "I must put on the collar again. I hope you understand." Re'ann stands up and pulls back her hair. Lortec secures the iron around her neck. "I will release you from the chains so that you may apply the balm to each other's backs." Lortec unlocks the chains attached to Re'ann's collar, then orders a guard to unlock the door. "There should be enough balm in that bag for the both of you."

Lortec exits the cell before the guard locks it once again. He says to Re'ann, "You asked earlier about our women. The ones who do *not* seek to have children. Orcneas recognize many different types of attractions. Males wanting males, females wanting females. Others, having little to no desire at all. We do not care how someone lives their life so long as it does not harm others. For *most* males, however, it is an honor to be chosen as a mate. Even with the losses from war, males greatly outnumber females."

"I never knew that," says Re'ann.

Lortec nods. "So when I tell you that we cherish our women and that they are precious to us, that is exactly what I mean."

"Hm," Re'ann ponders. "It sounds like being an orcnea female wouldn't be all that bad."

"You would make an excellent one," comments Lortec. "If not for your disgustingly bland skin."

"Am I really disgusting?"

Lortec shrugs. "I am not the one to judge the beauty of an elf. Perhaps Chance would like to offer his opinion."

They both look at Chance and wait. "Are you asking me if she's attractive?" asks Chance.

"It is difficult for me to tell," says Lortec.

Chance looks at Re'ann, feeling a bit awkward. "Yes, I would say she's pretty."

Re'ann smiles. "Thank you."

"Well, there you have it," laughs the general. "You would make an excellent prize."

"With all due respect, general," says Re'ann, "most women that I know wouldn't appreciate being referred to as a prize. It makes it sound as if we are just property to be won."

"Property, no," corrects Lortec. "But, to orcnea males, women are indeed a prize, and a valuable one at that. A female's affection is something that must be earned, and a male needs to work very hard to beat all others to *win* her favor."

"I guess when you put it that way, it doesn't sound so bad," says Re'ann.

Chance says, "I hope that someday we may be able to learn more about each other's customs. Assuming we survive the war."

What little smile there is on Lortec's face fades. "I would like someday for our sons to be able to have an ale together. However, it is too late for us. Tomorrow, when the High Chief arrives, we will most likely resume fighting. I will admit that you are not the monster I thought you to be. To be honest, I wish you were. It would make what I have to do easier. But make no mistake, I will follow my orders and do what is necessary."

Chapter 23
What's in a Name

Aboard the modern-day ship, Ariella is finishing lunch with Kelik and the others. Finishing her story, she says, "... and that's how we ended up here today."

Yentroc says, "I don't understand, is Eric Winters a private investigator in Florida *and* working for the port authority?"

"I somehow doubt he's both," suspects Kelik.

Rehma says, "Maybe we should contact the port authority and ask."

Without warning, Eric enters the room, saying, "I can save you the trouble."

"Mr. Winters, what brings you here?" asks Yentroc.

Kelik says, "We didn't hear your boat arrive."

"That's because I didn't arrive by boat," he replies. Eric looks at the gathering and can see their skepticism. He sets down a briefcase. "Don't worry, I don't mean to cause any trouble. Before I explain any further, may I speak with Courtney and Kyle privately?"

Kelik and Yentroc look at each other. "Very well," says Yentroc.

The three leave the room to talk just outside the door. Fidelma says quietly, "I can try to read his mind if we need to."

Garrett says, "How the hell did he get here?"

Ariella says, "I don't trust him."

Gelana speculates, "Maybe he works for the government."

Annalee asks, "What do you think is in the briefcase?"

Rehma warns, "I wouldn't open that if I were you."

"I'm not going to," she replies. "I just want to know what's inside."

Eric comes back into the room, followed by Kelik and Yentroc, who both look to be in shock. Rehma asks, "Is everything all right?"

"Everything is going to be fine," says Eric as he picks up the briefcase and brings it over to the table. "In fact, I think you are all going to enjoy this. I should say first that I know the origin of the coins you discovered."

"You do?" asks Rehma, questioningly.

Eric opens the briefcase. "It is a coin from a place called Runefell." Gelana and Rehma look at each other, wondering how this stranger could possibility know this. "More specifically," he adds, "it is from land called Bruen. The coin is a gold crown of Ravenguard, named after the ruling family hundreds of years ago. They lived in the city of Sheathelm."

"How do you know all this?" asks Rehma.

Eric smiles. "Because I was there once, long ago."

The room is quiet as everyone wonders if Eric's story is true. Ariella breaks the silence. "So if you've been there before, perhaps you could show us where it is."

"Oh, it's not on any map. At least on any map we have here," he says as he takes an envelope from the briefcase. "But unless I am mistaken, I believe you already know where it is. After all, these coins were found among the wreck of your ship."

Ariella, unwilling to give up the truth, says, "You mean my ancestor's ship."

Eric laughs lightly to himself. "You obviously don't remember me," he says as he hands her the envelope. "We met a long time ago."

Ariella removes a picture from inside and studies it. It is in black and white and taken outside a saloon. In the picture, Ariella sits front and center, flanked by Fidelma, Annalee, Garrett, and a host of young women. Trying to bluff, she says, "How old do you think I am?"

Eric looks at Garrett and says, "I think the four of you are a lot older than you appear. Don't worry, I won't tell anyone." He removes a ring from his finger, and an illusion spell ends, revealing Eric's true appearance. While he looks mostly the same, his ears are now long and pointed.

"Oh my god!" exclaims Gelana. "You're an elf."

"Yes," says Eric calmly. "Just like you, and your friends."

Kelik, suspicious, asks, "How do you know about us?"

Eric explains, "Well, one of my spells is to see through illusions. I knew you were elves, but I didn't know where you were from. As far as Ariella, I met her over a hundred years ago. I may not have figured it out, but she and her friends never thought it necessary to change their names. Ariella is not common, and Stormrage is unheard of."

Ariella sighs. "You'll have to forgive me if I don't remember you."

"Of course," he replies. "I only remember because of your name. I was passing through El Paso Texas when I came upon two men arguing. One of them shot and killed the other. He then drew his weapon on me, but I was able to deflect the bullet and kill him, instead. No one else saw what happened, but when the shots were fired, everyone nearby came running."

"I remember now," says Ariella. "They accused you of killing them both, and were going to hang you the next day."

"Fortunately for me, you and your friend here," he says, motioning to Fidelma, "visited me in jail and asked for my side of the story. You later convinced the sheriff that you saw what happened and cleared my name."

Fidelma says, "I could tell that you were being honest, but that wouldn't have been enough for the sheriff, so we had to make up a story."

Eric says, "The sheriff let me go in the middle of the night, but warned me to get out of town. By the time I visited El Paso again —under disguise—you were gone. I had forgotten about it all until a few years ago when I was hired to investigate a college man's death outside your club in Miami. When we met, I didn't remember you, but when you told me your name, I thought it was peculiar. I did some digging and found quite a bit about you, or should I say, your former lives." He tosses a folder on the table in front of Ariella. She opens it to find more pictures from her past along with articles from newspapers. He continues, "You helped free slaves during the Civil War, you owned the brothel in El Paso, you ran moonshine during Prohibition, and you worked as a nurse in World Wars I and II. You were a very busy woman, Ms. Stormrage."

Fidelma laughs. "I told you we should have changed our names."

"Okay, Eric," says Ariella. "You seem to know all about me. So, why don't you tell us about yourself?"

Eric shrugs his shoulders. "Sure. I was a part of an expedition to this world. When we came through a magic gate, we found ourselves in Stonehenge. Unfortunately, the gate back was damaged, and we were trapped."

"That's exactly what happened to us," says Kelik. "Well, except being part of an expedition."

Yentroc asks, "So what are you doing now?"

"I do investigative work," Eric answers. "Mostly for individuals, but occasionally I'll get hired by corporations. Have you ever heard of the Gantive Technologies Corporation?"

"I have," replies Rehma. "They research gravity and electromagnetic waves. They don't actually make anything, though."

"Correct," says Eric. "They have been working on ways to pinpoint gravitational anomalies." He looks at Kelik, "Like the ones created when you open a magic gate."

Concerned, Kelik asks, "Do they know about us?"

"They do, but don't worry. Your secret is safe."

"Are you certain? The last thing we need is the government dissecting us to see how we can manipulate nature itself."

"They're not the government. Though we do know that the government is also trying to investigate such anomalies."

Yentroc asks, "Who are they, then?"

Eric replies, "Fortunately, I have been authorized to inform you of Gantive Technologies' true origin. Do you notice anything familiar about the acronym for Gantive Technologies Corporation?"

"GTC?" ponders Ariella.

"Of course," says Kelik. "The Goblin Trade Company."

"Wait," says Rehma. "The Goblin Trade Company is here on Earth?"

"Well, sort of," replies Eric. "You see, in order for the goblins to operate here, they had to change their appearance, since humans tend not to be very accepting of other races."

Kelik sighs. "Many humans can't even stand their own race if they have different-colored skin."

"Exactly," agrees Eric. "It was always difficult to do business on Earth. To make matters worse, once man had begun to use electricity and radio, those who had magical aptitude began to suffer headaches, as I am sure you do, as well."

Yentroc says, "Yes, but fortunately we have been able to minimize the pain with an herbal tea."

Eric says, "While war is not unique to humans, they have always seemed to dedicate a fair amount of resources to finding ways to kill each other more efficiently. The goblins were able to capitalize on this for a while, but soon the other realms began to ban imported weapons. Then, when the modern technologies were tied to the migraines, it just wasn't worth the headache anymore for the goblins, pun fully intended. The Goblin Trade Company officially pulled out of this world, but there were a few that stayed behind."

"Do they have a way back to Runefell?" asks Kelik.

"Unfortunately, the GTC destroyed all of their gates to and from Earth when they left, stranding the ones that stayed behind."

"But there have to be other gates. Ones that didn't belong to them."

"You're right, of course. There are a few, like the ones at Stonehenge. I don't know all of the gates that they still have access to. But now that I know Runefell is where you're from, I can ask them if they know of a way back."

"Thank you," says Rehma.

Kelik asks, "How close is the government to being able to find me when I open a gate?"

"They're a long ways off," Eric answers as he closes the briefcase. "You're safe to use them if you wish. Teleportation is untraceable, though, and if you were wondering, that's how I got here today. I'll go now and ask my contacts about the gates. With any luck, I may be back with good news." Eric steps back and concentrates on his spell. A moment later, he disappears with a pop.

"Do you think we can trust him?" asks Yentroc.

Ariella replies, "I've known him for some time. He seems honorable, if slightly intrusive."

"How do you know him?" asks Rehma.

Ariella chuckles. "He's been investigating the death of a male college student who stepped out in front of a bus a few months ago."

"Does he suspect foul play?" asks Gelana.

"I believe he might."

"Why? Was there something unusual about it?"

Ariella shrugs. "Not really. The camera caught it all. It should be an open and shut case, but..."

"But what?"

Garret says, "One unusual death wouldn't raise suspicions, but Eric has come across a pattern."

"Are you suspects?" Yentroc inquires.

Annalee, Garret, and Fidelma all look at Ariella. She says, "I'm sure you all must be wondering how the four of us have managed to stay young."

Gelana nods. "As a matter of fact, I was. Does this have to do with the student?"

Kelik sighs. "Please don't tell me it's the same way you got younger during the third orcnea war."

Ariella raises an eyebrow. "And just what do you know about that?"

"There's a full account of that war and many of the people involved. I've actually been reading it again recently."

"The one that was written by that young historian's apprentice?"

"Yes, David Michael."

"I barely remember him," she says, thinking back. "He asked if he could read my mind for historical accuracy. I saw no harm in it at the time. So, he wrote a book about the war?"

"He did, and from what I read, you drained the youth from others to stay young."

The elves eye their visitors with suspicion, and Ariella says, "Before you start to judge us too harshly, you should know that those we chose to steal youth from deserved everything that happened to them. Fidelma made sure of that by reading their minds. They were rapists and murderers, among other things. We've never brought harm to an innocent man."

Rehma shakes her head. "Still, the number of years you would have had to take for all of you... How many had to die for you all to live?"

Fidelma says, "I think you are mistaken with our methods. Very few people ever died. Most of them we only took a year or two from while they were passed out, but, trust me, the ones that we took more from were the worst sort of monsters."

Kelik queries, "What about the college student's death that Eric is investigating?"

Fidelma, struggling to keep calm, explains, "That son of a bitch raped a dozen women, including one who was only sixteen years old. After we took a decade's worth of years, I used my magic to take control of his body. I made him confess his crimes aloud, and then I ran him into the streets. You'll have to forgive me if I show no remorse. After seeing what he did through his own eyes, I doubt any of you would either."

Garrett adds, "He's lucky, his death was quick. It shouldn't have been."

Ariella says, "Believe me, there is no shortage of monsters to keep us young."

Gelana, thinking deeply, says, "All these years, we were here together on earth, and we never once ran across each other. I just wish we met years ago." She stands up from the table. "If you'll all excuse me." Gelana leaves the room.

Ariella asks the others, "What's wrong with her?"

Kelik explains, "She had a child years ago, then watched as he and seven generations grew old and passed away. Her sixth great granddaughter, Linda, died last year in a car accident."

Ariella gets up. "That's horrible. I can't imagine what that must be like."

Yentroc says, "Now we all watch over the ninth generation, Gelana's seventh great grandchildren. She's never met them."

"And here we are," says Ariella, "humans, still as young as the day we first met. A reminder of what she lost. I'll talk with her."

Ariella makes her way around the table and out the door. She looks around and finds Gelana sitting in a chair by the port side railing. She takes a deep breath before approaching. "I remember the day you and Prince Galen took your vows. I must admit, I was almost surprised you went through with it, considering how stubbornly independent you always were."

"I sometimes wonder if I made a mistake then."

"How so? Because he passed away and you've survived?"

"Do you know what it's like... To watch helplessly as the ones you love most grow older and weaker until they can no longer go on?"

"No, I don't. But with each passing generation, a part of them lives on in something entirely new. Growing old is but one way to die. At least they got to live a full life. Never think for a moment that having a child with someone you loved was a mistake. Do you know what I have to remember Chance by?" Gelana shakes her head. "I've got nothing," says Ariella. "While I know you have suffered a great loss many times over, death is a part of life. You shouldn't let the thought of it keep you from living. Your grandchildren that live today are a part of you and the man you loved. I would give anything to have a fraction of Chance with me now."

Gelana sighs. "I know you're right, and I do plan to meet my grandchildren soon. It's just so hard."

"I would suggest that you enjoy the time that you are given to be with them while you can. You never know when that time will run out. And when it does, it's better to be able to look back on those times than have nothing to look back to at all.

"I just wish the fond memories weren't accompanied by sad ones, but I suppose it's up to me as to what I focus on."

Chapter 24
Soothing

In the apartment, Ambra says, "Does anyone else want to read now? My throat is getting sore and I'm thirsty."

"I can do that," offers Lyra.

Ambra gets up from the couch and heads to the kitchen as Lyra sits down and looks at the pages. She quickly finds the part where General Ka leaves the room where Chance and Re'ann are being held.

****

Within their cell, Re'ann takes one of the small jars of balm that Lortec left behind and walks over to Chance. "Let me put this on your back." He sits down facing away from her as she kneels behind him, looking at the blistering welts. "I'm sorry, I should have left you the other healing potion."

"We've been through this already," Chance replies. "It wouldn't have been very effective on me. It was better for you to use it."

"I don't know what my back looks like, but I can't imagine it's any worse than yours." She applies some of the balm to the top of wound, causing him to wince.

"He may have burned my back," says Chance as she continues to carefully cover the blisters, "but you were whipped until you bled, and after that, he branded you with that sword."

"The first potion took care of most of the lacerations. I only drank the second because you weren't going to use it."

"Still," says Chance, "I wish you would have just let him torture me. At least I did something to warrant it."

"How can you say that?" she asks. "You make it sound as if you're the only one the orcneas are at war with. In case you've forgotten, I've killed orcneas, too. When I dropped those fire elixirs on their ships, more than one perished in the flames. You may have killed more of them than me, but my hands are not without blood."

"You're right, of course."

"I know I am."

Chance shakes his head. "I can't help but think about what that shaman general said about burning to death. When you have mastered fire as well as I have, you learn not to fear it. Of course I've burned myself numerous times through the years attempting to master my spells, but I've never felt anything like the tip of that blade. I can't imagine burning to death, yet I've watched countless orcneas do just that at my hands, and never gave it a second thought."

Re'ann gently spreads more balm on Chance's lower back. "You can't let what he said get to you. It's not like you took pleasure in their suffering... did you?"

Chance hesitates to answer as he thinks deeply on the question. "I don't know," he finally says.

Re'ann puts down the jar of balm. "I've covered all the burns."

"Thank you," he says as he turns to face her. "Let me get yours."

Still kneeling on the ground, Re'ann turns around and lifts the back of her shirt. "You know, you're not exactly what I expected."

Chance picks up the jar and proceeds to wet his fingers with the balm inside. "And what exactly did you expect?"

"Well, first of all, I thought you would be taller."

Not only does Chance laugh, but so do two of the orcnea guards outside the bars of their cell. Chance says, "I feel as though people expect me to be as big as a goliath. You know, size doesn't really matter."

"You mean for spell casting, right?" she replies, trying not to laugh.

"Of course that's what I meant," he says, not finding any humor in her comment. "What else did you expect me to be like?"

"I'm not sure exactly how to put this," she replies. "Maybe I was expecting someone more angry than sad." She looks back over her shoulder. "Honestly, you're really depressing."

"To be fair, we're prisoners right now. It's not exactly a joyous environment."

"I somehow doubt you would be the life of any party. No offense."

Chance chuckles to himself. "None taken. You're not wrong about that. I don't particularly enjoy large gatherings. For some reason, I find myself in the King's Shield Inn quite often to watch the bards... but I usually sit alone."

"Why doesn't that surprise me?"

Continuing to apply the balm to Re'ann's back, Chance says, "That's not to say that I don't enjoy the company of good friends, but I don't usually enjoy the meaningless conversations with strangers."

"I see. Does this qualify as 'meaningless'?"

"Not at all. I wasn't referring to our current situation. I'm actually glad that I'm not alone right now. I just wish that they weren't making you suffer too."

"I knew the risks when I joined the drake riders."

"What made you join them in the first place?"

Re'ann shrugs. "I don't know. I guess I've loved drakes for as long as I can remember. When I was young, I would climb the spires of Elonfar just to get as close as I could to the sky where the drake riders soared."

"How did you become one?"

Re'ann smiles reflectively. "When I was twelve years old, I got my first job at the drake stables. I got to see them up close for the first time. They were so beautiful. It was before Belron became a captain. He let me pet Nimbus. I'll never forget it."

"They are wonderful creatures," says Chance. "It's a shame to have to fight against the ones the orcneas are using."

"Yes," agrees Re'ann. "I hated having to destroy them. I've worked with them half my life. I've even learned to communicate with them, though it is rudimentary. When I was fourteen, nearly a dozen eggs hatched. Their mother, a retired sky drake named Azure, only let a handful of people near the whelps. I was one of the fortunate ones. I got to hold and feed them."

"Is that how Cirrus became yours?"

Re'ann takes a deep breath. "Yes, he was from that litter." She laughs to herself as she thinks back. "Cirrus was always vying for my attention. He would stand at my feet and whine until I picked him up. Belron told me that when I left, he would howl at the gate of the stable for about an hour before stopping."

Chance puts the lid on the jar of balm. "I think I've got your entire back covered."

"Thank you," Re'ann says as she pulls down her shirt. She

turns around before continuing. "One night I woke to a howling outside my window. I looked out and found Cirrus at our font door, whining. He had escaped from the stables and tracked me to my house. The next day, Belron put a word in with the commander and asked me if I was interested in joining the riders."

"How old were you then?"

"Fifteen," she answers. "Cirrus was not quite a year old then, but he was already bigger than I was. Belron knew that Cirrus and I had a special bond. Even though it would be quite some time before Cirrus was ready to ride, he got permission to start training me. I studied long hours to learn how to calm and soothe a beast. Then I learned how to communicate with them."

"What did your parents think about all this?"

"My mother works in the gardens of Elonfar. Until I got the job at the stables, she was teaching me about plant and earth magic. My father is a baker. They were very supportive of me, even though my mother was worried." Re'ann looks around the cell and at the guards outside the bars. "Do you think I'll ever see my parents again?"

"I hope so," replies Chance.

Just then, Lortec enters the room, followed by the massive ogre Cron. They are carrying bowls of stew and mugs filled with the same healing elixir that Chance had the night before his trial.

Lortec opens the cell door before entering, while Cron waits outside. The orcnea general says to Re'ann, "You must go back to your side of the cell now." Re'ann nods and returns to where she was chained earlier. Lortec hands her the bowl and mug. "You will want to drink that after you have eaten." He bends down and picks up the chain from the ground.

Re'ann smells the mug and recoils from the odor. "What is it?" she asks as Lortec locks the chain to her collar."

"It will help you sleep," answers Lortec.

Chance asks, "Is it the same drink you gave me to the other day?"

"Yes."

Chance says to Re'ann, "It smells horrible, but it will help you heal faster."

Lortec takes the other bowl of stew and mug from Cron before giving them to Chance. "Sleep well, Na'Moon."

Chance gives a nod as Lortec turns and walks out of the cell. Cron closes the door before locking it. The ogre steps back and leans against the wall as Lortec exits the room. Chance can feel the weight of Cron's stare.

"You must be Cron," says Chance.

The ogre gives a nod and a grunt. Re'ann says, "I understand that you are the only reason Chance and I haven't been killed."

Cron looks around the room as if no one has spoken to him. Re'ann and Chance look at each other, puzzled. "It would have been wrong," Cron finally says. "Lortec gave you the terms of the fight, and you won, even if he would have preferred that you killed him."

Chance replies, "I would have preferred that he killed me, if it would mean bringing an end to this war."

"You may die yet, Slayer, but it will not bring the end of the war, at least not the way you want."

"Are you referring to the arrival of your High Chief?"

"He will be arriving tomorrow," confirms Cron. "Then your fate will be decided. It will not matter what Lortec or myself want."

Re'ann asks, "And what is it you want?"

"I want to return home," Cron says without hesitation. "I want peace and for all the things that Chance spoke of in his trial." He stares at Chance. "But I am doubtful that it is possible."

Chance sighs. "I have no doubt that peace will be very difficult to achieve. So many on both sides would prefer to fight 'til the end."

"Many of my people still have doubts about you, Slayer. Despite your words at the Colosseum, they feel you are still bloodthirsty."

"That is understandable, considering everything that I have done."

"They fear you," says Cron, "and with good reason. You are dangerous in battle, and your new dragon blessing makes you even more so." Chance looks at the markings on his arms and chest as the ogre continues, "I, however, do not fear you. I respect your abilities in combat, and I would never underestimate you, but you are not the ruthless animal that your reputation claims you to be."

"Lortec told us that you have witnessed true atrocities."

Cron nods. "I have looked into eyes of real monsters. Ones that have no pity, no mercy, for the women or young. I watched as they took pleasure in the suffering of my family. Their souls were as dark and cold as your fires burn hot. They left me for dead, lying in the blood-soaked streets of my village as it burned. I awaited death, but woke the next morning, weak, but alive."

Re'ann shakes her head. "I can't imagine what kind of person would do that."

"The worst kind," replies Chance.

"Yes," agrees Cron, "and when I look in your eyes, Slayer, I do not see that same soulless stare."

"That is kind of you to say," says Chance. "I wish I could tell you that I have always been that way, but in the last war, I'm not so sure that I *wasn't* a monster."

Chapter 25
Allen the Mad

In the dark of night, the *Trident* continues to lead the way toward the stronghold south of Sheathelm. An overcast sky makes it particularly difficult to see what is before them. While the captain sleeps in his quarters, his trusted crewman, Alex, is in charge of the night crew.

Alex checks his compass to make sure they are still on the correct heading when he hears the man in the crow's nest quietly call down, "A ship is ahead off the port side."

The few of the crew on deck rush to the side of the ship to have a look. Alex, too, squints as he tries to see what is ahead. Just as a large ship comes into focus, several small flames appear hovering above its deck. Alex warns the others, "Flaming arrows! Wake everyone now!"

One of the men rushes down to the lower deck, yelling, "We're under attack!"

Alex orders the man at the wheel to turn the ship 15 degrees to starboard, then says to the men at the side of the ship, "Ready the light." The men reach down over the port side railing and unlatch the tops of the long planks that run most of the length of the ship. On the bottom of the planks, hinges secure them to the ship's hull like long thin doors. Behind them a surprise waits to be revealed. As the ship's port side faces the mystery ship, Alex signals the men. "Now!"

The men release the tops of the boards, revealing hundreds of light stones. The stones are affixed to the center of a trough lined with polished silver. The bright light is of such magnitude, it illuminates the shrouded ship as if the sun were still high in the sky.

The men spot orcneas shielding their eyes, unable to see those aboard the *Trident*. The orcnea archers release their flaming arrows recklessly while the humans begin to pick off the enemy with crossbows.

Men emerge from below, including Marcus, James, and Mathew. A few of the arrows fired by the orcneas strike their ship.

One hits the main sail, threatening to catch it on fire. Marcus begins to bark out orders. "Mathew, put out that fire. Alex and James, prepare the whirl hammers. The rest of you, keep attacking them." The captain makes his way over to the wheel of the ship as Alex and James head towards the poop deck.

Allen comes up from below, followed by Vardik. Looking over at the other ship, Allen watches the orcnea archers ready another volley. The men continue to shoot the enemy with their crossbows, and some of the orcneas shoot back. Though the arrows were poorly aimed, three men are struck on the deck of the *Trident*. Allen rushes to the aid of one injured man while Vardik assists another.

On the poop deck, Alex and James begin to prepare contraptions resembling trebuchets, but smaller. Instead of standing upright, they are built with 45 degree tilts to the right. They are mounted on turrets that allow the users to aim the devices in almost any direction. Alex takes aim at the upper main mast of the orcnea ship, while James targets the foremast. Alex fires first. When he pulls the lever, the device flings a heavy iron weight that is attached by a rope to another weight. The two projectiles whirl around each other as they fly through the air, carrying another rope to the orcnea ship.

The rope connecting the iron weights becomes entangled on both vertical and horizontal ratlines of the enemy ship. James fires next, and soon two ropes connect the aft of the *Trident* to the masts of the orcnea ship.

Alex calls out, "We have them, Captain!"

Marcus spins the wheel of the ship, taking the *Trident* directly away from the orcneas. Alex and James scramble to secure the ropes connecting the ships to moorings on the deck. Several crew rush up the stairs with crossbows and take aim at their foes. Alex hurries down the stairs and yells into a pipe mounted on the exterior wall of the navigation room, "Start rowing!"

Several levels below, men sit on benches holding long oars. When the message comes through the other end of the pipe, they deploy their oars and begin to row. With the force of the men rowing and the wind in the sails, the *Trident* begins to pull away from the orcneas. The ropes attaching the ships become tight and begin to creak as they pull on the masts.

After healing one of injured men, Vardik joins Allen, who is applying pressure to the shoulder of another crewman who was hit by the orcnea arrows. Vardik casts a healing spell and the bleeding stops. "Thank you," says the man.

Allen turns his attention towards to back of the ship and watches as the orcnea ship begins to tilt. The shamans on board try to target the ropes with their spells, but have a hard time maintaining their balance. Several orcneas attempt to climb the ratlines but are shot by the crossbowmen.

"It's almost over," Alex says into the pipe. "Keep rowing."

Down below, men strain with all their might as they pull back on the massive oars. One man, standing at the aft of the room, keeps the cadence of the men together, calling out with every stroke. Even with the assistance of the wind, the ship is slow to move.

Topside, Matthew finishes extinguishing the fire on sails with a magical jet of water. He climbs the stairs to the poop deck to join in on the attack. With the enemy ship almost on its side, the orcneas are too busy trying to stay on the ship to be a real threat. He and others stand ready and watch as the orcnea ship begins to take on water.

An elven ship begins to flank the orcneas. Seeing the bottom of the hull exposed, they cast spells and throw them at the nearly overturned vessel. The spells take their toll and leave gaping holes. It doesn't take long for the orcnea ship to submerge. Alex cuts the ropes that tie the two ships together. Some of the men close the open planks on the side, concealing the light stones.

"Well, that wasn't so bad," says Jack.

The men begin to celebrate their victory. Matthew says, "Did anyone happen to notice if they were green?"

The crew laugh, and Jack answers, "Allen was right, they were orange." He turns to Allen. "Sorry I doubted you, mate."

"Don't worry about it," Allen replies. "I've never seen a ship overturned like that. What were those things you used against them?"

Marcus says, "Those are what we call whirl hammers. Alex came up with the idea, as well as the blinding lights on the sides of the ship."

"That was the easiest battle I have ever been a part of."

Alex humbly replies, "We were lucky it was dark. The lights made them easy targets and kept us relatively safe. As for the whirl hammers, positioning is everything. I wouldn't get too comfortable thinking all fights will go so smoothly."

Marcus says to Vardik, "Thank you for your assistance. It isn't very often that we have a healer aboard."

"Glad I could help."

Jack asks, "How much longer 'til we reach Sheathelm?"

Alex answers, "We have been making good time. We should be there shortly before sunrise, assuming the winds keep up."

An explosion from the aft of the ship grabs everyone's attention. The man in the crow's nest shouts, "More ships moving in!"

"Hard to port," Marcus orders the helmsman.

Allen makes haste up the stairs to the poop deck to have a better look. As the *Trident* begins to adjust its heading, the previously dark horizon before them is now illuminated with the casting of spells. A half dozen orcnea ships begin to pelt the fleet from Artos.

The crew readies their crossbows as one of the enemy ships closes in. Matthew summons a chunk of stone to hurl and begins to channel more strength into it. Allen rushes back down to the main deck, nervously awaiting what will happen next.

With the *Trident* back on its original heading, they nearly run head-on into an orcnea ship. Matthew throws his spell, damaging the hull of the enemy ship just as it begins to pass the *Trident* on the starboard side.

The planks rumble like thunder as the two ships scrape along each other's side. The men fire their crossbows as the orcneas shoot back with spells and arrows. Several grappling lines are also thrown by the orcneas as the ships slow to a stop. Allen draws his sword, knowing that the melee is just about to begin.

Marcus hollers over the sounds of battle, "Be ready to repel boarders."

Vardik draws a mace and says to Allen, "May your gods watch over you."

"Thank you," replies Allen. "You, too."

Dozens of orcneas flood over the railings and board the *Trident*. Several are killed the moment they step foot on the ship by the crossbowmen. Marcus wastes no time in engaging the reddish-skinned invaders. He slashes one with his sword before pressing the attack against a second.

Allen dodges as one of the enemies charges him. He turns and waits for an opening to attack, but the orcnea also waits. Jack swings his sword at the same orcnea. Though he is not successful, he causes a distraction. Allen steps forward and thrusts his sword into the orcnea. Jack and Allen give each other a nod before turning their attention back to the fight.

James does his best to stay behind the other men as he continues to cast lightning bolts. Though they are not as powerful as Ariella's, they are more than enough to disable a foe. The battle rages on as James and Mathew pick off the enemies one at a time.

Despite their success, there are losses on both sides. Jack is struck in the leg and falls to the ground. An orcnea stands over him, ready to finish him off, when Allen tackles the enemy to the ground. Letting out a yell akin to a battle cry, Allen uses both hands to drive his sword into the orcnea's chest. Allen grabs a knife from his victim's belt.

"Thanks," says Jack.

Allen, now incensed, doesn't hear him. He looks up and charges at the nearest orcnea fighting with someone. With the element of surprise, Allen reaches his arms around the enemy. Using the knife he just acquired, he stabs the side of the orcnea as he squeezes him tightly in a deadly embrace. Allen shakes him around like a rabid dog biting down on a squirrel as the knife mutilates the orcnea.

The young man throws his enemy to the ground before locking his gaze on another target. Allen rushes across the deck of the ship, slamming into another orcnea. Clasping both arms around him like he had with the last enemy, Allen begins to dispatch another foe. The orcnea cannot effectively use his sword, so he instead begins to bludgeon Allen in the back of the head with the hilt. The orcnea repeatedly strikes him, but in his enraged state, Allen is undeterred. He twists the knife as he continues to squeeze as tight as he can. Soon the orcnea's strikes cease, and Allen tosses him aside.

Covered with the blood of his foes as well as his own, Allen looks around once again. He finds the captain holding his own against one of the invaders, but soon two more orcneas join in and Marcus is outnumbered. Allen lets out another yell as he runs at the orcnea on the left. The captain impales the one on the right, and once again, the odds are even.

Unlike the other orcneas that Allen attacked, this one sees him coming. Rather than wait for an opening, however, Allen recklessly charges in. The orcnea swings his mace, striking Allen in the lower back as Allen wraps his arms around the orcnea's thighs. Allen pushes through the pain and lifts the larger enemy over his shoulder, forcibly slamming him onto his back.

The orcnea draws his own knife, but Allen dives and grabs the orcnea's wrist with both hands, losing his weapon in the process. With a firm grip on the enemy's arm, Allen proceeds to bite as hard as he can into the wrist. Allen can feel the tendons give as his teeth sink in. The orcnea loses his grip on the knife, and Allen quickly takes it. With blood dripping down his chin, Allen lets out a frightful wail as he drives the knife into its owner.

Marcus delivers a final blow to the orcnea before him before turning his eyes to Allen. With most all of the invaders defeated, he watches as Allen picks up the knife that he dropped and begins stabbing the downed orcnea with two weapons. With each blow, Allen's animalistic cries can be heard.

"He's dead, Allen," says the captain. Allen wails loudly to the gods above. By now, everyone on the *Trident* watches Allen's erratic behavior. Allen looks around frantically for another foe to attack. When he finds none, he looks over at the orcnea ship. A terrified orcnea begins cutting one of the lines. Soon others join him in an attempt to escape. Marcus looks at his victorious crew then at the enemy ship. "Attack!" he commands.

Allen is the first to cross. With a knife in each hand, he makes short work of the orcnea cutting the line. Shamans begin to aim their spells at the young man, but are shot by a barrage of crossbow bolts and spells from James and Mathew. Marcus and a handful of others cross over and slaughter the remaining orcneas in a swift and brutal attack.

When it is finally over, Vardik later finds Allen leaning over the railing of the orcnea ship. Vardik says, "Hey, Allen, let me have a look at you." Allen vomits into the sea several times before turning around. Vardik notices Allen is shaking uncontrollably.

"Are you all right?"

Dazed, Allen answers, "I-I don't know." He looks at his blood-soaked hands. "What happened? It's a blur to me, like a dream."

"We won," says Vardik. "You killed quite a few of them."

Marcus joins them. "You did well, Allen. You should be proud."

"Thank you," he mutters as he tries to control his shaking.

"You should get yourself cleaned up," says Marcus. "Right now we can't tell if you're bleeding or not. If you're wounded, we'll need to take care of it."

"Yes, Captain," he replies.

Marcus calls out to his crew, "I am going to need a few of you to man this ship. It's still in good shape, and we may find a use for it."

Some of men volunteer as Vardik assists Allen back over to the *Trident*. James greets them, "How are you doing?"

Vardik answers for Allen. "He's a little shaken up, but I think he'll be fine."

Jack rushes over and helps Allen down from the plank. Seeing all the blood, he asks the dwarf, "Is he all right?"

Vardik nods. "We have to clean him up to be certain."

"I'll get some water right away," says Jack before rushing off.

James and Vardik lead Allen over to the stairs so he may sit. By now, others have gathered around. Vardik asks, "Does it hurt anywhere particular?"

"I think I am bleeding here," says Allen, feeling the back of his head. "One of them was hitting me with the hilt of his sword."

"You're lucky it wasn't a knife," says James.

"I was careful not to grab anyone with a knife or dagger drawn."

Mathew says, "I wouldn't call your style of attack careful."

"It's one of the few things I remember," says Allen. "I knew he was hitting me, but I didn't really feel it. I remember thinking, 'I'm certainly going to feel this in the morning.'"

The gathering of men laughs. Vardik comments, "I am sure you *will* feel it in the morning."

Jack returns with a bucket of water. "All right, everyone, give him some room to breathe." He sets down the bucket. "It's warm, but not too hot."

Vardik says, "Let's get that shirt off."

Allen stands up and takes off his shirt. He winces in pain as Vardik slowly pours the bucket of water over his head. The water washes away most of the blood, revealing three cuts on his arms and a bruise, with a small puncture in the middle, on his lower back.

Vardik inspects each of the wounds. As blood begins to drip down the sides of Allen's head, he says, "I suppose I'll forgo the minor spell and get them all with one major spell." His hands glow white as he casts the healing spell on Allen. The wounds are soon mended.

Jack announces, "There he is, gentlemen, Allen the Mad, as good as new."

The inspired crew cheer loudly as Allen, embarrassed, bows his head humbly and blushes.

Day 26
Chapter 26
The Brothers Reonia

As morning arrives on the east coast, Arioch and a large group are gathered at the shore. The skies are empty, as the orcneas have moved the floating fortress further out to sea. Belron and the last remaining drake rider, Ashden, are also there. Arioch says, "We need to find where they moved the floating city to."

"Ashden and I will have a look," says Belron.

"I can help," says River. "I'll take Toren's drake."

Arioch says, "Very well, just be careful out there."

The three head out as a guard shouts, "Ships approaching!"

Arioch looks to the southeast, where the man with a spyglass was pointing. Coming into view is the armada of ships from Artos, along with the elven fleet. "The elves came back," says Arioch in amazement.

Baeldeth comments, "It looks like we'll have enough forces to take back Sheathelm, after all."

"We will once the ground forces arrive," Arioch corrects him.

On board the *Trident*, Marcus looks at the horizon. "I thought the orcneas had a floating city."

James looks out to sea and shrugs. "Maybe they brought it down."

"Let's hope so, because I still don't know what we would do to combat one." Marcus looks along the shore and spots the stronghold. "It looks like the *Red Dawn* is docked in the harbor. Bring us in closer and we'll take the longboat ashore."

Within the walls of the fortress, Belron climbs onto Nimbus's saddle. "I hope you weren't going to leave without saying goodbye," says Nicari as she approaches.

Belron replies, "I'll be back before you know it."

Nicari looks up at her husband. "That's the wrong answer. Now climb down here and try again."

The captain of the drake riders smiles as he climbs back down off his drake. He clears his throat. "No, my love, I was just about to tell you I was leaving."

"That's better," she says. "Where are you off to?"

"The floating city is no longer within our sight. We must locate it. In the meantime, the ships from Artos have arrived. We'll soon have enough forces to take back Sheathelm, but we need to know what the orcneas are up to."

"Well, be careful," says Nicari, concerned. "And promise me you'll never try to leave without telling me again."

"I won't, I promise."

A short time later, at the docks of the harbor, Marcus is greeted by King Arioch and a host of others, including Ariella.

The kings says, "Thank you for coming."

While eying Ariella, Marcus replies, "I must say, Your Highness, if not for my brother aboard the *Red Dawn*, I'm not certain we would be here now. That is not to say that I don't wish to help, but the council may not have found it fit to send us." He addresses Ariella. "May I see my brother now?"

"Of course," she replies. "Follow me." Arioch continues to greet more of the arriving forces as they make their way ashore on other longboats while Ariella leads Marcus to the *Red Dawn*.

As they walk, Marcus asks, "So, how have you been? I haven't seen you in a while."

"My life has been rather chaotic lately, but I'm managing."

"I understand that the orcneas are still holding Chance prisoner. I know how much he means to you. If you need anything..."

Ariella stops abruptly. "I said I'm managing," she repeats sternly.

They begin to walk again as Marcus says, "Ariella, don't be like that. I'm only trying to help." He grabs her arm and turns her to face him. "Listen, I know that you're a strong woman, and I know that you can't show your crew any sign of weakness."

"My crew has already seen me mourn for Chance when we thought he was dead."

"Of course," says Marcus. "But what you show the crew is only a part of your true feelings."

"And you're offering a shoulder to cry on, is that it?"

Marcus contemplates his next words carefully. "I was there when you were first allowed to come to shore by yourself. I was there at the Deep Mountain tavern in East Artos when you tried to drink yourself into a stupor in an attempt to forget about him. There was a line of men just waiting to take advantage of you. I took you back the *Red Dawn* to keep you away from them. Your father was in town, so you invited me back to your room. I declined, of course. Instead we sat up on the poop deck and you opened up to me."

"I was drunk," she argues.

"People seldom let others get very close, and you're no different. That night I got to see a side of you that was pure and honest, even if it was due to alcohol."

"That was a long time ago. I'm a grown woman now, and not some naive girl. Or did you forget about the other times we were together?"

Marcus laughs. "No, I haven't forgotten, nor shall I ever. Ariella, all I'm saying is that while people do change, deep down, our hearts remain the same. Love, the real kind, doesn't fade with time. And if you need someone to talk to, I'm here for you."

Ariella looks at him intently before turning to walk up the ramp. "What do you know about love? You speak of it as if someone broke your heart." They step onto the deck and she asks, "What was her name?"

Marcus looks around the ship before answering, "Her name is Samantha."

Ariella smiles and pretends not to know her. She says to one of her crew, "Go fetch Seth, please."

"Yes, ma'am," the crewman replies.

As he hurries off, Ariella walks up the stairs to the quarterdeck, Marcus following behind. She stops in front of the porthole to the lounge where Fidelma and her crew have been staying. Ariella asks him, "So, tell me about this Samantha. Why have you not told me about her before?"

Marcus explains, "When a man is in the presence of a beautiful woman, it does not help his cause to go on about another."

"Wait a moment," she interrupts. "Please tell me that we weren't together the same time that you and her were."

"No, of course not," protests Marcus. "I would never have done that to her. Samantha and I were together after you and I first met. She left me shortly before I saw you for the second time."

"Good," states Ariella. "I don't ever wish to come between two people in love."

Down below, Seth emerges from the stairway below deck. He looks up at the captain and his brother, smiling before making his way up the stairs to join them. He hugs his brother, saying, "I'm glad you came, Marcus."

"You had the entire family worried sick about you," admonishes his older brother as they end their embrace. "What were you thinking?"

Seth replies, "I was thinking that I would rather sail the seas like you than get married to Julia."

Ariella asks, "Is she really that bad?"

Marcus nods. "She is."

"I don't want to go back," says Seth.

Marcus replies, "First we need to worry about the orcneas. Then we can worry about returning home."

"Speaking of home," says Ariella, "your brother was just telling me about a woman from his past. Someone named Samantha."

Seth looks at Ariella, confused. Then, looking at the porthole, he realizes what the captain is up to. "Oh, yes," he says. "I remember her. Why did she leave again?"

Annoyed by the question, Marcus replies, "I don't know, she never said."

Seth shrugs. "She probably didn't want to be left behind in Artos as you sailed the world."

"I wouldn't have done that to her," says Marcus. "I would have taken her with me."

"Really?" asks Ariella. "Did she know that?"

"I never got the chance to tell her," says Marcus defensively. "She left without warning." He looks at Seth and adds, "Just like you did."

"I'm sorry," says Seth. "I wanted to tell you what I was doing, but I knew you would have warned Mother and Father."

"And what about Julia? I know what she's like, but you could have at least tried to tell her how you felt. Leaving like you did is nothing short of cowardice. She deserves the truth."

Seth shakes his head. "I told Julia countless times that I was not in love with her. She insisted that I would grow to love her. You're just upset that Samantha left without telling you why, and I don't blame you. That has to be hard for you."

Marcus sighs deeply. "I just don't understand. We were happy together. When our parents announced the engagement, it took Samantha and me by surprise, but I never imagined she would leave like she did. I never got the chance to tell her all the things I had planned for us."

Ariella asks, "What did you have planned?"

"It doesn't matter now."

The door to the lounge opens. Fidelma, Vindalia, and the twins exit. They are followed by Samantha, who stands at the entry looking at Marcus. As the other women walk down the stairs, Marcus looks at Ariella, confused. "What's going on here?" he asks.

"Why don't you ask her?" says Ariella, gesturing to Samantha.

Marcus turns his attention to his former love. "Samantha...? What are you doing here?"

"Does it really matter?" she replies.

"No, I suppose it doesn't. Did you hear all that?"

"Yes," she nods. "Can we talk alone for a moment?" She motions towards the lounge.

"Of course," replies Marcus as he walks towards Samantha. He passes her by, unable to stop himself from staring.

As Marcus goes inside, Samantha smiles at Ariella. "Thank you."

"I hope the two of you can work things out," says Ariella.

Marcus comes back to the doorway. He says to Ariella, "Before I forget, there's another matter I must address. It's regarding one of *my* new crewmen."

Aboard the *Trident,* Allen is on the main deck with Jack, Mathew, and James. The ship is now anchored, and the men watch as more longboats are taken to shore from the other ships. James notices one longboat returning.

"That looks like our boat, but I don't see the captain," comments James.

Allen looks over the rail at the approaching boat and immediately recognizes the long, red hair of Ariella. "Oh, no," he mutters under his breath.

"What's wrong?" asks Jack.

Allen starts wandering about. "I have to hide."

"Why?" asks Mathew.

James says, "I think because Ariella Stormrage is on that longboat."

"She'll kill me if she knows I'm here," says Allen, clearly worried.

Jack suggests, "Well, then, go hide in your hammock."

"Wait," Mathew interjects. "What if she asks about you?"

Allen sighs. "Then it means she already knows I'm here. In that case, just come get me."

The men get ready to greet their guest as Allen goes below and climbs into his hammock. He takes his blanket and covers himself completely, like a child frightened of the dark.

Up above, Ariella climbs aboard. James welcomes her. "Captain Stormrage, it's a pleasure to see you again."

"Hello, James," she replies.

"So, what brings you here?"

Ariella looks around the ship. After a few moments she answers, "You probably already know why I'm here. Where is he?"

"Who, ma'am?"

"Don't play stupid with me, James. Where's Allen?"

James, looking down, replies, "He's below deck in his hammock."

"Is he still asleep?"

"No, ma'am, he woke up hours ago."

"I see. So he's trying to hide from me?"

Jack says, "I'll go fetch him."

"No," Ariella shakes her head. "I have a better idea."

Moments later, Allen hears footsteps coming down the stairs. He listens as Ariella says to the others, "This is a nice ship you have here. This must be the crew's quarters."

"Yes, ma'am," says James as they walk over to Allen's hammock. Ariella points to her former crewman, completely wrapped up in his blanket. She looks at James, raising her eyebrows in a questioning manner. James quietly nods, confirming that it's him.

Ariella continues to speak as if she is unaware of his presence, "Well, I'm glad that Artos sent you." She removes her glove and proceeds to cast a small electric spell. As she holds out her index and middle fingers, a spark jumps between them. "Thank you for the tour, James. I should probably be going now." Allen sighs with relief just as Ariella touches his back.

The jolt causes him to jump and let out a yelp. Ariella forcefully pulls back the blanket, revealing the young man. Allen looks up Ariella, who is glaring back. "Captain, I can explain."

"Oh, we're past explanations, Allen," she snaps. "Now gather your things. We're leaving."

Climbing out of his hammock, he asks, "Leaving? Where to?"

"To the *Red Dawn*, where I can keep an eye on you and make sure you're safe."

"With all due respect, Captain, I don't need you to keep me safe anymore."

Jack interjects, "That's true, he killed twenty orcneas last night."

Ariella looks at Allen doubtfully. "Twenty?"

Allen looks down. "It was only six."

James says, "It was more than that. I think it was about ten."

Jack adds, "He was like a crazed animal. I never saw anything like it. The orcneas were scared of him. That's why we all call him 'Allen the Mad' now."

"Well, I don't care if he killed a hundred," says Ariella. "He's leaving with me."

Ariella starts to walk away when Allen tries to reason with her. "Captain—"

"Don't argue with me, Allen," she warns. "I'm in no mood. You're lucky I don't have a cat-o-nine tails right now."

"Yes, ma'am," he replies humbly.

"I didn't give you all that money so you could leave Marie behind and get yourself killed."

"I understand why you're upset, ma'am, but I couldn't do nothing."

"The orcneas already have Chance and my brother."

"Your brother?" he asks questioningly.

Remembering that Allen hasn't heard about Fernando, she explains, "It turns out that Mr. Greythorn is my brother, or half-brother, anyway. Neither one of us had any idea until I picked up that sword of his."

"So you found him, then?"

"Yes, I did. Not only that, but I found out that my father is still alive."

Allen nods. "Yes, I actually met him about two weeks ago."

"So you knew he was alive?"

"Well, yes. I would have told you, but I had no way of contacting you."

"Where did you meet him?" she asks.

Allen clears his throat. "Marie and I tracked Mr. Greythorn to Sheathelm. We met him there."

Surprised by the news, Ariella asks, "Are you telling me that the first thing you did when you got off my ship was go to the one place I warned you to stay away from?"

Allen retorts, "You only suggested that we stay away from South Haven until after the war, Captain."

Ariella asks James, "Do you think Marcus would mind if I borrowed his cat-o-nine?"

"Captain, please..." begs Allen.

Ariella grabs Allen's shirt. "The only thing I wanted from you, Allen, was for you to keep Marie safe. I can't believe you left her in Artos alone. What if something happens to her, or you?" Allen doesn't know how to respond. Ariella says to the others, "If you could all give us a moment alone, please."

"Yes, ma'am," replies James. He looks at the others. "Come on, let's go."

The men reluctantly leave as Allen awaits nervously for what Ariella has to say. Once they are alone, she stands before him. Allen, afraid she'll hurt him, is caught off guard when she embraces him and starts to cry. Allen puts his arms around her and says softly, "I'm sorry, Captain."

Still holding him tightly, she sobs, "The orcneas promised to kill Chance if we attack them. Now they have Fernando, and I don't know if he's even alive. You and Marie are all I have left of those I care for most."

"What about your father?" asks Allen.

Ariella steps back, regaining her composure. She laughs to herself. "I'm not really worried about him. I don't even know if he can die."

"Oh, yeah, that's right, he has the soul keeper spell protecting him."

"You know about that, too?" she asks.

"I was asking a lot of questions when I met him," Allen says with a smile, "including why he did everything he had done."

"And what did he tell you?"

"He said he did it to keep you safe."

Ariella nods. "That's what he told me, as well. I wish he wouldn't worry so much about me."

Allen smiles. "And I wish you wouldn't worry so much about me."

"Damn it, Allen, you aren't supposed to make a good point like that." The two laugh momentarily before she continues, "I can't help it, though, just as I'm sure my father can't help but worry about me."

"Captain, I'd like to stay. It's a good ship, with a good crew."

"I know," she agrees. "You're a grown man. If this is what you want to do..."

"It is."

"Very well." She laughs to herself. "I think Marcus was right."

Confused, Allen inquires, "What do you mean?"

"Marcus thought I needed a shoulder to cry on. He was right, though I wouldn't admit it to him. I'm going to head back to land now. Promise me you'll be careful."

"I promise, Captain."

"If you get yourself killed, I will find a way to punish you in the afterlife."

Chapter 27
Burying the Hatchet

Back on land, Vardik Craghammer is walking along the docks of the fortress. He comes across Lyra with her nose buried in a map. She looks up for a moment, and when she notices the dwarf, she says, "Excuse me, but can I ask you something?"

"Of course," Vardik replies.

Lyra holds out the map in front of them. "I have the old dwarven map of the fortress here, but I'm having trouble reading something." Lyra points to the map as she says, "This part is obviously the fortress where we're at now. It is clear to see the docks, the wall, tower, and even the chambers below." She then points to a long line leading north. "This is where the water comes from. My friends and I followed a tunnel until we came across an underground reservoir."

"You're correct. That is where the water comes from, but that symbol right there is not a reservoir," he says, pointing to the end of the line. "That is a dam."

"That's what I thought," says Lyra, "but we didn't find a dam. There is also no river on the map."

"It's an old map," notes Vardik. "It's possible the blue faded away."

Lyra holds the map up to the sky, facing the sun. She looks closely and sees a faint line passing through the symbol on the map that looks like a small segment of a wall. "I see it now!" she exclaims. "Thank you so much."

"Anytime," he replies.

Lyra runs to the large tent were the food is served. She finds Yentroc, Rehma, and Gelana. "Come on," she says, "we have to find the others."

"I saw them over there earlier," says Rehma as she points to the other side of the eating space.

The young women seek out the others, and once they are together, Yentroc asks, "So, what is this all about?"

"We have to go back into the tunnels," says Lyra. "I think if we cross over that deep pool of water, we may find a way into

Sheathelm."

"But there wasn't anything on the other side except fallen rocks," says Ja'noa.

"I know," says Lyra, "but according to this map, the source of water is supposed to be a dam, and if that's the case, it might be the same underwater dam that Sheathelm uses to draw water for the city."

Rehma asks, "How is that possible? Wouldn't the tunnels be flooded?"

Evelena says, "Most of Sheathelm is built much higher than King River."

"But how does that water get from King River to this fortress without flooding the tunnels?" asks Ja'noa.

Lyra looks at the map. "I think the dam is near the front of Sheathelm before the series of waterfalls along the south wall. It's high enough that a gradual slope could have been built all the way here. Keep in mind that this whole fortress is above the waterline. It's just built under the hill."

"I see," says Ja'noa. "So let's go."

The seven sisters of the Silver Moon head up the hill to enter the fortress while on the *Red Dawn*, King Arioch comes aboard looking for Ariella. When he finds Fidelma on the main deck, he asks, "Where is Captain Stormrage?"

Fidelma replies, "Red Beard is in the officer's quarters, and Ariella should be back shortly."

"Where is Captain Reonia?" he asks.

The door to the lounge opens as Marcus steps out. His hair is a mess, and he is out of breath. He finishes buttoning his shirt when he sees the king. "Your Majesty, my apologies." He begins to tuck in his shirt as Fidelma makes her way up the stairs. Samantha hands Marcus his vest before kissing him on the cheek. Marcus passes Fidelma as he heads down to meet with Arioch. Fidelma enters the lounge, where Samantha is putting on her boots. Without saying a word to each other, they smile and laugh.

On the main deck, Arioch says to Marcus, "When Ariella gets back, come find me. We need to start planning for what we do next."

"It looks like we won't have to wait any longer," says Marcus, pointing at the boarding plank.

Ariella steps onto the deck. "What can I do for you?"

The king explains, "When the floating city returns, we plan to bring it down. I thought that since your brother is possibly being held there, you would like to join us."

"Thank you," she replies. "I would. If I could bring a friend, I know someone who can could be useful in finding him."

"Absolutely." Arioch notes the size of Drake. "In fact, if we could use him as well, we need someone to help carry a barrel of black powder."

"You need someone strong? I may know someone who could help with that."

Moments later, Arioch and Marcus follow Ariella as she looks for someone. Soon they come across the massive goliath from the north. Ariella calls to him, "Sven!"

Sven turns around. When he sees Ariella, Sven looks disgruntled. When he spots the king, he smiles. "How can Sven be of help?"

Below ground, Lyra and the others have made it back to the small cavern with the reservoir of water. Looking across to the other side, they do not see a way to continue.

"Are you sure this isn't the end?" asks Evelena.

"Positive," says Lyra. "We have to get over to the other side to get a better look."

Kel'ana suggests, "Ja'noa and I could freeze the water."

"Good," says Evelena. "Do it."

"This isn't going to be easy," says Ja'noa. "This is a lot of water."

"We only need to freeze the top," says Kel'ana. "And it only needs to be wide enough for us to get across."

"But if it's too narrow, it won't support us," warns Ja'noa.

"Just hurry," says Rehma. "Or we may as well just swim."

Kel'ana and Ja'noa begin to concentrate. Their hands emit a blue glow as the water before them begins to crystallize. It takes several minutes, but eventually they complete their bridge of ice. Lyra carefully crosses, minding her steps to avoid slipping. The others follow, and soon they are standing on the other side.

Looking at the ground, Lyra spots some water coming out from under a fallen boulder leaning against the wall. "I think this is it," she says as she feels around the edge of the stone. "I think it's blocking another tunnel."

"It's too big for us to move," says Rehma. "Even if you did increase my strength."

"I can shape it," says Evelena. "Maybe if I narrow the base, we could tip it over."

Gelana walks over to one side of the boulder. "Rehma and I will try to roll it once you're done."

Evelena begins to cast her spell. The sound of rock crumbling can be heard. Shaping stone, however, is a more tiring spell than most. Evelena makes little headway before needing to stop and rest. Yentroc lends her strength to speed up the progress. After a few more tries, the bottom of the boulder is rounded. Gelana and Rehma begin the push.

"There is definitely something back here," says Gelana as the large stone begins to move.

Finally, the boulder rolls away from the wall and into the water, crushing the ice bridge. "You dropped something," says Kel'ana.

"Um, actually, we just rolled it," argues Gelana.

Kel'ana replies, "But it did *drop* to the bottom of water."

"All right, fine," Gelana relents. "But I'm not picking it up."

"Look, everyone," says Evelena. Where the boulder had just been, the women find a tunnel identical to the one they have been traversing.

Ja'noa says, "You were right, Lyra, it does continue."

"Now the only question," Lyra adds, "is whether or not we can use it to get into Sheathelm."

Rehma steps into the tunnel. "There's only one way to find out."

Under the food canopy in the fortress, King Arioch has summoned together all the high-ranking officers, including Princess Kianna, Isen, Prince River, Baeldeth, A'ranah, and most of the captains. Sitting on the hill, Kristieana watches the proceedings.

"May I join you?" asks Va'leen, standing beside her.

Kristieana looks up, confused. "I suppose."

Va'leen sits next to her. Looking at the gathering, she says,

"The end is near, I can feel it."

Kristieana sighs. "I hope whatever they're planning works."

"King Arioch is a brilliant strategist. I'm sure he knows what he's doing."

"How can you say that? We lost Sheathelm."

Va'leen retorts, "But in the process, the orcneas lost nearly five thousand troops, whereas we only lost one thousand. It's about survival, and had we stayed, we may not have."

Kristieana nods. "I suppose so."

They sit in silence, watching the others, until Va'leen says, "The reason I came here is to apologize. I haven't been a good sister to you."

After all the years of fighting, Kristieana isn't sure what to say. "Well, uh... Thanks. I'm sorry if I haven't been very good to you, either."

Va'leen shrugs. "I never gave you much reason to be. Do you remember the first time I challenged you?"

"Yes." Kristieana reflects on that time. "I was visiting Elonfar on my Rite of Passage. There was a festival going on and I met a man. I forget his name, though."

Va'leen laughs. "Their names seldom matter."

"I suppose you're right," she agrees. "Anyway, he and I were getting along, and I wanted to make a formal claim to him in front of the sisters at the festival."

Va'leen continues the story. "You were so confident that he was going to be yours. I remember the brash grin on your face. You looked as if you owned the world."

"I was just excited to be making my first claim. I didn't know how it would turn out."

"If it makes you feel any better, my first claim was challenged, too."

"Really? By who?

"I was challenged by Leewin La'harn."

"Oh, my!" Kristieana exclaims. "Did you win?"

"Sort of," replies Va'leen. "Back then, if a sister on her Rite of Passage tried to make a claim, it was tradition for someone to make her earn it. If they could not agree on a challenge, it defaulted to unarmed combat, and went until someone gave up or couldn't go on. Leewin got the better of me, but I refused to stop fighting. I managed to get behind her and hook my arm around her neck. She couldn't breathe and gave up, but that was only after she had broken my nose and busted my lip. I was a mess, and the man I tried to claim ran off."

"Oh, no," Kristieana laughs.

"Yeah," continues Va'leen. "I got my white bead for winning against Leewin, but also a black one for the denied claim."

"I guess I'm lucky you agreed to a less brutal challenge for my claim, though you did break three of my knuckles while disarming me."

Va'leen smiles. "There is no better way to knock a staff away from an opponent than striking their hands. The important thing is that you didn't let that one defeat stop you. You trained harder than anyone I've ever seen, and when the time came, you beat me."

"So, is that why you challenged me? To make me work harder and earn it?"

Va'leen shrugs. "I suppose. Over the years, the sisterhood challenged fewer first claims, and hardly ever bothered those on their Rite of Passage. But there you were, about to be handed a prize you didn't really earn. Your reminded me of myself at that age, with your confidence. You also reminded me of my sister, Sha'al, when she claimed Chance."

"You were there for that?"

"Yes, I was. I watched as she boldly announced to everyone that Chance was hers unless someone wanted to face her wrath."

Kristieana thinks back to the night she spent in Copper Pass. "I remember Chance telling this story to Evelena and Kel'ana. He said no one challenged her."

"No, they didn't. I was surprised, too. Even though it had become less common to challenge someone's first claim, I thought for certain there would be challengers for him. A few of my friends who saw Chance and me together over the previous weeks looked at me, expecting me to challenge her. Even Chance looked at me, though I couldn't tell what he was thinking. He was red-faced and embarrassed, but smiling. He looked content to be claimed, even if he was nervous. When no one stepped forward, she turned to him, and asked if he denied her claim. For a fraction of a second, I thought I noticed a hint of disappointment on his face before he looked away from me."

"Do you think he wanted you to challenge her?"

"I'll most likely never know. By then, it was too late. He accepted her claim, and she was given her first, and only, blue bead. After that, Chance belonged to her. We've never talked about that day since. I don't want him to question his time with Sha'al as if it may have been a mistake. Fate brought them together, and I have accepted that."

Kristieana sighs. "I assume from that story that you really care about him."

"I do."

"If I had known, I wouldn't have invoked neita. I'm sorry."

"It's all right," replies Va'leen. "I could tell that you weren't just doing it out of spite. You thought I was a danger to him."

"I did. I thought you were going to treat him the same as all the other men whose names don't matter."

"I would never do that to Chance. He's not like other men."

"I know. There's something different about him that I can't describe. It's an endearing quality, and yet, it's also a flaw."

"I know what you mean. He loves with so much passion, yet that same passion makes him fearful and indecisive."

"Yes," Kristieana agrees. "That's exactly what he was like in the mountains. One moment he was assertive, the next he was afraid of being hurt. He couldn't make up his mind what he wanted to do."

Va'leen nods, saying, "Few women want a man who isn't certain he wants to be with her."

Kristieana asks, "Do you suppose that's just as true about men?"

"Most likely."

"Then maybe Chance just needs to know how you feel."

"Perhaps." Va'leen ponders. "Maybe I should have said something. Then again, maybe he didn't feel the same. No, when it came to Chance, I didn't want to push him. If he had feelings for me, I wanted him to see it on his own."

"You speak of him as if he's already gone."

Va'leen looks down and shakes her head. "I want to believe we can save him, but it's not likely."

"I know," says Kristieana sadly. "If we do, though, you should tell him."

"It wouldn't make any difference if I did. Ariella Stormrage has his heart now." She laughs to herself. "On the bright side, she's only human. How long could she possibly live?"

Kristieana gasps. "That's terrible."

"I know it is. I shouldn't say such things. You know, I'm glad we had this talk."

"So am I."

Va'leen asks, "Have you seen Lyra?"

"No, not since waking this morning."

Seeing Sven, Va'leen says, "No matter. At least I can talk with him."

Chapter 28
The Old Code

Rushing out from the underground portion of the fortress, Lyra and the others look for someone to inform about their discovery. Evelena notes, "It looks like everyone is meeting under the canopy."

"There's Kristieana," says Rehma. "Let's tell her."

The young women approach their friend. Gelana says to Kristieana, "You're not going to believe what we just found."

"What?" she asks.

"Lyra just found a way into Sheathelm underground," says Gelana, excited.

"That's great," says Kristieana. "We'll have to tell Arioch and A'ranah as soon as the meeting is done."

"Shouldn't we tell them now?" asks Evelena.

Kristieana looks at the guards surrounding the meeting. "I don't think we'll be allowed in. Besides, they shouldn't be much longer." Kristieana's eyes spot Sven, who is now talking with Va'leen.

The other girls turn their attention to them, as well. Yentroc demands, "What is she doing talking to him?"

"More importantly," says Gelana, "what is he doing talking to her?"

Lyra looks away, searching for anything that might capture her attention. Kristieana says, "I was speaking with Va'leen earlier. She apologized for everything she had done. I'm sure she's doing the same with Sven." Lyra, absorbed into her own thoughts, doesn't hear her.

Now worried, Yentroc asks, "Are you all right?"

Lyra once again focuses on Sven and Va'leen. Va'leen, is now holding his hand, beckoning him to come with her. Without a word to her friends, Lyra starts towards them.

"Lyra, wait!" calls Yentroc as she starts to follow.

"Oh, this isn't good," mutters Kristieana.

The others all follow Lyra as she makes her way through the sparse number of soldiers on the hill. Neither Sven nor Va'leen see her coming.

Va'leen says to Sven while still pulling at his arm, "Come on, we'll tell Lyra the truth together."

As she turns around, Va'leen nearly runs into Lyra, who gives her shove, yelling, "Stay away from him!"

"Lyra, stop!" shouts Sven.

He grabs her arm, but she turns and swats his hand away. "Sven, don't move from this spot." Lyra grinds the heel of her boot into the soil. "I mean it. Stand on this line and wait until I'm done."

"Lyra, it's not what you th—"

"Now!" she commands pointing at the line. Gelana and the others look on, stunned, as Sven stands on the line.

Lyra turns around, almost running into Va'leen, who smiles and says, "My, my, it looks like the little mouse has the roar of a lioness. Tell me, runt, do you have the claws to go with it, or are you all talk?"

Without warning, Lyra strikes Va'leen on the side of her face with a closed fist. Everyone is astonished, including Lyra, who second guesses her own actions for a moment before becoming resolved once again.

Gelana rhetorically asks Rehma, "Did Lyra just hit Va'leen?"

"This isn't going to end well," worries Kel'ana.

"Lyra!" calls Yentroc. She takes a step towards her friend, when she is pulled back by Kristieana. "What are you doing? I have to stop this."

Kristieana shakes her head, "Lyra has to do this for herself."

Sven, also trying to intervene, says to her, "Lyra, it is not what you think. Va'leen was just telling Sven about other night."

Va'leen rubs the corner of her mouth. When she looks at her fingertips and sees blood, a sadistic grin spans her face.

Evelena asks Kristieana, "Aren't you going to stop this?"

"There's nothing to stop... yet." she replies.

Va'leen takes a step towards Lyra, staring her down. Lyra, both furious and frightened, doesn't look away, holding her ground. Wiping the corner of her lip again, Va'leen says, "All right, whelp, I'll give you that one. I'll even admit I had it coming, but don't try that again. You won't like the result if you do."

Lyra swallows before asking, "What were you talking about with Sven?"

Va'leen laughs as she takes a step back. "Oh, *now* you want to talk? We'll get to that in a moment, but first, I think we need to address another issue."

"What issue is that?" asks Lyra.

"If you really want me to stay away from what is yours, there's a simple way to ensure it." Va'leen looks around at the others.

When she makes eye contact with Kristieana, the red-headed elf shakes her head and silently mouths the words, "Please don't do this." No one else gets the message except Va'leen.

Va'leen looks back at Lyra and says, "All you have to do is claim him."

"Don't do it, Lyra," cautions Yentroc. "It's a trick. She'll just challenge you."

"She's right," says Gelana, "you don't have to do this."

"Of course not," Va'leen agrees. "If there is no claim, there can be no challenge. Then again, I could always evoke neita."

"Va'leen, stop," Kristieana finally interjects. "I thought we've moved past this."

"Relax," says Va'leen. "I wouldn't do that to her. I just want to give Lyra the opportunity to show everyone how she feels about him. I want to hear her say the words." She looks at Lyra. "You probably know all the words to the old code. What Amazon hasn't practiced them before heading out on their Rite of Passage?"

"So you won't challenge her claim?" asks Yentroc.

Va'leen smiles. "I didn't say that."

Sven, taking a step forward, says, "Lyra, please..."

"Sven!" Lyra snaps, without looking back. "I swear to the gods, if you have moved from that spot..."

Sven quickly steps back, looking at the ground to make sure he is exactly where Lyra told him to wait.

Va'leen smiles. "Look at how obedient he is. He's already yours, Lyra. The question is, is he worth fighting for?"

"Lyra," Sven begs. "Sven is not worth it. Sven does not want to see you get hurt."

Looking back over her shoulder, Lyra says to Sven, "A challenge does not have to be a fight."

"Lyra is correct," says Va'leen. "We would have to agree on the challenge. It could be anything. I'd even let Lyra decide."

Yentroc warns, "But if Va'leen wins..."

"Then I have to stay away from Sven," Lyra finishes.

Va'leen sighs. "It's not as if it would be forever. She could always try again. But if Lyra doesn't feel that Sven is worth taking the risk for..."

"I get to pick the challenge?" asks Lyra.

"Yes. Anything you want."

Before anyone else can say a word, Lyra says, "I accept."

"Lyra, don't," Gelana pleas.

"Too late," gloats Va'leen.

Lyra says, "For the challenge I propose—"

"I think you're getting ahead of yourself," Va'leen interrupts. "First you have to make the claim."

Lyra looks at Sven, who shakes his head. "You do not have to do this, Lyra."

"Yes," she replies, "I do." Lyra clears her throat. With her heart beating vigorously, she looks Sven in the eyes and announces, "I, Lyra, from the house of Dri'el, proclaim that this man belongs to me, unless he denies it." She looks around at her sisters and continues. "If any Amazon of the Silver Moon wishes to challenge this claim, step forth now and face my wrath." Lyra turns to face Va'leen once more. She stands before her, body shaking with anticipation, waiting for her challenge.

"Congratulations, Lyra," says Va'leen. "You've successfully made your first claim."

Confused, she asks, "You're... not going to challenge it?"

Va'leen shakes her head, "Even if I were to win the challenge, I would only be awarded one white bead, and then, because Sven would surely deny me, I would also receive a black one. Honestly, Lyra, this isn't worth getting dishonor over."

"So, that's it?" asks Yentroc. "She claimed Sven?"

"Yes." Kristieana smiles, relieved. "Unless Sven refuses her."

Everyone's eyes turn to Sven. He laughs. "Sven would never refuse Lyra."

Gelana, opening her pouch, says, "Lyra, I have a blue bead for you."

"No!" barks Yentroc. "I'm giving her the blue bead." Yentroc, holding out her hand to Lyra, continues, "I have been waiting a long time for this." Lyra takes the token of honor from her friend and smiles.

Sven says jokingly, "If Sven may move from spot now, he would like to see bead, too."

The women laugh, and Lyra says, "All right, Sven, you may move now."

As Lyra shows Sven the new addition to her necklace, Kristieana privately says to Va'leen, "I was worried that you were going make her 'earn' her claim."

Va'leen shrugs. "Like I said, it's not worth getting any dishonor over."

"I know that's what you told Lyra, but it was still nice of you."

"Lyra has been through enough already. She's more than earned this claim."

Sven looks over at Va'leen and Kristieana. "Wait. Va'leen, please tell Lyra what you told Sven earlier."

Lyra and the others look at Va'leen, waiting. Lyra says, "I don't know if I really want to hear more about that night."

Va'leen sighs. "Actually, I think you may enjoy this." She rejoins the group and explains to Lyra, "That night, Sven didn't invite me back to his room. In fact, he was quite insistent to go back alone. He had been drinking a lot, however, and it was easy to convince him to let me help. All that night, he had been going on about how he lost you, Lyra. When I got him back to his room, he just continued to cry over it. I helped him to bed, and he fell asleep immediately. I thought about leaving, but I was still too angry about the neita, so I slept on the floor. When morning came, I thought about telling him the truth, but then you showed up, and... I got angry all over again. I'm sorry, Lyra. I didn't mean for it to go on this long. I should have told you earlier. The important thing is, he was never tempted by me."

Disappointed that it took so long to learn the truth, but understanding, Lyra says, "Thank you for finally telling me. And I'm sorry about the neita."

Kristieana says, "For what it's worth, I'm sorry, too. And Va'leen, I revoke the neita."

"Thank you," says Va'leen. "I just hope I get to see Chance again."

Lyra's face lights up. "I almost forgot. We found a way into Sheathelm. We might be able to rescue Chance."

"Really?" asks Va'leen, optimistic.

"Yes, I just have to check on a map where we might find him. But we can get into the city from here."

"Then I will go with you."

"Wait," says Sven. "You are going into Sheathelm?"

Yentroc suggests, "You could come with us."

"Sven is supposed to help Arioch with attack on floating city."

Va'leen says, "But the floating city is gone now."

Kristieana looks out at the horizon. She notices a drake flying towards the stronghold. "That must be Belron returning."

Va'leen says, "I'll go tell my mother what Lyra found. You should all make sure you're ready to go."

"I'll go with you," says Kristieana.

As the two women leave, Sven asks Lyra, "Now that Lyra has claimed Sven, what does Sven do?"

Lyra thinks for a moment. She grins mischievously and says, "Well, the first thing you have to do is kiss me. Otherwise, it's not a real claim."

Gelana quietly asks Yentroc, "Wait, that's not a real rule, is it?"

Yentroc elbows her sharply. "Shh..."

Lyra continues to tell Sven, "It has to be a 'real' kiss, too. Not just a friendly kiss on the cheek, or a light peck." Lyra begins to blush.

"Sven can do that," he says as he takes Lyra's hand. He pulls her close and her heart begins to race. He lifts her chin with his finger as she reaches up, putting her arms around his neck. He slides his hand around to the back of her head, cradling it as he leans down. With her eyes closed, she can feel a light tingling as his beard brushes across her parted lips. She feels the warmth of his lips just out of reach as he hovers over her, making the moment last. Every shortened breath she takes feels as long as a heavy sigh. Pulling down on his neck, Lyra springs up onto her toes. Lyra's and Sven's lips finally meet. The sensation is exhilarating for Lyra, yet she can't quite shake the feeling that, due to her inexperience, her kiss is a bit clumsy. Doing her best not to over-think matters, she follows Sven's lead. He reaches around her waist, pressing their bodies together as their kiss becomes what can only be described as anything *but* a friendly peck.

While Sven and Lyra carry on, Yentroc holds out her hand to

Gelana. "I think now would be a good time to pay up." Gelana sighs before reaching into her leather pouch and pulling out a silver coin. Yentroc says to the others, "Come on, everyone. Who bet?"

Lyra and Sven pause for a moment. Lyra looks over. "What's going on?"

"Sorry," says Gelana. "I didn't think you would claim him. For the record, it's the best bet I ever lost."

Looking at the other young women digging into their pouches, Lyra asks, "You all bet against me?"

"I didn't," boasts Rehma. "I knew you had it in you."

"Wait," says Gelana. "Yentroc, you and I also made a vow to give a silver piece to whoever had the first claim. So you should give one of those to Lyra."

"But she wasn't part of it," argues Yentroc.

"So?" Gelana retorts. "We didn't specify that it had to be you or I."

Lyra grins as she walks over to Yentroc, saying, "I'll take one of those."

Yentroc hands her one of the four silver pieces as Gelana takes out another from her pouch. Handing it to Lyra, she says, "It's still the best two silver I've ever lost in a bet."

Yentroc says to Lyra, "We would have bet honor, but we weren't sure if it would have been valid."

Sven chuckles. "You ladies have interesting customs. Speaking of which..." Sven takes off his necklace of polished stones and seashells. He holds it out to Lyra. "Sven would like you to have this."

Lyra's eyes widen. "Are you sure?"

"Yes, is something wrong?"

"No. I just know how important it is."

Yentroc asks, "What is it?"

Sven explains, "It is necklace Sven's mother gave him when he became man. Goliath men are to give them to woman he loves. Sven loves you, Lyra."

Panic hits Lyra like a wave. Taken aback, she asks, "You do?"

"Yes, Sven does."

Lyra reluctantly takes the necklace. "I don't know what to say."

"You do not have to say anything. Just keep it as long as you wish to claim Sven. It does not have to mean anything more than that."

"But you just told me..."

Sven brushes back her hair. "Sven knows what he said, and you do not have to say it back."

"But I want to," insists Lyra, with tears welling her eyes. "I've just never said that before... At least, not to anyone other than my mother."

Sven smiles and says reassuringly, "They are not easy words to say, and Sven does not want you to say them until you are ready."

"I've let you down."

"No," he scoffs. "You make Sven very happy. Sven has lived a lot longer than you. Sven knows when he loves someone, but you are young. All of this is new to you, but you will figure it out in time. Until then, Sven belongs to you as long as you want him. You can say those words when you feel time is right, not before."

"Thank you for understanding."

Chapter 29
Rushed Plans

As Kristieana and Va'leen reach the canopy, there is a rapid dispersal of the gathering. Captains are running back to their longboats as generals and commanders prepare their men. A sense of urgency can be felt as people scramble about. As they make their way to A'ranah, Isen calls to Kristieana through the crowd. "Wait!"

Kristieana stops, allowing Isen and Princess Kianna to catch up. "What's going on?" asks Kristieana.

Kianna replies, "We just found out that the floating fortress is on its way back now."

"We have to hold off the attack," says Va'leen. "We need to get Chance out first."

Isen asks, "What are you talking about?"

Kristieana answers, "Lyra says there is an underground passage into Sheathelm from this fortress."

"If that's true, you'll have to go soon," says Kianna. "Belron reported dozens of ships being escorted by the floating city. Thousands more troops are on board."

"I have to talk with my mother," says Va'leen.

The four make their way through the bustling crowd until they reach Arioch and A'ranah. The king says to Kianna and Isen, "What are you two still doing here? You have your orders, now go find Ya'leigh and get to the west."

Kianna says, "Father, there may be a way into Sheathelm. We can rescue Chance."

Arioch asks, "Where?"

Kianna looks at Va'leen, who explains, "All I know is that Lyra claims she found a way through."

Kristieana says, "Lyra said it was underground."

"Father," says Kianna, "we can send our forces in."

Arioch shakes his head, "No, if she is talking about going in through the waterway here in the fortress, it does not go all the way through to the city."

Kristieana says, "She seemed certain that it does."

"Listen to me," says Arioch. "We have to stick the plan we've already made. Even if there is some sort of passage into Sheathelm, it will be flooded when we bring down the floating city. We cannot risk losing them, and we have to bring down that city now. Isen, you, Kristieana, and Kianna, find Ya'leigh and join Baeldeth and the other generals. We have to get everyone out of this stronghold before the floating city falls."

Isen asks, "What about Chance?"

"I'll get him," says Va'leen. "If the passage floods on my way in, I'll be safe in my shadow form. When I free him and Re'ann, we can make our escape another way."

A'ranah says, "Tell Evelena and the others to go with the rest of the forces that are leaving."

"I will," says Va'leen.

Kristieana says to her sister, "Be safe, and may the gods watch over you."

Va'leen embraces her. "You, too."

Isen, Kristieana, and the princess head out to find Ya'leigh as Va'leen heads back to the others. When she reaches them, she says to Lyra, "I'll take the maps that you have."

"I can hold them," says Lyra.

Va'leen replies, "Unfortunately, I have to go alone. The floating city is on its way back and apparently they're bringing reinforcements. The main priority is to bring it down as soon as possible. When it falls, Arioch says the tunnels will be flooded. Mother Elder wants you all to go with the others."

Sven looks down at the docks and sees Ariella waving to him. He says to Lyra, "Sven has to go now."

"You aren't going with us?" asks Lyra, confused.

"Sven is going to help bring floating city down. King Arioch asked Sven personally." He smiles. "They will sing songs of this day."

"All right," replies Lyra. "Just be careful."

Sven leans down and kisses her softly. "You be careful, too."

The goliath heads down to the docks as Rehma says to Va'leen, "I'm going with you."

"Me, too," says Gelana.

"I don't need you two to come with me," Va'leen replies.

Yentroc says, "Chance may be hurt. You'll need someone to

heal him."

"I can pick the locks if you can't find a key," says Ja'noa.

Evelena adds, "I can see through the stone in the walls to help find him."

"What if the tunnels become flooded?" asks Va'leen.

Kel'ana says, "Ja'noa and I can hold the water back. The passages aren't that big."

Va'leen sighs. "I assume you all want to come, then?" Kel'ana and Lyra nod their heads. "Fine, but we have to go now. The floating city is starting to come into view."

Lyra looks out to sea. Just over the horizon, the orcnea's floating fortress can now be seen. She looks at the top of the hill where the tower stands. It is crowded with soldiers. "We should go through the entrance by the docks."

The eight women walk at a quickened pace to the lower entrance to the stronghold. As they enter, Lyra runs into A'ranah. "Excuse me," says Lyra, not looking up.

The others all stop. Va'leen, embarrassed, looks down as the Amazon queen says, "Where are you all going? Didn't Va'leen tell you to go with the others?"

"No, mother," Va'leen replies, "I needed their help, so I asked them to come."

Evelena interjects, "That's not true, Mother Elder. She told us to leave, but we all insisted on going with her."

Rehma says, "The orcneas said they would kill Chance if we attacked. We can't just let them execute him. Kel'ana and Ja'noa can keep us safe from the flooding waters."

The Amazon queen eyes the eight women. "In that case, you should know that he is most likely being held in the dungeon below the Colosseum. Now go quickly. We are about to assault the floating city."

"Thank you, Mother Elder," Evelena says, bowing her head.

The women continue on as A'ranah joins Arioch near the docks, where a smaller gathering of troops await. In the center, several Amazons of the Silver Moon have shaped water into a flat, horizontal disc, low to the ground. Within the water's surface, Jadelyn has used her magic to watch the floating city from above. An image of one of the pyramids' tops is in view.

On either side of the water, logs are tied together to form an

'A' frame. Another log runs between them like a giant swing. Two ropes are tied to the middle of the center log with the other ends being held by two soldiers off to the side of the water.

A'ranah says, "This is as close as we can get to the floating city with our magic."

Arioch announces to the gathering, "Once the gate is open, Belron, Ashden, and Prince River will dive through with their drakes. As soon as they are through, the rest of us will rappel down the ropes to the top of the pyramid. Those of you who can safely jump or fly down will do so over at this side of the portal. Then, you will quickly but carefully, make your way down the side to attack."

Belron continues with the instructions. "The orcneas still have fifteen drakes under their control. Our first target is to take their beast masters out. Without them, the drakes will be far less dangerous, assuming they don't flee altogether."

Arioch continues, "After the drakes go through, my group will go next. We will make our way to the chamber where the magic crystal that keeps city in the air is located. All other groups are to engage the enemy forces and keep them from following us."

The Amazon queen warns, "Once we are through, we'll have to act fast. We must get inside the pyramid before they close the doors. It will be our only chance to bring it down. Once they realize they are under attack, they may have some way to bring in reinforcements of their own."

Arioch adds, "They will also warn the ships below if they perceive us as a threat."

"Remember," says A'ranah, "when you get the signal to escape, you will have less than a minute to activate your gate-stones and get everyone in your group through them. Be aware of your surroundings and don't wander too far from those who have the gate-stones. We didn't have as much time as we would have liked to create them, so there is a possibility, that one, or more, may fail. If that happens, you will need to go through another group's gate."

"Does everyone know what to do?" asks the king. When there are no questions, he concludes, "All right, Belron we'll open the gate once you're ready."

Belron nods. "We'll take flight immediately."

The captain of the drake riders heads for his mount when he is stopped by Nicari. "May the gods watch over you," she says to her husband.

Belron gives his wife a kiss. "Be safe, my love."

Nicari reluctantly allows Belron to pull away as he makes haste for the other riders. When he arrives, he looks at Ashden and Prince River. "Are you both ready?"

Ashden replies, "As ready as I can be."

Prince River adds, "Let's go."

The three riders take to the sky as Arioch says to the handful of Amazons surrounding the magical image, "Open the gate."

The women concentrate on the image of the pyramid, and soon the watery image on the ground is replaced with a magic gateway to the same point above the floating city. Belron, Ashden, and River all dive through, narrowly missing the edges. King Arioch is the next through, followed by Sven, Ariella, Fidelma, Annalee, and A'ranah.

Above the floating fortress, the drake riders take the enemy by surprise. Below them is a large gathering of orcnea soldiers in front of the entrance to one of the two pyramids. Beyond the soldiers, in the middle of the floating landmass, are fourteen of the drakes that remain under the control of the orcneas. They are bound to chains that are staked into the ground.

"Where's the sea drake?" Belron ponders aloud. He looks around for the beast master shamans, but doesn't find any. He calls out, "You two, take out the ballistas, and keep an eye out for the shamans."

As more elves and humans pour through the gate, Ashden and Prince River prepare their fire potions, splitting up and flying towards the rows of ballistas near the walls. Belron heads toward the other group of orcneas gathered in front of the far pyramid. It all happens so fast, there is no time for the enemy to react. Several of the heavy weapons are set ablaze, as well as a handful of soldiers.

Working their way down the side of the pyramid, Arioch and A'ranah lead the way, followed by the others. Spells and arrows fly as the orcneas ready themselves for combat. Arioch hits the ground first, throwing his spear into the chest of the nearest orcnea. The Amazon queen is the next one down. She stands next to Arioch as he draws his sword.

Sven jumps down the rest of the way to the ground. As he falls, he yells out at the top of his lungs to call forth the magical properties of his axe. "Hellfire!" The blade's edge splits the ground as it sends forth a destructive wave of intense flames. With almost no way to protect from such a spell, most of the orcneas are killed, only a few able to get out of the way. The group of enemies scatters in panic while more of the attacking forces engage them in melee.

Ariella warns, "Sven, be careful with that weapon. Don't forget what's in that barrel on your back."

Sven nods as Ariella, Fidelma, and Annalee quickly make their way into the entrance tunnel of the pyramid. There is a rumbling sound all around them, and when the women look up they see a stone slab slowing coming down to close off the tunnel.

"Arioch!" calls Ariella. "Hurry, it's closing."

The king retrieves his spear before rushing over with Sven. The goliath attempts to stop the massive stone door from falling into place, but it is too much. The men enter while A'ranah, now engaged in battle, makes quick work of the enemy before her. She turns and sprints to the entrance before diving under the closing door. The slab hits the floor with a deafening thump.

The passageway that the six now stand in is lit with magic stones along the walls. It is a wide hallway that extends twenty paces before splitting into a "T." An orcnea comes around the corner and is surprised to see them. He turns to run away, but Arioch throws his spear, impaling him through the back.

"Remember," says Fidelma. "We'll need to take one alive so I can find out where they are holding Fernando."

"Let's get moving," suggests Arioch.

Outside, Serena La'harn is in the thick of the battle. With her shield and spear, she engages one orcnea after another. A fierce thrust of her weapon, followed by a strike of her shield as she pulls her spear free, is more than enough to put an end to most anyone. If that wasn't enough, she also lets out a shout with every foe she vanquishes that rallies her allies while demoralizing her enemies. As foreboding as the orcneas are, this Amazon warrior is not intimidated as she strikes with both lightning speed and overpowering strength.

Not far away, Jadelyn catches a fire spell thrown from one of the surrounding towers. She turns and hurls it at an unsuspecting orcnea nearby. "We need to take those towers out now."

Adolayn eyes the nearest tower. "I'll see what I can do." She begins to summon a massive stone with her hands. She concentrates to increase its size until she reaches the limit of her abilities. She aims carefully at the limestone tower before her and releases the spell. The stone missile slams into the base of the fortification. Dust and stone violently explode, leaving a hole in the tower.

Yarwin throws a bolt of lightning at the orcnea guard in the top of the stone structure, but misses, instead hitting just outside the window.

Nicari says to Serena, "If we hurry, we may be able to free the drakes before the beast masters can take control of them."

"I don't know if that's a good idea," replies Serena.

"If we frighten them off, they may not return."

"Or, once they are free, they may attack anyway."

Nicari argues, "If they try to get us while they are still chained up, you're right, but if they try to get away from us, they will run."

Serena bashes an orcnea with her shield. "Fine, we'll try it. But if one comes at me, you won't have to worry about freeing it. It'll be dead."

Nicari nods and the two head to the middle where the drakes are kept. The orcneas at the other side of the fortress approach the middle as well, but are cut off when Belron drops two elixirs on the ground, creating a barrier of fire.

Nicari and Serena reach the first drake. It is an ice drake, and while it doesn't attack them, it does hiss. Serena walks straight up to the beast and, using her spear as a staff, she gives it a hit on the snout, yelling, "Back, or I'll run this through you!" The ice drake backs up, pulling hard against the chains. "That's right," she continues, "you better fear me."

Nicari takes her three-sided dagger and begins to strike the heavy lock keeping the beast chained to the iron stake in the ground. While a normal dagger wouldn't do, hers is forged from star steel, and is enchanted as well. With five rapid hits, the lock breaks and the drake is free.

Serena and Nicari watch as the blue drake takes to the sky. In a panic, and without the beast masters to guide it, the scaly beast flies away.

Belron calls to River and Ashden, "If the drakes flee, let them go."

Below the surface, the dwarf Corthag is speaking into the pool of water that allows him to communicate with the High Chief. "We're under attack."

The image of the orcnea leader says, "We'll send up some reinforcements soon. In the meantime, I will go to the shore and begin the final preparations."

In a ship below the floating fortress, the High Chief comes out of his quarters and onto the main deck. He says aloud, "The floating city is under attack. Use the gate-stone to return and help."

A massive ogre stands. He picks up a breastplate the size of an adult male human and puts it on. As other orcneas prepare for combat, the High Chief transforms into a giant eagle and hurries for the shore.

In the tunnels below the pyramids, Arioch peeks around a corner as the others wait quietly. He sees one orcnea guard standing outside a door. He motions to the others that there is only one.

Fidelma nods before walking out around the corner. She begins to cast a spell when the orcnea looks in her direction. The other five follow her with their weapons drawn, expecting a fight. Instead, the orcnea stands motionless, looking at them, seeming to be in a trance.

Ariella says in amazement, "It's working."

Fidelma replies, "Now, to get as much information as I can."

Sven and Arioch keep watch as Ariella, Annalee, and A'ranah watch Fidelma scan the mind of the orcnea. After a few moments, Fidelma says, "Fernando isn't far from here."

"So, he's alive?" asks Ariella, relieved.

"Yes."

A'ranah asks, "What about the power crystal? Is it where we suspect?"

Fidelma nods, "Yes, it is, and we better hurry. I just learned that the High Chief is on a ship below."

"We better move then," suggests Ariella.

A'ranah asks Fidelma, "Are you done with him?"

"Yes."

The Amazon queen takes her sword and drives the point up into the orcnea's skull from below the jaw. Even the battle-hardened Ariella cringes at the sight. Fidelma takes the lead as the rest follow. They make their way down another passage until they reach a corner. Fidelma motions for the others to stop. Peeking around the edge, she sees another orcnea standing guard. She walks around the corner like before and casts the spell to put the enemy in a daze.

The others follow her, and when the orcnea spots them, Fidelma's spell fails to take effect. The orcnea yells something in Orcneish and turns to run the opposite way. Fidelma quickly casts another spell and uses it to pull the orcnea back. The magic force drags the enemy until Fidelma moves her hands around, causing the spell to slam the orcnea into the wall. Just to be certain, she drives him back and forth several times into the unforgiving stone before releasing the spell.

Ariella and Sven look on, surprised. Sven asks, "When did you learn to do that?"

Slightly out of breath, Fidelma replies, "Several years ago."

Ariella grins. "You'll have to teach me it sometime."

From up ahead, the muffled voice of Fernando can be heard from inside a room, "Hello? Is somebody out there?"

"Fernando!" calls Ariella as she runs down the corridor. Soon the others join her outside Fernando's cell.

Fernando, peering through the iron bars of the door, says, "Ariella, I am glad to see you."

Sven looks at the lock on the door. "Stand back, Sven will get you out."

Fernando takes a step back as Sven swings Hellfire at the lock, breaking it easily. The door opens and Ariella rushes inside to hug her brother tightly. "I thought I lost you," she says, her words muffled by the embrace.

Arioch says, "I hate to break up this family reunion, but we have to get moving."

"What's going on?" Fernando asks as he puts his arm in front of his face to allow his eyes to adjust to the light in the hall.

Ariella explains, "We are going to bring this damned place down." As they begin to make their way down the corridor she continues, "Sven has a keg full of the goblin black powder. It should be more than enough to destroy the power crystal that keeps this place afloat."

"Good," Fernando replies. "From what I understand, the High Chief is coming. If you have a way to attack their ships, you may be able to stop him."

Arioch says, "He is in the fleet below."

"Come, we mustn't delay any longer," says A'ranah, glancing down the corridor.

As the group follows Arioch, Fernando says to Ariella, "You should know that Corthag is in this floating fortress."

"He is?" asks Ariella questioningly. "Where?"

Fernando shakes his head. "I do not know where he is now. I do know that he is helping the orcneas."

"Of course he would. He'd do anything for the right price."

"There is something else I have to tell you. Something he told me about the *White Feather*."

Curious, Ariella asks, "What is it?"

"It will have to wait," Fernando replies. "Right now, let's just get this fortress out of the sky."

Chapter 30
Songs of This Day

On the surface of the floating fortress, Adolayn pushes her abilities as she channels as much of her strength as possible into another spell. She hurls the summoned stone into the base of the same tower that she has been focusing on since the battle began. The tower collapses.

At the same time, the orcneas begin to emerge through a magic gate of their own. When the massive ogre appears, the Amazons' eyes widen. Armed for battle, the ogre is wearing a cast iron helmet the size a cauldron. Along with the breastplate for his chest, he has crude chain-mail sleeves to protect his arms. His legs are covered with a thick leather hide. An ogre without any armor is formidable. An ogre wearing this much armor is dire threat.

Serena and Nicari free the last of the drakes before frightening it off. They turn their attention to the orcnea gate and the massive ogre. Serena, unintimidated, tosses her spear to the side before drawing her sword.

"Be careful," warns Nicari.

Serena nods. "Let's give that creature a fight it won't soon forget. The bards will sing of it for centuries." The seasoned veteran charges at the ogre as he raises his spiked club above his head. With its upper body heavily protected, Serena looks to attack the legs.

Nicari follows behind her, watching out for orcneas. One of the reddish-orange foes tries to flank them, but Nicari is ready. She rolls to the side, avoiding the orcnea's attack. As the enemy swings his sword again, Nicari uses both of her three-sided daggers to stop the blade. She then uses her weapons to cut the orcnea's sword in half. As the enemy backs up, she hurls one of her enchanted blades into the orcnea's chest. The orcnea falls, and Nicari holds out her hand to call back her weapon.

Only a few paces away, the ogre swings his club at Serena. Despite the strength of the Amazonian elder from the house of La'harn, the weapon is too enormous to stop. She is struck by the club, and one of the spikes gouges her arm. The force of the hit sends her through the air and onto her back.

The rest of the Amazons begin to clash with the new orcnea forces while Belron circles above. The captain of the drake riders watches as the orcnea drakes fly aimlessly. Several fly away, while a few more stay close to the floating city.

Ashden says, "I don't think they are a threat. What should we do?"

Belron studies the field of battle below. "You and Prince River stay up here and keep an eye on the other drakes. I'm going to see if I can help down below."

As Belron prepares to dive, the ogre sets his sights on the wounded Serena. With his back to Nicari, he is open to her attack. The blonde Amazon tosses her twisted weapons forward. Not only do Nicari's Star Steel weapons return to her on command, but she can control their every move. The fine, three-sided blades levitate. She motions with her hand, sending them speeding into the upper back of the ogre.

As deadly as they are, the blades are diminutive compared to the broad back and shoulders of the imposing ogre. It does wound him, however, and he turns his attention to Nicari. She begins to call back her weapons as the ogre approaches, but before they return, Nicari is forced to dodge the deadly club.

The ogre's weapon slams against the ground, barely missing its target. Nicari catches her daggers while Serena makes it back to her feet. The ogre, still focused on Nicari, is caught off guard by Belron as he strafes the enemy from Nimbus's back. The sky drake's tale strikes the ogre's head, knocking his helmet off.

Serena looks down at the gash in her right arm. Unable to hold the sword properly, she grips her weapon tightly with her left hand. She sprints at the ogre as his attention is shifted to the captain of the drake riders. As she passes behind him, she spins around, striking the ogre in the back of the leg with her blade. The cut is deep, and the ogre instinctively swipes behind him with his club. Serena is sent flying once more. This time when she hits the ground, she falls unconscious.

With the ogre's back again facing her, Nicari seizes the opportunity to strike. Rather than throw her daggers, she decides to move in. Nicari approaches rapidly before springing into the air. She lands right on the shoulders of the ogre before driving the twisted steel of her dagger into his skull. Without the cast iron helmet, the ogre cannot withstand the deadly blow. The beast falls, trapping Nicari's leg under it. Covered with blood, Nicari struggles to pull herself free. She commands her daggers to attack an oncoming orcnea. The enemy is held at bay as she pulls herself free. The twisted blades finish off the enemy and Nicari calls them back to her before rushing over to check on Serena.

Below one of the pyramids, King Arioch and his group make their way down to the lower level. Arioch turns a corner, where they encounter Corthag and two orcnea guards. The dwarf greets them. "King Arioch, it's been a long time."

Arioch stands with his shield ready. "Corthag, I hear you've been helping the orcneas."

The dark-haired dwarf laughs. "They made me an excellent offer. Perhaps you'd like to make a better one."

Ariella pushes her way past the king while charging a lightning bolt. "The only offer you'll get from us is death." She hurls the spell at the dwarf, but Corthag is able to catch it. With the spell under his control, he throws it back. Ariella stands steadfast as the bolt strikes her. Unharmed, she asks, "Did you really think a little lightning would hurt me?"

"No, I suppose not," replies Corthag. "But how 'bout this?" Corthag begins to cast a spell. A dark sphere begins to form in his hand.

Arioch moves Ariella aside, saying, "We don't have time for this." Before Corthag can complete his spell, the king hurls his spear into the dwarf's chest.

Corthag's spell dissipates. He clutches the spear before pulling it out. Staring at the blood-soaked tip, the dark dwarf laughs maniacally. Arioch draws his sword and begins to move in. The two orcneas intercept the king, but with a quick parry and counterattack, the one to Arioch's right falls. The one on the left grabs the king's shield. As the orcnea pulls the shield to the side, the king drives his sword into the right eye of the attacker.

Corthag tries to cast another spell, but Arioch closes in. The fine blade of the king strikes the wrist of the necromancer dwarf, cutting his right hand clean off. Though the wound is not fatal to him, Corthag still cries out in pain. The king drives his sword into the gut of the dwarf.

Corthag falls to his knees. "You can't kill me. No matter what you do, I'll be back. Then I'll kill you, Chance, Red Beard, and I'll finish off the Greythorns once and for all."

Ariella, confused, asks, "What do you mean by that?"

Fernando stands before Corthag as Arioch takes a step back. He looks down and sees his family's sword in Corthag's sheath. Corthag grins. "Go on, take it. Use it to avenge your father's death."

Fernando reaches down and reclaims his sword. Ariella joins him, asking, "Fernando, what is he talking about?"

Fernando points the tip of his sword at Corthag's throat. "Orcneas did not kill our father and your mother. It was him."

"No," Ariella replies doubtfully. "That can't be true. Whatever he said to you, he was lying."

"I wish he were."

Corthag taunts, "What are waiting for, boy? Kill me. Just make sure you pay the same respect to Red Beard as well."

"Silence!" Ariella shouts. Turning to Fernando, she continues, "Can't you see? He's just trying to stir trouble. You can't trust anything he says."

Corthag says, "If you don't believe me, Ariella, then ask your father."

Ariella glares at Red Beard's former shipmate. "I intend to. Now, let's see if you can recover with your head removed." Ariella steps back as Fernando strikes his sword across the thick of Corthag's neck. In an instant, the dwarf crumbles to dust.

Fidelma says to her visibly shaken friend, "I'm sorry, I couldn't tell if he was being truthful or not."

"He had to have been lying," she says. "My father may not have been perfect, but he would never kill innocent people."

Arioch motions for them to continue moving. "I don't know if Corthag was telling the truth or not, but I think it may be best to keep this to ourselves and sort this out after the war. I know he's your father, Ariella, but if he is responsible for the *White Feather*, then he must be held accountable, and we just can't deal with that right now."

Ariella nods. "I'll do my best not to say anything, but I can't make any promises."

The group begins to head around another corner when a

fireball strikes Sven in the back. The large backpack with the barrel absorbs the ambush, leaving Sven unharmed. He turns to see a shaman at the far end of the passageway they had come from, and Ariella notices that the backpack is on fire.

"Sven!" she warns. "The keg is on fire."

Sven looks over his shoulder and can see the flames. He says to the others, "Run!" He then scrambles to get the backpack off before throwing it down the hall and diving around the corner. When the keg hits the ground, it breaks open, exposing the black powder inside. It explodes violently, sending a shockwave down the halls.

Moments later, Sven looks up from the ground, surprised to still be alive. He finds A'ranah standing next to him. She is concentrating on a spell that has created a magic barrier between them and the fiery explosion.

"By the gods," gasps Fidelma. "I thought we were dead."

A'ranah looks at Sven. "You did good getting that off of you."

"I should have put out the flames," says Ariella.

Sven gets to his feet. "Sven did not think there was time."

"It doesn't matter now," says Arioch. "We have to get to the power crystal and destroy it the way we did last time. Come on, we're not far."

The group moves on, except for Ariella, who is distracted by her thoughts. Fernando asks her, "Are you all right?"

She nods. "I'll be fine. I was just thinking about my father."

Out at sea, the *Red Dawn* and the other ships wait at a distance. They are far from shore so that if the plan is successful, the wave will not be as destructive. Torgus and Red Beard watch the horizon. The former crew of the *Sea Griffin* is also there. The twins, Faye and Janette, watch the floating city over the rails from the front of the ship.

Faye says, "I have a bad feeling about this."

Samantha says, "If things get bad, I want you and Janette to teleport yourselves to safety. Even if you have to go all the way home."

"But we don't want to leave you," protests Janette.

Samantha shakes her head. "I know, but it won't do any good to stay if this ship is going to be destroyed."

Vindalia says, "I've never had much love for dwarves, but if I had to be on a ship captained by one, the *Red Dawn* is the safest place to be."

"You girls stay close to me," says Samantha.

Seth joins the gathering. He says to Samantha, "I'm surprised you aren't aboard the *Trident*."

"Your brother wanted me to keep an eye on you."

Seth sighs. "I wish he would stop worrying about me. I don't need a watcher."

A loud thump is heard as the *Red Dawn* collides with something in the water. Red Beard shouts, "We're barely moving. What hit us?"

The lookout calls down from the crows-nest, "There's something moving in the water off the port side!"

Torgus leans over the rail to get a better look when the sea drake breaches the surface. He barely manages to get out of the way as the silvery-blue beast rises up next to the ship. Red Beard scowls, "Ya picked the wrong ship to attack, ya damned water demon."

The drake screeches before diving back into the sea. It uses its tail to swipe the deck as it submerges once more. Torgus dives out of the way, but his leg is struck. The gash in his thigh begins to bleed as he makes it back to his feet.

"Quick! Get below deck," Samantha orders the other women.

The twins begin to run, followed by Vindalia. Samantha heads for safety, as well, when she looks back to find Seth standing ready with his sword. "What are you doing?" she queries.

"My duty to the ship," he replies stoically.

"Come on, we don't stand a chance against that thing. Let the spell-casters deal with it."

"There are only two of them."

The drake emerges from the water again. Its front claws dig into the port side railing. It uses its water attack, and Samantha is struck by the jetting stream. The force knocks her down and begins to push her to the far side of the ship. Seth rushes in and swings his sword at the long neck of the drake. The distraction is enough to draw the beast's attention away from Samantha.

The drake lowers its head and slams it into the young man. Seth has the wind knocked out of him as he collides with the foremast. The drake steps onto the deck when it is hit by a lightning spell from Red Beard.

"I told ya, this was the wrong ship to attack," grumbles the old captain. He begins to summon another bolt of lightning when the drake turns around and swings its tail. Torgus and Red Beard hit the deck to avoid the drake's attack.

Just inside the doorway to the officer's quarters, the twins and Vindalia have made it to safety. The former Amazon of the Silver Moon begins to play her fiddle. As the tune's pitch climbs higher, an electrical charge builds up on her bowstring.

The drake begins to use its water jet again, knocking down several crewmen. Samantha makes it to her feet as she looks over and sees Vindalia charging her spell. Samantha rushes at the beast while its attention is focused on the two dwarves at the wheel. She impales the neck of the drake with her sword before releasing the grip on her weapon.

Leaving her sword behind, Samantha shouts, "Vindalia, now!"

The elf uses her bowstring like a sling and hurls the magical bolt at the drake. The protruding steel weapon acts as a lightning rod, making the spell more effective. The sea drake screeches in pain before turning to flee.

Before the beast can make it to the edge of the ship, it is struck again by Red Beard's lightning spell, as well as a fireball from Torgus. The drake falls dead, and the crew sighs with relief. Vindalia and the twins emerge from the officers' quarters as Red Beard comes down from the quarterdeck.

Torgus, still walking with a limp, asks the elf, "Was that you who cast that bolt of lightning?"

Vindalia nods. "Yes, that was me."

"Impressive."

"Thank you, sir."

Red Beard surveys the damage. "Let's get everything secure. There's no telling how much time we have left before that floating city comes down."

Torgus adds, "Assuming they're successful."

Red Beard looks to the fortress floating above the horizon. "They will be, no matter the cost."

Within the deepest chambers below the pyramids, King Arioch

and the others have reached their destination. Mounted in the center of a round room is a massive crystal the size of an adult dwarf. The room is twenty paces in diameter. The crystal, red in color, is affixed to the center of a pillar that reaches all the way to the top of the high vaulted ceiling.

They enter the room and close the door behind them. On the right side of the room is another doorway. Arioch rushes over with his sword drawn to check it out. Looking inside, he sees a smaller room with a stone table in the center but no one inside.

A'ranah asks the others, "Did you feel the mana drop when we entered?"

Ariella tries to cast a spell, but nothing happens. "There's no mana at all."

Fernando wonders, "Without any mana, how does this magic crystal work?"

Arioch says, "My guess is that the no mana zone only surrounds it. They most likely added it to protect the crystal from being destroyed by magic, like we did last time." He points into the smaller room. "When we brought down the last one, we opened a gate in this room. After we left, Tharidin launched a stone missile at it from here and teleported away."

A'ranah enters the smaller room. "There is still mana in here," she notes, creating a small fireball. She throws the spell into the main chamber. As soon as the spell crosses the door's threshold, it disappears. "I was afraid of that," she says with a sigh. "The whole room is protected from magic. We have no way of destroying the crystal without a keg of black powder."

"Yes, we do," says Arioch. "I'll stay behind and destroy it."

"That's not going to happen," argues A'ranah. "We'll just have to come back and destroy it later."

Fernando shakes his head, "By then, the orcnea ships will be safe. They will also be ready for us next time. No, we have to do this now. I'll stay and destroy it."

"No!" insists Ariella. "We didn't come up here and rescue you just so you can try to die again."

Sven walks over and studies the crystal as A'ranah says, "If anyone is going to stay behind, it will be me."

"Why you?" asks the king.

"I have lived a long and full life. My years outnumber all of yours combined. There is nothing new for me to experience."

Arioch takes her hand. "There has to be another way. I don't want to lose you."

"You won't have to," says Sven. The others all look at the goliath as he stands before the crystal with Hellfire drawn. "Sven will stay behind and make sure crystal is destroyed."

Fidelma shakes her head. "No, we'll find another way."

"There is no other way, and you all know this."

A'ranah says, "I already volunteered."

Sven replies, "You may have lived longer than all of us, but you have many more years to live than Sven. Arioch is king, and you are queen. Your people depend on you. Fidelma, Ariella, and Fernando all have family." Looking at Annalee, he continues, "And you, little one, have barely begun to live."

Fidelma argues, "But you have family, too, Sven."

"Sven left his family long ago. He is alone now."

After taking a moment to reflect on the half-giant's words, A'ranah says to Arioch, "I'll send the signal to the others to evacuate. We'll need to give them time to go."

The Amazon queen enters the other room and concentrates on a spell as Arioch and the others wait in the main chamber with the crystal. Arioch says, "You are a brave man, Sven. I'll make sure to buy you a drink in the afterlife."

Sven chuckles, "Just make sure you build big statue of Sven in center of Sheathelm."

"I will," says the king with a smile.

Fernando extends hand. "Your sacrifice will not be forgotten."

Sven shakes Fernando's hand. "Make sure they sing songs of this day, and make sure you keep smelling roses for Sven."

"I will do that, my friend."

Fidelma looks up at her former love with tears welling in her eyes. Sven wipes Fidelma's cheek, and says, "Make sure that when bards sing songs of Sven, they do not forget you. Sven's story would not be complete without you in it."

"You said you were alone," Fidelma sniffles. "What about Lyra?"

"Sven hopes she will understand."

"Is there anything you would like me to tell her?"

"Yes," he says sadly. "If you could tell her..." Sven falls silent as he struggles to speak.

In all the years that Fidelma has known him, she has only seen him in this state one other time. When she left him. Now, the goliath tries to find the words to tell his former love, so that she can relay his message to his new love. Fidelma takes his hand and pulls him towards the other room. "Come in here so I can read your thoughts," she says.

Sven follows her to the adjacent room. Fidelma reaches up with both hands clasping his face. She whispers, "Now you don't have to say it. Just think it, and feel it. I promise I'll make sure she gets your message."

"You would really do that for Sven?"

Fidelma nods. "Absolutely. Just close your eyes and think about what you want to tell her."

Sven does as instructed while Fidelma channels her spell. As Sven's thoughts fill her mind, the two begin to cry freely.

Trying her best to give Fidelma and Sven the space they need, Ariella spots three more large crystals on a table at the far end of the room. While they are not as big as the one holding up the fortress, they are still enormous. She says to her brother, "Fernando, help me gather these." Fernando and Annalee each grab one of the crystals as Ariella picks up the third.

Up top, the elves and the humans are making their escape through several magic portals leading back to the stronghold. Nicari struggles to help the wounded Serena to the nearest gate.

"You should leave me behind," says Serena.

"Is that what you would do? Leave me?"

"No," Serena laughs, "but I can carry you."

Nicari jests. "Well, if you weren't so heavy, I could carry you, too."

An orcnea charges at them, but is struck down by a stone hurled by Adolayn. She rushes over and helps Nicari assist Serena the rest of the way to the gate.

The women enter as the last Amazon of the Silver Moon sounds a horn before entering herself.

Down below, A'ranah says to Arioch, "It's time to go."

Looking at Sven and Fidelma, the king says, "We'll give them another moment."

Fernando watches as Fidelma finishes reading Sven's thoughts. Fidelma embraces the goliath, neither saying another word. Fidelma slowly backs away before turning and running to Ariella. Fidelma is comforted by her friend as Arioch takes out the gate-stone.

There is a thump at the entrance of the main chamber. Sven hurries to the center of the room and stands before the main crystal. He says, "Hurry, they're trying to get in."

Arioch says, "Let's hope this works." He crumbles the sandstone medallion, and a magic gate appears.

A'ranah and Annalee are the first to enter. Fidelma, Ariella, and Fernando follow them. The king says to Sven, "Good luck, and may the warmth of the light embrace you."

The king enters the gate as the entry door begins to buckle. Sven looks at the crystal as he draws back his weapon. "Forgive me, Lyra." As the door finally gives, Sven adds, "They will sing songs of this day."

Chapter 31
The Fallen

At the apartment, Lyra abruptly stops reading from the large leather-bound book. Struggling to hold back her emotions, she hands it to Ambra, saying, "If you'll all excuse me for a minute..."

"Of course," says Ambra. "I'll continue from here."

"Thank you," says Lyra as she heads towards the sliding glass door.

Laura watches her closely, noting the sadness in her expression. Lyra walks out onto the balcony to gather herself. As soon as she closes the door behind her, Laura asks, "Is she all right?"

Ambra nods. "She just gets emotional with this book." Ambra scans the page, trying to find where they left off. Soon she comes across the line and begins to read.

****

On the docks of Sheathelm, the orcnea's High Chief lands and transforms just as the explosion can be heard from the floating city. He turns and watches as the bottom of the landmass begins to crumble and fall. Carr Vork and Lortec Ka join their leader as the rest of the city begins to slip from the sky.

The High Chief says, "Carr, you and the other shamans will hold back the wave. Lortec, you will fetch Chance Na'Moon and the female elf, and bring them to me in the Colosseum while I begin to open the gate of banishment."

Lortec nods. "So, we are sending them to the same desolate place they imprisoned the dark dragon, Zetamat."

"Not exactly," replies the High Chief.

"Then what is our plan?"

"We are summoning the dark dragon, and Chance Na'Moon will be our gift to him once he arrives."

"You can't be serious." replies Lortec, clearly concerned.

"I am," says the High Chief. "I have been in contact with Zetamat for some time. He is ready to return, and when he does he will make King Arioch and all of our enemies pay." He looks at his general. "Is there a problem?"

Lortec shakes his head. "No, High Chief. I will get Chance Na'Moon at once."

Below the city, the Amazons of the Silver Moon are nearing where Chance is being held. Lyra, leading the way, suddenly stops.

Va'leen asks, "Do you hear something?"

"No," Lyra replies. "Something's not right."

Evelena says, "We've been walking in circles for some time. Are you sure you can find the way?"

"That's not it," says Lyra. "I know we're close. I just felt something. I don't know how to explain it, but something's wrong."

Va'leen says, "You all stay here. I'll go look up ahead." Va'leen quickly but quietly forges ahead as the others stay back. Soon, the dark-haired Amazon hears orcnea voices echoing in the tunnels. She makes her way to a corner, and as she peeks around it, she spots two guards standing in front of a heavy door. Further down the passage, general Ka and the ogre, Cron, come down a flight of stairs before turning in the direction of the door. Va'leen ducks back around the corner to avoid being seen before hurrying back to fetch the others.

On the other side of the door, Chance and Re'ann are locked away in their cell. Lortec enters the room, followed by Cron. The orcnea general says to the guards, "Report to the walls immediately. The floating city has been brought down, and we expect an attack soon."

The two guards looks at each other doubtfully, when the ogre snaps, "Now!" The guards take their leave.

As Lortec looks through his keys to unlock the cell, he says to Cron, "Make sure no one is out there." The ogre looks out the door as the guards make their way up the stairs.

"They are gone," says Cron.

"What's going on?" asks Chance.

Lortec opens the cell before stepping inside. "Chance, did you really mean what you said in the Colosseum? Do you really believe there can be peace between our people?"

Confused, Chance answers, "Yes... I did. Why?"

"I am setting you both free."

Re'ann inquires, "What do you mean by that?"

Cron also enters the cell as Lortec begins to explain. "My High Chief has betrayed us."

Out in the hall, Va'leen and the others have returned. Va'leen checks around the corner only to find the guards that were there are now gone. Fearing that they have already taken Chance away, she rushes for the door. "Come on," she says to the others.

Inside, Lortec unlocks the collar around Chance's neck as he continues, "You must return to your king and tell him that our High Chief plans to open the Gate of Banishment."

Va'leen enters the room with her dagger drawn. "Get away from him now, or I will kill you where you stand."

"Wait!" cautions Chance, as he puts himself between the door and the general.

"Wait?" Va'leen repeats questioningly. "Chance, what's going on?"

"He's letting us go," Chance replies as Lortec begins to release Re'ann.

Gelana enters the room as Va'leen motions for the others to stand down. Lortec says to them, "In a few moments my High Chief will set free the dark dragon, Zetamat."

"There may be time to stop him," says Chance.

"Perhaps, if I had time to prepare," replies Lortec. "But I was unaware of his plans until a short while ago. The Colosseum is well guarded, and I have not been able to spread the word among my men."

The ground shakes, and Va'leen says, "It's too late, the gate is now opening. We have to go."

Chance says to Lortec, "Thank you."

Lortec shakes his head. "I'll never understand why you thank me so much. This is not over yet. I have a plan, but it will take some time. Go now, with your friends. Tell Arioch that when the time is right, I will make my move. When that happens, it is important that our people fight together. When it is over, if we are both alive, you can thank me by granting me an audience with you and your king."

"Come on," says Va'leen to Chance and Re'ann. "Follow us."

Gelana says, "I hope we can find our way out faster than it took to find him."

Evelena replies, "We'll just follow the water upstream. It only comes from one source."

Cron says to Lortec, "What are we going to do now?"

Lortec shuts the cell door. "We will wait here in the cell and say they locked us in. No one will understand why we let them go."

"Good luck," says Chance. "May your gods watch over you."

Chance and the others exit the room into the passageway. They start to head back the way they came when an arrow strikes Re'ann in the back of her right shoulder. They turn to see an orcnea coming down the stairs. The guard yells out in Orcneish and begins to nock another arrow. Kel'ana quickly fires an icy arrow from her bow Glacies. The orcnea falls down the stairs, but is dead before he hits the floor.

"Hurry, more will be coming soon," says Evelena.

"Let me get the arrow out of you," Yentroc says to Re'ann.

As Yentroc removes the arrow, Ja'noa takes out a leaf from a pouch on her belt. She says, "Eat this in case the arrow was poisoned."

Re'ann puts the leaf in her mouth and begins to chew it as Yentroc heals her shoulder. Soon the sound of guards can be heard coming down the stairs.

"Let's move!" says Chance.

As the group begins to flee under the city of Sheathelm, back at the stronghold, Arioch and the group that assaulted the floating city are taking positions at the top of the hill to avoid the tidal wave that is soon to come.

Fernando comments, "Let's hope this is high enough."

"Even if it's not," says A'ranah, "it will be easier to hold back the water with magic this time. We don't have to worry about the entire length of a city."

Jadelyn approaches the Amazon queen. "Mother Elder, do you feel it? Someone has opened a gate, a powerful one."

A'ranah turns to Arioch. "Do you think the orcneas are bringing reinforcements from the Red Rock Plains?"

The king looks at Sheathelm. "Let's hope that's all it is."

Out at sea, as the enormous wave approaches the fleet of ships, Red Beard says to Torgus, "It's a good thing we're further out to sea, otherwise we may not be able to stop it."

Vindalia comes up to the top of the poop deck to join them. "Can I do something to help?"

Torgus nods. "We're going to create a trough in the water so when the wave arrives, it will fill it first and soften the blow."

"I can help with that," she says as she lifts her instrument to her chin. Vindalia glides her bow across the strings and begins to play a tune.

Torgus and Red Beard watch as the water below them begins to move. As the elven female continues to play, the water begins to part. Red Beard gives Torgus a nod. "Let's not make this lass do all the work."

The dwarves begin to add their magic to the spell while aboard the other ships, all spell-casters that can do so begin to follow the same procedure. After a short while, the water looks as though a shallow, wide canyon has been carved into it.

The water from the wave arrives, flowing over the edge and down into the chasm. While most of the water harmlessly fills the void, there is a thunderous crash as the wave reaches the near side of the trough. Mist fills the air, soaking the ships along the edge. Though they are wet, the ships are safe.

On the docks of Sheathelm, Carr Vork and the shamans manage to protect the shore from the incoming wave. As the water recedes, the general heads towards the Colosseum, where the dark dragon is being summoned.

In the center of the arena, a stone ring twenty paces in diameter lies horizontally on the floor. The sand that once hid the magic gateway from view has been blown away. The gate is now active and surrounded by dozens of orcnea soldiers. An enormous black-scaled neck begins to emerge as the forces back away, nervously gripping their weapons. The dark head appears as the massive creature—fifty paces in length—begins to climb out of the magical hole in the ground. Its claws dig into the sand, gouging trenches as it pulls the dragon forward. Its wide torso barely manages to fit through the stone gate.

The High Chief looks on, grinning as the enormous beast exits. Its long tail is the last part to make the journey from the other realm, and the magic gateway closes behind it.

The dark dragon surveys its surroundings. Its eyes seem to glow compared to the dark scales. With a voice so thunderous and deep that it can be felt as well as heard, Zetamat asks, "Where is Chance Na'Moon?"

Lortec and Cron enter the arena. Lortec says, "They escaped."

"How is that possible?" asks the High Chief angrily.

Lortec bows his head. "There was a small group that rescued them. Cron and I were locked in the cell as they fled. Dozens are in pursuit as we speak. We will get them back."

Cron, looking at the dark dragon, tries to hide his rage. Zetamat lies down and extends his wings. The right wing is noticeably damaged. The dragon says, "The banished lands have low levels of mana. I must take a moment to rest. I may not be able to fly, but I can still defeat King Arioch and his forces."

The High Chief replies, "Your efforts will be much appreciated."

"I will be ready to fight soon."

Carr arrives as the High Chief says to his generals, "Prepare everyone for battle."

The three generals bow their heads before leaving to make preparations.

High above, on the backs of their sky drakes, Belron, Ashden, and Prince River look down upon the city. When Belron spies the dark dragon, he says to the prince, "River, you go and tell Kianna and Baeldeth that the orcneas have summoned Zetamat. Ashden, you go and warn the ships. I'll tell Arioch."

While the three drake riders head off to warn the others, under the ground just outside the city, Chance and the Amazons have reached the underground reservoir.

"Our ice bridge has melted," says Kel'ana.

"We don't have time to make another," says Va'leen. "Kel'ana, can you and Ja'noa make it so that Gelana, Rehma, and Evelena can walk on the water's surface?"

"Yes," Kel'ana answers.

"Good. The rest of us have light armor and should be able to swim."

Kel'ana casts a spell on Rehma. "You should able to cross now."

Rehma steps onto the water gingerly. "It's working. Lyra, get on my back, and I can take you across."

While Lyra climbs onto Rehma's back, Kel'ana casts the spell on Gelana. Ja'noa casts the same spell on Evelena. Yentroc climbs onto Gelana.

Re'ann says, "I'll swim across."

"So will I," says Chance.

Va'leen transforms into a dark mist. She glides across as Kel'ana and Ja'noa cast the spell on themselves before making it to the other side.

Gelana helps Re'ann out of the water as Rehma pulls up Chance.

"Come on," Va'leen beckons them.

Chance cries out in pain as he is struck with a spear in the back of his leg. The others turn to see an orcnea on the other side of the water. Ja'noa quickly hurls her Star Steel daggers at the foe, killing him instantly.

Va'leen and Yentroc rush over to check on Chance as he lies on the ground in pain."I'll pull it out, and you heal him," says Va'leen. Yentroc nods. Va'leen removes the spear as Chance groans loudly through gritted teeth. Yentroc concentrates on her healing spell and the wound is repaired.

Chance rolls over and sits up before leaning back against a small boulder. He flexes and extends his leg to test it. "Thank you."

"Anytime," says Yentroc.

As the others start to leave once more, Rehma kneels down and offers her hand to help Chance get back to his feet. Chance grasps her hand, but as he looks over her shoulder, he spots another orcnea emerging from the dark passage on the others side of the water. Before Chance can warn the others, the enemy hurls a barbed tip spear at Rehma's back. Chance pulls at Rehma's arm with all his might. Not ready for such an action, Rehma falls to the side, narrowly avoiding the spear. Instead, the pointed weapon finds its mark in the Chance's ribcage.

The others turn to see what the commotion is all about to find orcneas flooding through the doorway. Kel'ana readies Glacies and picks one off as Ja'noa throws her Star Steel daggers once more. Gelana summons Infragilis and makes her way back to Chance as Rehma makes it to her feet. Evelena takes refuge behind her shield as she also makes her way back to the water.

The orcneas with bows begin to release their arrows. One strikes Yentroc in the arm, while another hits Rehma. Fortunately, Rehma's armor protects her from the arrow, but with the enemies on the other side of the water, there isn't much she can do to fight back. She casts a spell to increase her speed, hoping she will be able to do more with the precious time they have.

Gelana positions herself in front of Chance. Rehma checks on him, but finds him motionless. She looks for Yentroc and finds her ducking for cover as she holds onto her wounded arm. Though everything is happening fast, Rehma is able to study the entire cavern.

Re'ann is summoning a stone to hurl at the orcneas, while Kel'ana and Ja'noa continue to their attacks. Evelena is providing cover for Re'ann and Lyra. Va'leen becomes a dark mist and glides back over the water to where the orcneas are.

One of them swings wildly at the mist but it has no effect. Va'leen becomes tangible once more as she drives her dagger into the neck of the orcnea before her. As the orcnea next to her shifts his attention, Va'leen protects herself by creating an area of darkness around them. While the orcnea is blind within the spell's area of effect, Va'leen can see normally. She makes quick work of the enemy.

A shaman enters the battle with a magical spell protecting him from the arrows and spells being thrown by the Amazons. When the shaman spots the area of darkness, he begins to cast a spell. Va'leen emerges in her dark mist form and prepares to attack the shaman when his spell goes off.

A flash of light blinds everyone looking in the shaman's direction. It has a particularly powerful effect on Va'leen in her dark form. Her spell is interrupted and she falls to the ground, stunned. The shaman turns his attention to Evelena as she stays protected behind her shield. He casts a bolt of lightning, and even though the young Amazon blocks the attack, her shield offers little protection. The bolt sends a shock through her body, knocking her unconscious.

The situation rapidly gets out of hand for the small group. Rehma watches her companions struggle to see clearly while the shaman takes his time to target them with bolts of lightning. Gelana grabs Rehma's arm and the two move over to Evelena. Lyra throws a beam of light at the shaman before also taking cover behind Gelana and her magical shield, Infragilis. Unfortunately, the shaman's spell protects him from Lyra's attack.

"What are we going to do?" asks Rehma trying to remain calm.

"We have to get out of here," says Gelana. "You two carry Evelena. I'll go and cover Ja'noa and Kel'ana."

Lyra asks, "What about Chance and Va'leen?"

Rehma looks over at Chance. He is covered with blood and hasn't moved. "I think he's gone, and we can't reach Va'leen."

A lightening spell strikes Kel'ana, and she falls to the ground. Gelana says, "Now!"

Rehma and Lyra pick up Evelena and begin to flee, with Re'ann close on their heels. Gelana rushes over to Kel'ana and assists Ja'noa with picking her up. Gelana says, "Once we get them to safety, I want you to cast that spell on me again so I can cross the water."

"You're going back?" asks Ja'noa, concerned.

"I can take that shaman if I can reach him."

More orcneas enter the chamber. Va'leen manages to take on her dark mist form and cross the water before the shaman casts another flash spell. Va'leen cries out in agony as her spell is ended once more. She lands hard on the ground next to Chance.

A bolt of lightning strikes Rehma, and she falls to ground, dropping Evelena. Looking back, she sees the orcneas preparing more spells. A glint of gold light from Evelena's belt catches Rehma's eye. Upon further inspection, she spots the Horn of the Fallen.

Thinking back to when the horn was given to Evelena by the Moon Dragon, Lunarus, Rehma remembers the dragon telling them, *"I hope you never find yourselves is a situation that you will need it. You may blow into it if you wish. It will not do anything out of the ordinary unless it is truly needed."*

Evelena asked, *"What will it do if it IS needed?"*

The dragon replied, *"It calls for help from a long lost guardian."*

The memory fades, and with her body shaking from the effects of getting struck with a spell, Rehma pushes through the pain as she reaches down to grab the horn from Evelena's belt. Putting it to her lips, Rehma blows as hard as she can through the horn of gold and ivory.

The battle falls silent as a ghostly white spirit appears before Rehma. It is a female elven warrior in full battle armor. Her presence illuminates the entire cavern. The guardian spirit smiles at Rehma before turning to the orcneas.

In a fraction of a second, the warrior is across the water and begins to strike down the orcneas with blazing speed. Rehma watches as Evelena wakes. Gelana sets Kel'ana down and goes to check on Va'leen. Rehma joins her as the spirit warrior disappears down the passageway towards the city. Sounds of fighting can be heard from down the passageway as orcneas let out frightful yells. Then, there is silence.

Va'leen sits up. "What happened?"

"I'm not exactly sure," says Rehma.

The women are startled when Chance gasps for air. "Thank the gods, he's still alive," says Va'leen.

The ground rumbles as dust flies out of the passageway.

"It's collapsing," says Evelena.

"Let's get Chance out of here," says Gelana.

"Wait," says Chance, his eyes focused on the other side of the water.

The women turn around as the guardian spirit enters the chamber. "It is safe now," the spirit says, her voice commanding yet distant.

Chance smiles. "Teresa, is that you?"

The female spirit crosses over the water as everyone looks on in awe. "Chance, it is good to see you again." She kneels down. "Thank you for looking after my daughter, though I wish it did not come at so high a price."

"I guess we're even now," Chance says with a painful laugh and a cough.

"Mother?!" gasps Rehma, now realizing who the spirit is. "Is it really you?"

The essence of Teresa La'harn stands and faces her daughter. "Yes, Rehma, it's me. Let me look at you." She steps back and looks Rehma over. "You've grown so much. I'm so proud of you."

Still at a loss for words, Rehma doesn't know what to say. Tears stream down her face. "I miss you."

"And I miss you." Teresa takes her daughter's hand. "Never forget that I am always with you. I may not be always able to help you, or hold you, but I am always there." She kneels next to Chance. "I'm glad you were able to meet Chance and forgive him."

"Is he going to be all right?"

Teresa takes out a knife. She uses the ghostly weapon to slice off the shaft of the spear impaled in Chance. "He doesn't have much time left."

"Can't you heal him?" asks Va'leen as she holds Chance's hand.

Teresa shakes her head. "My skills are limited to those I had in life, though I am faster and stronger."

Rehma turns to Yentroc. "Can you heal him?"

Yentroc sighs. "We would have to pull out the rest of the spear. Even with my crystal, I think the damage is too great. If I hadn't healed him already, I might be able to help."

Teresa says, "You have to leave the spear in him until you get back to the others. The moment it comes out, he could die."

Va'leen squeezes Chance's hand. "Please hold on. We didn't go through all this for you to die on us now." Chance forces a smile.

Teresa stands and embraces her daughter. "My time here is up. I give you my remaining strength. Hurry, or he won't survive." The guardian spirit casts a spell. As Teresa fades away, a white aura emanates from Rehma before being absorbed into her body.

With a newfound strength, Rehma bends down and takes Chance in her arms. Though he is in pain, she knows she has no time to wait. "Come on," she says, "we have to get him back to camp."

Chapter 32
The Traitor

To the west, Kianna, holding the banner of Ravenguard, is with Isen, and Ya'leigh. They wait with, Baeldeth, and Kristieana as they look over the city of Sheathelm. Prince River is also there, on the back of the sky drake. River says to the others, "We should fall back to the stronghold now that the water is receding."

"With all due respect, my prince," argues Baeldeth, "there are more than enough of us to take on Zetamat."

Kianna, unaware of the orcnea general's plan, replies, "The dark dragon on its own is powerful enough, but we're facing the orcneas, too. Besides, most of the spell-casters that have any chance of hurting him were part of the assault on the floating city."

"So what are we supposed to do, run?"

The roar of the dark dragon can be heard for miles. They shift their gaze to the city and watch as Zetamat climbs over the walls of the Colosseum and moves towards the west wall. Kianna says, "We better start back now, then."

Baeldeth shouts out to the troops, "Fall back to the stronghold! Maintain your formation!"

"I'll do what I can from the sky," says River, taking flight.

As the prince takes to the sky, Kianna shouts, "Be careful!"

In the city of Sheathelm, orcneas scatter in the streets to get out of the dragon's way. Zetamat pays them no mind, stepping on many that fail to move.

At the front gate of the city, the High Chief is with Lortec, Carr, and Cron. They are perched on top of one of the towers next to the main gate, watching as the dark dragon makes its way recklessly through the streets.

Lortec snaps, "It was a mistake summoning him. He does not care who he kills."

"He will bring us victory," argues the High Chief.

"But at what cost?"

The High Chief eyes the general. "I will not be questioned by you. Carr told me how you have befriended our enemy. You are a traitor."

"I have not befriended anyone," retorts Lortec. "But you have made an ally with one of our worst enemies—or have you forgotten the dragon war? If anyone here is traitor, it is you, High Chief."

The High Chief looks at his generals. He asks the ogre, "What do you think of this, Cron? Do you stand with Lortec?"

The ogre general nods. "I do."

The High Chief steps back to the edge of the tower. Carr also makes room as the tensions rise. Lortec continues to stand his ground while Cron grips his mace firmly in his hands. The High Chief sighs. "If you stand with Lortec, then you can die with him, as well."

A bolt of lightning shoots forth from the High Chief's staff, striking Cron. It took no time at all for the spell to be channeled. Cron falls down the flight of stairs into the tower. As Lortec checks on his friend, the High Chief uses his staff to strike the general in the back with another bolt of lightning.

Undaunted, Lortec turns around before grabbing the High Chief by the collar of his shirt. "Your spells do not affect me."

"Unhand me," demands the High Chief.

"I will unhand you," says Lortec as he draws his knife with his other hand, "once I have gutted you." Lortec drives his knife into the belly of his leader. The High Chief tries to break away, but he is no match for Lortec's strength. The orcnea general proceeds to run the blade up the length of the High Chief's torso, nearly splitting him in two. As blood and entrails fall to the ground, Lortec grabs the High Chief's staff. As the last bit of life fades from the orcnea leader, Lortec throws him over the edge of the tower.

The orcnea general peers over the edge at his former leader when a dark spell hits him from behind. Lortec falls to his knees as he looks behind him.

Carr begins to cast another dark bolt. "Our High Chief may have forgotten the spells that affect you, but I have not. You may be protected from most of the elements, but not the dark college." Carr releases another bolt, further injuring Lortec.

"I thought you were on our side," says Lortec, his life fading. "You stood and watched me kill the High Chief."

Carr grins. "Only because I knew you could kill him. Now you and I are the only ones left in line to lead."

Lortec, struggling to speak, says, "If you want to lead, I will not stand in your way, but we must stop Zetamat before it's too late."

"I plan to," says Carr. "AFTER he has killed the humans and elves."

"This war is over," says Lortec. "It was lost with our troops at sea, and you are a fool to believe that Zetamat will not turn on us once he is done."

"My staff will bring him down."

Lortec shakes his head. "Not before we lose thousands more."

Carr begins to charge another dark bolt. "You have lost your way. Victory is within our grasp, and you would give it up."

"Perhaps you're right," says Lortec through gasps for air. "Maybe I have lost my way. Maybe peace is not possible. But you are wrong about one thing."

"Oh, and what is that?" inquires Carr.

"You and I are not the only ones left." Lortec's gaze shifts beyond Carr.

The shaman general turns to find Cron towering over him. Carr tries to release his dark bolt at the ogre, but his spell is not as fast as Cron's mace. The heavy steel weapon completely crushes the shaman's skull.

Cron grabs Carr's staff before his body falls down the stairs below. Lortec says, "I thought the High Chief killed you. I'm glad I was wrong."

Cron kneels to check on Lortec. "I am hurt, but not as bad as you. I will fetch you a healing potion."

"Good. I will need to be at my best if I am to offer any help against Zetamat."

"I'll be back soon," says Cron.

Back at the stronghold, Belron has already informed the king of their recent discovery. He is with Arioch and A'ranah, and they watch the dark dragon begin to climb over the wall of Sheathelm as it heads towards the troops now retreating from the west.

"We have to help them," says A'ranah.

"I'll try to keep his focus on me," says Belron. Then, commanding his drake, he says, "Up, Nimbus!" The captain of the drake riders flies upward.

Va'leen comes out of the tower. Out of breath, she says, "Mother, we have Chance. The general he fought in the arena let us go."

"He let you go?" inquires the king.

"Yes, but Chance suffered a wound in the escape. We have to help him. Rehma is bringing him up now."

"Yarwin!" calls A'ranah. "Gather a few of the sisters who can heal."

"Yes, Mother Elder," she replies.

Va'leen continues, "The general said that when the time is right, he will help us take down Zetamat. He said something about the High Chief betraying them. I think the general wants peace."

"I'm sure they do, now that we brought down that floating city," A'ranah comments.

Arioch looks back out at his forces. "Zetamat uses a dark breath spell. Do you have any ward spells for that?"

A'ranah replies, "I do, but nothing I have will be enough to protect you from his bite, tail, or claws."

"My sword will have to do for that. Now hurry, our daughter is in danger."

Out on the battlefield, the dark dragon gives chase to Princess Kianna and her companions. The orcneas, unaware of Lortec's plans, charge onto the plains as well. While the human and elven forces continue to fall back to the stronghold, the archers fire volleys at the pursuing enemy.

Zetamat stops and turns his head away from the arrows. The attack does nothing to the black-scaled behemoth. Zetamat charges a breath attack. Instead of fire, a dark ball of energy shoots forth from the dragon's mouth. The spell hits in the center of a group of archers. When it strikes the ground, it explodes, sending its dark energy everywhere. A half dozen perish immediately, while more are left wounded.

Prince River drops a fire elixir on the back of the dragon from above. Zetamat quickly releases another dark spell towards the prince, striking the side of the sky drake. The flying mount screeches in pain as it begins to lose altitude.

With River no longer a threat, Zetamat spots the princess once again, and begins to follow. Isen, seeing that they are the target, says, "Is it just me, or is it coming for us?"

Kianna looks at the banner in her hands. "It's coming for this."

Isen snatches the banner from the princess's grasp. "Ya'leigh, increase my speed."

"What are you doing?" asks Kristieana.

"The duty I swore."

Ya'leigh concentrates on her spell, and soon the world slows down for Isen. The princess's bodyguard says, "Keep moving towards the stronghold. I'll try to buy you enough time."

"Isen, wait!" calls Kristieana. But it is too late. Isen starts to sprint back towards the dark dragon, carrying the banner of Sheathelm.

Baeldeth sighs. "I don't suppose you have enough strength left to cast that on me?"

"I do," replies Ya'leigh.

"You're going to get yourselves killed," says Kristieana.

Baeldeth laughs. "I'd rather die fighting at my ally's side than live while they fight alone. He won't last long without me, but I can increase our chance of success. Now, cast it and go."

Ya'leigh casts the spell once more, leaving her exhausted. Kristieana and the princess assist Ya'leigh as they continue to retreat.

Toward the stronghold, Arioch is beginning to lead a charge with reinforcements. They are on foot, and the king realizes that if they don't hurry, they may be too late to help.

Prince River brings his drake in and lands safely near the stronghold. He looks up and spots Belron joining with Ashden on their mounts. Re'ann emerges from the tower in the stronghold. Seeing the prince with his wounded drake, she rushes over.

"Is he hurt?" she asks.

"Yes," replies the prince.

"Stand back and let me help." The prince backs away as the drake rider inspects the injured mount. The scales on its right side are scorched from the spell. Re'ann concentrates on a spell. "Let's get you healed up, boy."

Out on the field of battle, Baeldeth has caught up with Isen. "What are you doing?" asks Isen.

"You didn't really think I'd let you fight alone, did you?"

"I didn't think there was any reason for both of us to die."

"I plan on living to see tomorrow, and many days after that."

Isen stops running and drives the base of the banner's pole into the ground.

Baeldeth says, "I'll go right, you go left."

The human and elven archers fire another round of arrows. This time, they target the orcneas following Zetamat. The orcneas stop their advance and take cover under their shields. The dark dragon tries to hit Isen with its breath attack. Fortunately, his increased speed allows him to avoid being hit as he begins to flank the dragon. Zetamat faces Isen, turning his back to Baeldeth.

As they continue to flee, Kianna looks back. "It's working. They're actually doing it."

Kristieana hesitantly looks back to see Isen dodge another spell from the dragon. She watches as Baeldeth moves in.

With his focus on Isen, Zetamat leaves himself open to an attack from Prince River's bodyguard. Baeldeth slashes the left hind leg of the black scaled beast. The dragon roars, both out of frustration and because of the pain caused by Baeldeth's sword.

The thrill of damaging the enemy is short lived, however, as Zetamat pivots around, slashing his claws across Baeldeth's body. The powerful blow not only cuts into his armor, but sends him backwards over twenty paces. Baeldeth clutches his chest, trying to stop the bleeding.

Isen rushes in and tries to draw the attention back to himself by striking the dragon with his fiery morning star. He hits the other hind leg, but while the attack is a solid hit, it does little damage. Zetamat sweeps its tail around, knocking Isen to the ground. The dragon grabs Isen with his right claw, picking him up. The pressure is immense, and Isen can barely breathe.

A fire elixir burns the dragon's back. Zetamat looks up to the sky to see Belron preparing to make another pass. The dragon releases a dark bolt at the captain, striking Nimbus.

Advancing with the rest of the king's reinforcements, Nicari watches the sky drake crash to the ground with her husband. "Belron!" she cries. Still at a great distance, Nicari casts the same spell that Ya'leigh cast on Isen and Baeldeth. She begins to rapidly pull away from the rest of the king's forces.

The orcneas begin to launch spells and arrows at the troops in range. Zetamat, still clutching Isen in its claw, slams him to the ground with crushing force. Isen can feel his ribs crack as the wind is knocked out of him.

The dark dragon eyes Belron as he checks on his injured steed. Arioch, watching from a distance, says, "We have to attack now."

"We're still too far away," replies A'ranah. "Our spells will be weak." The Amazon queen spots Nicari nearing Belron. "By the gods, no." She begins to summon a spell in her hands as Arioch continues on.

Zetamat makes his way to captain of the drake riders as Ashden throws his elixir. The dark dragon ignores him, as the fire is barely a nuisance. Nimbus, badly hurt, hisses at the much larger dragon. The blue scaled drake puts itself between Zetamat and its rider.

"No, Nimbus," begs Belron. "Fly. Let's go."

Zetamat says with his low rumbling voice, "Loyal 'til the very end." The dark dragon opens its jaws, sending forth another dark bolt. Nimbus absorbs the attack before collapsing.

A'ranah throws her spell at her towering foe. But Zetamat rears up on its hind legs and uses its front claws to catch the spell. Surprised, the Amazon queen watches in horror as the dark dragon hurls the spell back at Arioch and the advancing forces. The spell hits the ground with a thunderous impact. Arioch and others are knocked to the ground.

Nicari is now close enough to her husband that she draws her twisted daggers and lets them fly at the dark dragon. Both daggers strike the beast in the chest. Zetamat grasps the weapons before pulling them out.

Belron, standing in front of his mortally wounded drake, now sees his wife. "What are you doing?"

Nicari joins him, standing by his side. "I couldn't stand back and watch. Come on, let's hurry."

"No, my leg is hurt. I can't run. Save yourself, please."

Nicari looks up at the dark dragon, who is now focused on them. Still clutching the twisted daggers in its claw, Zetamat prepares to throw another spell.

Nicari takes her husband's hand. "I love you."

Belron embraces her. "I love you, too."

The two lovers close their eyes as a spell strikes the dark dragon in the back. This spell causes Zetamat a great deal of pain. The dark bolt is sent harmlessly into the air as the dragon turns around to find Lortec standing atop the tower with Carr's staff in one hand and the High Chief's staff in the other.

"Traitor!" bellows Zetamat.

Using the staff of their former leader, Lortec is able to be heard by everyone as he speaks. "I am no traitor. The High Chief betrayed our people when he made a deal with you."

Arioch makes it back to his feet. He signals to everyone, and soon all the spell-casters begin to charge their spells.

Belron and Nicari open their eyes. With the dragon's attention elsewhere, they tend to Nimbus. Now safely with the others, Ya'leigh and Kianna stop running. The daughter of Chance draws her bow Incendia while the princess begins to summon a sphere of ice.

Zetamat edges closer to castle walls, saying to Lortec, "I offer you victory over your enemies, and you betray me."

The orcneas down below, as well as all the forces on both sides, hold their actions nervously as they listen. Lortec replies, "Everyone here knows what the elves and the humans have put us through. But few remember what you and your dragon slayer forces did to our people. It was before my time, but from what I am told, you left no survivors. You had no mercy. King Arioch and Chance Na'Moon may have driven us from these lands, but at least they tried to spare the women and the children. You murdered all." The orcneas, now curious, listen as their general continues. "You are just using us to enact your revenge on those who defeated you, and when you are done with them, you will no doubt turn your back on us, or worse."

Zetamat, slowly closing in on the tower, says, "When we are done with Arioch, we can move on to the rest of Bruen. We can rule all of Runefell."

"There has been enough death already."

"You cannot win without my help."

"After you are gone, I plan to seek an audience with Arioch to discuss peace."

Zetamat's laugh echoes for miles. "Arioch will take back everything you've gained. You will be banished to the north once again."

"I would rather live in the tundra of the north, free, than rule over rubble at the end of your chain."

"I've heard enough of this nonsense." Zetamat attacks the base of the tower with a dark bolt. The stone structure crumbles, with Cron and Lortec on top. They fall with the tumbling stone.

Zetamat turns its attention toward Arioch. "Now it is time for you to die."

A bolt of lightning strikes the dark dragon from its rear flank. Zetamat looks over to find a shaman, preparing another spell. A second shaman releases a spell, striking the beast, followed by a third.

Zetamat fires back with a spell of his own, killing several orcneas. "I will make you all pay!"

Arioch shouts to his men, "Try to avoid the orcneas!" He then gives the signal to his forces and the sky fills with spells and arrows.

The attacks rain down on the dark dragon. Zetamat's roar fills the air as the dark dragon flees toward the sea. Orcnea shamans continue to fire upon the fleeing dragon as it crashes through the streets of Sheathelm. Now badly wounded, the common foe reaches the water's edge.

The *Red Dawn* and the elven fleet greet the dark dragon with a barrage of spells of their own. Though he is in great pain, Zetamat manages to dive below the surface of the water and escape.

Back on shore, everyone focuses their attention on their original enemies. Arioch shouts as loud as he can. "Hold! Hold your attacks!" Though tensions are high, everyone heeds his words.

Arioch, flanked by A'ranah and a host of soldiers, checks on Baeldeth. Kristieana, Ya'leigh, and the princess head back to check on Isen. Baeldeth, barely conscious, looks up at A'ranah standing over him. The Amazon queen kneels down and casts a healing spell on her son.

Re'ann joins Belron and Nicari, hoping to help Nimbus. "You're free?" asks Belron. "Did Chance escape with you?"

"Yes. They're tending to his wounds now," she replies. Re'ann places her hand in front of Nimbus's snout to check for breathing.

"Do you think he'll make it?" Belron asks.

She looks back at her captain and shakes her head. "I'm sorry."

Belron finds comfort in his wife's embrace as the three mourn the loss of his companion.

Not far away, Arioch has reached Isen. With the orcneas standing at a distance, the king checks on his friend as Ya'leigh and the others arrive behind him.

Isen groans as he opens his eyes. "What happened?"

Arioch replies, "You kept Zetamat distracted long enough for Kianna and Ya'leigh to reach a safe distance."

"So they're safe?" he asks, not noticing them standing behind the king.

Kristieana crouches down and casts a healing spell on him, saying, "They are safe, thanks to you."

Isen coughs up blood as he forces a smile. "See, I told you I could do my job."

Kristieana smiles as she looks on, concerned. "Let me try to heal you again. I don't think my spell worked." She closes her eyes and focuses on her spell. The white light from her hands is absorbed into Isen's body. "Is that better?"

"A little," he replies. "But it still hurts to breathe." He coughs again, spitting more blood up.

Worried, Kristieana calls out for help. "Mother Elder! Someone, please, help us."

A'ranah rushes over, as well as Baeldeth, who keeps a watchful eye on the orcneas. A'ranah closes her eyes and passes her hands over Isen's body. When she is done, she sighs and shakes her head. "The damage is too great for my skills."

Princess Kianna asks, "We can revive him, though, right? If he passes, we can bring him back, can't we?"

A'ranah nods as she stands up. Kristieana says to Isen, "Listen to me. Whatever you do, don't go into the light. We'll bring you back."

Isen shakes his head. "I'm not worth the effort."

"What are you talking about? Of course you are."

"No," he insists. "Don't worry, there is no better way to die than doing one's duty. Not bad for a fool, huh?"

"Don't say that, please." Kristieana begins to cry. "I'm the fool, not you."

Isen takes a deep breath. "No, *I* am the fool. If there's a lever, I'll pull it. If there's a dark hall, I'll rush down it. If there's a light..."

"No, don't. Isen, we need you. The princess needs you to look out for her. Chance's children need you." She leans down and kisses him. "I... I need you."

Isen smiles. "You may miss me, but you don't need me."

"I love you."

With shortened breaths, Isen replies, "I love you, too..." Isen slowly exhales as he closes his eyes.

With teary eyes, Kristieana looks up at the others. "He's gone."

Ya'leigh wipes her face. "Let's get him back to the stronghold so we can try to resurrect him."

Baeldeth says, "I'll give you ladies a hand in just a moment." Then, turning his attention to Arioch, he adds, "We should go."

Arioch replies, "I must speak with their general."

"I don't think he survived," says A'ranah.

The king addresses the gathering of orcneas. "Is there a leader I may speak with?"

An orcnea in the far back of the group begins to shout something in his native tongue. Other orcneas turn their attention to the pile of rubble where the front watchtower fell. The ogre general, Cron, lifts himself from the mound of stone.

The orcneas watch, amazed, as Cron bends down and helps Lortec, still alive, to his feet. The army of orcneas begins to cheer as the humans and elves nervously observe. The orcnea general picks up both staves and begins to climb down the crumbled tower.

Lortec walks with a limp as the orcneas move out of his way. Eventually, Cron and Lortec reach Arioch, who stands stoically, without fear.

Face to face with the king, Lortec asks, "Where is Chance Na'Moon?"

"He was wounded in the escape," says Arioch. "He is safe, though, back at the fortress."

Ya'leigh grasps Kianna's hand, whispering, "Did you hear that? My father escaped."

Lortec says to the king, "I wish to sit and speak with both of you, when he is able."

"Come to the stronghold at sunset. We can talk then."

Lortec looks around at both forces. "I will see you then."

Cron and Lortec turn and walk away, leading the other orcneas back into Sheathelm. Arioch watches them until they are gone.

Baeldeth says to Ya'leigh, "If you can increase my strength, I shall carry Isen back to the stronghold."

Arioch says to A'ranah, "Can you get word to the fleets to hold their positions out to sea?"

"I'll do what I can."

"Good. If there is the possibility of peace, we don't want to ruin it by appearing to be a threat."

A short time later, as troops begin to file back into the stronghold, Lyra comes up from the underground chambers. She walks through the crowd, looking for one familiar face. Just as she is about to give up, she finds Fidelma talking with Fernando. When Lyra and Fidelma make eye contact, Fidelma drops her gaze, unable to look the young woman in the eye. The expression on her face confirms Lyra's worst fear.

Lyra disappears in the flood of people as Fidelma sighs. Fernando asks, "Who was that?"

"That was Lyra."

"Sven's flower?"

Fidelma nods. "I need to talk with her, but it will have to wait."

Lyra runs down the stairs into the lower portions of the stronghold. Crying as she clutches her chest, Lyra struggles to breathe. She makes it back to Yentroc, who is waiting in a hall outside a chamber.

"Lyra? What's wrong?" asks her friend.

Hysterical, the young woman only manages to croak, "It's Sven," before collapsing to the ground. Yentroc kneels and puts her arms around her.

Ja'noa, Gelana, and Evelena exit the chamber. No one needs to ask what has happened. Lyra makes it to her feet with Yentroc's help.

"Come on," says Evelena. "Let's get you back outside. I think the light and fresh air will do you some good."

Yentroc leans back against the wall. "I think I could use some fresh air, too. I'm not feeling so well."

Ja'noa replies, "You don't look good."

"I'll take Lyra up," says Gelana.

"I need to sit down," says Yentroc.

Yentroc slides down the wall into a sitting position. Gelana takes Lyra back up the stairs, as Evelena says to Yentroc, "I'll get you some water."

A short time later, outside the tower, Arioch and the others make it back to the stronghold. Baeldeth, still carrying Isen's body, asks, "Where should we take him?"

A'ranah answers, "We converted one of the chambers below to a healing room. Follow me."

The Amazon queen starts to lead the way when she passes Gelana and Lyra. A'ranah asks, "How's Chance doing?"

Gelana replies, "He's still unconscious, but alive. The healers said they've done all they can. We came up for fresh air."

Anxious to see her father, Ya'leigh maneuvers past the others to take the lead. Arioch stays outside, watching the city of Sheathelm as Ya'leigh leads A'ranah, Baeldeth, Kristieana, and Kianna down below. As they turn a corner, they find Kel'ana and Ja'noa in the hall with Yentroc.

Seeing Ya'leigh, Kel'ana stands in her way, just outside the door. "You may not want to go in there."

"What do you mean?" asks Ya'leigh.

Kel'ana tries to hold her back, saying, "There was a complication." Ya'leigh peers into the room and gasps.

"What do you mean, a 'complication'?" asks A'ranah. The Amazon queen moves Kel'ana aside and looks in to find Chance on a table in the middle of the room. In addition to the markings of the dragon blessing, Chance's skin is covered with dark veins.

Kristieana looks in and shakes her head. "Poison?"

Ja'noa sobs, "I'm so sorry. Everything happened so fast when we were escaping. When it was all done, I didn't think to check for it. Yentroc became ill first, just a short while ago. By the time I treated her and realized what was happening..."

Ya'leigh, ignoring the explanation, walks into the room. At Chance's side are Va'leen and Rehma. When they see Ya'leigh, they both stand up and make room, neither saying a word, as no mere words can help. Kianna, A'ranah, and Kristieana join Ya'leigh next her father.

A'ranah places her hand on Ya'leigh's shoulder. "It's not too late. We can resurrect him." Ya'leigh doesn't speak. She sniffs and nods her head. A'ranah says, "Isen will have to wait."

"I understand," says Kristieana.

A'ranah says, "I'll go make the preparations personally."

The Amazon queen leaves the room as Baeldeth enters. Standing over Chance, he says, "I swear to you, brother, if they can't bring you back, I will avenge you."

"No," cries Ya'leigh. "That's not what he wanted. He wanted peace."

"I know he did, and look where it got him. I'm sorry, Ya'leigh, but these animals don't understand peace."

"That's enough, Baeldeth," interrupts Kristieana. "Now, get out of here. You're upsetting her."

Baeldeth sighs. "I'm sorry. I know that Chance would want me to try to work things out with them, and I will do my best, but I can't make any promises."

The prince's bodyguard leaves the room, followed by Kristieana. Ya'leigh leans down and whispers in her father's ear. "Please, father, come back to us."

Chapter 33
Warmth of the Light

The light is blinding. So much so that Chance cannot see anything else. When his eyes come into focus, he looks at his hands, then down at his feet. Chance takes a step and can tell that there is a solid surface to walk on, though there is no horizon to walk towards.

"It's disorienting, isn't it?" asks a woman's voice. Chance turns around to find Rehma's mother, Teresa La'harn, standing behind him. Her body is as luminous as it was in the cavern.

"Is this the light?" asks Chance.

"No," replies Teresa. "It's this way, follow me." As the two begin to walk, Teresa comments, "I understand it was poison that killed you in the end."

Chance laughs to himself. "I suppose it's fitting to die the way Finna did."

"You'll be able to talk with her shortly."

"She's here?"

"We're all here." After walking a bit, Teresa adds, "You know, I've been watching over my daughter for some time. I must say I cried when she fought you in Copper Pass, and again in the atrium of the castle. I'm sorry she blamed you for my death."

Chance shakes his head. "It's not your fault. To be honest, I didn't blame her for hating me."

"I know. That brings me to my next point. After all these years, I'm sorry that you blamed yourself. If I had gone with you to be healed, you wouldn't have had to risk casting your spell in the middle of the fighting."

"I should have taken you further away."

"As if I would have let you," she laughs. "Chance, it's not your fault. It never was. Rehma knows this now, and I have to be sure you know it, as well."

"I guess so."

"That doesn't sound very convincing."

"I'm the one that chose that spot to heal you. I turned my back to the enemy."

"We were safe, Chance. No one could have predicted what was going to happen. If I had listened to you instead of fighting you... Chance, you did your best, and that is all I could have asked."

"Thank you."

"Now, there is someone else who would like to say hello."

As Teresa's eyes look beyond Chance, he turns to find his sister, Finna, standing behind him. He looks back to see Teresa is no longer there.

"Hello, brother," says Finna.

Chance gives her a hug. "I'm so sorry."

"About what?"

"The poison," answers Chance as they start to walk again. "I didn't think to check the arrow."

"It wasn't the way I would have chosen to die, but it's over now."

"I guess it's fitting that I died the same way."

"Are you angry with the girls?"

"For what?"

"For not checking the spear that struck you."

"There was a lot going on. Besides, they're young."

"Va'leen isn't, are you angry with her?"

Chance sighs. "I see what you are trying to do."

"Do you?"

"You want me to stop blaming myself for your death."

Finna smiles. "If you're going to take the blame for my death, then you have to blame them for yours. And, since you aren't doing that, I can only assume that means that, deep down, you know it wasn't your fault."

"I'm sensing a pattern here."

Finna stops walking. "If there's a pattern, it's one that you've created. Now, before I go, brother, tell Va'leen and Eveoh that I said hello."

"I..." Chance looks around to find he is alone. He carefully stares in each direction until he is surprised by the sudden appearance of another loved one. "Sha'al?"

His wife smiles radiantly. "It is good to see you," she finally says.

Chance rushes to embrace her. "I've missed you so much."

Holding him tightly, she replies, "And I've missed you."

Chance steps back to get a better look. "I can't believe you're here, or I mean, I can't believe I am here... with you." He laughs. "I suppose this is the part where you tell me that your death is also not my fault."

"Is it that obvious?"

"Just a little."

"Well," she smiles, "it's not your fault. You are not responsible for everyone's fate."

Chance nods. "I see that now. You know, all these years I have suffered with that guilt. I just wanted to be there for you."

Sha'al gently places her hand on his cheek. "You *were* always there for me."

"Now I can be again, forever."

Sha'al looks at him puzzled. "What are you talking about?"

"Dying," he replies. "I get to be with you again."

"Is that what you think is happening right now?"

"Yes," he replies, confused. "You're taking me to the light, aren't you?" Chance looks around and notices that the bright light that once surrounded him has now faded. "Where is the light?"

"It's behind us."

"It's colder here. What's going on?"

Sha'al replies, "Chance, your time in the light is not at hand."

"Why? Did I do something wrong?"

"You've done nothing wrong," Sha'al insists. She points in front of them to where the ground should be. Instead, it looks as though a magic gate has formed. On the other side is their daughter, Ya'leigh. She is crying and being comforted by Kianna. "Our daughter needs you. All of our children need you."

Chance shakes his head. "But I need *you*."

Sha'al waves her hand over the image. Now, instead of their daughter, an image of Ariella appears. "You don't need me. You just need love, like everyone else."

Chance looks at the image before turning back to Sha'al. "I'm sorry. I shouldn't have betrayed our love." He drops to his knees and begs, "Please, forgive me."

Sha'al pulls Chance to his feet, saying, "You did not betray our love. Love is not limited. You and your whimsical heart, freely giving love away. So many are afraid to give their love to even one person, and you love so many." She motions again, and this time Kristieana appears in the image.

"I'm sorry," he repeats, looking down.

"Do you love me any less?"

"No, of course not."

"Then don't be sorry."

Her words give him pause. He ponders them for a moment before saying, "This isn't the reaction I expected."

Sha'al laughs. "If I were still with you in life, I would fight for you, and I would let any woman know that you belong to me. But... you are not mine to fight for anymore."

Chance sighs. "I don't want to leave you."

"I know, and I don't *want* you to leave, but you cannot stay. There are so many people calling you back now. It would be selfish of me to keep you here."

"Is the war over?"

"For now. Arioch and Lortec have agreed to meet this evening to discuss peace."

Chance sighs. "Then they don't really need me."

"Lortec is not likely to trust Arioch, and my brother, Baeldeth, will not trust the orcneas. You are the best hope for this to work."

Chance looks at the image as it changes once again. This time it is of his own body laying on a stone table in the stronghold where the resurrection ritual is being performed. The dark veins that had covered his body are now gone. The image rises up out of the hole in the ground and the rest of the light fades. Chance, standing next to his own body, looks around to find a circle of Amazons holding hands surrounding him. They are all concentrating on the ritual magic to bring Chance back.

All that remains of the light from which he came is a portal. None of the Amazons seem to notice Chance or the portal of light. Sha'al, standing in the light, says, "Tell my mother that I miss her, and tell our children that I love them."

Chance shakes his head. "Please don't leave me here."

Ignoring his request, she says, "Tell my sister, Va'leen, that I'm sorry."

"For what?"

"I'm sorry that she stood by and watched as I took something precious from her. Tell her she deserves to be happy, too."

"Wait," says Chance, "I don't understand, what does that mean?"

He steps towards her, but Sha'al shoves him back. Chance is blinded by a flash of light, and suddenly feels a great deal of pain. Back in his body, he cries out Sha'al's name as he tries to sit up. From the circle of spell-casters, A'ranah opens her eyes, and rushes to Chance's side to calm him.

"It's all right," she says soothingly.

"Sha'al!" he gasps as he looks around frantically. "She was just here."

"You're back with us now. Try to relax."

Chance looks around the room one last time for his late wife before lying back and closing his eyes.

A'ranah looks around the circle of Amazons. She says to Jadelyn, "Go spread the word that Chance lives."

A short time later, Chance is escorted outside by Ya'leigh and Baeldeth. He moves slowly, as his body is still recovering.

Chance, continuing to tell his daughter what has happened to him, says, "Your mother wanted me to tell you that she loves you."

"I wish I could have seen her."

"I'm sure she would have liked that, too."

They walk outside the walls of the fortress as the sun hangs low in the sky. They are joined by a large group, all anxious to see Chance.

Baeldeth says, "I'm glad you came back to us, brother. I'm not sure how I would fare at being diplomatic if you were gone."

Though it causes him some discomfort, Chance laughs lightly. "Sha'al said that would be the case."

"What else did she say?" asks Ya'leigh.

Chance glances at Va'leen before answering, "There was one more greeting for someone, but it was a little more personal."

Ariella pushes her way through the crowd. Throwing her arms around Chance, she says, "Thank the gods you're all right." Chance winces in pain as Ariella backs away. "I'm sorry, I didn't mean to hurt you."

Chance says, "Ariella, have you ever met my daughter?"

"Yes, we've met," answers Ariella. "After we thought we lost you the first time. You know, Chance, you really need to stop scaring us."

"I would love to," he replies. Chance looks around the group. He asks Ya'leigh, "Where's Isen?"

Everyone is quiet as Ya'leigh tries to find the words. Baeldeth finally says, "He died well, brother."

Chance, at a loss for words, nods. Ya'leigh says, "They are trying to resurrect him now."

"Good," says Chance. "And what about Sven?"

Another silence falls over them. Ariella sighs. "He died bringing down the floating city."

"Are they going to try to bring him back as well?"

Ariella shakes her head. "He stayed behind to destroy the crystal. There was no other way."

Chance begins to deal with the loss of Sven and the potential loss of Isen as Ariella embraces him. Va'leen makes her way back through the gate of the stronghold. She is walking down toward the docks when Nicari catches up with her.

"Hey, are you all right?" asks Nicari.

Va'leen stops walking. "Yes, why?"

"No reason, but if you want to talk about anything..."

"Thanks for the offer, but I'm fine."

"Are you?"

Va'leen closes her eyes to calm herself. "What do you want me to say, Nicari? Chance just returned from death, and while he was there, he spoke to Sha'al. Now, he is being comforted by his first love. What is there to say?"

"I don't know," Nicari replies. "But if there is more you wish to discuss, I'm here to listen."

Va'leen places her hands on Nicari's shoulders. "Thank you. I know you're trying to help, but the truth of the matter is, I just want Chance to be happy. If that means being in the arms of a pirate whore, so be it."

"Va'leen, that's a bit harsh, don't you think?"

"I know," she sighs.

"You should tell him how you feel."

"What, and add to his confusion and woes? No, now is not the time."

"When will it be the time?" asks Nicari.

Va'leen ignores the inquiry as her eyes shift to the top of the hill where a large group of forces begin to make their way down to the docks. The group is led by King Arioch and Ariella. Fernando and Fidelma are also with them.

Still weak, Chance stays behind with Ya'leigh and Baeldeth.

Coming into port is the *Red Dawn*. The group takes formation around the section of dock where the ship will be moored. Ariella anxiously waits to see her father, and hopes to find the truth about the ship her mother died on. She wants to know what really happened aboard the *White Feather.*

Chapter 34
Digging Up the Past

It takes some time, but the *Red Dawn* is eventually secured to the dock. Samantha and Vindalia are the first to disembark. Fidelma rushes up and gives Samantha a hug.

"I'm glad to see you," says Fidelma. "Are the twins safe?"

"Yes," answers Samantha. "They're fine."

"Come on," Fidelma says as she tries to hurry them. "I'll explain in a moment."

The three women clear the area when Red Beard makes his way down the boarding plank. Arioch, attempting to keep him from becoming suspicious, greets him cheerfully, "I'm glad the wave wasn't a problem for you."

Red Beard gets to the bottom of the plank. "Aye, 'twas not a problem at all."

Standing next to the king is Ariella. Fernando waits behind them, trying to keep his calm. Red Beard, noticing the scowl on Ariella's face, asks, "Is everything all right?"

Ariella clenches her fists as Arioch does the talking. "Well, we aren't exactly sure. We do have a question for you, if you don't mind me asking."

Now curious, Red Beard replies, "Sure. What do you want to know?"

Ariella, unable to keep her thoughts to herself any longer, says, "Tell me it's not true, father."

"What are you talking about?"

Fernando and Arioch stare at him as she says angrily, "Please tell me Corthag was lying. Tell me the *Red Dawn* is not responsible for the *White Feather's* demise."

"Hmm," Red Beard grumbles to himself. "Is Corthag here now?"

Fernando replies, "He is not. He was helping the orcneas aboard the floating city. He told us that the *Red Dawn* attacked the *White Feather*. He said there were no orcneas, and that he himself killed our father." Fernando draws his sword. "I removed his head, and unless you wish for me to do the same to you, I suggest you tell us everything."

Red Beard eyes Arioch. The king says, "I was there when he said it. I know Corthag is capable of anything. I'm hoping you have a good explanation. Otherwise, I'm going to have to place you under arrest."

"I understand," Red Beard replies with a nod. Looking at Ariella and Fernando, he continues. "What Corthag told you was partially true. There were no orcneas." Ariella holds back tears as she shakes her head in disbelief. "Corthag did kill your parents, but, I promise you, that was not the plan. We did *not* attack them."

Fernando points the tip of his blade at the dwarven captain. Arioch places himself between the two men, saying, "Let's hear the whole story before we act rashly."

Fidelma says, "I can read his mind to make sure that what he says is the truth."

Red Beard asks, "Tell me lass, can you share memories as well?"

"I can," she confirms.

"Good. Then instead of me just telling you what happened, I can show you."

"You can do that?" asks Fernando.

Fidelma says, "While I read his mind, I can share those thoughts with someone who holds my hand. I can show two people what he remembers."

Fernando asks Red Beard, "Do you remember what my father looked like? Or Ariella's mother?"

"Aye, though barely."

"It doesn't matter," says Fidelma. "The spell will clarify any lapses in the memories. They should be as perfect as if they just happened."

Fernando says to Ariella, "Did you hear that? You can finally see what your mother was really like."

Ariella shakes her head. "No, I-I can't. I don't think I can do this."

"Why not?"

"I can't watch her die," she sobs. "I just can't."

"It's all right," says Fernando reassuringly. "I will do it."

Fidelma says. "First, I'll need to get inside his mind."

"I won't resist," says Red Beard.

Fidelma moves closer before placing her hand on Red Beard's forehead. She concentrates on her spell. "I'll let you guide us through your memories as you speak. If you try to lie to us, I'll know it."

"Ya won't get any lies from me."

Fidelma takes Fernando's hand and says to Red Beard, "All right, then. Go on."

Red Beard says, "We came across the *White Feather* as evening was setting in. We had been out to sea for some time and were running low on supplies. The *White Feather* was carrying a lot of cargo bound for Northwind. Desperate, we decided to steal some of it."

Fidelma and Fernando relive that night as Red Beard's memories come back to him.

****

We had arranged a trade with them. We sent over a couple barrels of rum in exchange for water and food, but inside one of the barrels we hid a secret. Corthag didn't need to breathe and was able to stay inside one until nightfall. Peering through a hole, he waited until it was clear before breaking out.

We had done this several times in the past. It was routine to us. Once most of the crew had turned in for the night, Corthag would cast a spell on the watchmen so they, too, would fall asleep. Then, he would throw the cargo that would float overboard, and we would scoop it up in the *Red Dawn* as we followed behind them.

Most of the time we would only take a few items. If we took it all, there would be no doubt who was responsible. Since we limited what we stole, it would seem to them as if some cargo had simply been miscounted or come up missing at the docks. It was a way for us to survive when we couldn't find work.

Unfortunately, that night our luck ran out. Corthag started to unload some of the cargo when he was spotted. Torgus and I heard some yelling and decided to order the *Red Dawn* to close the distance. The yells soon turned into cries of terror, and by the time we got there, it was too late.

Corthag was able to wipe out the entire crew. At the time, we had no idea how he was able to do it, but because of his soul stone, they couldn't kill him. Only Ariella's and Fernando's father was able to slow him down, but he, too, would eventually fall to Corthag's dark magic.

When we boarded, we came across a horrifying sight.

"How could you do this?!" I asked.

"They attacked me," he replied. "I had to defend myself."

Torgus said, "You should have escaped."

Corthag shook his head, "They knew who I was, and what ship I was from. I would have just killed the one, but they kept coming."

That's when we heard the cry of pain from Ariella's mother in the navigation room. Torgus and I rushed to check on her and to see if there were more survivors. Ariella's father was nearby, already dead. As it turned out, she was the only one left. Her hair was almost as red as the pools of blood that she laid in. She had a gash on her head and a stab wound that just missed her heart. It was clear that she was late into her pregnancy, and it took all I had to keep myself from attacking Corthag right there and then.

****

Fernando gasps at the image. "She is beautiful."

"Aye," agrees Red Beard. "That she was."

Ariella reluctantly takes Fidelma's other hand. Soon, she, too, can see the memory of her mother through Red Beard's perspective. Tears begin fall down her cheeks as her adoptive father continues the story.

****

"Please," she begged. "I don't care what you do with me, just please, don't hurt my baby."

I took her hand in mine and said, "No one is going to hurt you or your baby."

We healed her the best we could, but the rest she was going to have to recover from on her own. Corthag asked, "What are we going to do now?"

I jumped to my feet and slammed him against the wall. "You'll be lucky if you don't spend the rest of your life in the brig!"

Corthag stood right there and stared me in the eye. "Are you going to turn me in?"

I didn't know what to say. It's not like we were strangers to killing people, but this felt different to me. I said, "Gather their food and water, but leave everything else."

"Why?" he asked, clearly upset that the wealth aboard the ship wouldn't be coming with us.

I said to him, "Anything that could be tracked to us has to stay. If we are linked to this, we will go back to being hunted again."

"What about her?"

I looked the poor woman over. Crying, she said, "I promise I won't say anything. Your secret is safe with me."

Torgus said, "I can make a potion that will help her forget the last few hours."

"Good," I said. "She'll come with us, and we'll sink this ship. As far as anyone else will know, the *White Feather* was attacked by orcneas. We got here just in time to save her, but no one else."

Torgus said, "I'll get to it, then, and tell a few of the crew to gather the supplies."

As Torgus and Corthag left, Corthag stopped at the dead body by the door. He bent down and picked up the Greythorn's sword, saying, "I'm at least going to take this."

*****

Fernando does his best to study the memory of his father through Red Beard's eyes. He notes the light hair and small pointed ears. "Our father was a half-elf."

"Aye," confirms Red Beard. "It is one of the reasons we never thought he was Ariella's father." He continues.

******

We didn't discover until later that the sword was useless to us. I took it from Corthag and put it with my personal treasure. I'm not sure exactly what possessed me to keep it, but I'm glad I did.

As preparations were being made to leave the ship, Ariella's mother went into labor. Torgus returned to help me deliver the child. Unfortunately, the birth did not go smoothly, and by the time it was done, she had lost more blood. She was weak and fading.

I was the first to hold Ariella's tiny body in my hands. She was the most beautiful sight I had ever laid my eyes on. Something so pure and innocent surrounded by anything but. I cleaned her up and handed her to her mother.

She said to the infant, "My sweet Ariella, don't cry. Everything is going to be all right now. I just wish I could be there to watch you grow up."

And with that, she handed Ariella to me. She grasped a locket around her neck saying, "Please, take this and give it to her when she's old enough."

"I will," I promised as she handed it over. "I'll see that she finds her way home. Where are you from?"

Unfortunately, she was already gone. Torgus found the letter she had started to write, but it wasn't much help.

****

Red Beard says to Ariella, "I should have given you that letter long ago, but I had buried it away, and wanted to forget."

Fidelma ends the spell as they open their eyes. Fernando asks, "What did you end up doing to Corthag?"

"We put him in the brig," says Red Beard. "We held him there for couple of years, but he told us that if we didn't let him out he would start telling everyone the truth. We didn't see any other choice."

Arioch asks, "How did your whole crew keep silent about it for so long?"

Red Beard explains, "Most of the crew took the potion that Torgus made to make them forget. When they asked about Corthag, we simply told them he killed someone unprovoked."

Arioch asks Fidelma, "Is everything he said the truth?"

"Yes," she answers.

Arioch sighs, "Well, I suppose I'll leave you all to discuss this matter amongst yourselves." The king signals for his troops to disperse.

Ariella stands silently, fighting the rage inside. Red Beard says to her, "My dear, I'm sor—"

"Don't," she snaps. "Don't say it. Don't say another word to me." Red Beard nods as Ariella walks past him to board the ship. She walks up the plank before turning around. "I want you to gather your things and get off my ship, and don't even think of telling me the *Red Dawn* isn't mine. After what you took from me, this ship is the least you can give me back!"

"Aye," he mumbles softly. "It's all yours."

As Red Beard makes his way up the plank, Fernando and Fidelma follow. Torgus comes out from the officer's quarters and is met with slap across the face by Ariella as she shouts, "You! I looked you in the eyes a couple weeks ago, and I asked you if there was anything else you were keeping from me."

Confused, Torgus asks, "What is this all about?"

"I know the truth," she replies angrily. "I know what really happened on the *White Feather.*"

Torgus sighs. "Then you know it was Corthag's doing."

"Save it!" she snaps. "As far as I'm concerned, all three of you are to blame. Now get your things and get off my ship."

"Ariella..."

"Now!"

Red Beard says to Torgus, "Come, my old friend. There's no use in arguing with her. Her mind is made up."

Torgus nods as Ariella continues on towards the lounge. Once inside, she slams the door behind her. Enraged, she walks over to the far wall and grabs the portrait of Red Beard off the wall. With a shriek, she smashes the painting on the table before collapsing to the ground.

Chapter 35
The Dusk of War

As the sun sets, in the west, the orcnea general Lortec Ka and the ogre Cron approach the stronghold with a half dozen of their soldiers. King Arioch has set up a table outside the walls at the top of the hill. There are torches surrounding the area, and six chairs on each side of the long table. Chance, Arioch, and A'ranah are joined by Prince River and Baeldeth. They stand on one side of the table behind their respective chairs as the orcneas approach.

"I'm glad that you have come to talk," says Arioch.

Lortec and Cron take positions behind two of the chairs on the other side of the table. Lortec replies, "I am grateful that you have granted us an audience."

A'ranah says, "Let us hope that from this point forward we can continue with words instead of violence."

"I'll admit," says Lortec, "it wasn't easy to convince my people that this was the right path. Some of them wanted the war to continue."

Baeldeth says, "Trust me, some of us feel the same."

Lortec laughs. "I am sure it would be a good fight, son of the Silver Moon, but I am here to put an end to the bloodshed. I am here to build a different future." Then, looking at Chance, he adds, "A future for my son, and a future for your people's children. Or am I the only one who saw wisdom in Chance Na'Moon's words?"

"No," says Arioch. "You are not the only one. Now, please, have a seat." The representatives sit at the table, save for Cron, who is too big to sit in the chairs provided.

Lortec says to Chance, "I understand you were wounded during your escape. You don't look well."

"I'll be fine," says Chance, trying to hide the pain.

"I have brought you a few items," says Lortec. He motions to two of the soldiers, who step forward with a chest. They place it on the ground and open it. Inside is Chance's armor and swords.

"Thank you," says Chance as the orcneas close the chest and step back into their positions.

"I have one more gift," says the orcnea general. He pulls a

large gem, strung on a leather necklace, from his pouch.

"What's this?"

"It is the crystal from Carr Vork's staff. It possesses the spirit energy from your friend's drake. I felt she may want to decide its fate."

Chance takes the crystal. He can feel the presence of the creature's spirit within. "I'll make sure she gets it."

Arioch says, "Now then, if you are really here to discuss peace, let us start. The first item of business is nonnegotiable. You will pull back all orcnea forces and return to the north side of the Northwind Range."

"My people," begins Lortec, "have roamed these lands since long before you humans and elves ever set foot on them. We will return Sheathelm to you, but the city of Northwind will remain ours."

"Unacceptable," replies the king. "I understand that many years ago, these were once your ancestor's lands, but that was before the great collapse. Most human ancestors did not come here by choice. The collapse brought them here."

"Yes," Cron agrees. "And since that time, our peoples have had many conflicts. Each time, we have been pushed further back to lands that can barely support us."

"And what do you propose?" asks Arioch.

Lortec replies, "The orcneas keep Northwind and enough land to farm and support it."

Arioch says, "We cannot simply give you a massive city that our people built. Besides, it would be isolated from the rest of the orcnea territories."

"But it would give us much-needed access to better food sources," retorts the orcnea general.

"If food is your concern," says A'ranah, "I'm sure we could arrange a trade agreement."

"That would leave us dependent on an outside source to survive," argues Lortec. "We must remain independent."

Arioch replies. "But what about your shamans? Can't they grow food?"

"Chance and I have already discussed that," says Lortec. "We do not wish to become dependent on the use of magic for food. Mana levels can shift and wane over time, like the ocean tides."

Chance says, "You would only need to use magic for a couple of years. If you plant the right crops, they can make the soil fertile for other plants."

A'ranah says, "Chance is right. If you need, we can give you seeds to plant so that after a few seasons you wouldn't need to use magic."

"That would be helpful," says Lortec. "But if there is to be true peace, then we cannot be forced to stay beyond the Northwind Range. We must be able to move freely about the rest of Bruen."

"The lands on this continent have already been settled," says A'ranah.

Lortec replies, "We are not looking to expand our borders. We only wish to travel without fear of being attacked, and possibly to open trade with other cities."

The king ponders a moment before answering. "I cannot speak for the other territories, but if you would like to open trade within Sheathelm's influence, I am open to that idea—provided that no troops enter our lands."

Lortec nods. "Of course."

"So it is agreed?" asks Arioch. "You will pull back to the north, abandoning Sheathelm and Northwind. In exchange, we will assist you with your agriculture and allow for trade within the eastern lands."

Lortec stands up, saying, "That sounds agreeable to me. Cron, do you have any objection?"

The massive ogre shakes his head. "No."

The others stand up, as well. Arioch says, "I expect our people to be allowed to travel in your lands, as well."

"Yes," replies Lortec. "It would be difficult to assist us otherwise."

Arioch says, "I'm afraid I don't have any formal agreements to sign."

"That will not be necessary," says Lortec, "so long as you and Chance will give me your word, then what we have agreed upon here will be honored."

Lortec looks at Chance, who extends his hand. "You have my word."

The orcnea general shakes both Chance's and the king's hands before saying, "And I, Lortec Ka, give you both my word that as long as I am High Chief, there will be peace between my tribes and your people. We will stay the night at Sheathelm, and leave in the morning."

The two groups part ways and Chance heads back into the stronghold. After searching for a short while, he finds Re'ann, sitting with the young Amazons on their Rite of Passage.

Seeing Chance, Re'ann jumps to her feet and embraces him. "You should be resting. Come on, sit down."

"I'm fine," he insists. "I was actually looking for you."

"Oh?"

Chance pulls out the crystal from Carr's staff. "Lortec gave me this to give to you."

Re'ann's eyes widen. "Is that..?"

Chance nods. "It is."

Re'ann nervously asks, "Can you feel him? Is he in there?"

Lyra and the others circle around, and Chance answers, "Yes, he's in there, and if I'm not mistaken, he's happy to see you."

Re'ann gasps. "He can see me?"

Chance nods. "If my understanding is correct, captured souls can hear and see normally."

He offers the crystal to her. Though the crystal itself is clear, it emanates a faint blue glow. Re'ann hesitantly reaches for it, unsure what to expect. Once she makes contact with it, she is overwhelmed with both joy and sorrow.

"I can feel him," she says with a smile. "And you're right, he's happy."

Chance says to the others, "Could you all give us a moment, please?"

"Sure," says Rehma. "But, first..." She embraces Chance. "I'm glad you're all right."

The seven sisters give Chance and Re'ann some space. Seeing concern on his face, Re'ann asks, "Is something wrong?"

Chance sighs. "I'm just sorry that your attempt to rescue me cost your drake its life."

"That wasn't your fault," replies Re'ann.

"I know, but still, I can't help but feel guilty. I don't know if I would have survived without you."

Re'ann, scoffing at the idea, says, "Carr said he wasn't allowed to kill you. I think you would have been fine."

"I feel anything but fine." After a short pause he continues. "What you went through for me, I can never repay."

"Now, you listen to me," Re'ann scolds playfully. "Don't you dare feel sorry for me. I don't need you to repay me. You suffered for me, as well, and we survived together."

"But—"

"No buts," she interrupts. "Because of you, I'm already a hero. I pulled you from the sea when the orcnea ship exploded. And while I may not have successfully rescued you from the Colosseum, my attempt was still daring. Because of that, the Amazons of the Silver Moon have decided that I can join them if I wish. I just have to follow them on their Rite of Passage."

"Re'ann, that's great. Any idea what house you'll join?"

"I'm not sure yet, but I'm thinking Dri'el."

Chance laughs. "That would make us brother and sister."

"Great, that's just what I need. More bothers." The two laugh.

Chance eyes Va'leen, who stands not far away. He says to Re'ann, "If you'll excuse me, I have to talk with someone."

"Of course," she replies. "I'll see you later."

Re'ann rejoins the seven sisters as Chance makes his way over to Va'leen. The raven-haired Amazon says, "Shouldn't you be resting?"

"That's what Re'ann said."

"Well, we're right."

Chance nods in agreement. "I will get some rest soon, but first I needed to talk to you."

Va'leen smiles, taking Chance by the arm. As they start to walk down to the water, she asks, "And just what would you like to talk about?"

"When I was in the light, I also saw Finna."

"You did? What did she say?"

"She told me not to blame myself for her death, but she also wanted me to tell you hello."

"I really miss her."

"So do I," Chance replies. After walking a bit more, he continues, "When I saw Sha'al, she also wanted me to tell you something." Va'leen stops and looks at Chance, waiting for him to finish. "It didn't make much sense," he continues, shaking his head. "She said she was sorry that she took something from you that was precious while you just stood by and watched."

"She did?" she gasps, holding back tears.

"She also said you deserved to be happy, too. Do you know what she was talking about?"

Va'leen reflects back to the moment when her sister Sha'al claimed Chance after the Dragon War. She remembers the way she felt for him then, and still does now. Forcing a smile, she shakes her head, clears her throat, and lies. "I don't know. I'm sure whatever it was, it was as important to her as it was to me, maybe more."

"It was the last thing she said to me before I woke."

"Thank you for delivering the message. It does mean a lot to me."

Chance spots Ariella approaching them. Va'leen turns to see what he is looking at.

When Ariella recognizes who Chance is with, she says, "I'm sorry. I didn't mean to interrupt." Still distraught from the fallout with her father, she adds, "Chance, when you get a moment, I really need to talk to you."

Before Chance can reply, Ariella turns to head back to the *Red Dawn*. Va'leen says to him, "Did you hear what happened between her and Red Beard?"

"Arioch told me," he says. "I can't imagine what she's going through."

"You should go to her. She needs you, and I know how you feel about her. Now, be a good pup, and go after her."

"So, I'm a pup again?"

"What can I say, old habits are hard to break."

"Thank you," says Chance as he gives her a hug. "We'll talk later."

As Chance starts towards the *Red Dawn*, Nicari approaches Va'leen, asking, "Did you finally tell him?"

"I swear to the gods, Nicari..." she laughs. Then, sadness fills her eyes.

Noticing the sudden change, Nicari says, "Something's wrong. You can tell me, you know."

Va'leen explains, "Chance was just telling me what Sha'al said to him while he was close to the light." She takes a deep breath before continuing. "I think she knew how I felt about Chance, or at least her spirit knows now. She told Chance that I deserved to be happy, too."

"And what did Chance say?"

Va'leen shakes her head and chuckles. "He didn't know what she was talking about. He's as clueless as he's always been."

"So, you still haven't told him."

"No," she replies as she watches Chance walk up the boarding plank to the *Red Dawn*. "He's happy now."

"But are you?"

Va'leen ponders before replying. "Whether or not I'm content will not change how he feels. For now, as long Ariella makes him happy, I'll take solace in that."

"I don't understand how you're taking this so well."

Va'leen laughs lightly. "Not long ago, you and Chance were but children. Even now, you're still young. When you reach my age, a decade can pass without noticing. I've known Chance for twenty years, and I'm sure I'll know him much longer. Forcing him to choose between myself and his first love wouldn't end well for any of us. And as morbid as this may sound, my patience can outlast the lifespan of a human."

Aboard the *Red Dawn*, Ariella sits at the table in the lounge. She pours herself a drink when there is knock at the door. Before she can respond, Chance enters. Seeing that she is distressed, he closes the door behind him.

Ariella stands up as he says, "I heard about your father. Are you all right?"

Holding back tears, she shakes her head. Chance rushes to her and takes her in his arms. She sobs, "Everything I thought I knew was wrong. He took everything from me, Chance. My parents... you... everything."

"I'm here now, and I promise, I'm not going anywhere."

Chapter 36
Hello, Goodbye

Back at the apartment, Kelik has returned from the ship and is in the hallway with Gelana and Yentroc. "Are you ready to meet them?" he asks

"No," Gelana replies with a laugh, "but I have to do this sooner or later, I suppose."

Kelik opens the door, and they enter. Josh rushes to greet them, calling, "Uncle Kyle, Aunt Amber is at the end of the book finally."

"Wow!" he replies as they walk into the living room. "You must have been reading all day."

"We have," says Ambra with a disgruntled tone. "You can finish the rest. I know how much you like telling stories."

"Sure," says Kelik as Josh sits on the couch next to his sisters.

Laura, looking at Gelana, asks, "Who is this?"

Kelik leads Gelana over to the three kids. "This is your Aunt Angela."

"On whose side of the family?" Laura inquires.

"Your mother's," replies Gelana. "I'm sorry, we've never met before."

"Can we finish the story now?" asks Josh impatiently.

"I can read it," says Gelana. "If you don't mind, that is."

Laura shrugs. "It doesn't matter to me. Are you familiar with it?"

Gelana smiles at Kelik and Ambra. "I think I remember hearing it once."

Yentroc finds a chair to sit in as Lyra comes in from the balcony. "Oh, hello," says Lyra. "I didn't know you all were coming."

"It was a last minute decision," says Yentroc. "Is Kel'ana around?"

Lyra gives Yentroc a stern look, and asks pointedly, "Is *who* around?"

Realizing her mistake, Yentroc laughs nervously. "I must have been thinking about the book. I meant to ask, is Danielle around?"

Ambra replies, "We got a text from her a short while ago. She should be back soon."

Gelana, looking at the book, asks, "So, where did you leave off?"

Ambra flips through the pages until she finds the place she stopped. "Right here," she points.

"You're almost done," Gelana comments.

"I would hope so," laughs Laura. "We've been binge reading for the last two days after Uncle Kyle started to tell us the story."

Gelana looks back down at the pages. After skimming over the page, she says, "Oh, these are the sad parts."

Lyra motions to Yentroc. "Do you want to join me on the balcony?"

"Sure," she replies.

As Yentroc and Lyra excuse themselves, Gelana starts the conclusion to the book.

******

A long line of Amazons of the Silver Moon file out from the underground fortress through the tower at the top of the hill. Waiting for them are Ya'leigh and Princess Kianna. Seeing the depressed looks on their faces, the two become concerned.

When Jadelyn appears, Ya'leigh pulls her aside. "So, what happened? Did it work?"

Jadelyn shakes her head. "We tried resurrecting Isen twice, but it didn't work. I'm sorry. If we were able to try sooner, perhaps it would have."

Ya'leigh and Kianna look at each other mournfully. Kianna says to Jadelyn, "Thank you for trying."

"Of course," she replies. "Do you know where I can find Chance?"

"He's..." Ya'leigh looks around, disoriented, as she tries to think. "I think he's down at the water."

Jadelyn nods. "I'll go tell him."

Ya'leigh and Kianna make their way down the stairs and through the underground passages until they reach the room where the resurrection ritual was attempted. Lying on a stone table in the center is the body of Isen. Standing at his side is Kristieana. "It's not fair," weeps the red-headed Amazon. "He should be alive."

The two young women approach their former bodyguard and stand next to Kristieana. Ya'leigh looks down at him, noting the peaceful look on his face. Trying to lighten the mood, she says, "I always figured he'd die doing something stupid, not heroic."

Kianna laughs lightly as she wipes her cheeks. Thinking back, she says, "Like taking that gem from the statue in Cold Rock?"

"Exactly," replies Ya'leigh.

Kristieana listens, unsure what to make of their comments. She smiles to cover the sadness, and adds, "I told him to stay away from the light, but do you think he would listen to me?"

"Curiosity always seemed to get the better of him," Kianna comments.

Ya'leigh nods. "Like the time he put on that cursed crown. He was lucky he didn't get possessed by the spirit inside."

The women fall silent in a moment of reflection. Kianna speaks softly. "I'm going to miss you, Isen. May the warmth of the light embrace you."

Ya'leigh and Kristieana both repeat the blessing. "May the warmth of the light embrace you."

Chance enters the chamber. Ya'leigh rushes over and embraces him. He kisses his daughter on her forehead. "I just found out they were unsuccessful."

Kristieana says, "We might have been successful, had we not had to wait so long to try." Her words seem pointed, even angry.

Chance moves closer to the table. "Would you give me a moment alone, please?" The princess and Ya'leigh nod before heading out the door. Kristieana starts to follow them when Chance says to her, "Wait."

Kristieana stops as Chance looks out the door and down the hallway. When his daughter reaches the stairs, he turns back to Kristieana. "I know you're upset right now. So am I. So, if you want to take your frustrations out on me, then let's have it."

"What are you talking about?"

"You blame me for the failure of the resurrection."

"I didn't say that."

"You didn't have to. I can tell by the way you're looking at me even now."

Kristieana fights with her own emotions, trying to keep her anger from boiling over. Chance, frustrated himself, prods her by saying, "If you didn't have to spend so much time resurrecting me first, then Isen may still be here now."

"It's not fair!" she snaps. "They rescued you. They had you back here. You were safe. Why didn't anyone take two seconds to check you for poison?"

Chance shakes his head. "Do you even know what we went through during the escape? We almost didn't make it at all."

"I know," says Kristieana, trying to rein in her temper. "I heard."

"Everything happened so fast, and by the time we got back here, I'm sure everyone else thought that the girls had already checked." Chance walks back to the table. "Look, I know you want Isen's death to make some sort of sense. We all want to know why we lose the ones we love, and no, it's not fair. It rarely ever is. Just promise me you won't say anything to the girls. They feel bad enough as it is. They don't need to feel weight of Isen's loss."

Kristieana sighs. "I won't." She looks down at Isen's body, forces a smile, and says, "The fool probably ran towards the light the first moment he saw it, anyway."

Chance smiles sadly. "Trust me, given the opportunity to do it again... that's exactly what I would have done."

Down at the water's edge, Lyra looks out over the sea. She is sitting alone, listening to the waves crash against the rocks. Holding on to the necklace Sven had given her, she rolls one of the pearls between her thumb and finger.

Fidelma approaches unnoticed. She watches Lyra for a few moments before reluctantly saying, "I'm sorry if I'm interrupting, but can we talk?"

"Of course," she replies, feigning happiness as she gets to her feet. Not sure what Fidelma has to say, Lyra anxiously asks, "What did you want to talk about?"

"I'm sorry I didn't come to you earlier," says Fidelma. "I didn't quite know how to do this. I have a message for you... From Sven." Lyra grips the necklace tighter, whitening her knuckles. Noticing this, Fidelma asks, "You really cared about him, didn't you?"

Noticeably uneasy, Lyra nods. "I loved him. At least I think I did."

"That's not something people are usually uncertain of," remarks Fidelma.

"I suppose so," Lyra replies. "I've just never felt that way before."

Fidelma takes out a small white crystal. "This is called a memory crystal. I used it right before Sven brought down the floating city. I was able to read his thoughts and save them perfectly onto this." She holds it out to Lyra, who hesitates before taking it from her.

"How does it work?"

"It requires a spell, but for now, I can cast it and share the thoughts with you until you learn how."

"His thoughts are in here?" she asks as she studies the crystal.

"Sort of. It contains his message to you as well as some of his emotions."

Lyra stares at the crystal. "I don't know if I can do this."

Fidelma places her hand on Lyra's shoulder. "I understand if you're not ready. We can do this later if you wish, but you really should hear what he had to say. He most certainly loved you. The fact that you have that necklace is proof that he thought the world of you."

"I'm sorry," apologizes Lyra. "I know this can't be easy for you."

Fidelma shrugs. "I'll be fine. What Sven and I shared was a long time ago. I was so angry with him, I almost forgot that I loved him. The spells that I learned over the years to know when I was being lied to are both a blessing and a curse. The curse is having your world shattered when you learn that most people will lie to get what they want. It's hard to look at the world the same way when you can see past all the lies. The blessing is when you find someone who truly loves and cares about you. Then, you *know* it's true, and all doubts are erased. It's one thing to hear someone say they love you, but it's another to actually feel it."

Lyra holds up the crystal. "Is that what this does?"

"Yes. In his final moments, I asked Sven to think of you, and think about what he might say to you. When he did, I was able to read those thoughts and place them inside. When you experience it, it will be as if he is speaking to you directly, and then at some points, you will be able to feel what he felt for you."

Lyra looks again at the crystal. "I think I'm ready."

"Are you sure? We can do this later."

"No. I want to do this now, before I change my mind."

"All right," says Fidelma. "I have to hold the crystal in one hand and you have to hold my other." Lyra hands back the crystal as Fidelma takes her hand. "Now, close your eyes and clear your mind. Tell me when you're ready."

Lyra takes a deep breath in an attempt to calm her nerves as well as clear her thoughts. After a few breaths, Lyra says, "I'm ready."

Fidelma concentrates on the crystal in her hand, and soon, in Lyra's mind, a memory begins to play out. A memory that is new to Lyra. To her, it's as if Sven is standing before her. She tries to reach for him, but her hand passes through him like he's an illusion spell.

She calls to him, but he cannot hear her. She watches as Sven says, "Lyra, Sven hopes that this works and you get this message. Fidelma told Sven to think of you, and she would make sure you got it. Is Sven doing this right?"

Lyra can hear Fidelma's voice say, "Yes, you're doing well, keep going."

The image of Sven smiles. "Lyra, you have saved Sven. Not only his life, but you have saved his soul. For years, Sven has felt alone. Sven can die happy, knowing what it was like to love again. Sven hopes that you will not be angry with him for doing this. Others have volunteered to stay behind, but Sven is best choice. It is better this way."

Lyra's cheeks are soaked with tears as she hears Fidelma's voice tell Sven to concentrate on his feelings and his memories of Lyra.

For Lyra there is flash of light, and then images begin to bombard her. First is the memory of Lyra throwing snow at Sven and telling him that she is not a little girl. In the next, he is looking down at her as she curls up, asleep, next to him. Along with the memory comes a feeling of warmth and being content, washing over Lyra as the next memory fills her head: Lyra reading to him. Though he can read the words, Sven guiltily enjoys the closeness of the encounter.

The next memory is one that Lyra cannot remember on her

own. It is of the night in Ogre's Mead, and she is drunk. She relives the events through his eyes, and even though she tries to kiss, him, he refuses. The feelings of respect that Sven had for her fills her heart.

Images of Lyra in the dress she borrowed from Kianna are next. While standing at the top of the stairs in the royal library, Sven was in awe of her beauty. Lyra has never seen herself in that way, but now, knowing what she looked like through his eyes, she can't help but smile.

The next memory, while embarrassing for Lyra, is one that Sven remembers quite differently. After having been knocked down by a wave, ruining the same dress, Lyra is back on the docks with Sven. Though she is a mess, Sven tells her that he can see her true beauty when he looks in her eyes, and that nothing can make her more beautiful than when she smiles.

The memories end there, as Sven appears before her in her mind like before. He says to her, "It is time for Sven to go. Perhaps if legends are true, he will be back in four hundred and forty-four years. Sven only has one regret, and that is he wishes that he could belong to you longer. Sven loves you, Lyra." Then, speaking properly, he repeats, "I love you. Goodbye, my sweet Lyra."

As the spell ends, Lyra gasps, "I love you, too." She is brought back to reality and finds herself on the shore, still holding Fidelma's hand. "Is that it?" she asks.

"Yes," answers Fidelma. "That was it."

"Thank you for doing that."

"Of course."

"He really loved me."

"Yes," agrees Fidelma. "He really did."

"When he first told me that he loved me, I didn't know what to say. I panicked and couldn't say it back. I know now that I did love him, and do love him. Why couldn't I say it?"

"It's not easy thing to say, especially when it's real."

Distraught, Lyra says, "I feel awful. He professed his love to me, and then died not knowing if I felt the same."

"He knew," says Fidelma. "Trust me, he knew."

✱✱✱✱✱✱✱✱

Back at the apartment, Lyra and Yentroc overlook the city from the balcony. The sliding glass door opens as Josh calls out, "It's OK, Aunt Nica, Uncle Kyle says we're past the sad stuff now."

"Thank you," says Lyra. "We'll be in shortly."

Josh closes the door, and Yentroc asks, "Are you all right? You've hardly said a word since we came out here."

Lyra shakes her head, "I don't know what came over me. I haven't thought about Sven in years."

"He was your first love," says Yentroc. "It's okay that you still have feelings. I think you always will."

"I know, but it's been so long now. I thought I'd be able to read this to the kids."

"Well, I think reading it made it all come back to you."

"You're right. You know, I dreamed of him from time to time for centuries before he finally stayed out of my dreams. Part of me was hoping that he really would come back to me after four hundred forty four years. I guess that's not how the universe works."

"Come on," says Yentroc. "Let's go back inside."

Chapter 37
Loose Ends

Gelana says to the kids, "This is the last chapter."

"Really?" Laura asks questioningly. "How do they wrap up everything that's been happening with one chapter?"

Kelik says, "Unlike the rest of the book, which tracks each day, the final chapter summarizes what happens a week after the war ended."

"What happened to Red Beard?" asks Josh. "Did they hang him?"

"No," laughs Kelik. "While Arioch was upset, they ultimately decided that the deaths of those aboard the *White Feather* were the fault of Corthag."

"Corthag didn't die when Fernando cut off his head, did he?"

"No, he didn't."

Laura interrupts, "Would you two just let Aunt Angela finish reading?"

"Sorry," apologizes Josh.

Gelana laughs, "It's okay, are you ready now?"

Josh nods and Gelana begins to read again.

*****

One Week Later

Not wanting to wait to return to Artos, Allen convinced his captain, Marcus, to release him from his duties. Marcus agreed, and while the *Trident* stayed off the coast of Sheathelm waiting for the orcneas to make it back to the north, Allen rushed back to East Artos as fast as he could. Now, entering the city for the first time in weeks, Allen can feel his heart pounding as he makes his way to the inn where he and Marie had been staying.

Upon entering, he finds Marie washing a table. When she's done, she picks up her bucket and starts to head toward the next. Allen stands there watching her when she looks up. Upon seeing him again, she drops the bucket, spilling the water on the floor. She rushes to Allen, crying tears of joy.

"I was so worried about you," she cries into his chest as they embrace.

"I told you I would return," says Allen.

"But we got word that the war ended a week ago, and you said you would return in a week."

"I know," he says as is he strokes her hair. "I hurried as fast as I could. I made it just in time."

"So, it's all over?"

"Yes."

Stepping back and looking at him, she asks, "Did you get hurt?"

"The only thing that hurt me was being away from you for so long."

Marie laughs as she wipes her face. "Allen, you're so sweet."

"Come on, I'll help you mop up the water. It's a skill I'm still good at."

"Did you have to fight?"

"Just once," says Allen as he picks up the bucket from the floor. "I made some new friends. When they return, you might hear them call me 'Allen the Mad.'"

"Really? Why?"

Allen chuckles. "Let's get a mop and I'll tell you all about it."

Back at Sheathelm, Princess Kianna is standing with Prince River in the ruins of the Atrium. Kianna says, "I wish you didn't have to go back to Elonfar so soon."

"I'm sorry," says River, "but it's been a week since the orcneas left. They are almost completely on their side of the Northwind Range now. Mother and Father want me home so I can help arrange the aid of food that was part of the peace agreement."

"I hope I haven't offended them by not becoming your wife."

"Nonsense," scoffs the prince. "They like you. You may not be a full-blooded elf, but you are the daughter of A'ranah Ree, and my parents respect your father as well. If anything, they will blame me for not being good enough for you."

"That's ridiculous. You are more than good enough for me. Please understand, it's not like I don't want to marry you, I just want the choice to be ours and not our parents'."

River takes her hand and kisses it. "Well, when I return, I plan to ask you again. Not as prince to princess, but man to woman. I hope you'll say yes then."

Kianna blushes. "I guess you'll have to come back to find out."

At the west gate, Chance and Arioch are with a large gathering as the elven forces prepare to leave. Ya'leigh is next to her father's side. Baeldeth says to her, "Make sure you keep your father out of trouble."

"I'll try," she replies with a laugh.

"It was a pleasure meeting you, Ya'leigh," says Baeldeth. "I can see your mother in your eyes."

"Thank you. It was nice to meet you too."

Baeldeth grins at Chance. "Well, brother, I'm glad that we've survived another war."

"Thank you. We couldn't have done it without your help."

"That's what brothers are for. I'll always have your back."

River and Kianna join the gathering. River says to Arioch, "Your Majesty, please let me know if there's anything more we can do to help."

"Thank you," says the king. "Have a safe journey and give your parents my best regards."

"I will," replies the prince as he and Baeldeth climb onto the backs of their horses.

Baeldeth gives the order for the troops to move out. Not far away, Belron climbs the back of the drake Blue Wing. Nicari is about to join her husband on the drake's back when she hears Va'leen call to her through the crowd.

Nicari turns as Va'leen teases, "I thought you were afraid of heights."

"It's better than walking all the way back to Elonfar."

Va'leen laughs. "I suppose it is. Before you and Belron leave, I wanted to ask you something."

"Sure, what is it?"

"If I paid a visit to Elonfar, could I stay with you?"

Nicari smiles. "Of course. Is everything all right? You're not leaving the sisterhood, are you?"

"No, not just yet," replies Va'leen. "I just need a little time away for myself."

"Well, you're more than welcome to stay with us."

Va'leen gives Nicari a hug. "Thank you."

Nicari takes a deep breath before rejoining her husband. Wrapping her arms tightly around his waist, she says, "All right, let's go." The captain of the drake riders takes to the sky with his wife clinging to his back.

Down at the docks, the *Red Dawn* and the *Trident* are both docked. Ariella has made a clean start, settling her accounts with almost all of her crew. Now, Ariella and Fidelma are co-captains of the ship. Lyra and her friends have volunteered their services in exchange for transportation. Re'ann, the drake rider, has joined the seven sisters on their Rite of Passage with the Amazon Queen's promise that she will be able to join the sisterhood upon its completion. Trisha and Lee, from the King's Shield Inn, have also joined the crew. Along with Annalee and Vindalia, the crew of the *Red Dawn* is now mostly women.

Fidelma gives Samantha a hug. "I'm going to miss you."

Samantha replies, "Make sure you stop and visit us."

"I will, just make sure you tell me when you're going to take your vows. I don't want to miss it."

Samantha nods and jests, "Just make sure if you come, you keep an eye on Ariella."

The women laugh as Ariella protests, "That's not fair and you know it."

"I know," agrees Samantha, trying to control her laughter. "I just couldn't resist." In a serious tone, Samantha adds, "It was a pleasure meeting you, Ariella. Please, take good care of Fidelma."

"I will," says Ariella.

Fernando says to Marcus, "Well, my friend, you are a lucky man. Samantha is quite a woman."

"She is, indeed," Marcus agrees as he puts his arm around Samantha.

Fernando says, "Samantha, I will never forget the time we spent together." Samantha looks at him, puzzled, as he continues. "The time that you stomped on my head to keep me from escaping, or the time that you drugged me to put me to sleep... I think my fondest memory will be the time you gagged me with a pair of your drawers and beat me with a bamboo rod."

Marcus gasps. "By the gods, Samantha, what did you do to

this man?"

"Nothing he didn't deserve," replies Samantha with a grin.

Marcus says, "Well, Mr. Greythorn, I wish you the best. Please help Ariella look after my brother, Seth."

"Absolutely."

Marcus says to his brother, "I just hope our parents aren't too upset with me for not bringing you home."

Seth comments, "I would be more worried about Lucinda."

"You're right," agrees Samantha. "She is going to be furious that you're not going to marry Julia."

Fernando says, "Just make sure you don't tell her that the *Red Dawn* is now a ship full of mostly women."

Samantha smiles mischievously. "I may just have to mention that to see the look on her face."

Marcus shakes his head. "That's terrible, but I have to admit, it may be worth seeing."

They laugh before Samantha and Marcus board the *Trident*.

A short time later, as the ship makes its way out to sea, Chance and Va'leen join Ariella and the others at the docks.

"Ariella," says Chance. "I'd like you to meet a friend of mine, Va'leen."

The women look at each other coldly. Everyone around, except for Chance, can feel the intensity at that moment. Ariella says, "We've already met, but it is a pleasure to see you again."

With a smirk on her face, Va'leen replies, "Oh, no, the pleasure is mine."

"Wait, when did you meet?" asks Chance.

"When you were captured," answers Va'leen. "I introduced myself to her. I wanted to see the woman you always went on about when we were fighting together in the Dragon War."

"Oh," replies Chance, unsure what to make of the situation.

"Well, this is awkward," Fernando says quietly to Fidelma.

Ariella says, "Chance, could we have a word?"

"Sure," he replies as he comes closer to Ariella.

Ariella puts up her hand. "No, I mean I would like to talk with her."

"Oh, this is awkward, all right," Fidelma whispers to Fernando.

"Va'leen and I are just friends," says Chance.

"I know," says Ariella, trying to sound sincere. "I just want to talk with your friend, one woman to another."

Now nervous, Chance looks back at Va'leen, who shrugs, saying, "Of course."

The dark-haired Amazon walks off with the red-headed captain, leaving Chance alone to wonder and worry.

"So," says Va'leen, "I heard you were leaving soon."

Ariella glares at her. "You would like that, wouldn't you? For me to get out of your way so you can get your claws into Chance."

Va'leen shakes her head. "You know, jealousy doesn't become you, darling."

"Oh, I'm not jealous, if that's what you think. I'm just trying to save you the effort."

"That's sweet of you, but don't worry about me. It takes no effort for me at all to be there for him as his friend."

Ariella sighs. "You and I both know how you feel about him. Even though you won't say it."

"My feelings for Chance are not relevant, and I assure you, woman to woman, I will not ever move on Chance. He is happy with you, and I will never come between him and his happiness."

"By the gods, you really do love him, don't you?"

"He sees me as a friend, and that is exactly what I will be for him."

"I wish I could tell you that it makes me feel better to hear you say that, but it doesn't. It's like I told that sister of yours, Kristieana, I think. Sometimes you don't have to get in the way to be in the way. "

"Well, let me say this, then: The only way something will ever happen between Chance and myself is if he pursues me, and I think you and I both know that's not likely."

Ariella looks back at Chance, who looks uneasy. She says to Va'leen, "So, I have your word, then? You will not seduce him?"

Va'leen smiles. "You have my word, woman to woman."

The women walk back as Chance sighs with relief, glad that they're not fighting. He asks, "Is everything all right?"

"Of course," replies Va'leen. "I'll talk to you later."

"Oh, all right," he replies as Va'leen makes her way back to the castle.

Ariella says, "We're about to leave. Would you like to join

us?"

"You know I can't."

"I don't mean to stay. Just long enough to send us off. You can fly back to Sheathelm at any time."

Chance looks at the *Red Dawn.* "I suppose I could do that."

As Chance and Ariella board the ship, Va'leen is approached by Kristieana as she enters the castle grounds. The red-headed Amazon says, "I heard a rumor that you're taking a leave from the sisterhood. Is that true?"

Va'leen nods. "Yes, but it's nothing permanent."

Kristieana looks at the rubble where the atrium once stood. "Are you going to stay here and help Chance with Sheathelm?"

"No," Va'leen says, shaking her head. "As a matter of fact, I want to get as far away from this city as possible."

"I don't understand..."

Va'leen sighs. "Sometimes it's necessary to distance yourself from the echoes of the past in order to see the present more clearly." She smiles and adds, "You should come with me."

"What? Are you joking?"

"Not at all. We would make a great team, you and I. When we're not fighting, that is."

"Where were you planning on going?"

Va'leen shrugs. "It's been a long time since I've visited the Amazons of the Blood River. I was thinking of starting there."

"I've never been to the southern continent."

"So, does that mean you'll go with me?"

Kristieana nods. "I think I'd like that."

Back aboard the *Red Dawn,* the ship is ready to get underway. Ariella and Fidelma are both at the wheel, where a new pedestal has been added just before it. A large orb is affixed to the center. Fidelma instructs her friend, "Now, just place your hand on the orb and think about the ship floating up."

"I'm nervous," Ariella replies.

"Relax. The goblins tested it this morning. It works wonderfully. If you would rather I fly her first..."

"No, I can do it." Ariella insists as she places her hand on the orb. She takes a deep breath and concentrates. The ship lunges forward, causing the crew to lose their balance momentarily.

"Easy," cautions Fidelma. "Now, take her up."

Ariella thinks about the ship flying, and soon the *Red Dawn* begins to rise out of the water.

A large crowd on the docks watches in awe as the galleon floats upward and into the air. Powered by one of the massive crystals that Ariella managed to take from the floating city, the *Red Dawn* does not require a balloon to aid in its flight. Instead, thanks to the cooperation of the goblins, the ship can be completely powered by magic.

As they continue to rise up, Fernando and Seth look out over the railing at the city of Sheathelm. Fernando says, "You know, you are probably the luckiest man in all of Runefell right now."

"Why is that?" inquires Seth.

Fernando chuckles. "We are the only two men on a ship with over a dozen beautiful women. What I wouldn't give to be your age right now."

"I suppose," Seth replies with a laugh. He looks over at the other side of the ship at the Amazons on their Rite of Passage.

Gelana and Yentroc both smile and wave at the young man. Then Gelana nudges Yentroc, saying, "I claim him."

"You'll have to fight me first," replies Yentroc.

Kel'ana laughs. "Here we go again."

Most of the women find it amusing, with the exception of Lyra, who excuses herself before heading below deck.

Rehma, admonishes her friends. "Now look what you've done."

Yentroc sighs. "I'll go talk with her."

Down below, what was once an open common crew quarters is now divided up into cabins. Inside one of them, Lyra makes herself comfortable in her hammock. Yentroc comes down the stairs and stands outside the door to their shared room. After working herself up to it, Yentroc enters. "I'm sorry, Lyra," she says, standing in the doorway. "Gelana and I didn't mean to upset you."

"I know," Lyra replies sadly. "The two of you should be able to have your fun without worrying about me, though. I don't want you to stop on my account."

Yentroc puts her hand on Lyra's shoulder. "You know, someday you'll claim another man. I just know it."

"I don't know." Lyra shrugs. "Maybe... someday. Right now, I just want to forget about everything."

On the upper deck, Ariella says to Fidelma, "You can take over now." As her friend takes the helm, Ariella grabs Chance's hand and leads him up to the top of the poop deck. "Isn't this wonderful?" she asks with a gleaming smile. "I can fly now, just like you. I can go anywhere I want."

"You're right," he agrees. "It is wonderful. I'm so happy for you."

Repeating the words that Chance had once said to her years ago, Ariella says, "Now that I can fly, I shall soar to the sky. No ocean or sea shall keep you from me."

"I hope you do... Come find me, that is. I wish I could go with you, but the city of Sheathelm needs me."

The smile on her face fades. "I know. I'm just worried I might lose you again anyway."

Chance forces a smile. "You won't lose me. You know where I'll be. On that note, where are you heading to next?"

"First," she answers, "we're going to New Waterford. Fidelma's going to introduce me to more of the family." She looks down at Fernando on the lower deck and adds, "Then we're going to Bastion to get that bounty off my brother's head."

"Well, be careful. Bastion is a dangerous place."

"I'm familiar with it," she laughs. "And it's more dangerous for those who would mess with the *Red Dawn*." She looks down at the mostly female crew and adds, "I don't think I've ever had a more capable crew. From what they told me, most of them can cast some sort of spell they can attack with. And since we can fly now, no other ship would stand a chance."

"Well, good luck, and if you get into trouble, you know how to reach me." Chance holds out the crystal that once belonged to Trisha and Lee.

"I'm not just going to call you when I get into trouble." Ariella smiles. "I plan to speak with you every night before I go to bed."

"I look forward to it." Chance looks back at the city of Sheathelm, now further away. "I should be going now."

He leans in and kisses Ariella on the forehead. Trying to hide her disappointment, Ariella smiles. "I love you."

"I love you, too," he answers genuinely. Chance then turns to the railing before climbing over and jumping from the ship.

Ariella rushes over to the edge and looks down as Chance

transforms into his eagle form. Behind her, Ariella hears Fidelma say, "The ship is on a steady heading now." When Fidelma notices the sadness in her friend's eyes, she asks, "Are you all right?"

Ariella nods. "I'm fine, but I don't think Chance is."

"What are you talking about?"

"All week long, he's seemed distant. Like his mind was somewhere else."

"I wouldn't worry too much about it. I can tell he meant it when he said that he was just friends with that Va'leen woman."

"I'm not worried about her," insists Ariella.

"What is it, then?"

Ariella sighs. "I think that no matter how long it's been, Chance's heart belongs to a ghost in his past."

Back at Sheathelm, Chance lands on the windowsill to his room. He transforms and hops down to the floor. He walks over to his dresser and places the communication crystal next to a bowl of water. He then picks up a small painted portrait of his former wife. "Why?" he asks, staring at the image. "Why wouldn't you let me stay? I'm forever lost without you."

Chapter 38
The End of the Beginning

At the apartment, Gelana closes the thick book. "Wait!" Josh exclaims. "Are you done? Is that it?"

"That's the end of the book," explains Gelana.

"What a terrible ending," comments Laura.

"It's not that bad," says Kelik.

"Yeah, it is," insists Laura. "First of all, they should have never killed Sven. He was like my favorite character—right after Ariella—then, on top of that, Chance is left miserable?"

Kelik replies, "To be fair, this isn't the end to Chance's story, or for that matter, the Amazons' story, either. Really, this book marks the end of the beginning for them."

Kel'ana enters the apartment. When she enters the living room, she is surprised to find so many visitors. "Oh, hello," she greets them. "I didn't know you all were coming by."

Gelana says, "It was a last-minute decision on my part. I thought about it and figured I should probably meet the kids."

"We just finished the story," says Josh, sounding disappointed. "We didn't like the ending."

Yentroc says to Kel'ana, "We told them there are other stories."

"Oh, yes, of course," Kel'ana replies. Then, looking at Lyra, she asks, "How many other books are there?"

Lyra thinks for a moment. "I guess it depends on what kind of books you're looking for. If you want to follow the current story line, there are a few more. First, you have the book about the rest of the Amazons' Rite of Passage."

Gelana says, "Then there's the one about the time Lyra returned to see Lunarus after she learned how to read dragon."

"Oh!" exclaims Haley excitedly. "Can you read that one next?"

Lyra smirks at Gelana as she says to the kids, "There's also one about how Gelana claimed and married a prince."

"No way!" replies Laura. "She would never settle down."

There is uncomfortable laughter in the air from those who

lived through the events mentioned. Kelik says, "I think it may be best if, perhaps, we read them in order. Starting with Ariella's trip to Bastion."

"Great," says Josh. "Can you come tomorrow?"

Kelik laughs. "I'm afraid I can't tomorrow, but perhaps next weekend."

"Right now," Kel'ana says to the kids, "you three need to go to bed."

"Wait!" protests Laura. "I have to go to bed, too?"

"Yes," replies Kel'ana. "You don't have to go to sleep, but I'd like to be able to talk with your aunts and uncle and catch up."

"Fine," Laura sighs, disgruntled.

As the three kids go get ready for bed, there is a knock at the door. Kelik says, "I'll get it."

"Thanks," says Kel'ana.

As the women are left to converse, Kelik opens the door and is surprised to find Eric Winters. Kelik looks back in the other room before stepping outside the apartment and closing the door behind him.

"How did you find me?" asks Kelik.

Eric answers, "I was able to track the gate to the Daily Scoop. After that, I just did some research. It really wasn't that hard, but that's unimportant. What IS important is that I think I can help you and your friends return home. That is, of course, if you want to."

"I'm listening," says Kelik, curious.

Inside, Kel'ana asks the others, "So, where's Rehma?"

"Still on the ship," answers Gelana. "You know she hates gate travel."

"You two are not going to believe who we met today," Yentroc says to Lyra and Kel'ana.

Before they can reply, Gelana says, "Ariella Stormrage!"

"She's alive?" inquires Lyra. "How is that possible?"

"How do you think?" Gelana asks rhetorically. "She's been using the steal youth spell."

"Not only that," continues Yentroc, "but Fidelma, Annalee, and Garrett are still around, as well."

Lyra chuckles. "That's crazy. We were just reading about most of them tonight. How did they get here?"

Yentroc explains, "The short version is that they got sent here through a gate that ripped the *Red Dawn* in half shortly after we got here."

Kel'ana sits in one of the chairs. "What about Chance? Was he with them?"

Gelana shakes her head. "No. Although, according to Ariella, Chance was looking into every lead on magic gates he could. Ariella just happened to come across this particular gate while chasing after Corthag. She suspects that Corthag knew of the gate and set a trap for her. She also said that every gate on this side seems to have been destroyed."

Lyra sighs. "So there's no way back."

"I wouldn't be so sure," says Kelik as he rejoins the conversation.

"What do you mean?" asks Kel'ana.

Kelik finds a place to sit. "That was Eric Winters at the door."

"The guy we met in Bermuda?"

"Yes," answers Kelik. "But what we found out today is that he, too, is an elf."

"So we're not alone here," says Lyra.

Yentroc nods. "We always assumed there were other elves around, but we never could prove it."

"What did he want?" asks Yentroc.

Kelik, summarizing his conversation in the hall, says, "He told me that the Goblin Trade Company does have access to what they believe to be the ruins of Atlantis."

"So it is real," ponders Lyra.

"Apparently so," says Kelik. "And according to him, there are a few gates that survived the Great Collapse. He wants me to go with him tomorrow and have a look."

"Can I go with you?" asks Lyra. "I can read any written language."

"That's sort of what got us here in the first place," says Gelana.

Lyra's gaze drops to the floor as an awkward silence fills the room. Kelik finally suggests, "Let's not dwell on the past. If you want to go with me tomorrow, that's fine by me."

"Thank you," she replies, forcing a smile. "And I promise not to touch anything."

"Don't worry about it," says Kelik. "What happened to us

years ago was a fluke. It's not your fault."

Gelana sighs. "He's right, Lyra, and I'm sorry. I didn't mean to blame you."

"It's all right," she replies. "It *is* my fault that we all got trapped here. I just hope that maybe now we can finally go home."

"Is that what we're going to do?" asks Yentroc. "Go back to Runefell?"

"Why? You don't want to?"

"I don't know. We've been here so long, I've become accustomed to it. Even with the headaches."

Kel'ana adds, "And what about you, Lyra? You just got married a few years ago. Would you really ask your husband and children to leave this world behind to go with you? Or would you leave them behind?"

Lyra, unsure of her answer, replies, "I guess I never thought that much about it."

"Well, I think it's time we do," says Yentroc.

"Why don't we see if there is really a gate back to Runefell first?" says Kelik. "Then we can worry about what to do next."

Gelana says, "Whether there's a gate or not, what are we going to do about Laura? Her headaches are only going to get worse, and we're the only ones that know the cause. I think it's time we told her the truth."

From the hall, Laura, who has gone unnoticed, asks, "What truth are you talking about?"

The others are startled. Kelik asks, "How long have you been standing there?"

Laura, who looks visibly concerned, replies, "Long enough to have lots of questions."

Gelana smiles. "Whatever you want to ask, we promise to tell the truth."

"I don't..." she stutters over her words. "I don't know where to begin."

"What did you hear?" asks Kelik.

Laura takes a deep breath in an attempt to calm her nerves. "I heard you talking about Runefell as if it was a real place that you're all from." She looks at Gelana. "I heard you call Aunt Nica 'Lyra,' like from the stories. But that's impossible."

"Well..." Kelik begins, "it does *sound* impossible, but what if I told you that magic was very real, and that Runefell is also real?"

"I would say that you all are playing an elaborate prank on me."

Kelik nods. "I know this will be hard for you to understand and accept, but the stories that you have heard, including that book over there," he says, pointing to the account of the Third Orcnea War, "are real. And all of us are people in those stories. My real name is Kelik Na'Moon, son of Chance Na'Moon."

Ambra adds, "And I am his sister, Ambra."

Laura shakes her head, laughing. "No way. I don't believe any of this."

"Of course not," says Kel'ana. "Why would you? Let me show you a little magic to help prove it."

Kel'ana concentrates on a spell and summons water. It floats above her hand like a wet globe. She then shapes the water into a flower before freezing it into ice. Kel'ana takes the frozen sculpture and hands it to Laura, who reluctantly grasps it.

"How did you do that?" Laura asks, amazed.

"It's magic," Kel'ana replies. She then removes a ring on her finger that hides her true appearance. Kel'ana's ears take on their natural long, pointed form. "My real name is Kel'ana Ree."

Still doubtful, Laura says, "I don't know how you did all this, but it's really good. Were you ever a magician?"

Kelik says, "Like we said, it's magic. Real magic. No tricks. Let me show you something." Kelik walks to the center of the room. "Here I am." He then teleports himself to the doorway of the kitchen. The air pops as it does when someone uses the spell. Kelik says, "Now, I'm here."

As Laura begins to understand, she suddenly feels faint. "I don't feel so good." She quickly makes her way to the couch as the others move out of her way to make room.

Kelik says, "I know this can be quite confusing, and even scary. But I promise you, there is nothing to be frightened of."

Laura thinks for a bit. She looks at the woman she has always known as her Aunt Nica. "If you're really Lyra, from the books, then you can become invisible. Show me that, and I'll believe you."

Lyra looks at the others and shrugs. "I can do that." In an instant, Lyra disappears. Her disembodied voice continues. "If you want to feel that I'm still here, put out your hand, and I will hold it."

Laura stands from the couch and hesitantly extends her hand before her. She feels the grasp of an invisible force. "I can't believe it!" Laura gasps. "It's real?"

Lyra ends her spell, reappearing before Laura as she continues to hold her hand. "We're sorry we didn't tell you sooner, but we wanted to wait until we thought you were old enough to handle it without telling others."

Kelik says, "It is very important that this remains secret."

"I won't tell," insists Laura. She looks around the room at the others. "So, if you're Lyra, and she is Kel'ana, and they are Kelik and Ambra..." she looks at Yentroc, "Who are you?"

The dark-haired Amazon smiles. "I'm Yentroc."

"Of course," laughs Laura before turning her attention to Gelana. "Then if I remember the stories correctly, you must be Gelana."

"Very good," she replies. "There is one more thing you need to know about me." Gelana glances at the others, who give her a reassuring nod. "I am your ancestor. Your eighth great grandmother, to be exact."

Laura laughs to herself. "So I'm a descendant of an Amazon of the Silver Moon?"

"And a great prince named Galen," adds Gelana.

"I know him from the stories," she says excitedly.

"Yes," says Gelana. "Now that you know the truth, there is so much more we have to tell you."

Ambra steps in. "Like how to fight your headaches and what they mean."

"What *do* they mean?" she asks, concerned.

Ambra smiles. "It means that you have to capacity to learn magic. Unfortunately, technology has made earth an almost unbearable place for spell-casters to live. At least in most places."

"Are you going back?" asks Laura. "To Runefell, that is."

Kelik says, "We don't even know if we can go back yet."

Now excited, Laura says, "Oh, I want to hear all about it. What is it like? How did you guys get here? How many worlds have you been to? There's so much I want to know. Like how do I cast spells?"

"Let's just slow things down," laughs Gelana. "You have just had your whole world change. I promise we'll tell you everything you want to know, but it may be best to sleep on it."

"I don't know if I'll be able to sleep tonight," replies Laura.

Ambra quips, "I can give you something to help you sleep."

"No, that's all right. I promise, I'll get to sleep somehow."

Gelana says, "I'll come by and visit soon. Maybe I can tell you about our time aboard the *Red Dawn*."

"That would be great!" Laura exclaims. "I want to hear about everything."

"Very well," laughs Gelana. "As we said, the Third Orcnea War was just the beginning."

###

Epilogue

A warm fire crackles away within a small pit surrounded by a gathering of people. A woman with thick glasses and unkempt dark hair closes a thick book. She looks at two young girls—ages ten and twelve—within the group of onlookers, saying, "And that is how your mother first learned the truth about who she really was."

The older one looks at her mother, Laura—who is now in her early thirties—and asks, "So you never knew you could cast magic until you were older?"

Laura's brother, Josh answers for her. "That's right. On Earth, it would have been dangerous if the wrong people knew what your mother could do."

"So how did you get here?" she asks. "I thought the gate took you to Runefell."

"It did," answers Laura. "But the gate of banishment brought us here."

"That's when we defeated the Talon Knight," says Josh.

"Well, *we* didn't exactly defeat him," corrects Laura. "We had some help."

Laura's younger daughter asks, "Why didn't you stay in Runefell?"

Haley, now a young woman as well, answers, "We would

have, but the Dragon Emperor captured us and sent us here."

Laura laughs. "I'm sure Alicia will tell you all about it... *tomorrow* night. But now it's time for bed."

"Ugh," the girls whine in unison.

The woman with the thick glasses, Alicia, chuckles. "You heard your mother. Now, off to bed."

As the children leave the campfire and head towards their primitive home with Laura, Josh picks up the thick book that Alicia was reading. "It's amazing," he comments. "Just a few short years ago, we were just kids reading from a book very much like this one. Now here we are, reading about ourselves."

Alicia shakes her head. "It's not amazing at all. We all exist in the minds of gods. And we are all gods to everything within our imaginations. Everything we dream is a story to be told, just so long as we are willing to tell it."

###

Thank you for taking the time to read this book. I hope you found it as enjoyable to read as I did to write. If you have enjoyed it, please take a moment to give it a positive review.

Thanks!
Shawn Sodman

About the Author

As long as I can remember, I have always been a daydreamer. In fourth grade, it became more of a distraction than normal. My grades were marginal, and at the end of the year I was informed that if I were to continue on to the fifth grade I may find it too difficult. Ultimately, my parents and the school left the choice up to me. While it was a hard decision, it was not one that I regret. I repeated the fourth grade with my best friend at the time, who was also struggling. One silver lining was that I was going to be able to hear my teacher, Mr. Sheathelm, read from *The Chronicles of Narnia* by C.S. Lewis for a second time. Out of all of the books that he read, *The Voyage of the Dawn Treader* was my favorite. Despite the fact that I had to repeat the grade, Mr. Sheathelm became my favorite teacher.

My short attention span and daydreaming didn't end there. To this day, I often find myself thinking of places within my imagination. I have even wondered if I spend more time daydreaming than thinking about reality.

Loose Ends

As you may be able to tell, I have left this series open to add on to at a later date. I have already developed several stories in my mind, including the ones mentioned in the story itself. At this time, I plan to take a short break from this realm and try my hand at a science fiction novel. I do plan to revisit this in the future, barring an untimely death. The stories I have in mind are what happens with Ariella and her crew in Bastion and what happens one year after the Third Orcnea War. I can then write about Gelana and

Prince Galen. As one of my readers/editors once pointed out to me, I have five hundred years of time to fill in.

Aside from those three stories, I have plans to tell the story about what happens when those who choose to return to Runefell go back to find out that much has changed since they left. There is also the possibility to tell the tales of what happened BEFORE the Third Orcnea War, including the Dragon War, how King Arioch rose to power, and even the Second Orcnea War. So many possibilities! I only hope to find the time to tell them all.

Sven

Sven was without a doubt my favorite character. I even plan to write an entire book about his life leading up to this series. So why, then, did he get killed off? There are several reasons, but the first and most important reason was that his self sacrifice was the most emotional. Out of the main characters, his death would be the most moving.

In a way, the readers did experience what it would be like for Chance and Fernando to die. Characters even grieved for them, and said their goodbyes. To have one of them killed off in the end would have been anti-climatic.

Isen's death, while emotionally moving in its own right, lacked the same shock value. And while I could have killed off one of the main seven young Amazons, I told myself that I wasn't going to do that from the very beginning.

One of the other reasons was simply that there was nowhere else to take Sven and Lyra's story. They jumped through all the hoops and Lyra made her claim to him towards the end. I already had plans for future writings that included all of the seven sisters in mind. And while I did have some interesting ideas about Lyra meeting Sven's family, I still feel like the relationship ran its course. I didn't think keeping Sven around for five hundred years would make for an interesting "Happily Ever After." I think at some point something would have to give, leaving readers disappointed.

Alternate Endings.

For quite a while I had what I thought to be the perfect ending to the book. It wasn't until I was nearly finished that I changed it. While it may seem odd to leave the main hero distraught and "lost" at the very end of the trilogy, I wanted to convey that this was still just the beginning.

Still, I did have a happy ending (of sorts) before I started mucking with it. The original ending was going to start off with Chance looking out at Kristieana, who would be sitting alone on the docks. A'ranah would then tell Chance that Kristieana could use a friend, as they had both just lost Isen. Chance would admit that he didn't know how. While it would be sad, Kristieana would soon be joined by the seven sisters, and they would cheer her up.

Meanwhile, Chance would return to his first love, Ariella, who would be sitting on the *Red Dawn* gazing at the ocean over the railing. The idea I had was that he would join her and the two would re-introduce themselves to each other, re-living the first time they met. It would end with Ariella looking up at him with a smile.

It was a bittersweet ending that I really liked for quite a while. While writing the second book, I even had the two re-enact getting to know each on their date. It was to help set the stage for that final scene.

Later I decided I wanted to add another element to that same idea. Instead of the seven sisters coming out to Kristieana, I had the idea to have Va'leen come out instead. I figured the two would make up and Kristieana would revoke the neita. Then the idea was that Va'leen would go seek out Chance. Then I was going to cut to Chance sitting on the dock, and just when the readers expect Va'leen to find him, I was going to have Ariella come across him instead. The two would re-live their first meeting just as before, but once it was done, I would cut back to Va'leen, just off in the distance, watching the exchange. From that point I was going to have Va'leen say to herself, "Good luck, pup, I hope she keeps you happy."

Aside from those endings, I also had an entirely different one in mind involving Lyra. The idea being that Lyra would be walking along the coast alone as she reflects on her time with Sven. Instead of Fidelma joining her, it was originally going to be her closest friend, Yentroc. As Lyra would sob about not telling Sven that she loved him, the final words in the book would be that of Yentroc telling her friend, "He knew... he knew."

Out of all those ideas, I was able to salvage most of them in some form or another. There were several emotional conclusions as well as a new beginning when the *Red Dawn* took flight. From there, however, I went back to the dramatic flair that I always seem to be drawn to. Instead of ending with Lyra or Va'leen, I stuck with the main tragic hero. No matter how many options Chance had open to him, I just couldn't help but think that the more realistic ending for him would be that of sorrow. He had just seen his former wife, and I wanted the weight of that encounter to be more believable. Besides, I have the advantage of knowing exactly what the future has in store for him, and trust me when I say that this is only the beginning.